KARNA

THE KING OF ANGA

During the Iron Age of India
around 900 B.C.E.

Kevin Missal

SIMON &
SCHUSTER

London · New York · Sydney · Toronto · New Delhi

First published in India by Simon & Schuster India, 2021

This edition published in 2021

1 3 5 7 9 10 8 6 4 2

Simon & Schuster India
818, Indraprakash Building,
21, Barakhamba Road,
New Delhi 110001

www.simonandschuster.co.in

PB ISBN: 978-81-951317-9-2
eBook ISBN: 978-81-951317-0-9

Typeset in India by SÜRYA, New Delhi

Printed and bound in India by Replika Press Pvt. Ltd.

1

Twin sons…a mother with black blood in her…

He was there. Right there, in the depth of monstrous trees intertwined with vines like some crooked old lady hands. His mother was there too. Not his real mother, though. But the one who accepted him when he was ousted by his royal family. She taught him everything about kingship and the ways of warfare, whatever she knew. On the last day though, when he was prepared and ready to go back to the world, she asked for a *dakshini*.

And he asked her what was it that she wanted, to which she laid a sharp, steel knife on the mossy ground. And whispered: "*Kill me.*"

Girivraj, Magadha, modern day south Bihar

Jarasandha woke up, drenched in sweat.

The dreams. *The cursed dreams!*

He clenched the satin sheet and looked up at the ceiling. Lying naked there, Jarasandha didn't look a day over forty, with a stylish dyed beard and cropped hair. His neck was almost non-existent and his bulk was of a wrestler, with thick arms and a broad waist. He turned on his side to see the empty part of his bed and touched it. There was a time his wife would caress him and put him back to sleep. But that was over. Long time back.

She was no more.

He was the King of Magadha, the mighty kingdom of the north-west and he had no queen except for the ones you needed to have to create alliances with city-states. There was no emotion involved, just strategic practicality when it came to signing these marital contracts.

And before he could go back to sleep, away from his thoughts and the dreams of his past, Jarasandha heard an urgent knock on his brass door.

It's late at night. Who could it be?

Wearing his golden, saffron dhoti while the knocks continued, Jara walked to the door, bare-chested and glistening with the leftover sweat, a string of Rudraksh beads wrapped around his arm and a pendent of a trishul hanging from his neck.

He opened the door. Standing in front of him, was his chief of command. A man as pale as a *vetaal,* the creature Jara's old nan used to orate about under the mindful eyes of the moon. Bald from head to toe, he had a habit of chewing tobacco in the corner of his mouth.

"You should have a good reason to be here, Gonanda," Jara said.

He looked weary, as he nodded and bowed, saying, "Yes, your highness. I do."

"What is it?"

And with a dramatic sigh, he said: “The Vijaya dock has been attacked.”

Jara wasn’t supposed to go. In fact, a king must only see matters at the court and not on the field. That is why he had so many generals and lieutenants; they were meant to do that. But it was the Vijaya dock. A yard of forts and buildings set in the north of Ganga, which acted as a shipbuilding and trading centre for Magadha. It was an important port from where they would set their ships to travel far west towards the Greeks or the Egyptians.

“You don’t have to go,” Gonanda said.

But by then, they had reached the common roads, a pebble strewn path towards the exit gates of the royal palace.

“You know why I am going.”

There was one ship, holding cargo. An important one, that would have been leaving the harbour the next day. And he was only wishing and praying to Lord Shiva under his breath, hoping it wasn’t destroyed. But it was a fool’s errand to think that way.

He sat on his chariot, without armour, placing the sheathed sword on the side, while the chief sat on his stallion. Along with the hundred men behind them, they raced forward towards Vijaya, under the blanket of stars and a foggy moon.

As the gates opened, Magadha lay in front of him, enveloped in night, brimming with exciting lights like fireflies. It was indeed a beautiful kingdom. While his palace was on a strategically higher ground, the city was laid out with two-storey buildings and narrow roads, bricked kiln walls and high towers with bowmen ready to strike. The walls were fortified with thorn gates and forts which his men held to protect his people. It was a structured society, working day and night to make Magadha a kingdom to be reckoned with.

He turned on his side, on his comfortable seat, to watch the chief, who was riding with him, when he asked: "Do we know who attacked the dock?"

"Negative," said the chief. "Your highness, I am sure it's a bunch of marauders and robbers. Who else?"

If it is, the damage would be less.

But the stars were not in his favour, he could feel it. He could feel it in his gut like a punch, that something far more sinister was at work.

He was going in the dead of night, leaving everyone behind, for cargo. And he was hoping against hope that the cargo was safe.

It better be.

2

The distance was long. And the journey was tiring. While they had camped in between, it took them hours to reach the Vijaya port.

The long journey gave Jara some time to reflect on things he had ignored. One of them being his complex relations with another city-state like his.

Aryavarta, which was the northern part of Bharat, was comprised of multiple kingdoms known as janapadas, loosely translated as city-states. Cities like Anga, Vanga and Mathura came under this title. And then there were the Mahajanapadas, which had created a reputation of their own because of their skilled strategies, army control, width and the girth of the size and economy. Magadha, fortunately was one of them, and its deep-rooted ally and an enemy at the same time—Hastinapur—was the biggest kingdom as well.

Jara always detested the relationship with Hastinapur. It was complex. At certain parts, they had good relations and at other parts, they were quite a behemoth to deal with. Jara had to be nice to them to not create an entire *mahayuddh*. Otherwise, that would be unpreventable and casualties would be in millions, government would fail and they would be fighting for castles made of ashes. And so, cold war had prevailed, with smiles and laughs masking their real intentions.

A turning point had come when they had formed a treaty, a truce of a kind to divide their favourite timberland, Anga, into two. One half would be given to Jara and another to Hastinapur. While it happened and everyone went home happy, recently Jara's part of Anga was reaping really good timber from which he was making ships that could make his naval system strong.

And so, fearing these new developments, Hastinapur had been distant. Cold, to be clearer. While Jara liked them to be away, his chief of command had told him that it could be a sign that Hastinapur was rethinking their position with Magadha.

But the truce continued. At least, for now.

They had reached.

He noticed an eerie sense of melancholy presided over the docks—strewn with corpses of his men laid flat on the ground, arrows with tips of iron thrust inside their fleshy heads, their eyes or their chests.

Jara dismounted from the chariot, his eyes scanning the dock. He was at an open complex, where a half-finished ship of wood and timber was placed and his workers, all from the impure caste were standing with their hands folded, bowing to him. They were not hurt. The robbers didn't think of hurting them.

While his chief questioned the people, Jara with two guards behind, walked. It was approaching dawn, the sun rising like an orange beacon. His face shimmered with the light of the skies, as he came close to the port where the holy river Ganga cascaded. There were his large ships and while the docks had corpses, the ships weren't harmed. Nor burnt. They almost felt untouched.

He grinned like an idiot. Relief washed over his face. The cargo would be safe.

"Open it for me." He ordered his men to put the plank on one of his ships on to which he walked. For a moment, he admired the beauty of the innovative ship with a hull that was in the shape of a bull, his favourite animal, a bow that was strong and a mast that was almost fifty feet high to resist tough winds.

He went down, passing the quartermaster's cabin and inside the wine stables, to reach the lowest level, the one that would have his cargo and in it, to check, he opened the doors to find...

Nothing.

Empty.

Everything was gone.

A drowning sensation engulfed him and he felt weak in his knees but he didn't show his emotions. All the boxed cartons, the cargo, was burnt.

As if...

As if...

The attack at the dock was aimed at this. *This* particular cargo.

This was no attack by robbers. It was a strategic play.

The cargo was important because it held large amounts of gold and silver which was going to one of the Greek island tribes—the Ionians—in return for their draught horses. These were no ordinary ponies. They were tough as nails and faster than ordinary ones and this deal, if carried out, would have been beneficial for Jara's cavalry, which was the weakest in his state.

He was in a hurry because he couldn't just put another set of gold and silver cargo together and set the ship sailing. It had to go at a particular time. Ionians were quite particular about timing and they were insistent that it should reach within thirty-two sundowns or they would cancel the deal.

But now...

Even if he brought all the gold and silver on time, to build a ship that would travel all the way to the Greek Islands and back with more than hundreds of horses... would take a lot of time. And a lot of money.

He had already lost so much.

He continued to look at the empty space, with an empty heart.

Whoever did this, shall pay for it.

Jara walked back to the dock and by that time, his chief had put the carpenters and the workers of the dock in front. They were partially naked, with exhausted eyes, and they were all kneeling in front of him, with tears in their eyes, begging for their lives, saying they had no role to play in it, while Jara's soldier was flogging them.

There was a man in front, a carpenter, a bushy-moustached one, who had his palms clasped.

Jara towered over him, anger biting his very bones, as he asked through his clenched jaw: "Who was it?"

"We didn't s-s-see, your highness."

"I had a hundred men here. All of them dead. How is it possible that you didn't see anything?"

"I-i-it happened so fast. We had taken rest and we were sleeping when our men began to go down. One after another. Arrows came out of nowhere. It was a silent attack," the man said. "And when we did see, a few of us, we saw a figure on the ship, your highness. He was throwing cargo from the ship and on to his boat, and he left with that."

"A figure?" Jara knelt down, next to the man, sneering at him. "What do you mean a figure?"

"A man, your highness."

"Just *one*?"

The carpenter nodded. "There must be others, but we only saw one. And it was not like we didn't try to stop him. We approached him. He looked at us. We told him to not take it, that it was your cargo. We begged..." the man was shivering by now. Jara couldn't expect him to stop a vicious archer like that.

"Did you see his face?" Jara asked.

"It was hidden in the shadows."

What an enigma.

"What did he say?"

"He said..." the carpenter whispered the final words of the killer.

Jara's blood ran cold. "Thank you, my friend."

He came on his feet and moved towards the chief of command.

"Do you think they were involved?" Gonanda asked, still chewing tobacco as always.

Jara shook his head. "They are too feeble. But kill one or two, to set an example. I don't want to lose workforce over this."

The chief nodded. "How is one man capable of killing one hundred of our men?"

Jara had no words for a moment. He paused with uncertainty.

"We lost our contract with the Ionians and that's what this man wanted," Jara said. "He didn't want us to have the horses. But I'm sure he's not working alone. He has allies. Strong ones, otherwise how would he have known about our deal with the Greeks?"

"Spies?"

Jara nodded. "And who would have spies keep an ear out towards us?"

The answer was simple.

"So what does this mean?"

The carpenter had told him, whispered to him the final words of this heinous, vicious predator, who had said before leaving on his boat: *With compliments from Hastinapur.*

Jara looked at the chief, sternly, declaring what he should have done a long time back when he was warned by Gonanda continuously: "We are going to war with Hastinapur."

3

Hastinapur, Capital of Kuru Kingdom, modern day Meerut

Suyodhan fell on the ground. Out of exhaustion. Out of pain, that vibrated in his tough arms.

He knelt next to his mace, on which he was taking his support. He had been practicing with his mace for hours now and he would continue to do it even if his body killed him. He had to be a better warrior. A perfect one.

Better than those Pandava parasites.

Only few years earlier, the bright eyed Suyodhan had learnt his throne was at risk when the Pandavas had come from the forest and his father had accepted them. After all, the Pandavas were Suyodhan's first cousins and his father's nephews. The five of them were considered a partial heir even though their father, Pandu, the heir, had strictly given the throne to his blind brother and had gone off to the woods to be a hermit—otherwise, he would have been the king. To be a saint, and an ascetic. He did it for his own religious reasons. But Kunti, the mother of the Pandavas, brought her children back to *snatch* the throne of the mightiest city of Bharat—Hastinapur—when Pandu died. She acted innocent, saying she did it because she wanted her sons to grow in a healthy environment and not in the woods anymore.

All lies.

Picking up his mace, he began to do the three sixty degree turn of it. In his anger he did it faster, his arms tightening, his legs weakening and he grew exhausted and dehydrated because his body was losing water quickly, his head slowly loosening up…

Parasites.

A strange energy ran through his veins. The Pandavas for the last couple of years, had continued to be under Suyodhan's family's care. They began to cling on to them. And then, when Dronacharya, the mighty royal guru was tasked to train the royal kids in Ujjanak, Suyodhan thought him and his ninety-nine other brothers would be the chosen ones, but the Pandavas clung along there too.

Bah!

He had always loved his father, but the man was blind as a bat and his judgments were not very different. Once, he used to be a manipulative strategist, but now he was just someone whose position you could usurp.

He should have never accepted them in the first place.

Now they had reached the point where they would be participating in Rangbhoomi, the Tournament of Arms, which was organised by Dronacharya to showcase each royal kid's talents and what they had learnt under Drona's tutelage. They would also compete with each other.

It was to take place the following week and Suyodhan was going to fight the vile brute of a man, Bheema, in a mace fight…

He smashed the mace on the ground, as if he was splitting logs of wood. Then with all his strength, he picked the mace and went forward again, plummeting it on the ground, letting the spray of red, dusty sand swirl thickly in the air.

He was in the training complex, closed from the top except for a small opening from where a beam of light fell. Swathes of sand surrounded him, and he almost felt like he was in a desert.

He fell down on it, collapsed, slowly immersing himself in the sand, as the fire torches were lit around, casting an orange gaze on his bronze frame.

I will prove in Rangbhoomi that I am better than Bheema.

I will prove that I am the rightful heir to Hastinapur.

He lay naked in the bathtub, leaning against a wooden rail, as a maiden trickled cold water from her terracotta jar.

Then she dipped the jar in the tub, taking more water and doing the same all over again to Suyodhan.

After every practice this was his ritual. To be bathed and pampered. His body felt weak. His skin was itchy and soft. He had his arms flayed, his eyes closed as he heard the light humming of his servant Meena, who sang the tune his mother, Gandhari, used to sing when he was a child.

"Do you think I will win?" Suyodhan asked her.

She was quiet, her humming stopped.

"Do you think I will win?" he asked her again.

"I don't know, crown prince. What do you believe in?" her voice was like nectar.

Suyodhan opened his eyes and watched her delicate frame. She was small in stature, especially since he was over six feet in height. Her jaw was definite and her eyes were like a fish's—big and watery. Her lips were tender and lotus-like and she smelled of sunflower seeds. "Wash my beard," he ordered.

She took a jar of water and began to clean the hair on his chin, his cheeks. It had grown, he knew, and it would itch after every practice.

"The Mesopotamians believe that beards are a sign of courage, virility and strength. Only the royalty have the right to have a beard and thus the Greeks adopted this same method," he said, repeating what he had learnt from his guru Drona during his foreign relations studies. "Do you think beards are nice?"

Meena tightened her jaw and forced a smile when she said, "I find them sensual."

Suyodhan grinned. He could feel her fingers tracing his jaw and his lips, when he slowly began to suck on her thumb, his tongue lolling around the fabric of her skin. His eyes were closed, but he could hear her moan, just a bit.

His hands went for her, cupping her buttocks and pressing them hard. Meena flinched and went red when Suyodhan opened his eyes to look at her.

She knew what she had signed up for when she became Suyodhan's personal servant. He was famous for bedding the maids and his nurses. And especially after practice, to let go of the exhaustion in him.

He groped her and brought her inside the tub. She was still in her clothes, but he didn't let her open them gently. He ripped them apart, uncovering her bosom. His mouth ceased to speak, but hers moaned, when he pressed his teeth against her nipples and sucked on them, softly in the beginning and then hard, biting them. He brought her between his legs and thrusted in her, when she mumbled:

"Crown prince...oh...crown prince..." whispers, echoing gently.

"Call me king." He grabbed her by the hair. "Call me Your Highness."

"My king! My king!" She moaned loudly and he could feel the energy in him meet hers.

Yes. I am a king.

Then he heard a cough. But it didn't come from either of them.

He sharply turned around, shoving Meena in the water, who was still grabbing her wits about her. She looked flustered and unsatisfied, when Suyodhan turned to see a tall figure with a thin moustache standing, a purple turban on his head, a tunic over his body. He had a very decent air about him.

He was Suyodhan's living and breathing uncle—Vidura.

"I always believed that a bath is a man's private business," he said.

"Which makes me question, why is the prime minister of Hastinapur here to interfere with my privacy?" Suyodhan came to his feet and ordered Meena to wrap a shawl around his manhood.

"I wouldn't have if it wasn't urgent."

"What is it?" Suyodhan's face went grim and stark with worry.

"It's Jarasandha," Vidura replied. "He has just declared war against us."

4

By the time he had reached the war room, his father and his guru were already there, deep in discussion.

Dhritarashtra, his father, was on his throne, smaller than the one from the common halls, as he calmly listened to Drona who was leaning on his cane. Suyodhan noticed how his father was a meek, timid man with a long robe, pale eyes and silvery hair that danced over his shoulders. He wasn't wearing his crown tonight and his hair was all over the place, probably woken up suddenly from his sleep by the news.

Guru Drona, on the other hand, had a back problem because of which he would lean on his wooden stick. He had a snowy beard, with white hair and a wrinkled face. He displayed wisdom beyond his years, by just the look of it. He didn't see Bhishma Pitamah, but then he was on a campaign in the east, and he must have not returned.

"Have they come?" Dhritarashtra asked.

"Yes," Drona responded.

Suyodhan walked forward and in the war room, he noticed the glistening gaze of the fire lamps, illuminating the shadowy grounds where the map of Bharat was designed and painted by the best of artists. Wooden figurines, half his height would be used to put on the map as a way to strategise.

"Stop right there," Drona ordered Suyodhan and he did.

He paused. Bowed. And said, "Guruji, what is it that has happened?"

"These are dark times, son," his father responded. "War has fallen on us. By our own ally."

"And why does he have a change of heart?" Suyodhan asked.

"He feels we are antagonising him. The scroll we received clearly stated that he was hurt by the action we took against him at Vijaya dock a fortnight back," Drona said, chuckling to himself. "What a funny excuse to fight us, since we clearly didn't attack the dock."

Suyodhan raised his brows. "Indeed. Jarasandha is not a man we should make an enemy out of."

His father nodded. "You speak right, son. It's a waste of our resources and time and frankly, our economy."

"Should we ask for truce?" Suyodhan suggested.

Vidura, who had been silent for a while with his hand rolled up against his chest, came forward at that moment. "Unfortunately, he wants only blood, my dear nephew."

"Gah, and he's smart." Drona patted the cane on the ground, making a *tak tak* noise. "He knows if he attacks the great Hastinapur, he would be vanquished. But that's not his plan," the old guru began to walk around the map of Bharat until he reached where Suyodhan was told to halt and tapped on the location, "It's here. He wants this."

Suyodhan bent down, to see the map and found the name of the place written in Devnagiri: *Anga.*

The timberland of Bharat. One of the finest places where wood is found and made. If anyone knows progress in maritime, they know it comes from the land of Anga.

"In the scroll, it clearly stated he expects us in sixty sundowns along the river Champa, where the war will take place," Vidura added. "And he has already reined in his people from his part of Anga, so we don't ride surgical strikes on them. He's taking this quite seriously."

There was silence in response to what the prime minister said. A shrug and a sigh followed from the king.

"He was always unsatisfied with the truce we made," Dhritarashtra said, with a defeated sigh. "His goal and purpose is to raid the foreign lands and the more the timber, the more the ships and the more the raids."

"Your highness, you are nice to say such a thing, but you have forgotten one thing. The reason why he wants to raid the foreign lands, is to gain enough army to defeat Hastinapur." Drona responded shrewdly, scratching his beard thoughtfully. "He's an infected dog who's slowly spiralling into madness. He might not bite today, but he will one day. And personally, we don't want that."

Dhritarashtra nodded.

Suyodhan coughed a question, "If I may ask, what made him think we attacked him?"

"A soldier," Vidura answered. "He thinks we sent a soldier to loot him and kill his men."

"Gah!" Drona groaned. "It must be his own man and he's using that as an excuse. Can I suggest something, your highness?"

Dhritarashtra nodded. "Yes, guruji."

"Let's just end this. Let me lead the army..."

Vidura snapped. "With all respect to you, guruji, you haven't stepped once in Anga. He has an upper hand when it comes to the knowledge of Anga."

"And also," the king added, "you are the guru of my children and nephews. You have a far more important role to play here than in a petty battle."

"Yes. I believe personally we should hand this over to Devi." Vidura smiled in relief, as he referred to the Senani of Anga, who ruled from Dhritarashtra's part. She was the only female general in Dhritarashtra's army. "She knows the Angan politics, has dealt with Angan soldiers and knows the land inside and out."

"But she's not a Kshtriya," Dhritarashtra mulled over. "And she's a woman." Devi was sent for day-to-day affairs, not for battles. "We need someone smart to lead them." He paused, taking a puff of air in his mouth as he was about to recommend some general when Suyodhan said, "Your highness, I have a suggestion. An unorthodox one, but one that makes most sense."

"Don't recommend yourself, fool," Drona grunted and Suyodhan felt a stab of embarrassment. "You are still a student."

"I wasn't naming myself. In fact, guruji, I was naming someone who was unable to graduate from nowhere else but your school, but he still managed to learn everything from you. He also learnt from *your* master, Parsurama, attaining the secret of Brahmastra and he knows Anga by heart. Because he was born there. Anga is in his blood," Suyodhan explained.

"By the thunderbolt of Indra," Drona clenched his teeth, spitting as he said, "I hope you are not recommending *him*."

Suyodhan defied his guru's order, as he walked further and bent down next to his father's legs, touching his feet.

"Who is he?" His father asked, unknowing of the man who could be Hastinapur's secret weapon.

"He was born by the name of Vasusena, a peer of mine and a man with a heart of gold," Suyodhan said. "Karna."

5

Doors were slammed, and Drona and Vidura were asked to leave the room as they both hated the idea, leaving Dhritarashtra and Suyodhan alone.

Drona had said—*He's a suta. A charioteer's son. He will ride the battle into the depths of carnage for us. I kicked him out of my Gurukul because he was weak and he had no talent.*

Vidura had said—*He's just a boy. Few years older than Suyodhan. He can't lead the battle.*

But Suyodhan asked for a private audience, just to make him understand the logic behind this statement of his. So, the king allowed it, to Suyodhan's surprise.

And he felt close to his father. He felt like he was talking to his father and not a king anymore, who walked and who wanted to be guided to the table where the goblet of wine was kept. And from there, he took a sip and leaned on the table.

"Have you drank till now?"

Tons.

"No, father."

"What a sad liar you are. Unlike me." He proudly filled another glass and handed it over to his eldest son. "Have it while we enjoy the prison of temporary vanity we have created for ourselves."

They took a sip together and stayed in silence. And then his father said, "When will you tell me your reasoning behind choosing Adhirath's son?" He called out Karna's father's name, the man who was a bootlicker to Dhritarashtra, someone who listened to him unquestioningly.

"Do you know about Karna?"

Dhritarashtra shrugged.

"I remember, Adhirath had come and requested me to let Karna be a part of Drona's Gurukul. I took pity on the Brahmin and so I agreed. I ordered Drona to do so even though Karna was stripped off his royalty. Drona was... well...let's say he was not happy initially, so I asked for a test to be taken, to see if Karna was fit to be there. And Drona did so. I remember, Adhirath had wept at my feet that Karna had passed the test and he would be entering the Gurukul as a pupil. Drona was happy to choose him, said he had calibre. Then one wonders..."

"Yes. Why does he hate him now?" Suyodhan nodded.

"He must have a reason."

Suyodhan mulled over it. Karna was a *suta*. It had a meaning. He was born inter-caste, the son of a Brahmin father and a Kshtriya mother. And an inter-caste offspring was often treated poorly. *Could that be the reason?* Or because he was the charioteer's son?

"If you don't mind father, you were the one who made Karna's father a charioteer."

His father nodded, albeit a little annoyed. "He was looking for stature." He referred to the idea of how major kings like Dhritarashtra used smaller kings like the King of Anga as a driver. It was normal. The king of the Asmaka dynasty, for instance, had been his general for long. But it was done out of respect for the major king and a bit of compulsion, not out of love for him.

"He was the king of Anga. I am sure he would have liked that title more."

Dhritarashtra didn't say much about that. He was quiet. "He wanted my help and I helped him. So that's your logic? To tell my old friend's son, to help me in this crusade?"

"I want to show you something. Let me guide you."

Dhritarashtra was reluctant and then he joked, "Can I bring my wine goblet?"

Suyodhan chuckled, as he grabbed the decanter and handed it to his father. "You can bring it all."

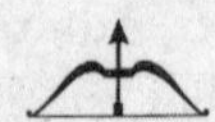

They walked together, crossing the recess and moving across the carved out corridors which had strange murals and paintings, sculptures of love gods and warriors before them. There was a sculpture attached to the ancient walls of the palace, which was of Bharata, the light of the fire lamp lingering on it. Bharata was their ancestor, the one who had founded this land and made it synonymous to his name. Then there was the sculpture of a turtle, who was supposed to be Kurma, the second incarnation of Lord Vishnu.

Suyodhan guided his father, who drank, and on reaching the terrace, they found the land that stood before them, intertwined with slices of the Ganges River that flew within it. Beautiful large towers which had giant elephant sculptures, towered over the quiet city that brimmed with silence in the late night.

"The wind..." Dhritarashtra felt it, smiling, "you brought me to the terrace."

"You know."

"Of course. I have lived here my whole life, son."

"Yes. But you must have ignored the peepul tree next to the terrace." He made him feel the twining branches that had crept in the crevices of the terrace.

"Indeed. One doesn't notice the simplest of things," Dhritarashtra was curious. "And what is that sound?" It was like a cold, sweet flute sound.

"It's of a robin. It sings at night."

"Indeed. So what is it you want to show me here?"

"Robins are the most underestimated birds. I know this, because I research the different breeds. But they are also the toughest, having speed, depending on the weather."

"And what are you trying to imply through this?"

"Karna might not be your ideal choice, but he's the right one, for this job."

"To lead an army?"

Suyodhan nodded. "And be the king of Anga."

Dhritarashtra turned in annoyance. He was perturbed. "That would mean we won't have any influence on Anga."

"Karna will swear fealty to me, when I become the king. That would be better than having Adhirath as a puppet king and a driver. The Angan are sentimental people. They care about who they are ruled by. How many rebellions have you faced ever since you took over Anga? How many suppressions and casualties did you have to make? You aren't like Jarasandha who tortured them to do your bidding so you were never able to reap profits from timber. But Jarasandha did. In the Angan people's eyes, you are a tyrant, a usurper even though you didn't shed blood, you are no better than Jarasandha. You are a mad man who has taken over their land. They loved Adhirath, but Adhirath was not a warrior and he had to be pulled down, which was a wise decision by you. He was a Brahmin. But Karna isn't. He's a Kshtriya even though he isn't. He exhibits all the signs of one. And the Angan would fall in love with him."

"How does that solve our problem?"

"It does. Because right now General Devi has less support on the army front from the Angan military. We know we can't send men from Hastinapur. It's a waste of resources and men. If Karna leads them, he has the correct birthright and the people of Anga would fight with him. You won't have unnecessary rebellion when you vanquish Jarasandha."

Dhritarashtra leaned forward on the marbled railing, eyes closed. He was thoughtfully mulling over this. If these words had come from someone else, he would have not even thought twice and rejected it. But it was his eldest son. "Have you been in touch with him?"

"It's been a few months since he has returned from Parsurama and he's living in Malinipur. I had paid him a social visit and we talked," he said to his father. "He's doing charity. Helping people. He's making them love him and they are."

"Is he a good man?"

"The best I know."

"And..." curiosity burnt in his father's voice, "...does he really know the secret of Brahmastra?"

Suyodhan smiled. The famed weapon of mass destruction. Legend said that Lord Brahma himself created the missile to kill thousands of people and the blueprint of the missile was given to only a few people. And the ones who did have the secret, couldn't divulge it. Not even on their last breath. Suyodhan knew only two people who had it: Drona and now, Karna. And he was definitely jealous of his friend.

"Yes father, he knows."

"That could be helpful for us. A man who knows so much about warfare and the ultimate weapon could defeat Jarasandha," he said, absent-mindedly. "But..."

There was a thick layer of tension that rose and Suyodhan, with a streak of sweat trickling down his face, waited for his father to say something.

Dhritarashtra sighed. "He has to promise one thing, then. Swear fealty to you and come to your aid when you need it. And only *if* Jarasandha is defeated—and it's a big *if*—he will be rewarded as being a full stature king. But for now, he will be interim."

Suyodhan nodded obediently.

"He's a boy. A young blood. And I don't want to spare my good men on it but I also don't want Jarasandha to feel I will *give up* my timber stronghold without a fight. He *only* gets Devi and her army of people. If he wants more armies, he has to get it himself or pay me for it."

"Yes father."

"And when he does vanquish Jarasandha and becomes the king, he has to give me the same timber percentage as I am being given now; regardless of the rebellions, I still get good profit of the timber I sell." He paused, a weak smile on his face. "But I won't put Devi and her men to rule my part of Anga then. It will be all his, his autonomy, his rules except for the percentage which I would still require." Even though Dhritarashtra was an understanding king, he was always concerned about the economy. He would worry too much about what went into the treasury and what didn't. "I hope you deliver the terms quickly to him."

"Sure, father, I will. I don't think he will have an issue."

"Good then, I'll make the scribes organise a decree for the same and send it across to the messengers to deliver the news," the king said.

"Thank you for listening, father."

Dhritarashtra nodded.

"Also, son?"

"Yes?"

He turned around, his arms holding on to Suyodhan's chiselled arms. "You are a good man and a good warrior," he smiled. "But that robin analogy...please don't repeat that to anyone. It was just dumb."

Father and son, both had a hearty laugh that night.

6

Suyodhan had lied.

Karna wasn't in Malinipur. He was not even near Anga.

In fact, he was here. In Hastinapur. He was just concealed; hidden from the right people.

And so early in the morning, when the sun was close to rising, Suyodhan had taken his best mare wildly across the ascending paths of the hills, which lay adjacent to the city. He didn't alert his men to accompany him, which they would by the royal decree. He concealed his face and head with a turban and its flaps. And he had escaped from the window.

Riding on the horse, he made his way through the lush greenery, passing the elevated and majestic Pandeshwar temple, realising he was entering the thick of the forest that lay in the hills. It was chilly there; biting cold underneath his skin. His face was impassive, the joy of his plan being accepted by his father hidden behind the placid features.

As he was coming closer, he could see the sky and the earth were meeting and the sun which was rising, had cast its orange flares over him. He was coming close to the sun—so close, that he was almost glad that morning was breaking. There was a certain positivity around whenever the sun was out.

Suyodhan escaped the trenches of the clearing and moved close to the cliff, when the hooves halted and his body jerked, his vertebrae feeling a strong impact. But his back was straight, just how he was taught.

He dismounted, for he saw his friend in front of him. Close to the cliff. In fact, on it. One shove, and he would fall to his death. But he had the poise of a dancer. One of his legs was on top of another, while his hands were clasped together in a *pranaam* towards the sun.

Suyodhan had asked him why he always worshipped the sun to which he had said, because his mother had taught him to do so. Radha was her name. She had said that the sun was the most powerful deity out there, a helper of humans, giving them a new lease on life everyday. And then, when he had recently met him, Karna had told Suyodhan that when you did breathing exercises in front of the sun, you were in greater control, you were more patient and it helped a lot in archery—the form of warfare that Karna practiced. He had learnt it in the north, with Parsurama.

Suyodhan waited. Knelt down, he began to play with the pebbles and looked straight, while Karna performed different breathing exercises in front of the sun. And for a moment, Suyodhan thought that Karna and the sun…they became one. It burned brighter.

And when Karna stopped, he did a *pranaam* once again, and Suyodhan said:

"It's done."

His friend turned. His face hidden by the sunlight's

glare. Suyodhan couldn't see whether he was happy or sad about it. He must be happy. He wanted to be the king of Anga.

That was why he had killed all those men. That was why he looted Jarasandha.

He wanted to trigger a battle between the two kingdoms since he knew Jarasandha would not attack Hastinapur directly and would go for the stronghold of Anga, since it was easier. It was closer. Jarasandha's Magadha and Anga had one division and that was the Champa River.

And who told Karna about the gold being sent to the Ionians? Well, it was Suyodhan of course, who had his spies deliver the information.

The crown prince of Hastinapur had helped Karna internally, by making a fool out of his father. He wasn't even sure whether Karna would be able to defeat Jarasandha. He just knew he had to do it.

And it was not because of friendship. It was because of a *debt* he owed to Karna.

"You'll be the interim king for now. It will be announced through the royal decree. I have done everything you have asked for. Am I free of the debt?" Suyodhan asked.

"You always were."

He was, as Karna hadn't forced Suyodhan to help him become the king. He just asked. But out of the debt that he carried for his friend...he did it. "Well, consider us even." He came to his feet. "I hope you win this battle. I have put in a good word for you. You won't have an army too. Do you have any idea how you'll defeat Jarasandha?"

"No," Karna said, still concealed by the glare of the sun. "But I'll figure it out. Thank you."

"See..." Suyodhan paused. Concerned. Worried. He didn't know whether he should say it or not, so he placed his words carefully, "If you win against Jarasandha, I know you will not aid me to become the king of Hastinapur. The swear of fealty towards me is full of shit and I know that. You hate my father for taking Anga from your father even though he did it thinking about your father's betterment. He did it for him. You hate Jarasandha and frankly..." he paused, "...I don't mind it. I understand your rage towards them. I might be repaying my debt towards you, but I am also correcting the wrongs of my father. So apologies from him."

Karna came forward then, escaping the glory of the sun, and his face became visible. Golden, shimmering eyes, with bronze flecks, perfectly sculptured skin and hair that rested on his shoulders. He had *kundalam*s hanging from his ears that glinted and shone light over Suyodhan.

"You are right. I won't aid you," Karna said, and Suyodhan was instantly disappointed. "But the sins of your father are forgiven by this help of yours. I just have one request. One more."

"What is that?"

"Announce that I am the king of Anga at Rangbhoomi. Make your father do it."

The moment he said it, Suyodhan froze in shock. Rangbhoomi was a prestigious event which had all the Kuru elders and the ministers and an audience of hundreds of people coming, even the allied kings and their daughters, sons and soldiers. By bringing and showing off Karna to everyone, it would be a stupid move. He was not even royalty of Hastinapur. He was an outsider. He was a charioteer's...

I don't want to say it.

"Why?"

"I have my reasons."

Suyodhan sighed. "I can't promise you that. You wouldn't even be allowed in the centre to perform…"

"Let me worry about that." He had a grin on his face and Suyodhan recognized this grin. He knew it very well. It meant one thing. He had something running in his mind, something devious.

"Fine, Karna."

"Yeah?"

"Yes. I can't promise but…" he heaved, "I will try."

Karna chuckled.

"What is so funny about it?"

He didn't respond, as he walked away to get his tunic. "Nothing," he said after a pause, "you said the same thing when I told you to spill beans about Jarasandha."

And with another chuckle, he left Suyodhan in a troublesome contemplation. But no matter how much he was scathed by the issue, he continued to think one thing:

Why does he want to announce his kingship title at Rangbhoomi?

With a thud of the hooves, leaving swirls of dust and crunched leaves on the ground, Suyodhan fled.

He didn't promise, but he knew he would do it.

And Karna remained there, bathed in the glory of the sun. He was quiet.

You have no idea how much I hate your father,

Suyodhan, and I won't forgive him so easily. Karna thought. Because he knew the truth. He had learnt it himself. One can only wonder how much you can learn from bribing a royal guard of the palace, which Karna had done.

You think what he did to my father was good for Anga? Karna shook his head, smiling at the naivety of his peer. *You thought wrong.*

Because the truth is out there and you don't want to see it.

But I did.

7

Thirty years earlier, outskirts of Anga Pradesh...

The moment he stepped into the war, everyone knew they were in trouble.

King Jarasandha of Magadh had that reputation; of a man who makes losing seem a part of winning. And here he was, standing firm and bulky at the forefront of his army. He was a short man, compared to his muscular soldiers. He had a thick neck and shoulders that went above as he crouched a little, like a creature ready to hurl.

He had a scar on his upper lip and ears that were purplish like a sore thumb. His hair was dyed orange, since it was popular at that time to do so. The foreigners did it to beautify themselves.

He sat on a tamed bull, unlike his comparatives who were all on stallions. His hands were over the saddle, as he watched the army in front of him.

The army that belonged to his enemy—King Adhirath of Anga.

He wanted Anga. For one reason.

But he wouldn't say why.

Hush.

He would never. Rumours had spread about why he wanted it so bad, but he let the rumours continue without clarification.

"Have you got so bored of playing chopat with me that you seek bloodshed?" A voice came from behind him.

Jara turned to see a jet-black-haired Bana enter on his stallion with a smile, as he feasted on a roasted mutton leg.

"Bana," Jara said, referring to his old friend with glee and delight, from the kingdom of Assam. "You don't want to lose more of your coins to me."

"Oh please, I was going to win."

Jara sniggered under his breath. He had been playing with Bana for the whole duration of the war.

And now that he had entered, he wanted it to be the last day of the war.

He was getting tired that his army hadn't finished off Anga's smaller army. He had thought he would just rest in his tent, play his game with his ally and friend Bana who had brought his men too for the battle. In fact, not only him. His other ally, King Damaghosha of the Chedi dynasty, had sent him a few thousand men for the battle in return for a hefty sum of money when they would conquer Anga.

All were supposed to be paid when the battle was won and they had placed the gamble on the most successful king of India—Jarasandha.

The man had not lost a battle to the point that rumours flew that he was an Asura, or perhaps even a Devta.

But he was a man. A shrewd, smart and a tough man.

"What is the plan though?" Bana asked.

"You don't have to be here," Jara said, staring at the other end of the bloody, sun-soaked desert where spears were plunged, rats were scurrying about and the heat was killing.

Their army was yelling; screaming. Drums were being beaten. They were forming up. Their commanders were rallying.

"No, wherever you go brother, I go. You know that," Bana smiled and so did Jara.

The one friend he could count on was him. And Jara was not a warm man, but he knew even if he was in trouble in the dead of the night, Bana would come to assist him. No matter how much trouble he was in already, which was a lot—since he was a voracious womaniser.

But that's a tale for another time.

Jara waited for his messenger, who had come by now on his mule, and he was breathing and panting harshly.

"Your highness," he began, "they are forming the Krauncha Vyuha." He referred to the battle formation in the shape of a heron.

Jara nodded.

"Going offensive, are they?" Bana added. "They have balls I must say, brother."

That was not expected from a king like Adhirath, who was always on the backfoot. Perhaps he was tired of losing and wanted to perform a massive strike.

"What is the plan?" Bana asked again.

Jara knew. Oh, he knew. His mother had taught him everything about formations, about war and how to tackle them. He still missed those moments of him spending time with her in the forest as she would explain the different battle formations over sand with the help of a stick. And she would tell him, for every offensive strike, one cannot be defensive.

But just create the illusion that you are defensive.

"Makara formation!" Jara yelled, specifying which one.

And so it did. The large drummers with their huge rods were smashing and creating havoc in the background. All his infantry, cavalry were being created and manoeuvred into a...

FISH!

Yes. It could either be a fish or a crocodile. He wanted a fish.

He saw Adhirath's army moving forward. He didn't blow a conch or a horn. He lifted his hand.

And hurled it forward.

The soldiers did indeed fall into a fish formation and began to move towards the enemies. For anyone who would be watching the war from the skies, the point of making a Makara formation of a fish is stupid. It's a defensive approach to a Kraucha formation, which had a beak in the front, to use as the greatest offence, while the wings of the formation would be used as a way to attack the outer flanks of Jara's army.

But Jara had a plan.

He always did. And he had instructed his senani how to go about it, while he watched from far.

"Have you heard of Matsya?" Jara asked Bana.

His friend shook his head. "Who is that?"

"Oh, the first Avatar of Lord Vishnu. What a story it is!" Jara felt his blood rush through him, recalling what his mother told him. "You see, there was a Yadav king called Manu, the first human, our progenitor. One day, close to the ocean, he found a fish. It was in a terrible condition."

The mouth of the Makara formation was the first to go in—hitting head on with the Kraucha formation.

The beak of the heron pierced the fish's mouth, almost killing hundreds of the infantry. The swords clashed and clanged. Blood was spilled. Javelins were thrown and the horses fell on the ground, crashing like the wheels of the chariots that the cavalry rode on.

What a mess it was. A beautiful, chaotic mess under the sunrise.

So many of Jara's men died—just laying waste.

And while Adhirath's army rejoiced that they had pierced the mouth of the fish, one of their soldiers noticed something.

The mouth of the fish, the infantry that they had just killed—they were slimmer and they had visible ribs and less armour on them. They had sunken cheeks and paled skin.

They were being starved off. And no soldier, is starved, *ever*. But the prisoners are.

The prisoners...

No.

The soldiers of Adhirath realised.

They hadn't killed the soldiers of Jara. They had killed the decoy.

"...And Manu was just sad, so petrified," Jara said, "that he took the fish in his hand and put it in a jar filled with water."

Bana listened and he looked confused by why this story was being told to him. But Jara, nevertheless, with a sly grin, continued.

"What he didn't realise was that this ordinary fish was more than just a fish. It was divine. And so..." he swivelled his head back at the field, seeing his army expand.

Just like that.

It had begun to grow. As the mouth of the fish had been fended off, most of the heron's beak was inside the mouth. The fish grew from all sides. His men began to expand their formations that they covered even the wings of the heron, the flanks of Adhirath's army on each side.

"The fish grew and grew..." Jara smirked, "...to the point that Manu could not keep it in the jar."

And it looked so grand in the field—Jara's army—the fish was about to swallow the heron.

Adhirath's army realised that the mouth of the fish was *supposed* to die so they could enter the mouth and then they get trapped, while the fish grew and covered their wings too. Their cavalry was being slaughtered.

And they tried to reach the tail of the fish. They tried to attack it, hoping it might break the formation and perhaps pause the expansion of the fish.

While, the fish on the other side was reaching for the heron's tail, tail being the reinforcements. The fish was attacking them viciously. Blood was shed and bones and flesh were scattered all over.

But now, the entirety of the heron formation was inside the fish and they were crowded by Jara's army.

The actual army, which began to slash and cut their way through Adhirath's army.

The soldiers were dead. Arrows were being flung.

But most of the infantry had reached the tail.

And when they did, to attack the reinforcement of the Makara formation, they realised—

Oh no.

Jara with his bull was waiting.

Everything happened in a frenzy after that.

He just rode in towards the tail of the Makara formation to be a part of his army. It had never happened before. The king was always supposed to be the spectator, but Jara was more than just a king.

He was a warrior. The hero of his land. Magadh Samrat.

With his scourge and his raging bull, he began to pummel his enemies left and right. His lash with blades, swinging in all directions as it scratched and stabbed and plunged into bodies. His blood was raging, his mouth had gone dry and his eyes were red.

He had even forgotten Bana, who was too much of a coward to go into battle himself.

He struck the enemies, while the horns of the bull were massacring the horses that came in between. He saw his men fighting, while the chariots were being toppled.

And then he felt it.

It was a searing pain…it was an arrow in his chest.

For a moment, everything came to a standstill. And he halted his bull, but it would be still raging…

So he fell from it.

He fell on the ground, his scourge still in his hands, as he tried to take a deep breath.

Come on.

And he pulled the arrow out. He clenched his fist and bit through the pain that was coursing through his veins.

He began to bleed from the chest and the moment he was about to surrender to the pain, in the middle of the war…

He felt another sharp jolt of it.

A kick.

It sprung at his ribs and he was tossed on the side. His scourge didn't leave him. It was still latched in his fist, as he tried to look through the dizziness to see a soldier of the enemy just in front of him.

He had a blade.

He was coming for Jara. And Jara didn't wait. He flung his lash towards the enemy's hand which then circled it, the blades piercing his palms and then he pulled the blade from the hand.

The soldier's weapon fell and his palm went bloody as he began to scream.

Jara didn't wait any longer. He didn't want to use his weapon anymore. He was hungry for some muscle-to-muscle action.

He sprinted towards the soldier and like a bull, smacked him in the chest with his head.

He fell over the soldier, grabbed hold of his head and began to squeeze it like a watermelon. His thick, wrestler hands gripping the forehead. The eyes of the soldier bulging out, blood spewing from his mouth, tears just swimming and sweat pulsating—and the head…

It *burst* open.

8

Adhirath knew he was fighting a losing war.

As he watched his men return from the battlefield, wounded and scarred, some carrying the dead along with them on their backs—he felt nothing but fear. It all seeped in, dark and morose. The second wave of the attack against Jarasandha was an absolute disaster, leading to nothing but Adhirath's army being crippled.

Across the dusty and bloody field was the canvassing army that belonged to the evil king Jarasandha. The man was the ruler of Magadha, one of the finest mahajanapadas, who dealt with the likes of the Egyptians and the Greeks in matters of export and import of the most precious metal out there in modern India: gold.

And he had a bigger army, bigger stallions and the biggest of all elephants, bought from the Persians.

Jarasandha knew he was going to win this. It was just a matter of time.

Adhirath rubbed his chin, shrugging off his fear and entering his tent, his senani—the commander of chief of his army—following him. Adhirath could feel his cheeks reddening, his mouth going dry as he fell on the ground, trying to catch his breath.

"Your highness," his senani grabbed hold of him, "you'll be fine, please take care of yourself."

Adhirath leaned against his muslin cushions as his senani handed him wine that he drank and spat on the ground. Tears rolled down his eyes, as he said: "Satya, I believe we are done. He has fifty elephants and ten thousand men while we have only one thousand and with each attack, we lose more. The next one will surely be our damnation."

His senani remained quiet, a grey-haired, balding man who was with Adhirath since he was a child. "When the title was passed down to you from your father, the army didn't believe in you, your highness. You were a Suta. Your father was a Kshtriya, surely, but your mother was a Brahmin. And thus, you were born a Suta. They felt a mixed breed can't be our king. Only a true Kshtriya can. But I chose to stand by you because I believed in you going beyond your caste. I believed in your merit."

"But...but..." Adhirath should have felt good about these honeyed words, but he only felt warm tears all over his red face.

He was a healthy man and getting his bronze armour, gauntlets and knee-pads fitted on him was a task to behold for his squire and manservants. He had girth, and no muscles. When he would walk, he appeared to be a bumbling fellow.

And thus, this incompetent man was given this royal kingdom of Anga Pradesh, the eastern stronghold of India but still a minor kingdom.

It was not a kingdom that was popular for arms and warriors. It was a peaceful kingdom, concealed from the rest of the country. It was not a kingdom popular for anything but having the best of timber. Oh yes, the timber would be cut down and slacked on the backs of the muscled labourers to be supplied to the shipbuilders and make the best of ships. Building naval forces was on the rise in India now since they had opened their doors to the world and timber was in high demand. No kind of wood other than timber had what it took to make a ship stay afloat on water and stand tough against the waves.

And Anga Pradesh came to the forefront—no more concealed, hidden. It faced the scrutiny, the brunt. It was no more a kingdom of nothing, but a kingdom of exponential possibilities of prosperity. Everyone wanted to get their hand on it, taste it.

Thus, Jarasandha wanted Anga Pradesh for himself. He wanted the monopoly of timber production only in his name and not in Adhirath's.

"We should have prepared for this day," Adhirath contemplated. "I believed we would have no opposition for we were nothing. But now, with no army on our side, we have no choice but to surrender."

"A king doesn't have to be a warrior, but the best businessman," his senani said. "And when your business goes down, what does a merchant do? He finds investors, someone who can keep him afloat."

"What do you suggest?" Adhirath arched his brows, instantly keen by this suggestion.

The senani, Satya, clenched his jaw as he told him the plan. "Your highness, I believe it's time to take help from your friend—the Supreme King of Kuru Kingdom—Dhritarashtra."

Days had gone by, and while remnants of Adhirath's army fought against the forces of Jarasandha in their limited capacity with the help of Satya—Adhirath waited in his wife's tent for his friend and the king, Dhritarashtra.

His wife, Radha, was pale as the moon, lying down in between the cushions, with an artificial hue blossoming on her face from the candles that burnt by her bed and the smell of lavender incense infiltrating Adhirath's nostrils. She was weak, but still she had life in her almond coloured eyes. She had a definite jaw and a small forehead, with straight, onyx hair.

"This is the third time," she said.

He nodded. Third time is the charm, they said, but here it was—his damnation. While he lost his battles on the ground every day, he lost a battle at home too. A battle of natural causes. His wife had her third miscarriage and they were in the tenth year of their marriage, with no sign of a child, no sign of an heir.

"It's probably because you came here," Adhirath fought back his tears.

"No," she shook her head. "Remember the day we got married and I promised to walk the path that you will walk? I continue to uphold that view."

"The battlefield is no place for a pregnant woman," Adhirath announced, even though he knew it would enrage Radha, who was a modern, progressive woman.

But she was quiet.

And so he continued. "There are flies, there is heat, not all the necessities are available, I mean it's our fault this time..." he broke into a cough while tears streamed down his face.

"No," Radha held his palms, "it's probably what the gods want from us. They don't want us to beget a child and it's fine. We are...well..."

She was trying to pacify him, but he knew it was not enough. He had only loved one woman in his life and that was Radha. Ever since he was very young. Ever since, he was just a prince.

"What is the status of the battle?" she asked.

"He has taken over Champa," he announced gravely. He had to break it to her sometime, so why not now? Champa was the capital of Anga Pradesh, a thriving city made of watchtowers and fortresses, also their home, where they had spent ten years—now lay sieged by his enemy, Jarasandha.

A deep, uneven sigh came from her. "So you mean we can't go back?"

"Yes. We have no home. We can station in Malinipur," he referred to the neighbouring city of Anga Pradesh.

"But..." he could see tears trickling down from her eyes. "I built that palace with my own hands, decorated it and crafted it like a child. How can I...how can I..." she had a hard time speaking, her lips dry as she turned and her back was towards Adhirath.

She sobbed and he put his arms around her but she shrugged away.

Rejected by her, Adhirath could not feel any more useless than he already did. Pursing his lips, he waited in silence for a while, his deep, unsettling breath being his only companion when he heard from outside the tent:

"Your highness? May I come in?"

Adhirath allowed and Satya entered through the

golden tent flaps, his sword dangling from his belt. He had a worried look.

"What is the status of the battle?"

"We lost, your highness, and two of our elephants have been spiked and bruised. They won't live to see another day, but we will still take care of them, for they served us well," he said.

Adhirath nodded, as he continued to speak, in the midst of his wife's sobs, "What of Dhritarashtra?"

"He is here, your highness, with his ten thousand men. And thus I came to inform you," he said.

Adhirath smiled in relief. He had sent one pigeon and even a messenger to his friend and he had come with a battalion, ready to strike Jarasandha.

But the uneasy, horrible question was—what would he want in return?

9

For a warrior and king like Jara, he had felt insecure and worried only *two* times in his life.

One was when he was abandoned with his twin brother in the forest by his father.

And *now*.

He was waiting outside the tent, while his wife, Usha, was giving birth to his child. He was sweating. He was wounded, with Ayurvedic medicine slapped on his scars. It still hurt, but he didn't mind. Pain was a part of life, he had realised long time back. Pain was glory. And pain was important. For those who don't suffer, don't learn. For those who don't allow themselves to feel pain, are cowards.

"She'll be fine," Bana said, who was standing in the corner, anxiously waiting with Jara. "She's the strongest one," he referred to the many wives Jara had.

It was not out of infidelity that he had wives across his conquered nations. It was because he had to build relations with them. And marriage was a pact, a contract to build it.

But Usha was different.

When he had come to Kashi with his men and his

father, he had seen her while entering the bridge, close to the river Ganga. She had looked at him and she didn't even glance at him a second time.

Later, they met and shared a conversation. Jara was intimidated. He was just a buffoon. A wrestler, with a sharp mind that he didn't use. Usha was different; more outspoken, very snide. But she began to like him when she saw a gentle soul behind the tough physique. She noticed that Jara carried scars deeper than his flesh.

She was the only one who knew about his life.

About his father abandoning him and his brother.

About him finally returning *alone*.

His father, Brihadratha, challenged him to wrestle. If he won, he could win the throne.

And Jara did.

Thus, he became the heir again.

But what his father didn't know was that the reason why he was so agile, so mentally fit, was because of his stepmother.

The bhisak, the physician, came out of his wife's tent and the nurses rushed to him with jugs so he could wash his hands. Jara's attention from the past shifted to the present.

Jara and Bana came close to him.

"How is she?" he asked.

The bhisak wiped his face as he said, "She's fine. She's resting." And then he placed his hand on Jara's shoulder even though it was forbidden to touch a king like that.

But Jara didn't mind, as the bhisak said: "Congratulations, you are blessed with two daughters."

Jara watched the two infants in his bulky arms, as he played with them while Usha, with a weak smile, watched him, lying in between the cushions, a colourful sheet over her frame.

"I am sorry," she said, as her smile faded.

Jara stopped dancing with his daughters and looked at his wife. He clenched his jaw, as he said: "About what?"

"About not bearing a boy."

Jara knew this conversation would come up. He had promised her he wouldn't have an affair with the rest of his queens because he loved her and wanted to have the heir of Magadh from only her. But now…

"You are free to go and be with the others," she said, turning away. And Jara could feel she was biting hard the sourness. "I have been a disappointment."

"No, you have not. You have blessed me with daughters and for that I'll always be grateful," he said. "Do not feel that way, in any possible manner. We shall try more for an heir, but I am more than happy to have these two little cherubs."

Usha nodded. She didn't seem convinced but Jara knew that over time, he would convince her.

He had not been a good husband. He had too many demons of his past to tackle and that had resulted in him having Soma as a drink. It was like a drug that would make his head swish and move around to the point he would become violent. Even to the ones who he loved.

But he had to take it. He was addicted to Soma. It was the only way to escape his past.

Due to the effect of Soma, he had also hurt Usha by being verbally and physically violent, something he regretted a lot.

"I promise you," he said. "I won't use the drink again."

She looked up and coughed a laugh. "What made you change all of a sudden?"

He could see she was angry and at the same time, remorseful. She was a woman of honour and she would have never stayed in the marriage if it wasn't for his constant pleas and apologies for hurting her when he was intoxicated.

He would defensively say that whenever he drank, he would become a different man.

But that was not enough of a reason.

"My daughters," he said. "They will make me a better man. And their happiness, will be my happiness. Their sadness, will be my sadness. I promise you that."

Usha nodded and then she lay out her arms.

Jara came and hugged her with his daughters still in his arms. They remained in that position when Bana came through the drapes of the tent and said with a grin:

"Oh what a sight!"

"Chaidya, meet them!" Jara excitedly said.

Bana watched the children and played with their fingers, until he broke the unfortunate news to Jara, whispering: "Dhritarashtra is here with his army."

Jara knew his enemy. He had dealt with the Kurus but Dhritarashtra was a stubborn, greedy man. He clenched his jaw, as he realised that the last battle was won by Jara and Adhirath was desperate. It was obvious, he would call for support.

"What should we do?" Bana asked. "His army is trained by *the* Bhishma Pitamah. We are no match to them. You know that, especially since we have been fighting for weeks now and our men are tired."

Jara always knew that it was important to back off when needed and to strike when you were fully prepared.

He had taken over Champa, the capital of Anga. He had control in most of the towns and villages surrounding the city.

So he was all right for now.

"Tell them to rein it in and pull back. We must return for now," Jara said.

"You give up so easily?"

Never.

Jara shook his head. "Don't argue. Just pull back."

10

What would he want? The thought raced in his mind, but he shrugged it off for now.

Adhirath embraced his friend as tight as he could, before making him comfortable on the cushions to discuss the war.

They were alone. For now.

He watched his blind friend, who he had grown up with, playing in the fields of Hastinapur which had now become Dhritarashtra's capital. He had grown unkempt and lanky, with a swollen face, marble coloured eyes, wispy greyish hair that fell over his gold and sapphire laced robe.

The Kuru Kingdom headed by Dhritarashtra was the supreme kingdom of Bharat with the mightiest army at their disposal. Their army, after all, was trained by their commander-in-chief: Bhishma Pitamah.

While Adhirath had heard a lot about Dhritarashtra's uncle, he had never seen the man. But his presence in their army led them to be so strong that no other kingdom would fight back.

And thus, Kuru Kingdom established their superiority by growing their tentacles over minor kingdoms like

Vanga, Kalinga and Gandhara. They wouldn't conquer them, but made them their vassals. These minor kingdoms would pay tribute to the superior kingdoms and would get their protection in return.

Adhirath never wanted this, for Anga Pradesh was his domain and only his. Dhritarashtra had respected that and never even offered.

Until now.

The tides had shifted and the times were different.

Adhirath wanted to begin, but the silence became his enemy and he felt the tremors of awkwardness, while the fruit basket was kept in between for them to have. "Um… uh, so your highness…"

"Have I told you how I got the crown?" he began.

He had heard rumours, but he said: "Please, do tell."

"I was born blind and they say it was because of the wrath of the gods. Even though I was the oldest son, my brother got the throne until he decided to leave the materialistic world and seek asceticism. When my brother, Pandu, left for the woods to become a sanyasi, I was told I would be the king only because they had no choice. My uncle Bhishma couldn't be the king because he had vowed not to, even though he would have been fitter than me. And my half-brother, Vidura, is of a low caste, thus he couldn't hold the title of the Superior King, the Maharaja." He smiled to himself. Adhirath knew that even if he had been in Vidura's position, he couldn't hold it, for he was a Suta. The title of Maharaja can only be given to a Kshtriya. "My blindness was my weakness in front of my comrades until they saw what I did with other kingdoms. I usurped, I formed treaties and I made Kuru a dynasty to be remembered for the next hundred years." He paused. "And when I see you, you have your own problems, you are underestimated every day like me for you are a Suta, yet you have shown your brilliance by calling me here and making a choice."

"Choice?"

"Yes, for the betterment of your kingdom." He smiled.

Adhirath could feel he was not talking to his friend, but a king. And a very callous one, with a placid smile and a pallid skin. The man gave him shivers down his spine, but Adhirath with his knees on the ground, and his arms on his thighs, listened to the Maharaja carefully.

"Jarasandha is as big of an enemy for you as he is to me. To win against him, will be my greatest honour. He sits in Magadha and he has distanced himself from the Kurus," Dhritarashtra explained. "He gives no tribute and also hurts my friends. For me, he's a sinister scoundrel and he must pay."

"Yes, yes," Adhirath hurriedly smiled and touched his friend's feet, to which Dhritarashtra pulled him up. "Please help me, your highness. My men falter."

"I will. But I risk my men for your soil. What would they get in return?" he asked.

Adhirath noticed the way he asked his friend. He put the blame on his soldiers, even though they were enlisted warriors of the state. Adhirath could never believe that the boy who played *chautaranga* with him would grow up to be such a diplomat.

"I'm ready to be your vassal, your highness. Just like Vanga or the..." he began to name other kingdoms.

"That is brilliant. But with your kingdom, the work

is more and the reward is less. The war that we will fight with Jarasandha will continue for years," he began. "The battle you fight today is just in the frontiers of Anga Pradesh. It will take me a week to get rid of it but Jarasandha won't give up so easily. He will continue to attack, especially when I've come to know that he holds Champa. The war with him over Anga will continue and for that…I wouldn't just take a meagre tribute from you."

"Then?" his breathing hitched, sweat trickled down his nose.

"I will station my senani in Malinipur, the other stronghold of Anga. And he will rule and execute. For sure, you will hold the title of the king, but you will be stripped off your duties." His words came as daggers being plunged in Adhirath's back. "My senani will report to me on a daily basis of the civil war that we will fight against Jarasandha." He paused, licking his thin lips. "And for all of this, I shall be taking half of your timber production."

"Half?" he went pale. "But your highness…"

"Jarasandha already controls half of your kingdom. So in a way, I'm just getting fifty per cent. But fifty per cent of what comes from the unconquerable cities and towns of Anga. In return, I'm saving you today and I promise you that Bhishma will take care of your army and teach them, so you aren't on the backfoot the next time you face such a situation."

Adhirath was glad about the Bhishma commitment, but then that was just one good thing in a series of disadvantageous things. Jarasandha was taking over Anga, and so was Dhrithashastra in his own way.

"And what of me? What will be my role in all of this?"

"Much greater than being a meagre raja. You will be your supreme king's eyes and ears and guide. You will be my charioteer," he smiled, placidly. "Just like the Panchala king is my minister of finance as well as the raja of his land, you will act as a part of my office."

Charioteer? *A king, turned into a driver?*

Adhirath didn't want to speak out his anger, but his eyes were bloodshot as he watched the blind king who couldn't *see* his fury. He wanted to attack the man, and renounce his friendship with him.

But did he have a choice? If he said no, he would die along with his wife and his men.

"For how long?" he quietly asked.

"Hmmm?" Dhritarashtra hummed.

"For how long will this last?"

"Till, of course," he smiled profoundly, "You or your heir…" he spat at the word for Dhritarashtra knew that Adhirath didn't have a son or daughter, "…are fit enough to rule Anga and lead an army to get rid of Jarasandha."

He didn't even know when that would happen. That seemed like a far-fetched, fairy tale dream.

"So, do we have a deal?" he brought his hand forward.

And with clenched jaw and gritted teeth, he kissed his owner's hand as a sign of acceptance.

11

They had met in the middle, once the battle was over.

On a rainy night, the camp was set for the two men, while guards circled around them. A musician played the flute in a corner, while a tabla was being beaten harshly on another. The rain was severe, like the two men who were concealed in the shadows of the night.

"Nice plan, your highness," Jara said, a grin on his face.

Dhritarashtra, on the other hand, was sombre. He didn't show any emotion of joy or sadness. "Thank you for being a part of this. And congratulations on your new daughters."

Jara nodded, munching on peanuts from a brass cup. "You know, the thing is," he chuckled, "I never expected your scroll in the middle of the bloody battle asking me to partner up with you and in return get fifty per cent of Anga. I could have gotten it all, but…"

"Lose your people and waste your time. This idea—isn't it smarter?" Dhritarashtra asked. "Instead of wasting our men, we would reap from our planning."

"Indeed. I am all for bloodshed, but this sounds better," Jara nodded again. "How did you convince that fool Adhirath?"

"He respects me too much to see how much I have gained from him," Dhritarashtra said. "But this needs to be not spoken of. Our alliance. In a few months, we will make an announcement saying that after so much bloodshed, we have agreed on a truce. We will sign that truce and this informal meeting of ours will become legitimate."

"And everyone will gobble up the idea? Even Adhirath?"

"He will believe it's better to sign a truce instead of continuously fighting and destroying his soil."

"Indeed. So it's decided. Champa is mine since it's closer to the Champa river. Malinipur is yours." Jara grinned, as he crookedly watched the blind man. He filled his cup from the wine bottle and asked: "Should we celebrate?"

Dhritarashtra nodded, taking his cup, smashing it against Jara's and then sipping from it.

"You know, everyone thinks I'm the bad man, the evil Jarasandha of Magadh ..." he snorted a laugh, "...wait till they see that true devious nature of yours."

"No one will." The king of Hastinapur spoke with a sharp shift in his tone. "Let them all think...that I am just a poor, old blind man, good for nothing."

And Jara noticed Dhritarashtra grinning at his triumph. He could only think one thing, after all this.

What a fucking bastard.

12

In the present...

The stage was set, for blue blood to be spilled.

It was like a colosseum with more than a hundred people, sitting in a semi-circular stadium. An excited crowd had gathered from small towns, villages, fishing settlements; even ascetics in their saffron attires had heard the news and stationed themselves to see the spectacle.

The ones who came from afar, camped outside the city walls, on land that sloped towards streams of water. Around the colosseum, thousands of fire torches were lit up, for people were waiting for Rangbhoomi and were staying the night outside.

Inside, the people were segregated according to their castes. Drummers and trumpeters could be heard making joyful, stirring music.

The royalty and the elders of the Kuru clan were stationed above everyone, on their own lavish balconies having grapes, apricots and wine, while their servants were fanning them.

Dhritarashtra was with Gandhari, his wife and the mother of Suyodhan. For the sake of being like her husband, she chose to wear a cloth over her eyes, to not see even though she had the ability of sight. They both had orators in the corner of their thrones, informing them what was happening around them.

In another balcony was Kunti, the mother of the Pandavas. She had braided hair and looked younger and sharper, with big, bold kohl-lined eyes and some thin jewellery around her neck. She was awaiting to see her sons perform and there was hope that they would be better than their cousins.

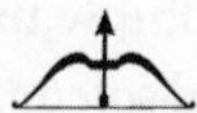

There were terraces belonging to different allied kings, one being Draupad who was with his daughter Panchali and his son Shikhandi. Born as a woman, Shikandi identified himself as a man growing up and while Draupad had a hard time accepting this fact, Panchali loved her brother, whichever way he wanted to be.

"You should be excited," Shikhandi teased Panchali while their father was busy drinking. "You are going to see Arjun."

Panchali grimaced. Arjun, one of the Pandavas, was indeed a handsome man, with features of divine origin, but he was also arrogant about it. And Panchali hated that. "I am here to see Dhristhadyumna only. No one else."

Shikhandi chuckled. The siblings were far away from the land of Panchal, their kingdom in the foot of the Himalayas.

Bhishma Pitamah, with his snowy beard and his pale armour, accompanied by his silent commander Kripa, was on his own terrace when the worried Vidura told him:

"This idea is bad. Pitting cousins and future princes against each other would just create more antagonism between them."

Bhishma didn't believe that. He believed in the idea that they should know each other's strengths and weaknesses, and this was the perfect way to showcase it. "Do not fret, prime minister. My grandchildren are tougher than your weak-minded soul. They know this is just a competition."

"Indeed," Kripa agreed solemnly, the chaser of Bhishma and a dog with a wagging tail for his master.

Vidura didn't take offense, but sighed. The old man was a defeater of champions and an honourable man, but he was also someone who believed in violence more than being a pacifist, unlike Vidura.

He should have never returned from his bloody campaign with Kripa, Vidura thought as he took a sip from his drink made of honey and milk.

A mysterious figure lurked in the bottom of the audience's seats, moving closer to the wooden rails where the guards were standing. Beyond it was the heat from the sun mixing with the sand, the plain field where the action would take place. He could smell the sweat, the stench of rotten teeth and dirt, as he moved past the people. Tall like a giant, the figure reached the railing and stood there, his head covered in a muslin shawl, his perturbed lips concealed.

The field he saw in front of him was of red dust and red earth, but in the middle, he could also see an elevated platform. Zigzag staircases lead up to the platform, which was made of marble and granite and the finest stones—ruby and sapphire—glimmered in the corners. Weapons of all kinds were displayed out front, from javelins to swords to maces. It was for the warriors. The young blood!

The stadium was created for this. And only for this. How much money would be spent on this, the mysterious figure didn't know. But it was a waste. Inciting rivalry between brothers is the worst.

And thus, with these thoughts, the eyes of the figure rolled towards the balconies in the erected towers where the royalty sat and his face turned towards the ministerial terrace, where he saw an individual.

Someone he knew.

I have come here because of you.

Suyodhan knew why Karna wanted his kingship to be announced at Rangbhoomi.

It was to belittle Arjun and impress Panchali.

That would be the reason, of course. What else? Karna always had an affinity towards Draupad's daughter and he hated Arjun for what he had done to Karna.

Even I would.

He coughed and remained in the corner, where it was dark. He was quiet. Really quiet. The sound of the clanging swords and the bowstrings being tied could be heard when he swivelled his head and looked at his cousins. And his brothers.

He was within the stadium walls, which was a closed waiting ground for the warriors.

One by one people would lead. Do something of their own.

Time passed and his anxiety got the better of him. Especially when he saw the brute. Bheem.

The man was big. A giant among them. Close to seven feet tall. Unevenly shaped face, bullish nose and curly hair. He had a big jaw and his eyes were crystal blue, just like the armour he wore. He had a heavier mace than Suyodhan, and he was talking to his brothers and patting their backs.

Suyodhan could feel his blood rushing and his eyes growing dark. His pupils contracting, his fingers growing icy. Memories began to stir. Memories from his past. During the Gurukul days.

When Bheem used to drown him. Shove him. Throw him in the mud and punch him in the face.

"Are you okay?" he heard a voice. It was far. Far away from the corner, it seemed.

He looked up. He was drenched in sweat.

It was Sushasan. His brother. One of the closest ones.

"Yeah, yeah, um..." Suyodhan's mind was racing. "How was your chariot racing?"

"Good. Everyone applauded," Sushasan smiled, kneeling down and Suyodhan saw his brother's bright green eyes, like his own. He was a delicate man and was told by Drona to show off his chariot racing skills.

Everyone had one skill to show. Suyodhan was supposed to break trunks of trees with his mace, but Bheem asked for a mock fight. It wouldn't be bloody. It wouldn't be brutal. It would be fun. Drona contemplated and agreed, to fuel the healthy fire. And that night when he had learnt of this, Suyodhan couldn't sleep. His palpitations were strong.

"I think you should not fight Bheem."

But then I'll be called a coward.

Oh no. That wasn't possible. *I have to show I am worthy of the crown.*

And all the elders here, they would see him in all his might and strength, showcasing the attributes of a Kshtriya.

"That's not possible."

"He wants to embarrass you in front of your parents. He wants to show he can beat you..."

Suyodhan kept shaking his head. He was frustrated. He felt strange. He felt the hooves of thousand horses racing inside him, thrashing him to pulp.

"Then I have to prove him wrong." He looked at his young brother and traced his fingers across his scalp, kissing him on the forehead. "You need to understand, by doing this, I will prove that *we* are the ones the people should respect and follow."

"But what if you lose?"

Suyodhan paused. *Why* would he say that with such earnest eyes? But he controlled his anger and said, "Then we are not fit to rule Hastinapur."

"And what about Arjun?"

That was a problem too. Arjun would show off his archery skills. He was a protégé, a genius in the art of archery since he was just five years old, he had held a reed bow and made it his friend, companion and lover. While people would sleep, he would train.

No one was tougher than him and even if Suyodhan won against Bheem, Arjun would show off his skills which were close to being divine. He had done impossible feats with the bow and arrow. And he would do the same again.

"But he's not competing with anyone?" Suyodhan asked for surety.

"Because *no one wants* to compete with him. Bheem is slow, challenged, and a brute, but Arjun is a genius. Even if you slow him down in archery, he will usurp you with his tactical mind."

Reminds me of someone. Suyodhan chuckled.

"So you are saying the crowd will cheer for him and love him even if he's fighting alone?"

"Yes," Sushasan said.

There is one way though. To embarrass Arjun or come close to embarrassing him.

That path had a name.

And it was Karna.

He was the only one good enough to be close to Arjun, even though he wasn't nearly as good as him. For Karna wasn't a protégé. He wasn't a genius, gifted by the gods. He grew into a powerful archer, over time. With practice. And with patience.

I should have told him to come. I am not even sure he's here.

"Well," Suyodhan said, "let's hope Arjun messes up."

"Best of luck."

Sushasan nodded and hugged his brother before leaving him alone. This distraction was good for him.

He knew the drums were beating and saw the entrance to the doors open, and he saw the light in front. He could hear Drona, standing on the pedestal in his white dhoti and a white string across his red skin, announcing the names of Suyodhan and Bheem.

I am next.

And his eyes met Bheem's. Locked in a fierce gaze. He knew that look. It clearly meant that even though this was a mock fight…

Bheem would not spare him.

13

As he entered the bright open stadium, carrying his mace, he could feel the pressure building inside him.

He could feel the noose of Yama—the god of death—around him, fastening around his neck and dragging him across the halls of fire and brimstone.

I have never been this afraid.

He touched his beard, stroking it, his icy fingertips touching the warm skin. He had never felt like that and the more he witnessed Bheem, the more he was afraid. The man towered over Suyodhan, and as they came to the elevation—the crowd jeered.

For whom, that would be decided by the fate of the fight.

They reached the pedestal, standing on each side of their hunched guru, who scowled and yelled standing above the crowd:

"I welcome now, my two favourites. The greatest of all mace fighters. While others feared defeating each other in the name of blood rivalry, these two looked above it and are fighting to show each other's prowess. On one side, I welcome thee the leader of Kauravas—Duryodhan…"

But that's not my name!

He almost cried out under his breath but Drona had a way with choosing names. After all, he had renamed Karna from Vasu.

"The man who fights viciously."

Suyodhan's name meant 'the one who fights righteously'. He made it the opposite.

"And on my other side, is the giant who can rival the creatures of the mountains, the rakshasas—Bheem!"

People jeered. Clapped. Drums were beaten.

Drona then lowered his voice and came closer to Suyodhan, saying: "I hope you make your father proud."

Suyodhan nodded.

"I heard what you did about Karna. You shouldn't have. I felt it was…it was a personal attack." He nodded. "And that's why I've told Bheem to not be lenient with you." His smile was plastic.

Suyodhan's blood ran cold. Perhaps people knew about Suyodhan convincing his father of Karna's position against Jarasandha. After all, Dhritarashtra had signed the decree and shared it amongst his inner council.

Drona hated Karna. And for reasons only both of them knew.

What had he done to deserve this?

With a frown, he left.

Leaving the two in between.

Suyodhan stared at Bheem, who was just grinning, his crooked teeth protruding out of his mouth. His face looked broken and battered.

Bheem used to hate how Suyodhan was such a good looking boy. He was young. And he was forced by Bheem to taste the shit of the cows and thrown against a tree, breaking his ribs. When he would complain, Drona would punish Bheem to sit outside in the sun and face the brunt of the heat.

But that's it?

Drona was a cruel teacher and because of that—Suyodhan was mightier than he used to be.

Before Suyodhan could wait for the drums to stop beating and the jeering to stop—Bheem raced towards him, plummeting him to the ground.

His head struck the ground, a pinning, searing pain flashing against his body, as he saw the recoil of the mace moving towards him.

With swiftness.

And he turned.

And turned, *again*.

The mace was missing him by inches, otherwise his head would be pulp.

The heavier facade of Bheem was over him, his thighs tightened around Suyodhan's waist and it was like being sat on by an elephant.

Suyodhan brought his fist, instead of his loosely handled mace against Bheem's face—breaking his jaw in the process, the salty trickling blood washing over Suyodhan's face, as Bheem lay wrecked.

The moment Bheem looked a bit confused after absorbing that blow, Suyodhan shoved him away and kicked him in the face again—

This time Bheem held him by the feet.

And grinned.

He was about to twist Suyodhan's leg and that would have been the end of the fight—when Suyodhan brought the mace he had in his hand and smacked it right across his left arm, leaving a thundering wave of discomfort on his face as he groaned.

"Why did you bully me so much?" Suyodhan asked, trying to loosen his feet and stand up on his own, while Bheem was on the ground. "Why? *Why*?" He could feel the tears trickling down his face and his voice becoming inaudible amidst the cheers of the crowd.

"Weak," Bheem said, coming to his feet and spitting a bloody spat. "You were weak. Malnutritioned, washing your snot and drinking milk to get some strength in you. Mother used to say, he will be your king. Ha!" he chuckled as if it was a joke. "You? And a king? My cock would serve the crown better."

When he said it, Suyodhan didn't wait. He restlessly went forward, dashing next to him as Bheem took advantage of his furiousness and dodged...

Manoeuvering cleverly and smacking him in the back.

Suyodhan fell on the ground. And before he could turn and dash, he felt the mace smack his face...

Breaking his nose. His teeth. Splitting his forehead with scars. His eyes were closing...and his face was growing soft, his future, present and past coinciding at the same time...when he saw Bheem's face, who said:

"But I was wrong."

Suyodhan, through the bloody, crimson face of his watched Bheem, whose big, bulgy eyes had softened.

"You are strong." He didn't smack the mace. Not any longer. Because if he did, he would have killed Suyodhan. "You have become strong and I fiercely believe that you do have the pride to be a king."

He put his hand forward. The crowd had gone silent. It was a hand for friendship. For acceptance.

"I apologise for whatever I did. In the past. I was a child," Bheem sighed, heaving. "I was insecure of my height and I picked a fight with anyone who would succumb to me."

Bhishma Pitamah, the grandfather of the Kauravas and Pandavas, was grinning; chuckling and clapping. His full white teeth glimmering in the light.

Vidura, standing in the corner, was curious. With hawk eyes, he asked: "You knew this would happen?"

Bhishma turned to the Prime Minister; a simpleton, born of a low caste, but with a sharp mind. However, not sharper than the old man. "The Pandavas are flawed children but they will grow into a reflection of mine. I just knew. What Bheem did, he did out of what he thought was right. They have my blood."

"And what about Suyodhan?" Vidura leaned forward. "Do you think he will forgive Bheem?"

A flash of uncertainty flitted across Bhishma's face. He looked troubled instantly.

"Well, we are about to find out now."

This is not how it should have turned out to be.

But Drona told Bheem to go tough on him, and even then Bheem disavowed his advice and did what was better.

He became a bigger person.

But am I?

Suyodhan took his time. He looked at Bheem. His hand was flayed. He was reeking of blood too, by now. And his mace had fallen from his hand.

He was without arms. Weak.

There was an opportunity to strike him. But should he?

"Let's not fight brother. Let's..."

It's too late.

Suyodhan gripped his mace and ushered a massive strike against Bheem's face, breaking open his cheek and his face and tossing him on the ground, almost gasping for breath. With the red face, instead of using his mace anymore, Suyodhan skid across his cousin and grabbed him by the throat, choking him.

No one was jeering anymore.

Bheem was tapping the ground to surrender, but Suyodhan didn't leave him. He had gripped him tightly.

"*Brother...Brother...*" Suyodhan snarled. "I am not your damn brother. I will kill you. I will destroy you, you pile of shit."

He could feel Bheem's strength ebbing away, slowly his taps were less...and everything was in a state of numbness.

Suyodhan could not see anything but fire and brimstone. Just like before. But this time, it was him who had ignited it.

"SUYODHAN! SUYODHAN!" cried a familiar voice.

And hands grabbed him by the torso, pushing him away. Bheem choked and coughed as he was loosened from the grip, spitting on the ground and catching his breath, while the bloodshot eyes of Suyodhan remained on the man who interfered in this fight.

His guruji.

"Have you both gone mad? I didn't send you both to kill each other. There is no winner here," he whispered and then smiled at the crowd, while his two wrestlers were lying down, waiting for the soldiers to come and pick them up. "Everything is fine. Everything has been calmed down. Whoosh! What a fight, eh? Well, the next one is very important..."

And Suyodhan felt the background voice fading, as he was taken indoors on a wooden stretcher. His eyes drawn to the crowd where he could hear none of the names being cheered.

No Bheem. No Duryodhan.

If we fight and if we kill each other to better ourselves in the eyes of others, would we not get acclaim? Is a violent act against someone reciprocated with a moment of silence? But they cheered when we began. Perhaps humans like the illusion of violence, more than the act itself.

He remained calm. Still shaken, though, by the path Bheem had taken. His eyes drew out one person in the crowd, before the darkness enveloped him.

And that one person, underneath a cowl, was wearing a breastplate with the symbol of the sun carved on it.

14

Rajmata Kunti was quiet, as she had seen the bloodshed of one of her sons, and with each trickle her heart drowned even deeper into misery.

Was it right to bring them here? To make them succumb to the tyranny of their cousins?

But Pandu, in his dying breath had told her—"*I was supposed to rule, but I became an ascetic. But by default, by virtue and by dharma, it should be our children who should be the kings of Hastinapur.*"

And with that thought, that confidence that she would get the throne easily—she pleaded with Dhritarashtra. The blind king was many things, but to his blood he was a loyal man. In fact, he had detested it when he was given the crown, said he only saw darkness and could not guide his people to light. And so when she returned, he welcomed her.

A selfless man.

Regardless of what she had heard about his tactics towards the helpless or the spiteful—she respected Dhritarashtra the most. He could have easily slaughtered her children and her too, but believed they had the rightful claim to the throne as well.

But sitting here, facing the bitter wind, and gazing at the field that was crimson from the blood that had coursed through Bheem's body—she regretted it.

I should just go. I can't see them getting hurt again. And again.

But then she heard the announcement. Drona with his trademark cane and hunch, walking onto the pedestal, avoiding the filthy blood and speaking as loud as he could: "I bring someone to you now, who I love more than my son. He is not just a gifted archer, but he's my saviour. A day back, I was attacked by an alligator and while all my pupils gathered their wits, it was him, who penetrated the eyes of the alligator and killed it. His fingers are as quick as the velocity of his arrows..."

She knew who it was. A smile came on her face. Arjun. Her protégé. Ever since he was a child, she told him he was the son of Indra. She used to continually convince him of that. She had learnt from one of her priestesses that if the child believes he's the son of god, he would do impossible feats later. It was a foolish desire to make their children great.

But Pandu, her husband, didn't leave any stone unturned. He made her go through *niyog* five times with different priests who worshipped different gods. It was a way of imbuing the powers of gods in their posterity. Albeit, he was obsessed with the idea of having perfect children, divine ones actually, because he was so entranced by spiritualism and religion. He studied science too, the idea of gene and the passing of it.

Kunti gave in. Like she always did. Now seeing Arjun walking towards his guruji, touching his feet and looking splendid as ever—with his grey eyes and a beautiful smile, wavy hair and a chiselled body—Kunti felt she did the right thing.

Even though there was no proof that Arjun had the power of Indra in him—he was still as mighty as the sculptures of Indra would be. Handsome as a hawk and quick as a snake.

"For Arjun, the son of Indra," Drona called him, "he will fight the one animal that lived close to the skies and faced thunder in its habitat. The animal that is not found in Bharat, but in the lands beyond it. Yes. Our Greek friends were kind to give it to us as a gift..."

The Greek? Kunti leaned forward on the railing, worried eyes gazed for an enemy to rise, but she only could see a large iron grilled cage being brought forth, covered in a satin shroud. The cage was rolling and toiling, creating sounds similar to a monster from the depths of Pataal Lok.

Who or what is he combating? Oh no.

"It took thirty men to rein him in and an entire fleet to bring him here. Sedated. Sleeping. Larger than any creature out there. I present..." Drona signalled at the cage, "The Boar of Mount Erymanthos."

The shroud was lifted and the only sound Kunti made was of a terrible, shaking shriek.

15

"THAT'S ONE BIG BOAR!" cried Shikhandi.

Panchali almost let out a gasp of shock, as she watched with rising horror the field which would have pieces of Arjun's flesh scattered around in a few moments from then. The creature was large, like a bison, with thick legs, three horns and tufts of fleshy hair protruding at the onyx, scarred skin. The boar was growling and almost confused, when let out of the cage.

The first thing it did was—

It mauled the closest soldier to death; pulling out his intestines and the heart. It began to chew on it and then looked up at Arjun, who was now left alone with just his reed bow and his obsidian bladed arrows.

Shikhandi, with his cropped hair and bangles hanging from his ears, began to get excited. "Do you think he will survive?"

Panchali wasn't sure. But seeing Arjun, who didn't look perturbed at all by the sight—she was confident that he could. She had known him when she used to look up to him. She was young. Younger than him, and he was a fascinating, good-looking boy. And now, he was not just good looking…he looked like a soldier from the stories her father used to tell her. Of Lord Ram and Lord Parshuram.

He was divine.

Let's see if he wins.

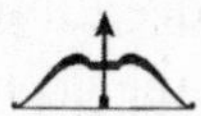

Arjun breathed.

He didn't look perturbed, staring at the creature in front of him; his breath steady and his eyes tracking the boar's each step. The creature was definitely confused. It didn't know where it was, but it surely knew that the person in front of him was about to attack.

Arjun wouldn't but…he would take his time. Patience was the key….

And suddenly the boar charged!

His patience went in the trash as the boar moved for Arjun, and he dashed to the corner, pulling the arrow and stringing it across the bow and aiming at the boar.

But the animal was too fast and he made his charge again, grunting and making retching noises, as it used its three large horns against Arjun…

He rolled over. The musky, red sand at his back.

He just had to have one shot. That would be enough. But the boar was not letting him concentrate. Its hooves were making thunderous quakes, leaving swirls of dust behind. The jeering of the crowd and the gasping and the hurraying was a distraction too. Archery was always good at night. You only had yourself. And no one else.

Feel the arrow.

He closed his eyes and the moment he could feel

the ground shaking and the sound of the boar coming close...

He somersaulted in the air.

Suspended in air, he shot the arrow. Incisive. And swift.

It instantly plunged deep into the flesh of the boar's head and it collapsed on the ground.

Arjun rolled over and came to his feet.

People cheered even more.

And he smiled.

It's over.

He looked straight at the crowd and at his mother Kunti, and then Panchali. Beautiful, seductive Panchali with her auburn locks of hair and her long, slender frame. She had a worried face.

Why?

And then he knew, as he could feel the quakes again. He turned...

But it was too late.

The horns pierced inside Arjun's chest and dropped him down on the ground, as the boar who was injured but certainly not dead, shoved him away with its horn. Arjun's piercing pain continued, and he could feel the sand and the dust around him, as he coughed blood all over his chest. He could hear his mother's loud cry, but struggled to come on his feet.

He realized his arrows and bow were yards away.

And the boar was charging again.

Blood pumped inside of him, rushing in him, as he began to stagger towards his bow. His only weapon.

COME ON!

He left his bloody wound and grabbed the bow, reaching for one arrow and shot it.

It hit the charging boar's eye and for a moment, the creature seemed confused.

Arjun was ready, as he came on his feet, still struggling and quivering. He had managed to lose the quiver and his arrows were scattered, but he grabbed one more and weakly looked at the bow.

I can do this. I am Indraputr.

And as he came forward, he shot another arrow at its eye...

He shot it.

But the arrow missed the mark.

No.

The boar was repulsed by all of this, storming with such fury that Arjun could see his demise. It was right in front of him. Gasps were heard and the moment was close...

When the boar turned. It was not going for Arjun anymore.

But towards the people.

It smacked the guards who were between the audience and the people, and broke through the wooden barricades, moving up the stairs and killing anyone that came in between. There was a lot of screaming and shock and horror, as the royalty fell out of their seats and numerous soldiers moved in the direction of the carnage.

Arjun was himself taken aback, but instead of saving the people—he rested. He couldn't move. Pain had grabbed him by the throat too tightly.

I should. I have to.

And as he did, he could see his brothers and cousins coming out, while soldiers were nearing the massive boar, but they were unable to stop him. They were too afraid, as it was breaking the stage and ripping apart the standing areas when…

Multitudes of arrows, of fire and poison smacked against the boar.

Right in the eye. All of them. With such precision that the boar was flung away in the corner as it collapsed.

It happened so quickly that Arjun was still contemplating as to what just took place. His eyes were wide open in shock.

And then he looked towards the direction from where the arrows had come.

And all the eyes of the people joined his too. Locking in on the person.

Removing his shroud, and letting everyone see his bow and arrow—with its golden plate and kundalams…

Arjun knew just by the look of it.

He was the same boy who he used to humiliate when they were kids.

Karna.

16

Karna hated Arjun.

But the hate was not for the humiliation he had suffered fifteen years back by the famed archer, it was because he couldn't handle the bloody boar. It attacked the public. The Rangbhoomi was cancelled. Medics had appeared and taken away the victims of the boar. And Karna, who was expecting his royal hood be announced was—

Disappointed.

And here he was. In the common halls of Hastinapur's Royal Palace. Ivory laden walls and marbled floors, with red carpets and yellow curtains made of Persian muslin. The halls were big. More than a hundred soldiers, decked in their shields and armours, wearing the emblem of an elephant, which was the motif of the Kuru clan. The elephant, in all its glory, represented wisdom, which apparently was Kuru's possession.

I beg to differ.

The royal families were still there, all murmuring and looking at each other in surprise while the feast in the dining hall was being prepared for them. But for now, the feast was the least of their concerns, even though rats scurried in Karna's stomach.

He was standing next to his old guru, Drona. And Arjun stood at the other end, while all the families had fixed their hawk eyes on them. Bhishma had a foul face, gazing at Karna, while Panchali was shocked to see her old friend Karna in the audience.

The news of Karna leaving Drona had reached the ears of everyone and he had disappeared for a good three years. No one had heard from him. None, except Suyodhan, his father and Dhritarashtra. And then, everyone speculated he had died, only to return at the Rangbhoomi now.

They were in front of the king. Dhritarashtra was in a foul mood, with a frown on his face and clenched fist, while Gandhari was pacifying him, rubbing his arms.

"Guruji," he snarled, "you have disappointed me. Rangbhoomi was supposed to be an entertaining event, but you made it violent and disgusting. More than ten people died and the ones who didn't die, were severely injured."

Drona's head was low, his arms resting on his cane. He looked embarrassed, turning red.

The lighting was low, as the fire lamps breathed orange, but only on some. The golden hatched windows allowed the moonlight to shine.

Karna turned to one side, his eyes darting to his father, the king's driver, who would roam around like a dog on a leash, who was pale as a ghost, watching him with utmost sincerity and shock. He was the opposite of what Karna looked like. He was a bit on the healthier side with a big belly, and a thinly trimmed moustache, oiled. He wanted to hug his father. But he couldn't. He was in front of the king.

"It was never meant to go out of hand. My intention was..." Drona began.

"The intention is never dangerous, but it leads to dangerous consequences," the king said.

Karna found Suyodhan, with a broken arm and a bandaged face. He was not looking like himself and neither was Bheem. Arjun, on the other hand, had no wounds on his face, but his torso, which had stab wounds, was being carefully treated by an Ayurvedic doctor.

"I apologise, your highness. You are right," Drona glumly nodded.

The king turned towards Karna. "And you...who are you?"

With the splendid sun emblem on his breastplate and his kundalams, Karna thought he would be recognisable. But he held no pride when he announced, "Karna, your highness."

"Karna?" The blind king raised his brows. "Indeed." He knew the name. After all, he had just made this man a king. "You have done an important job by saving these people. And for that, we all are grateful. But what were you doing hiding in the shadows?"

He could hear the sound of gurgling distaste coming from Arjun from the other end, who was bowing.

"I am an honest man, your highness," Karna replied. "And for that I should say, I had come here to fight Arjun but that plan went to disarray when he couldn't handle the boar and I had to do it for him."

There was a mighty chuckle amongst people. The Kauravas especially, who loved the dismissiveness Karna had just displayed towards Arjun, who was now flustering with anger and disappointment, but didn't speak a word.

"Fight Arjun? How did you plan to do that?" The king asked, raising his brows.

People murmured amongst themselves.

"Challenge him in front of everyone."

There was a scoff from the Pandava's side. It was Bheem. He couldn't help but gleefully remark at the absurdity of the statement.

Dhritarashtra turned to his brawny giant of a nephew. "Why does it amuse you, boy?"

"Your highness," Bheem said, standing next to his brothers Yudhistr, Nakul and Sahadev, who were all angry with Bheem for being so cocky with the king. "I apologise for my candour, but I believe the rules clearly state that only royalty will duel with royalty. And as far as I remember..." he glared at Karna. "Vasu is a son of a driver and a suta. I mean..." he chuckled again, nudged by Yudhishtr.

Karna gritted his teeth and he wanted to bash the big fart of a man, especially when he saw the despondent look on his father's face, the lowering of his eyes and a tightening of the jaw. He could feel his chest drown in his father's misery. Once a king, now a driver. And Karna couldn't help but feel pity for him.

Dhritarashtra was about to speak, when Suyodhan interjected: "May I, your highness?" He was sounding professional and brutishly incisive.

"Yes, son," the king said, in a harsh tone.

"I believe the news has not been revealed, but..." Suyodhan turned to Karna and smiled. It was a warm one.

Is he really doing it?

"But, Karna is a king."

And at that, he could hear another set of gasps as Karna couldn't help but grin.

Yes, I am.

The sutaputr glanced at Suyodhan again and smiled. It was not of distaste, but out of respect towards an individual who didn't have to announce it like this, but he still did.

"King? What king?" Bheem retorted. "He's no king!"

"Yes, he is." The king spoke softly, breaking Bheem's candour and frustrating him. "Only a few are aware of it now, but he is an interim king of Anga. For *now*."

Whispers broke out. Smiles and frowns were everywhere. The hatred came especially from Bhishma who Karna knew wouldn't like a non-Kshtriya to be ruling as a king of their prized stronghold in the west. "We are threatened by the forces of our once-ally Jarasandha and for that, we are using every means to fight back. He plans to take what he always wanted to—Anga. And I chose Karna to lead Anga and its people to fight against Jarasandha, as the Maharaja of Bharat."

Karna didn't care to look at anyone else, but only his father. He was teary eyed. Broken and restrained in a tight clasp of sadness and joy.

I have done it, father.

When he had told Suyodhan he had reasons for the kingship to be announced in the Rangbhoomi, it was not just to challenge Arjun and embarrass him with his royal status—it was also to show his father, who he knew would be where the king was...

That he had brought the crown home.

17

"May I speak, your highness?"

The voice that was silent for a while, finally spoke with much indulgence and gravitas, after the sudden announcement of Karna's royalty.

"Yes, Arjun?" The king allowed.

"I believe if Karna is royalty, then I can accept to fight him."

"Now?"

"Whenever you wish."

"You are wounded."

Drona turned to Arjun and rasped: "It's not worth it."

Arjun grew quiet. But Karna, now spoke: "I accept to do it now."

"Yes," Arjun agreed standing in his guru's shadow. "We will see who's better then."

The Kauravas clapped their hands in agreement, as did the Pandavas. The brimming energy was nowhere close to what it was earlier. Excitement raged in their guests' eyes and the royal guards whispered to each other, betting on who would win.

"And fling your arrows into our guests' eyes? No, thank you," the king chortled. "We have already faced too many deaths today, but…" he paused, "may I know Karna and Arjun, why you despise each other so much?"

Arjun looked at his rival, while Karna did the same. *Because you are arrogant. You are full of pride, and you think you are the son of god, when you are nothing but made of human flesh,* Karna thought. He didn't know what was running in Arjun's mind, but he was sure he had his own reasons. *And because of that day…that day, fifteen years ago. What you did.*

"I do have an idea, if you both seek to duel and if the guests seem to like this idea."

He clapped his hands and the guards appeared, with their swords and shields.

"Hand over your weapons, men."

Arjun was given a bronze sword while Karna was given the same.

"What is this?" Arjun asked.

"Your weapons. You both are excellent archers. But what about your prowess in swords? We shall see."

Karna, as he was holding the sword and the shield, was feeling weak. It felt like it was not him. It felt alien. The weapons belonged to someone else and for a while, he was confused. But then…

If this is how I have to defeat him, so be it.

Drona moved, with a spiteful expression on his face, as Karna and Arjun, began to circle around dramatically, sizing each other up sharply like eagles. Arjun looked pale and beaten up in his bandaged crimson torso; the stitches must have opened. He was already sweating and his eyes were hazy. But he still had the fire, the energy driving him. He wanted to kill Karna for humiliating him in the Rangbhoomi.

Fifteen years back, Karna was shown his worth by Arjun.

Today, he had that opportunity.

Arjun came forward with a basic jab of his sword, which Karna deflected with his shield, while he elbowed him in the torso—the place where he was already hurt. Arjun stepped back in pain, groaning, as sweat trickled even further.

Karna was patient. He was in his place. His breastplate was on. He had the upper hand. He had all the power to defeat his rival easily…

When Arjun came forward again, instead of attacking instantly, he went for Karna's knees.

The sutaputr jumped and rolled over, smacking the shield on Arjun's back and shoving him on the ground.

Arjun stomped and came on his feet, growling in anger as he threw the shield away and began to smack Karna's sword repeatedly…with as much aggression as he could, to which Karna deflected and the clanging of the blade came about…

When Karna with all his strength pushed him on the ground, he heard it…

"*NO!*"

Before the fight could be over, the voice came from the audience, hidden and concealed, he saw a middle-aged woman, with grey streaks of hair.

He had seen her enough.

"Rajmata Kunti," said King Dhritarashtra, "what is it?"

"I can't see my son get killed. Not here. Not for nothing."

The king chuckled. “He will not. Arjun is holding his ground well.”

Karna and Arjun were still in the same position, tightly grabbing the hilts and pushing the swords on to each other. Karna was impressed that even though Arjun had lost blood, enough to sleep for the night, he still had the power to fight him.

“But…”

“Only the King can stop a royal duel in his own halls, Rajmata Kunti. You may witness the winner or the loser soon. Sons, continue.” The blind king was feverishly leaning back and enjoying, as the orator continued to whisper in his ears what was happening in the duel.

Karna shoved Arjun in the back, and Arjun for a moment, was dizzy, until he began to blindly attack Karna, who threw his sword away and smacked Arjun in the torso, with the sides of his shield. Arjun scowled and yelled in agony, when Karna…

Threw his shield away too.

He heard whispers, but Arjun fell on his knees and his sword was still with him.

“What happened?” Dhritarashtra asked.

Karna looked up at the king. “It’s an unfair fight. I have my armour and he doesn’t. Also, he’s weak. And he’s helpless. And he has his mother who longs for him. I know one thing. I can’t fight one who is not on a par with me. When Arjun is fit and ready to duel again, I shall.”

“You fucking piece of shit!” Arjun snarled. “Fight me,” but he choked and fell on the ground. His voice had power, but he didn’t. He was looking like a feeble child.

“But by doing so, boy, you would be giving up, which

means you would *technically* lose the duel?" the king asked. "He still has his sword on him. Take it away and you might win the duel."

Karna saw the sword Arjun clung on to. Like an infant's toy. But he refrained and shook his head. "I don't know about Arjun, but if I was at a disadvantage, I would expect my enemy to give up too."

The blind king nodded. "Well, so be it. Arjun wins."

But there was no clap. Only sympathy. No applause. Just pity. Arjun was carried by Bheem, who with poisonous eyes watched Karna. Leaving him be.

"Come here," the king called Karna.

And he did. Walking up to him, passing his silent wife Gandhari, Karna could feel the anger rising inside him, involuntarily, as he came close to the king reeking of wine, whose eyes were cloudy and pale. The wrinkles were deep and hair was wiry. He looked like someone Karna would punch, for betraying his father, but he was the Maharaja. The king of kings.

Karna had to be in a position to fight him, enough to punch him.

"Yes, your highness?"

"You are a good man, boy. But remember, these morals, these rules, they don't apply in a war. A day will come," his voice was a raspy whisper, "that you will meet someone who doesn't follow them and he shall use it against you. Don't forget, that day might be near."

Karna paused. He was tempted. Almost, yes. But then, he should expect such derogatory ways of looking at a human being. After all, he was a degenerate himself—feeding on other people's kingdom like a *pishach*, a flesh-eating demon.

"But then, your highness, who would be the bigger man? Me or him?"

And there was another pause, as a sick, gut-wrenching smirk spread across the king's face.

The blind king scoffed. "Believe me, boy, *no one gives a shit.*"

18

And while the royal guests celebrated whatever they were supposed to celebrate, having a feast in the halls where the trumpets were being played and the food was the best mutton and chicken, hunted fish and ducks—Kunti was in no mood to socialise and rejoice.

She knew people had died that day and while they were of low castes, low births, and the royals would not spare a thought before going on with their lives, she couldn't. So she stayed in her room.

But there was one more reason. It being him, who made her feel she had seen a ghost. In the form of...

Karna.

He was wearing her armour. Her kundalams...

They were hers.

She didn't want to think. She was biting her lips. On her mattress, being fanned in her room, watching the windows and the specks of moonlight.

I should talk to someone. Someone, at least!

She began to run through the ideas. Who could it be? Who was wise and understanding but also had the genius to tell her what to do?

Vidura...but she was not close to him.

Dhritarashtra...a good man, but today he showed an absolutely remorseless facade. A different one, than she was used to. Her trust in him was no more.

She couldn't tell her children...

Maybe...Drona. He was an Acharya, but also detested Karna as poison in his eye. For reasons only they knew.

There was someone else.

Someone who was neutral.

She should see...

Arjun was sitting glumly, when he was slapped by his giant of a brother on the back, who was drowning himself in wine.

They were at the warrior complex made of brick and mortar, with linen curtains and to go from a prestigious bloody place to a degenerate place—it took them just three jars of wine. Everyone was singing, dancing and the whores of the city had come to impress the warriors. The king and queen had left before the place had become a land of sins. Even the elders were nowhere to be seen. Only the Kauravas, who were at the other table, a hundred and one of them—so many of them, all from different mothers.

Gandhari was just the face of the Kauravas, but only three held her blood and flesh—Suyodhan, Sushasan and Sushala. Yuyutsu was there too, but he was born of a maid. The rest of Arjun's cousins were not legitimate, all hogging like the boar he had fought earlier that day. Fat as pigs, born out of wedlock or out of infidelity by the womb of low births. The king was a fascist lord, believing in bedding hundreds and the same trait had been transferred to Suyodhan. And being the king, Dhritarashtra had accepted all the children and put them in the palace.

"You should not take it to heart, what happened today," a familiar, soft voice said and he turned to see his oldest brother, Yudhistr, with his curly locks of hair and an enchanting smile. He was the smallest of them all, with an oval face and smart eyes, but he was not handsome like Arjun or a brute like Bheem. In fact, he was the opposite of everyone in the family, but he had that…that aura of a leader. A quiet restraint, and he spoke with diligence. He wasn't drinking or eating like the rest of the brothers, since he never indulged in vices. Bheem, on the other hand, had two wenches on his lap and was sucking their tits out in the open. No sort of worry about anything.

He reminded Arjun of Uncle Vidura.

"Panchali saw everything," Arjun spoke, with a defeated sigh. "It breaks my heart, the fact that she might…think of me as a worthless boy."

Yudhishtr nodded. "So that was why you wanted to fight Karna? To impress her?"

"She always liked him more than me."

"How does it matter? Her father likes you more."

Arjun scoffed. "I am not going to end up marrying her father, or her brother." And then he turned around, looking at this dungeon of lust and perversity. The royal people, the ones who didn't shed blood and sweat today, were in the dining halls of the royal palace, where Panchali would be with her father. He should have just gone there, but Bheem had forced him to come here instead and revel in between the thighs of the exotic wenches from around the world. They all pooled in money to bring these women, the money they'd saved up and not many around the palace knew of such things going on. Even Drona, their tutor who was probably asleep in his quarters by now, snoring while dreaming of finding redemption in the king's eyes after today's events.

"I should talk to her."

"It's always her, you know. People don't realise that," Yudhishtr said. "Whatever you did, you did it for her. All the practice, all the love for archery—you wanted to be the best for her."

Arjun didn't say anything. He was a born archer. But he recalled how Panchali had seen him practicing once. She was eight and he was barely twelve and she grinned. Asked him to teach her and he did. They giggled. They talked. He knew then, he wanted to be with her. It was like...it was her...only her, always her.

"I should go to her hall, talk to her."

"She could be sleeping, Partha," Yudhishtr called him by his housename.

But Arjun didn't care to listen, when Bheem slapped him on the back again and it felt like a thunderous wave crashing against him. He said: "Listen, stop worrying about her and meet Bhanumati."

Arjun was introduced to a tall girl who could easily have been rivalling Bheem's height. She was slender and beautiful but Arjun found nothing attractive about her.

"Her thighs can choke you if you like that stuff," Bheem said. "Why don't you let her choke you?"

Arjun groaned, as Bheem chuckled. Bhanumati was standing almost naked, wearing a transparent cloth that showed her erect nipples. She had an aquiline nose and she was proud of it, with an exotic accent she knelt down in front of Arjun and spoke: "I can pleasure you the way I pleasure the African men."

Arjun came on his feet and pushed her to the side. "Thank you. But I'll be fine." He looked at his older brother Yudhishtr while Bheem was disappointed by Arjun's behaviour. "I should meet her."

Yudhishtr glumly nodded.

And Arjun, without a second look, went forward.

Kunti entered by parting the curtains and stepped on to the crimson carpet, to find herself in a lavish, fountain-studded room with a weapon case on the side and a terrace that opened up to another fountain.

"What is it, Kunti maa?" A booming, hoarse voice could be heard.

She turned to see where it came from and he could not be seen, but then she moved towards the terrace, to see the shadow move and there appeared the man, the god himself.

Gangaputr Bhishma Pitamah.

He had white locks of hair till his chest and a muscled body that could rival a young lad, even though he was the oldest of them all. A golden rim was clasped around his thick muscles, while a dhoti of gold and white was wrapped around his waist. He had blue eyes, like water.

"How did you know it was me?"

"Your footsteps. You walk carefully, tread as if you don't belong here."

"But I don't."

"You do. Hastinapur is yours. Pandu was the rightful heir, but he forfeited, for what..."

To be an ascetic and obsess over having divine children. He would do experiments, play around with nature. He wanted the perfect children and he knew his seed wouldn't be perfect.

"Yes, I know. But still, these halls are lonely. I have no one I can trust. The only person I know is you, who is good towards my sons and Gandhari's sons," she bowed in respect and knelt down.

Bhishma remained there, his arms tightened and crossed against his chest. "You are worried. What is it?"

"I have to tell you a story."

"You have come here to tell me a story?"

"It's an important one."

"Indeed. Speak. I'll listen."

"A long time back, when I was a child, barely fifteen years old, I had fallen in love with a man. He was sixteen and he was a shishya of Guru Durvasa, a worshipper of Suryadev."

"Hmmm."

Durvasa was a name to be reckoned with, for he was popular for being synonymous with the word "anger". He would be angry about every little thing.

"We fell in love and I got pregnant. At such a young age, I had no knowledge of what to do. He left with Durvasa and I followed him. And so, when Durvasa found out about us, he told us we could stay with him till the child was born and then the child would be under their care. I was fine with it, and so I did as told." She was almost getting teary eyed as the stars were twinkling and she heard the hoots of the owl in the background. "But then as I was near the due date, I noticed changes in Durvasa. When the child was finally born, Durvasa took him, and I learnt that my lover and him...they had planned to kill the child. For he was an abomination, a son of a child and a student. He had to be killed. I snatched the child and ran...and ran...

"Until I reached the banks of your mother, Ganga. It flew like a hopeful ravine and I knew I had no choice but to drop the child in the water. And so I did, but I made sure I gave him my breastplate, the one made in the kingdom and my kundalams, the one I was gifted as a child. I gave it to him because I wanted him to be protected by these gifts which were lucky for me as a child. I knew I couldn't go back to my father nor could I give it to Durvasa...so I dropped the basket with the child in it..."

"What are you getting at, woman?" Bhishma came close, towering over her.

Her bangles glinted, as she could feel the sourness in her mouth. "I believe Karna is my son."

Bhishma raised his brows. "Why do you think so?"

"He wears what I gave to that child of mine. Do you think..."

Bhishma didn't let her finish, but grabbed her by the shoulders and pulled her up, gazing at her with his steely eyes. "Have you told this to anyone else?"

"No. I didn't know who else to..."

"Good. Don't mention this ever again," Bhishma said.

She shivered, her spine growing cold. "Why?"

"Because even if he is your son, it is not his karma to be under your care, for you to be his mother."

"But…but I could be his mother…"

"The gods don't want that. If they did, he would have been like Arjun or Yudhishtr. But he's not. That boy was born out of wedlock and for all I care, he's not your son, but a mistake."

She couldn't believe she was hearing these words from a wise man like Bhishma, but he was serious and determined about it.

"He has the right to know."

"Kunti, my dear girl," he hugged her and said, "when you came over here from the woods, it was me who convinced the king to take you in. You know why? Because I saw his sons. They were…well, let's say…they were not fit to rule Hastinapur. I have been the protector of the throne for years now even though I do not sit on it. It is my duty to choose the best successor. But when I saw Yudhishtr, the young boy with wisdom beyond his years, I found the heir to the throne. I do not speak of this to anyone, but I believe so firmly. He's the oldest and the wisest of them all. He comes from Pandu's blood and he's the right one. But when you tell this story, the people of Hastinapur will cast doubts on…Yudhishtr. They will think that he's not the oldest one."

Yes. Karna is.

"That mistake of yours was born before everyone and for that, he would be rightfully sitting on the throne." He flared his nostrils, tightening his arms around her meek ones and she could feel the pressure of the Gangaputr. "And I know that the blood of my father, King Shantanu of Hastinapur, whose sons Pandu and Dhritarashtra are, is the only bloodline who will inherit that throne. Not some kid who was too busy impregnating women rather than studying the art of spirituality."

"But isn't Yudhishtr born out of a priest too?"

"By the laws of *niyog* but, my dear Kunti. The laws of *niyog* clearly state that if the husband is unable to impregnate their wife, they can request a pandit to do so, and that son would be the husband's even if the husband's seed is not in the woman. It's the law. And I follow the laws. But Karna was born out of sheer lust between you and that boy," he rasped and she was hurt by his cruel words. "In *niyog* there is no lust, just determination to continue posterity."

Kunti nodded. But the choice of priests...Pandu had gone to great lengths to find the perfect priests to impregnate her. He was obsessed with having perfect children. Divine. He had checked hundreds of times whether the priests had the capability, what talents they possessed since genes is one thing that would be passed on from the priest to the child.

"I can't let a sutaputr sit on the bloody throne that I have for years protected. He's a nobody and let him fight his petty war with Jarasandha. But when it comes to Hastinapur, he shall not set foot around it." Kunti teared up, feeling guilty of leaving the child and being wracked by uncertainty whether Karna was her son or not. "If you have to tell him, so be it. Tell him when the world ends and when the fiercest of all wars rages. But not now. Otherwise, you will be harming your true blood son's reputation and claim on the throne and not even I could help you then, dear Kunti." His voice softened, but she could see the sheer manipulation Bhishma was capable of now.

He didn't want anyone but Yudhishtr even though rightfully it should be Karna, who could contest for the throne.

But it was fine.

Yudhishtr was more important than Karna. Far more. She wasn't even sure if Karna was her son or not. He could have stolen or bartered that breastplate.

Though she knew, even if she could not tell him—she should talk to him.

Just once, to see whether he *really* was her son.

19

Karna was sitting outside, looking at his dreary hands that pained due to the blisters caused by grasping a sword for a while. He had no armour on tonight; it was kept in his quarters along with his weapons.

He looked down at the warrior's complex, where the soldiers practiced. It was a dome-like structure and at night, the wenches looked like fireflies with their transparent, glowing clothes while walking around inside the complex. Karna knew that wasn't allowed, but Suyodhan must have arranged it and the elders—they just turned a blind eye to it, as if it didn't matter, as if it was part of being a warrior, to be pleasured by women.

The complex was far from the royal palace, yards away, adjacent to the woods. That was where the celebration of the Pandavas and the Kauravas was taking place; they were enjoying to the hilt, as they should. He should have been there along with the people of his age, but he was invited here to this feast by the king, to a more solitary, quiet event of whispering and chortles. He had seen Panchali often. They exchanged glances from afar, but did not speak. He was mindful; confused, whether he should approach her or she would.

But she didn't. And by that time, as the warriors celebrated and would continue to do so till morning, the feast was getting over. The royalty would be going back to their quarters to sleep.

That's when he saw the familiar figure moving towards them.

The sound of the trumpets were heard from the halls, but the courtyard was fairly empty except for the bards and the drunken men.

He had not been able to talk to his father.

Correction: he couldn't bring himself to talk to him.

So he was outside. Away from him. Away from everyone.

But his father found him. As he saw him walking, Karna wanted to tightly embrace him, but he remained restrained. Perhaps because a lot of time had passed by. He had last seen his father perhaps five years back, when he was bidding farewell to him, his mother and his brother while leaving for Gurukul.

In between, he had an opportunity to come and meet them, but he didn't. He had a *promise* to keep.

"It's you," his father spoke in disbelief. "In the flesh."

Karna was quiet. *Should I hug him?*

"I should congratulate you, your highness," Adhirath mocked.

"Father..."

Adhirath didn't sit next to him. He remained still. Karna could see that he missed his son but at the same time, he could see he was angry.

And he had good reasons.

"We thought...I...I thought you were dead. You were

gone from the face of the earth and I had no idea where you were. I sought messengers from all over the country and they never found you."

"I was in the north. At Parsurama's," Karna said, bowing his head a bit with shame.

"I sent letters to..."

"I got them," Karna nodded. "The last letter..." he paused. He choked up thinking about it.

It was the time when he had been ousted from Drona's Gurukul at the pinnacle of his last year of graduation and he thought of defying his guru and leaving for the north, to complete his studies in martial arts—when the letter had arrived. It was his father who said his mother was ill...really ill...and she was close to death. That he should take leave and return. Instead, he cried. He wept because he could not be a part of her death, during her last days. He had a promise to keep.

"And you didn't come," Adhirath's eyes flashed with agony, with hurt. "I expected you. I expected a response."

"I know, father," Karna said. "Is she..."

"Yes. That year itself."

Karna clenched his jaw. There was a tinge of regret, but he was still proud of what he did: of being close to fulfilling that promise.

"How's Shon?" He asked about his brother.

"You don't get to question me," his father's voice cracked, with tears in his eyes. "You don't deserve answers. How dare you not come back during your mother's last days. Have you no feelings, no emotions? Do you think you are adopted and that's why you can treat us like that?"

Karna bit his lip. That was not it. *I am adopted, but you both were always my parents,* he wanted to say, but he was quiet.

"And now you come, make this grand entry and expect me to open my arms for you?" Adhirath's eyes were red.

"I don't expect anything father."

"You are a stranger to me. Four years. Four years of no response; of silence. Shon and me...we lived without you and without your mother. I believe, we will continue to do that now." He paused, as Karna remained quiet. He had nothing to say in response but only blabbering nonsense. He had a justification, but until he achieved that justification, he didn't want to say anything. "It is mighty kind of you to do that for Anga, for your soil, I believe. The king chose you for a reason as his close friend, I should suggest you not let him down. But if you think you can do what I couldn't, then you are wrong. There will come a time when Jarasandha will feel you are nothing and he will partner with the king and it'll be over soon. Your crusade, the promises to you...they'll be done for. And you'll be left in the cold like me." Karna could hear the concern in his voice and even though he was detesting his son, he still loved him. Karna could see that. "I could take the shame, the embarrassment of driving a bloody chariot. I do not want the same fate for you and Shon. I wanted you both away from it, all this bloodshed, war, politics. It's not in us, to be this way, that's why I gave up years back."

You were manipulated.

"And while you left me, I made sure Shon joined an ashram and worked hard to become a priest. He will live a happy life."

Adhirath began to move again, when Karna reached for his feet and called out: "Father?"

Adhirath turned. His face flustered. He didn't say anything.

"Did you ever return to Anga?"

"What do you mean?"

"When I left, when mother wasn't there, did you return to Anga?"

"There's nothing left there. There's just chaos and blood and…it's not the same as it used to be. It has changed tremendously and has become a land of reap but no sow, due to deforestation. Timber is being sold like hotcakes. Your mother was right," he scoffed. "She told me, if I sided with the king, I would lose half the kingdom too and we would have no Anga. But then I had no choice. I was weak. I STILL AM WEAK!" His voice cracked, hurt. "But I can't see my sons go down that road. Because I know they'll fail too."

"I want to right the wrong," Karna said weakly. "Anga is ours and I'll make sure it'll remain ours."

"At what cost?" The moonlight slivered over his face.

"Everything," Karna impassively responded.

He scoffed, "Your thirst for power is wrong."

It's not power I seek. It's the promise I have to fulfill.

"You are right about one thing," Karna said. "You are a weak man. But you are wrong about another. *I'm not.*"

Adhirath was stunned by his son's staunch approach but he didn't say anything. Shrugging, he left.

Karna sat back but he didn't feel like doing anything. He felt strange and alienated, rejected by the man he wanted to show in the morning that he had become the king of Anga, to make him feel proud but instead this happened. He felt rejected by him and he wanted to sob and weep for that fact. *How things get twisted.* But it would not divert him from the sparrow's eye that he sought. He had to reach his destination even if he failed everyone in the process.

Shon was a good swordsman, but father pushed him to be a priest. *That's wrong*. Just because he was weak, doesn't mean his progeny would be too.

All his life, he battled being called a sutaputr. An intercaste inbred. Rejected by society. Society intended him to be a charioteer, just like his father, but he didn't want that fate. He thought his father would be different since he was a victim too. But he also thought that Karna was worthless and he would lose the war. In fact, Karna was sure everyone thought that way.

And now, he had never imagined he would be rejected by the one person whose identity he carried all his life.

Though he knew there was one person who wouldn't reject him. One person who was always sweet to him.

Panchali.

She could be here. He should meet her. She was, after all, looking at him earnestly. It had been years, he had not met her, but he would now.

Because he was leaving the next day for Anga. To prepare for warfare against Jarasandha.

As he raced across the tulip gardens, his memory too raced back to the days when he had met her, to the point where he was humiliated by the treacherous, vicious Arjun.

Those were both bright and dark days.

It was a time when he was not called Karna...but Vasu.

20

12 years earlier...

City of elephants, it was called.

And behold, it was.

Vasu had only heard of the place from the people around him. Uncle Satya had told him a little and while he had stayed back in Anga to continue his secret military expansion that one day Vasu would lead—Vasu and his family had left for Hastinapur. He didn't want to go to the place where the usurper Dhritarashtra lived, but he couldn't say no to his parents for no reason.

The entire royal family was invited to Hastinapur for Chhat Pooja—the prestigious festival for Suryadev. In fact, lots of other royal families, allies of the Supreme King, were called and they were given hospices to stay in the palace itself. Dhritarashtra had been there in person to welcome them.

And while Vasu didn't like all of this, he couldn't help but appreciate the beauty and the marvel of the city of elephants, the city of wisdom and the city of the greatest architecture.

From far, Hastinapur had large fifty feet elephant

statues made of marble and granite, while there were outposts—four of them—to make sure no enemy could enter. There were watchtowers and basilisk gates made of thorns, but those were now decorated with roses due to Chhat Pooja. The entire city was situated on a hillock and the roads zigzagged to the top of the hill where the great palace was.

Large walls acted as defence and little fortresses and ashrams were on each side where the senanis as well as the priest resided. There were bazaars, bustling with energy and there were slums which formed the underbelly of the city.

There was a temple, huge in size, circular in shape, with outer circles smaller than the ones inside. On top of it, the idol of Goddess Kali resided.

"That's the Pandeshwar temple," his father explained. "This is where the sons of Pandu and sons of Kauravas are taught the Puranas and the Smritis by the great sage and guru, Acharya Drona."

Drona…

The name.

Vasu knew the popular name so distinctly, he had heard about him ever since he was born.

And he knew this visit for Chhat Pooja, could be an opportunity for him to impress the old man.

He had only heard about Drona—a wandering sage, who met the fabled immortal Lord Parshuram and through him he got the opportunity to be an acharya for the royal children. His favourite pupil being Arjun, of course, the master archer. He had heard everything and now because of Chhat Pooja, he would be seeing everything closely.

As they entered the palace, they were adorned with garlands and tikas. Vasu saw up close the lavender gardens of the palace and the hanging pots of lilies. There were ponds with fishes and everything was so beautiful, so rich in texture compared to Anga.

In comparison to this, Anga Pradesh seemed like a poor man's island.

Vasu saw a small complex made of gold, having four tight walls with two or three guards and cherry trees lined next to those walls. It seemed to stand out in comparison to the other places in the ground.

"What is that?" Vasu asked, since his father knew most of the places here. Even three-year-old Shon got excited and looked up from his mother's caress to see what his brother was pointing towards.

"That, my son, is the great Royal Stable, where the Maharaja's chariot rests."

"So much security for a vehicle?"

"It's not just a vehicle. It's made from the pearls that are found in the depths of the Arabian Sea," his father said. "No one is allowed to enter except him, me and a cleaner."

"Wow." Vasu was enamoured by the idea, since it was the chariot that the warriors rode on except that Dhritarashtra was a thief, but that didn't devalue the purity of what a royal chariot stood for. "So I can't see?"

"No. Don't be mad," Adhirath shushed him.

Vasu was definitely disappointed. But the rebel that he always was—he decided to do something drastic.

He decided to see it nevertheless.

As the midnight oil burnt and the entire palace was shut—

Vasu made a move.

And his move was quite simple. Tiptoeing to the Royal Stable and passing through the gardens, he hid inside the bushes to see the guards in front of him. They were moving on the side of the wall and they were all holding spears.

Getting caught by them would be an issue. And it would bring big shame to his family. So he had to be careful. He crossed the garden, crouching as he made his way to the trees that were right next to the walls of the Royal Stable.

Vasu noticed a cherry tree which he realised he could climb. And without further thought, he did so. Pulling himself up, he made his way to the top and dangled from the long branch that lopsidedly hung like a woman's wrinkled hands over to the other side of the wall.

His hands felt the pressure, almost reddening from touching the scratchy twigs leaving minor scars on his skin.

The guard who was doing the rounds, walked underneath him as he dangled from the top. Vasu only hoped that the branch wouldn't make a sound of any kind or his sweat wouldn't trickle down on the ground that would alert the guard, who was busy checking something under his feet.

Vasu felt something close to his legs and he could feel it even more clearly as it began to move up his dhoti when he realised, what it was: *a rattlesnake*.

He managed to hold back his scream. Because if he screamed, he would be caught instantly for trespassing and the consequences wouldn't be pretty. The snake slowly moved upwards and looked at him, hissing.

Uncle Satya had always taught him not to alarm any snake. Let them feel safe and secure, and they will respond with no danger.

While the guard remained underneath, so did the snake remain close to him. Vasu couldn't fathom that to see a simple chariot, he had to go through such trials.

That was when the snake turned back. A sigh of relief escaped from Vasu's mouth when he noticed fangs being plunged out, and the snake's mouth opening…

He's going to bite me!

He instantly shook his leg and the snake flung itself down, on the guard, who was taken by surprise and struggled to get rid of the snake.

I don't have much time. Here it is…

His heart was in his mouth as he took a leap of faith, his chest thumping and his mouth opening, letting the breeze just smack him like a mace.

He rolled over to the other side, his feet bruising in the process, his knees rubbing against the ground.

He made a little squeak and blood rushed in his ears, as he realised the sound would lead the guards to hear him.

He instantly hid close to the golden, glittering shed, just lurking in its shadows while he waited for the guards. He caught his breath and calmed his pulse.

I hope this is worth the effort.

Vasu realised that no one was coming to check on him. With a triumphant grin, he walked about the shed, his eyes scanning for a door through which he could enter.

Crouching and tiptoeing, so the guards who were inside the walls couldn't hear or see him, he walked to the door and entered slyly.

And once he did, a short breath escaped him as he witnessed...

Oh, by the heavens!

His breath seized again and he exhaled in shocked delight. Delight because he saw the chariot which was golden and bronze, the seating was muslin and the reins were ivory. Sapphires and rubies added to the gleam. The chariot was huge, it could almost seat five to six people.

And it had an aura.

The pearls, as his father had told him, were lined up perfectly across the side as decorative elements. For sure, as his father suggested, they had come out of the water. Dhritarashtra must have taken help from the Naga people, who were the fisher community; they worked in isolation unlike the other tribals, like the rakshasas or the vanars.

Vasu walked around the chariot, noticing the finesse and looked at the seat. Oh, the seat. He ignored everything else in the world and just focused on the wars, the battles the king must have fought on this. Battle chariots during the yug he lived in were the prime movers of the battle, used by the greatest men and the greatest of heroes. Dhritarashtra was an aberration in this case, but then that man was a king, no matter how ruthless he was towards certain kingdoms.

Uncle Satya had told him of the grand tales of Lord Ram, Lord Parshuram and Bhishma Pitamah, who was after all a living legend, uncle to the king himself. All the heroes used chariots and fought wars for valour, for duty.

Vasu had this sudden urge to be just that. That's why he had come. That's why he had broken his father's rules and laws of the palace, to be here.

To feel like something he had never felt all his life.

A king.

To be seated on the throne and the chariot. And the seat, it made him feel like one.

I will be that. Soon.

Vasu pulled himself up and sat on it. For a moment, he could feel it—in front of him, all the creatures and his enemies. He could imagine he was in a battlefield and he had a bow and an arrow that he was swinging across enemies of all kinds.

And he continued to do so, until the door of the shed opened in front of him with a voice saying...

"I finally got permission from the king and I wouldn't squander it for another day. I have to see the chariot." It was of a girl, who entered while Vasu was playing makeshift archery.

Behind her, was a soldier, who followed her. "But Rajkumari, he has said you can see it anytime you want and the night isn't the best time..."

The girl who had entered was younger than Vasu and she looked up at Vasu with absolute delight and horror.

Vasu looked back at her.

Her mouth was wide open. So was his.

But then, he noticed how vibrant and beautiful she was. She had brown eyes and fair, cherubic skin with freckles under her kohl-dipped lashes. There was a headgear and a necklace of diamonds and crystals.

Time stood still altogether thanks to her beauty...

There was an awkward silence and when the soldier saw Vasu—it didn't help.

"Rajkumari Panchali," said the soldier, "I believe we have an intruder."

21

If he was told that the great Bhishma Pitamah wanted to meet him, he would have been happy…

But under ordinary circumstances, of course.

This wasn't ordinary. This was frightening. This was a circumstance where he was a trespasser and a rebel and an insubordinate, the black sheep of the royal family of Anga Pradesh.

Vasu stood silently in the chambers of Bhishma, the commander-in-chief and the head of security for the king. But the man wasn't there.

Vasu waited, as his thoughts meandered towards Panchali. He had heard the name from his uncle; she was the princess of Panchala, who was beautiful and nice and gracious. She was allowed in to see the chariot, because she was a princess while Vasu was rejected outright by his father because…

He wanted to question his father about this.

He stood, next to Vasu, impassive as always, an embarrassed expression on his face. He didn't speak to Vasu. And that was worse than shouting. It was when your parent had given up on you.

The chamber doors opened behind them, and Vasu

heard the large footsteps echoing as the figure in front of them stood there, before circling around them and then sitting on the cushion.

There was a red drape behind, two hanging pots and a lamp burning. There was a short table over which documents of yellow colour were placed and scattered.

The man, Vasu saw, was a hulking figure. Almost above seven feet tall. He was broad as a wrestler with tight, vein-popping muscles. His eyes were crystal blue, like the Ganga river he was apparently born close to. He was called Gangaputr. His hair was white and snowy, pulled back, his thick mane that coiled and wound, next to his breastplate.

It was Devavrat, also called Bhishma—the man who had vowed to protect the throne of his father, Shantanu.

But his eyes were tough and bloodshot.

"Pranaam, Commander Bhishma," Adhirath bowed.

Vasu didn't, as he was in awe of the man in front of him.

"Do you have no manners, boy?" Bhishma asked.

Vasu then realised and bowed as well.

"I see you are a rebel," Bhishma said as he picked up the grapes from the fruit basket. "Someone who breaks the rules, when you could have asked for permission."

Vasu didn't say anything. His head was lowered and his hands were at his back.

"Do you seek forgiveness?"

"Yes," Vasu earnestly nodded.

"Then explain to me why you did it."

Vasu was shy. He didn't know why he did it, but it was all about the curiosity, the nature of the chariot, the significance of it. "I wanted to see what my father drives for your highness."

And then he heard it. There were some footsteps in the room, but he didn't turn around. The footsteps stopped close to the windows. From his peripheral vision, Vasu realised there was someone else there.

"It's simply a chariot," Bhishma sighed.

"For you," he raised his brows, "but for me it makes me work more."

"Work? Heh..." he chuckled, in a gruff way, "work for what?"

"To be the heir of Anga, to be the king, of course, Lord Bhishma."

"King, I see," Bhishma came on his feet, as he walked around the nineteen-year-old Vasu. Even though Vasu was shorter than Bhishma, his frame was tough. He was six feet five inches and he had a muscular build. "What makes you think you can be a king? A king is someone who follows rules, not breaks them."

"No, my lord," Vasu recalled what Uncle Satya had taught him as he matched his eyes with the icy glare of the Gangaputr. "A king is someone who has to break the rules for the betterment of his kingdom. In fact, he's the only one who can afford to do so, while giving the illusion that he's a rule bearer."

"Really? Which king does that?"

Every atom in his body was rejecting this answer, but his instinct said to go with it:

"The very ones that rule us, Lord Bhishma."

"Adhirath!" Bhishma scowled, and Vasu's father instantly fell on Bhishma's knees. "Your son has quite an attitude. Does he mock your king by speaking such ill-fated words?"

"Commander," Adhirath whimpered and anger rose in Vasu's blood and veins, "he's a child. Please forgive him. He has no idea what he speaks of."

"That's where you are wrong, driver," Bhishma sniggered and the word *driver* pierced through Vasu's skin. "He knows too much." A smile appeared on his face, as if in a very sinister, mocking way.

"He's not a driver, my lord," Vasu said, through gritted teeth, what his mother had told him since he was a child, informed him his real status and not the one that was forced on them. "He's the rightful king of Anga."

"Your father is nothing but a driver, son," Bhishma said with a straight face. "And if you think you can take the kingdom from him once you grow up, you are wrong. You won't have the strength to do it, because you are after all, a sutaputr, son of a sarthi, a driver. And a king can only be a Kshtriya. No more. No less. Only a Kshtriya rules the stead and the ones who are not Kshtriya, become victims of the war." He signalled at the man at his feet. "Look at your father, son. He was a suta and thus he lost to Jarasandha. A suta knows nothing. A suta is just a... vermin. You can't be a king. In fact, you can't be even close to it."

Vasu had so many things running in his mind, but the only thing he could say right then was: "Watch...me... try."

And at that, Bhishma was taken aback. Adhirath had come on his feet and he had begun to slap his son on the head for speaking with such hostility to the honourable Bhishma Pitamah.

The old commander stepped back and ordered: "ADHIRATH! Your son…he's a nuisance. You have served your highness for a while and for that, I am ready to lock him up only on the day of the Chhat Pooja. He should not be allowed to witness the beautiful, grand festival that celebrates Suryadev."

"Lock up? My lord, he's not an enemy…he's…he's…" Adhirath began to shiver.

"He's a trespasser."

Vasu nodded and told his father: "I'm ready to take the punishment. Lord Bhishma, thank you for being so forgiving."

And he turned as the soldiers came to take him. That was when Vasu's eye caught the figure next to the window who had slithered inside the room at the beginning of the meeting.

He saw the matted hair, the gray beard, the man with a twisted mouth and a crouched body. He held a cane in his hand and he had a smile on his face. He was wearing a saffron angavastram with a saffron dhoti.

Vasu didn't know who he was, and so he walked off with Adhirath on his side. And the last words he heard from the room while exiting were:

"It's very rare to see such guts in a young boy like him, Devavrat," the mysterious man's voice spoke. "Perhaps he can bring those guts on the field too."

"Guts that shouldn't be encouraged," Bhishma sighed, finally revealing the mysterious man's name, "Drona ."

22

Chhat Pooja was celebrated during sunset in the best possible way. The parvaitis, who were the worshippers, mostly women, had fasted, drank no water even and moved to the majestic riverbank of Ganga. There was Kunti, Panchali, Gandhari, wives and daughters of other kingdoms. They had their friends and family behind them, watching them. The women had arghya, which were the offerings to the setting sun in winnow baskets that held sweets, kheer, thekua, fruits like sugarcane, sweet lime and banana. Folk songs were being played on sitars and flutes. Drums were beaten.

The Maharaja stood along with the other rajas and his senanis and the commanders. Food was being cooked by the finest of cooks that had come from around the world but only the vegetarian kind.

But Vasu was nowhere to be seen. He was frustrated he couldn't be a part of the prestigious Chhat Pooja celebrations and it bothered him.

He was locked up in a small cell and his parents were almost teary eyed to see their son in such a place. But he didn't feel bad. He had stood up for his crown when his father wouldn't do it. He had stood up to being called a driver's son. He was much more than that.

Bhishma was a ruthless, callous man, Vasu realised. He was Pitamah to his grandsons—the Kauravas and the Pandavas. But not to anyone else. He was a cold-hearted warrior and Vasu respected him till the time he had demeaned him.

As night fell and the moon became his ally, specks of moonlight entered through the iron grills of the cell's window. Vasu saw a figure emerging from the darkness.

He was sheepish and he rubbed his eyes to find the figure glowing in saffron. The figure had a headgear on, a nice jewel hung across the neck, a chunni that glistened.

He realised who it was.

Panchali.

Vasu couldn't help but smile as she came close to the grills; she had a thali in her hand.

"Are you here, son of Adhirath?" she asked. "I was told you were here."

"Yes," Vasu meekly responded, coming on his feet and showing himself in the moonlight.

They both stared at each other, when she broke her silence: "I am uh...well I actually sneaked in to give you this." She showed the thali.

"Sneaked in?" Vasu was curious.

"My handmaiden is busy talking to jivagribha," she said about the police officer of the cell, "she's very good at talking so, um..."

"So you can come here and give me..." he looked at the sweets, the laddoos and the kheer. "Sweets?"

She nodded. Her eyes, Vasu noticed, were round and brown, like the bark of a tree. But they weren't the normal kind of brown. They were almond and rich with colour, like honey. Oh yes, honey was the right word for the beauty of her eyes. And the only other pair of eyes that had ever caught Vasu's attention was Supriya's.

The very thought of her made his chest heavy and his mind began to bring back the dastardly memories of the past.

It made him sad. So very sad...

Vasu shrugged, to see the present. And surprisingly, it was beautiful.

"I am not a very rude person and it was rude of me..." she began in an apologetic tone, "to put you in a position where you were locked up. I didn't want to do it. I genuinely thought you were an intruder and not a..."

"A prince?"

"They say you are a driver's son, though," she said with curiosity. "How do both ends of the spectrum work?"

"It's too complicated to explain."

"Try me?"

"Perhaps later."

She nodded; impassive, as if she could understand every word of it, as if she didn't want to rebel against it, or retort. "I feel you are someone who's always facing the brunt of other people's actions."

Vasu wanted to say yes, but what was the point of feeling sorry for himself? "So you brought me prasad. That's very kind of you."

"Of course, since you couldn't come to the pooja and mother always says you have to give prasad to everyone who you find important and nice and to every good-natured person. Here..." she brought a golden spoon and dipped it into the kheer and offered it to him.

Vasu took it. Eating it he felt the sweet taste spread in his mouth. Then he smiled, and she smiled back. "I'm good-natured?"

"Seems like it," she grinned.

"How long do you plan to stay in Hastinapur?"

"Oh, I leave for Ahichatra in less than five days." She referred to the capital of Panchala, which was in the northern part of the kingdom, acting as the bed of the Himalayas. "Will you be out before that?"

Vasu nodded. "Yes, tomorrow."

"We must meet!" she exclaimed. "In better conditions than this," she paused.

Vasu wanted to compliment her and tell her how beautiful she was. Say better things to her but all he could muster was: "Thank you for bringing me the prasad."

She nodded, almost feeling disappointed. "I must go. Hope to see you soon." She winked.

Vasu smiled.

Hope to see you soon too.

23

A day later, when he left the lock-up, the one thing that he had in mind was: Drona.

After listening to the scolding of his mother and the silence of his father, Vasu had decided to leave for Pandeshwar Temple where Drona was last seen. His mother had told him that Drona had begun admissions for students for his Gurukul for the present term, that would commence in summer. His mother got to know when one of the other queens shared that their child had been accepted by Drona.

Vasu almost felt left out. He didn't know the selection process had already started. And there was this gut feeling in him that reached his throat and choked him.

"GO! GO! Perhaps you still have time," his mother had said. "Convince him!"

Vasu rushed, his chest firing up in the process. And when finally he reached the temple grounds, his hands were behind his back when he found himself in the circular structure.

And there was no one. The temple grounds were empty. He moved around the garden, hoping to find a soul, perhaps Drona. He wanted to prove his worth;

show he was more than just his caste. But there was not a soul.

Instead, he found Panchali.

Along with a young boy who was holding her by the arms and was teaching her how to shoot an arrow. In front of them, there was a goblet, on a broken bark of a tree. Panchali was giggling and Vasu could see that they were flirting with each other.

He felt a tug; a jealous tug.

"What are you doing here, sutaputr?" A voice came from behind him.

Vasu immediately turned to find a scrawny, lanky man with a cane in his hand on which he leaned, a crooked mouth in which he chewed on the betel leaves.

"Pranaam Acharyaji," he bowed, joining his hands, "I seek your audience. I hear you are looking for students for this summer term. I would like to take admission."

He raised his brows. "Ah. And why is that?"

"To become powerful and be a warrior."

"To become a king, is that so?" He began to circle around Vasu, looking for the lies in his words.

Vasu didn't want to lie. "Yes."

"But what makes you think I will select you?"

"I'm a good archer."

"AND SO ARE THE OTHER HUNDRED STUDENTS I HAVE JUST ACCEPTED!" he yelled. "Being just *good* in something is ordinary. You have to be great. The best! I have hand-picked most of my students for this term and unfortunately I have no more place left, especially for a sutaputr. You are late."

"But I didn't know it had even started..."

"What you know or what you don't doesn't matter. You should have known," he said. "If you were so great, I would have known about you and I would have taken you. You are mediocre at best."

"You haven't seen me! You haven't even give me an opportunity!" Vasu protested.

"A true leader seeks the opportunity when there is none, he does not wait for an opportunity to strike him."

At that moment, Vasu realised that Panchali and the boy next to her were paying attention to what was being said. He felt embarrassed.

"What is so special about you?" he asked.

"I can show you, Acharyaji."

"I'm..."

And then he came in front, inches away from Vasu; his eyes gray like stormy clouds. "Bhishma was right in what he said in the room. You are not a Kshtriya, sutaputr. So stop your daydreams. Be a driver or perhaps be a minister. But a king...bah! That is a dream a sutaputr should not possess."

And with that, he began walking towards the temple.

Vasu clenched his fist. He was angry; petrified. He wanted to smack the ground and bring the skies down on the ground. But most of all, he wanted to punch the old man.

Vasu felt insurmountable anger. He wanted to cry. He was feeling sorry for himself. He knew Drona was doing all of this just because he was a sutaputr. There was no other reason behind it.

And then he did the unthinkable.

He stormed towards Panchali and the boy.

Panchali asked: "What happened? Why were you quarrelling with Guru Drona?"

But Vasu didn't want to answer that.

He only had very little time.

"Give me one arrow and a bow," he said to the boy next to her.

"Who is he, Panchali?" the boy asked.

"Just give it to me!" he ordered the boy.

"This is my bow."

"Give it to him," Panchali sneered. "It's just a bow."

"No, I was teaching you," the boy said. "How dare he just come out of nowhere...I don't even know..."

Vasu didn't wait. He shoved the boy forward, grabbing his quiver and his bow in the process. He eyed Drona, who was staggering towards the temple doors.

The boy retorted and retaliated, but didn't come forward, as Vasu had the weapon on him.

He strung five arrows around the bow and aimed towards Drona.

"What are you doing..." Panchali was about to let out a scream. "Are you going to kill him?"

Vasu took a deep breath.

And shot the five arrows.

Panchali closed her eyes. So did the boy next to her.

Vasu didn't. In fact, he saw what he had done made Drona pause in his step. He was frozen in surprise.

At the gate of the temple, where Drona was about to enter, the arrows had aligned around the corners of the door—without even hitting Guru Drona...*once.*

It was *this* precision that made Drona turn with delight and surprise.

Vasu grinned.

Panchali saw it and instantly began to clap at his prowess. Drona was shocked and the boy next to Panchali was frowning with anger.

"You are pretty good, Vasu!" she exclaimed and turned to the grimacing boy. "Well Arjun—I believe you have finally met your match."

24

While that day was quite an adventure and he regretted humiliating a guru like Drona, Vasu ignored such thoughts and concentrated now.

Here. With her.

Yes. Her.

She was sitting right in front of him, as they were boating in a small pond where swans were swimming. There was a forest around them and hares could be seen, grazing on the grass.

It was her idea, to be here. Panchali.

She had come to his room and knocked on it, early one morning. And she wanted someone to go with her. Vasu agreed readily but he also knew Panchali had invited him after what happened with Drona.

He rowed the reed baton, guiding the boat on the pond, silently watching her. She had anklets that made a *cham-cham* sound and her earrings dangled lopsidedly touching her shoulders. Her hair was in a tight knot, braided. Her lips had cherry-coloured paste, to make them look more glossy.

Vasu kept admiring her beauty when Panchali said: "I have to be grateful for two things to you."

"What?"

"First that you forgave me for...you know...putting you in a prison."

"Second?"

"To actually show that arrogant Guru Drona what you are capable of," she grinned.

Vasu couldn't help but smile, though Drona hadn't got back to him ever since. He was just stunned after what Vasu had done and left. After that, there was no news whatsoever. Vasu wondered whether he was rejected and if he was...then it was fine. Uncle Satya could teach him. He couldn't just keep begging to Drona.

"I presume you don't like him."

"No one does. He's pompous and he's rude. He was against me spending time with Arjun, his star pupil. Though you are better at archery than him."

"Do you like him?" he quietly asked.

"Who?

He referred to the Pandava. He knew little about Arjun, ever since he had the opportunity of taking his bow and arrow and targeting his guru. Vasu knew he had angered lot of people in Hastinapur. Arjun was, in fact, a protégé. He had begun using the bow and arrow since he was a child and he was a focused boy. He was the son of the earlier king, Pandu, before he became a sanyasi and died in the forest. Their mother, Kunti had come with her five sons—the Pandavas—and requested Dhritarashtra to stay in the palace. Dhritarashtra agreed—to Vasu's surprise, since he was after all a cold-hearted man.

Perhaps there was more to him than Vasu was aware of.

"Arjun?" she asked and then Vasu noticed that she had blushed. "Oh no, he's well…he's talented and he's intelligent, but he's a bit arrogant because he has so many followers around him who keep saying how good he is."

"Perhaps he might be that good."

"He is, but remember one thing, arrogance gets to the best of heroes and topples them," she smiled. "Do you think you are arrogant, Vasu?"

Vasu didn't know whether he was. He knew he was good at archery, but he wasn't pompous about it. "I don't think so."

"That's good. I kind of knew that. You are…you seem like a nice person."

"Seem?" he raised his brows.

She giggled. "I'm just glad you have taught that Drona a lesson. You know, my father and Drona…they were the best of friends when they were young. Drona, at that time, was a poor Brahmin boy before he was taken in by Bhishma to become the Rajguru of Hastinapur only because they had the same teacher: Lord Parshuram."

"Before you continue, I wanted to ask: is he really immortal? Does he exist?" Vasu was always curious about it.

"He's a Vishnu avatar. Of course he does. I've never seen him though."

Vasu was not satisfied with the answer. This was all very religious and not at all realistic to him, but he was quiet, as she continued with her story about Drona and her father:

"My father made a promise to Drona as a child: when they grew up he would share everything in half with him. So basically, my father becomes king of Panchala down the road while Drona gets poorer and even has a son, Ashwatthama. Drona, realising his good friend has become king, goes there to ask for half of the kingdom. My father tries to reason with him saying when he had made that promise to him as a child, he was innocent, he didn't know any better. Drona got angry…really angry. And he promised to take revenge." She rolled her eyes. "The story sounds dramatic, but it serves it's purpose: to show how opportunistic Drona is."

Vasu was quiet. Promises made as a child were often not taken seriously. But then…this was just one side of the story.

"That's why he doesn't like you?"

"Yes," Panchali nodded. "Also, because apparently I distract Arjun. Why would I distract him? Ugh!" She scowled, until her eyes fell on the pond and it widened. "By the graces of Lord Vishnu, Vasu! See!"

He turned to find a glowing fish just swimming around their boat.

"It's a dragonfish," she smiled. "Look, it's bioluminescent."

Vasu couldn't believe there was a fish like this that existed in the world, just glowing in front of him underwater, lighting up the rest of the pond.

"Can we touch it?" she asked, confused.

Vasu didn't know whether they should, but he dipped his hand in the pond and slowly reached over to the fish, just patting it. It was slimy and very sensitive.

"Yes, you can. I think it likes it."

"Oooh, ooh," she grinned bringing the hand down, but getting nervous.

Vasu brought his hand closer to her hand and asked: "May I?"

She nodded; her eyes still locked on the fish. Vasu grabbed her palm and dipped it in the water and they both felt the fish. But Vasu didn't look at the fish. He was looking at her and he was smiling. For some reason, the glowing fish felt a tad bit faded in front of the luminescence that Panchali's smile had.

"I love Hastinapur," she looked up and in the background, with Vasu, she saw the beautiful city of elephants just canvassed over the horizon. "I wish to stay here. Panchala is half the beauty of what Hastinapur is."

Because they have beautified it on the money they earn from others—Vasu wanted to say. But then, he remained quiet.

As they neared the banks of the pond, Vasu saw a familiar figure, standing impassively—waiting for them. His ears were red and his cheeks were pink. His stormy grey eyes like Drona's, watched Vasu with bloodshot anger.

It was Arjun.

Vasu tied the boat to the bank, as Panchali greeted Arjun: "Oh well, here you are!"

"What are you doing with him?" Arjun asked like a brat.

"Well, your guru doesn't like the fact that I am with you, so," she entwined her arm with Vasu's, "I thought I'd spend time with Vasu."

"He's a sutaputr!" Arjun groaned; speaking just like his guru.

Vasu noticed he was a bit younger than him and had this constant frown on his childlike face.

"You have disrespected me, sutaputr, by stealing my bow and arrows," Arjun flared his nostrils, "and you have disrespected my guru."

"In my defence," Vasu grinned cheekily, "I asked you nicely."

"You do not use another archer's bow. And you demean me by showing you are better than me." Arjun shook his head. "You are not." He came closer to Vasu but he was not even half his height. Vasu towered over the young lad. "Guru Drona says I am the best archer he's ever seen."

"I'm sure you are," Vasu chuckled.

"You don't believe it," Arjun sighed. "Well, to show Panchali and to calm my senses, why don't we have a... well...a contest?"

"I don't care about your senses, kid," Vasu grimaced. "I don't want to prove to anyone how good I am or how bad."

And he began to move away with Panchali, when Arjun said: "Oh well, I can help you get admission into the Gurukul."

Vasu halted. Frozen. He swivelled his head to see Arjun, who was grinning, as if he got Vasu by the tug of his heartstring.

"Oh yes. I asked Guruji what you wanted from him," he paused, playfully chuckling. "My recommendation can be quite useful to you. If you win, of course, you'll be *in* the Gurukul. And you shall travel with us to Ujjanak and learn martial arts and modern warfare."

Vasu arched his brows. He could show the little brat

that he was better than Arjun. But then… "What if I lose?" he asked. He had to know his odds.

"Well, sutaputr. You are a son of a sarthi. You will then…" he shrugged, as if showing he was thinking about it when he had already thought about it, "oh well, what should I say? Ummm…you will drive me and Panchali on the roads of Hastinapur on my chariot to show everyone that you just have attitude and arrogance and I used my skills to put you in your place."

Panchali shrieked. "Arjun! That's nonsense. You shouldn't do that. I have told you so many times to not use your pride like this."

Arjun seemed unaffected. He was just grinning as if he was savouring this. Vasu remained unmoved; his jaw tightly clenched as he watched Arjun for a while and then looked at Panchali.

"You don't have to do this," Panchali said. "Don't do this. Seriously. You are much above this competitive nonsense."

Vasu wanted to get into the Gurukul.

And he was leaving the next day to go back to Anga. This was his only opportunity.

"Fine," Vasu said, letting Arjun sigh with delight. "Let's have a contest."

25

Vasu knew Arjun was better trained.

He had Drona as his teacher since he was a child, while Vasu had himself and Uncle Satya. And yet here he was, competing.

Like a fool? Perhaps.

They were in the woods. And the first thing Vasu noticed was that where Arjun was taking him there was an old oak tree which had a twig from which a reedy sack of gold was hanging. He had his horse with him, with a saddle that carried other sacks of gold.

Arjun had already come prepared.

Vasu and Panchali were standing together, while Arjun was waiting with his bow and arrow. He turned around, and said: "The plan here is to…let out one coin of the sack."

"One coin?"

"Oh yes. One coin." He walked to the sack. It was small. Handful, one could say. Arjun gripped it tighter, to show there were coins in it. "You have to hit it in such a way, and I don't know how you will do it, that only one coin comes out of it. No more. No less."

That is impossible.

Vasu began to strategise. Even if he hit the sack in such a way, there was a possibility that he would create a big enough hole in the sack for more than one coin to exit.

How will Arjun be able to do it?

"Do you want to go first?" Arjun asked, with a smile dancing on his thick lips.

Vasu didn't want to. Best to always first see how tough your competitor is. "Since you allowed this competition to happen between us, why don't you do it?"

Arjun froze for a moment, as if he expected Vasu to adhere to his vanity and go forward with it.

"Fine," Arjun shrugged. "I would love to. Remember..." he began to string an arrow in his bow. "If I win this, you will have to drive me around."

Vasu gritted his teeth. He didn't want to be insulted like this.

"And if it's a draw?" he asked. "If you do it, and so do I?"

"Then we shall try it again. And then again. Till someone loses," Arjun said. "But it's impossible. For this to happen, is quite a rarity as you see, this isn't an ordinary contest."

Vasu nodded.

He wanted to see Arjun's technique, wondering how he would do it; to have one coin out of the sack.

Arjun got prepared. Vasu could hear him take a deep breath and call out to Indradev to support him in this venture. And he said, how the storms and the wind were going to help him, under his breath.

Vasu could see he had almost closed his eyes and was just focusing on the arrow. That was it. Vasu craved that much dedication. At this point, he was envious that Arjun could reach that focus in such a short amount of time. He wanted to know how he did it. What was the secret?

And then, he shot.

It was unpredictable. It was sudden. Vasu was taken aback.

And then he heard.

The clanging of the sack.

And a coin making a noise.

Just falling on the ground and rolling off.

Vasu's eyes couldn't believe that only one coin had come out. The arrow, instead of stabbing it, had slithered the corner of the sack, just enough for the coin to pop out. And the arrow then hit the trunk.

For a moment, Vasu couldn't believe this had happened. He swallowed a lump and he walked to the sack, to see the cut Arjun's arrow had made. It was so clinical, even from far off. He was almost fifteen yards away from the sack.

"This is..." Vasu began.

"Genius? I know," he raised his brows. "It's your turn."

Vasu was scared; petrified. Suddenly he felt sorry that he had accepted a challenge from a trained archer. But then, he calmly walked to Arjun and took an arrow, with the bow.

He adjusted it, when he heard Panchali's voice:

"You don't have to do this Vasu."

Actually, this is what I have to do.

Vasu aimed at the corner of the new sack that Arjun had just hung on the twig. His eyes were locked on the sack, the turned corner of it.

I have to hit that.

But the chances of doing so were just impossible. And Arjun had achieved that feat. For someone who is so obnoxious and pompous—Arjun was indeed a genius.

I can't do the same. I have to do it differently.

He began to strategise.

"Always make use of your surrounding when you are crowded, boy," Satya had told him. A long time ago.

Surrounding? Vasu realised there was a way. A smile came on his lips.

He closed his eyes too. He let his ears prick over the breeze. He let the smell of daffodils and orchids infiltrate his nostrils. He did everything to feel every element of the nature around him and finally tried feeling the arrow. And soon, the arrow, it became a part of him. It was him.

And then he shot it.

There was a tug in his heart, his nervousness had reached the peak.

He couldn't lose. He couldn't be embarrassed like this.

"What the..." he could hear Arjun's gasp.

Vasu opened his eyes to see where he had hit.

It was at the twig and not at the sack. The twig, when hit by a pulsating arrow, broke and the sack fell on the ground. And Vasu had calculated that the sack was not quite high, for it to fall harshly and let so many coins disperse. Plus, he had noticed, the sack was only a wee bit closed from the top, so not many coins could pop out. Only one would, with difficulty.

Vasu, Panchali and Arjun saw that a coin did escape the pouch and it lay a few metres away from it.

"You did it!" Panchali grinned, hugging Vasu sideways.

Arjun, angrily, walked around it—to check. And then he said, "Sutaputr! I believe you should come and see this here."

Vasu arched his brows as he walked with Panchali and saw what Arjun was pointing towards: another coin did indeed slip out of the pouch, but only partially.

But it was touching the ground. The earth.

No.

"You can't count that, Arjun," Panchali protested. "That is allowed."

"Let him answer that," Arjun smiled. "Tell me, sutaputr, would an experienced archer allow even such a tiny mistake or would he seek perfection? I leave it to you."

Vasu clenched his jaw. He knew Arjun was right. In the Gurukul, there was no place for mediocrity and Vasu just proved that he was mediocre. He didn't want to say it and he knew, every atom in his body was rejecting what he was about to say: "Where is your chariot?"

"I don't like this," Panchali protested.

"But this was a bet," Arjun said. "Driver! Please take it forward."

And under the sunset orange sky, Vasu reined the horses in front as he took the chariot and began to roam around the streets of Hastinapur. Every person from the city saw him. Some gasped. Some chuckled.

With a heavy heart and a tearful face, Vasu took the chariot up the zigzag roads which led to the palace and as he moved inside the palace—

He saw Adhirath, and his mother who had come out to witness the event. There were Arjun's brothers too, who were mockingly laughing just like Arjun, who was just glad he had proved to be better.

Tears began to stream down his face as he saw in the farthest corner of the palatial grounds—Drona, crouching over his cane and just narrowly gazing at Vasu.

He felt an even harsher tug. He had never felt so lowly. He had never felt as if the elephants of Hastinapur had crushed his hopes; his dreams. He could feel his heart just diving deep in the depths of the ocean and he could feel himself being drained of all energy. But however he felt about it, he realised, he was not good enough. He realised, he was just another...

And then he saw him. The man in the white armour and snowy beard. He had come to watch the spectacle.

Bhishma.

The very man Vasu had challenged that he will show he could be a king.

And now...he was a sarthi. Nothing but a driver.

That was his destiny.

Arjun just showed him his fate.

Bhishma could have intervened and stopped this nonsense, but he was chuckling under his breath. Vasu could read Bhishma's expression: *This was for being oversmart.*

And then he left.

"Stop it, Vasu! You don't have to do this anymore. Arjun," Panchali rasped, "you have humiliated him enough."

And as Vasu halted the chariot, Panchali rushed out, leaving Arjun alone.

But Arjun was unaffected, as he dismounted the chariot and came in front, to see Vasu.

He flipped the coin on the ground, the very one from the sack and said: "Here's your tip, driver."

Vasu didn't pick it up. He was just silent, his head low, to not show that he was crying. Vasu knew that he would not come to Hastinapur. That he would leave archery. And he knew that he was not good at these things.

And then he walked away, before stopping again.

"Nevertheless," Arjun said, "you are a talented archer. Guruji should take you in. Even though I have shamed you, like you had shamed me by trying to get close to Panchali when I liked her, I will still talk to him for you." There was this softness in his voice, as if he had made a total, tidal shift.

And then he left.

As his family packed to leave for Anga, Vasu remained where he was: in his room, leaning against the rails of the window and looking at his view from the top of the palace, with a parchment clasped in his hand.

He was supposed to read it. But he refrained from it. Not now, he thought. In a while, he processed.

All of Hastinapur could be seen, as well as the vultures and eagles that scurried in the skies. The sun was glistening red as of now, shining bright on his body when he heard something.

They were footsteps.

He turned to see, it was his potbellied father Adhirath,

with his bushy moustache, a turban on his head and in an orange angavastram.

Vasu sighed and then turned away.

"Have you come to tell me I was wrong to compete with Arjun just like how you told me to not speak cruelly to Bhishma?" Vasu asked.

"It shouldn't have happened to you," he said. "Arjun was not being nice."

Vasu shook his head. "It doesn't matter. Everyone knows who I am now. Everyone knows what *you* wanted me to be."

"I'll be honest with you, son. I also want to see Anga ruled by you, by my son, but the politics of the state is not in our favour."

"Then we make it in our favour."

"It's not that simple."

Vasu shook his head. "You are a coward. And I'm not." He gritted his teeth. "But because of your caste, your profession, I have to carry that stain all my life and no one will look at me beyond that." He sternly watched his father's disappointed, sad face. "Don't forget, father. It is because of *you* I will never grow above my identity. I hope you realise that."

Adhirath lowered his head as he began to move towards the door's entrance and then stopped. "I have talked to Dronacharya. He has agreed to take you in at my behest. Dhritarashtra convinced him too. You can start your term during summers."

For a moment, Vasu felt remorseful for saying such spiteful things to his father who had got him the admission. But then he also let his ego come in between and his ego didn't let him bow down to his father. His ego made him speak harsher words, that he internally regretted but externally he had to speak out; out of pure spite.

Vasu scoffed. "After this humiliation, you think I'll go to the Gurukul? Never. I have this much self-respect."

He nodded. His father didn't argue further. He left.

Vasu was breathing hard. He could not believe how much anger he had inside him. And he had no place to vent.

But then he saw the parchment he had been holding on to.

It was from Panchali and had been given to him by a servant earlier that day…

He unfolded it, to read:

Vasu,

It is unfortunate as to what happened and for that I am partially responsible. I should have protested more. I should have said something. But I didn't. I will never forgive myself for that. But all I can say is, it was lovely meeting you during these days. I can assure you, I have found a friend in you that I hadn't thought I ever will. If you happen to be around Panchala, please meet me. I would like to see you again.

Panchali

"Me too," he smiled, letting his anger fade a bit, "me too, Panchali."

26

Chariots were being readied with a silent hum, Vasu was sitting in the corner of the courtyard, playing with his fingers.

He was still in a glum mood and Panchali's letter was a silver lining, though not enough to grant him a beaming smile. He could see his father, who he was not talking to. There was a cold war going on and he didn't like that.

And while the chariot was almost ready to leave for Anga, he saw a familiar figure walking towards him.

With a cane that made a sound as he walked, Vasu saw him: Guru Drona.

He had that snide grin on his face that he had always had; Vasu instantly went down on his knees and touched his feet.

"Guruji."

"Such respect? I believe you didn't give it to me the first time we met," Drona said with a chuckle.

"But wasn't it Commander Bhishma that I was insubordinate towards?"

"We met outside the temple."

"No, guruji, we met in the room and you were in the shadows. I noticed your cane."

At that, Drona smiled. "And that's why I am here, son. Stand straight."

Vasu did so and Drona grabbed him by the shoulders. "The king wants me to take you in because your father begged him to, but I personally feel I am not taking you in because of them. I don't care what someone says. I choose according to my wishes and I see something special in you."

There was a flicker of hope. Vasu couldn't believe he was hearing Drona saying that to him and he was being honest; genuine.

"I firmly believe you will fit right in the Gurukul and your father told me you don't want to go now because you were humiliated yesterday. Listen, son, the boy known as Arjun is born with archery in his blood, but you were not and yet you were good at it. That speaks volumes about what you can achieve if I give you a proper education. Now you sulk and cry about how you were humiliated and treated like a nobody, or you come to my Gurukul and become a somebody. There's a very thin line between success and failure. And that is how much strength you have to continuously fail and to stand up and fail again. The cycle goes on," he paused. "Ego is man's biggest enemy. Don't let it hinder your judgement in joining the Gurukul. I'll see you there."

And saying that, he left.

Vasu was stunned. With such simple but effective words, Drona had convinced him. He didn't ask Vasu whether he would come. He told him he had to be there. There was dominance. There was surety.

He wanted to become somebody and he knew under Drona's guidance, he would.

If a great guru like Drona can believe in me, so can I.

And he turned to his father, who had talked to Drona and even though Vasu knew he wouldn't be talking to his father for a while, because he felt awkward and embarrassed as a stupid, indignant child—he knew he was grateful to him.

A reassuring smile appeared on his face as he locked eyes with his father, who looked back at him with conviction.

Let's see how my life changes.

27

Present day...

Karna had a handful of pebbles, when he reached under Panchali's window. It was on the first floor, just gleaming with green, thick vines and pulpy roses that intermingled. Silver moonlight beamed on the glass, as Karna took one pebble and lightly with precision hit it.

He waited. No response.

He did it again. He was in the crowd, next to the willow that sprouted apples. And he was in his loose tunic, that showed the ridges of his muscles, a dhoti and saffron chappals, with ears that glinted with kundalams. Worn by him since birth, his mother had told him it had come with him in the basket. Initially, he was saddened by the idea that someone abandoned him, but he grew to realise it didn't matter. He had a mother and her name was Radha. No one else.

Another pebble. A *tak* sound. And the moment it hit, the window opened.

For a moment, he smiled and then it wavered and disappeared when he saw it was a brutishly naked man, with hairy chest and a loincloth that showed enough skin to disgust him.

"What are you doing, you idiot?" The man scowled, scratching his balls.

"Oh sorry, I uh..."

Wrong window! Wrong window!

And then he heard a giggle. He looked at the other window. Was it from there it had come? He turned back and saw her, bright as the night, shining under the stars, the smile of a supernova. She was in her nightgown, a shawl wrapped around her and her hair was loose. She had no jewellery on her and she looked beautiful as ever, even more so than she used to do.

It had been years he had not met her, and longing was an understatement as to what he felt for her.

"What are you doing here?" he asked, incredulously. His hair was tied in a ponytail by a reed string.

"I can ask you the same question."

"I was uh...actually, I thought this was your window."

She nodded. "I was coming to meet you. I waited for my father and my brother to go to sleep and then I came, in the dead of night, hoping you would be at the feast still, even though only a handful of drunkards were left there."

Karna smiled, realising she had come to meet him too and it was just something he couldn't believe. Even after years...she cared.

"Well, I was one of them."

"You don't drink. I know."

And they began to walk. Stroll would be the right word, as they moved across the tulip garden, the one where Karna had jumped over to the royal stable. And met Panchali for the first time.

"How have you been?" Her voice was soft.

"I have been...well...not the best."

"You finally went north and learnt the secret of Brahmastra I believe?"

"Yes, I did."

"And what is it?"

"I can't say, but it's not what I expected it to be."

"What else did you learn?" She sounded excited but mature too. Her voice wasn't the childish one that it used to be.

"I learnt what a Nagastra is. I mean I thought in the beginning it was really to tie a bloody snake to it and shoot, but no, it's the poison of the snake that the blade is dipped into and..."

She was chuckling.

"What?" he asked, confused.

"Your eyes glow, when you talk about this."

They had reached the royal stable and from up close, it looked the same, but the soldiers outside had changed and perhaps a lot of other things would have changed inside too.

"The chariot is of no more importance, you know," she said.

"What do you mean?"

"Earlier, it was the king's vehicle into battle but the king himself hasn't gone out of his kingdom for the last several years. Now the chariot is more of a rusted, forgotten memory." She walked to the guards, who didn't even flinch, as they entered the royal stable, as if it was no more a big issue, as it used to be earlier.

The passage of time surely corrodes once-cherished things.

They walked inside the stable and the glimmer of the chariot was no more.

"He rides another vehicle, if the king has to go somewhere," Panchali said. "To the kingdom, to see his people, but it's not a war vehicle. This once was."

Karna knew it had been a long time, but the chariot was broken.

"Have we become like this?" he asked her.

"What do you mean?" she was circling around the chariot.

"This thing. Like this, time has rusted us."

"I think materialism fades, but not feelings, or emotions. They are eternal," she smiled, reaching close to him and darting her eyes at him. "When was the last time we met?"

"When the fires were started in your kingdom," he said, remembering that memory.

It wasn't a very fond night to remember.

"No, it was after. When you left Gurukul and on your way to the Himalayas, you stopped at Panchala and we met."

He raised his brows. Lowering his gaze. *She remembered.*

Perhaps she didn't want to. And perhaps that's why, he didn't mention it. But she did. There was a crinkle in her eyes and her lips were pursed and her eyes were stark.

"Three years," she nodded, "it's been three years since that night."

"Did you miss me?" Karna smirked.

She didn't have to say. She didn't have to even look at him. Her body was loose and her frame was weak. She looked like a child now, just helpless, and she was closing her eyes and thinking. Perhaps of that night.

"Can I kiss you?" he asked her, leaning forward, inches away from her lips.

And she opened her eyes. They were standing on hay, the sound of the horses neighing was in the background, while the smell of metal and hay permeated the air. It wasn't appealing, but they didn't care.

"Things have changed in three years, Vasu." She called him by his birth name. Only few were allowed to. Only few knew.

"But you told me emotions don't fade."

"They don't. But circumstances do."

"What are you trying to say?" he moved back, arching brows.

"My father...he wants Arjun to be my groom," she said, with a hiccup and a pause. She didn't even look at him.

Karna was struck for a moment. Confused. "But wasn't he...didn't he...is your father crazy, if you don't mind me asking?"

"He favours strength. The brawn."

"But Arjun..." he wanted to say such spiteful things. "And I did the right thing. What he did...it was the opposite."

"I know, I know," she was pacifying him, but he pushed her away. "He just feels, even though what he did was wrong...he's someone I should spend my life with because he will protect me and he's Hastinapur's true gem and archer. If he won't be the king then Yudhishtr will and I'll be part of Hastinapur's royal family."

She said it as if it was a prestigious thing and he remembered how she always wanted to immerse herself in this vanity.

"I can't give you that, but I am a king now. Anga. It's not as pretty as Hastinapur..."

"Don't say that. Do you think I want to marry Arjun? I don't. I don't care about Hastinapur anymore. I..." she stopped.

Even though they were not far physcially, they felt like there was a distance of miles between them. They wanted to reach and embrace, but they were held back by...even they didn't know what it was.

"Is there a chance...between us?"

She was confused. "I don't know. I...I don't know anything. I can't defy my father but also...I don't know," her chest was heaving.

"Your father is an idiot," Karna said finally, flaring his nostrils.

Panchali clenched her jaw. "And you are an idiot too. For leaving for the Himalayas...alone."

"I couldn't have taken you," he growled. "It was a dangerous place."

"And I am a dangerous girl," she came close, smelling of mint.

He didn't wait. He couldn't. He grabbed her by the hair and pushed her against the chariot door, pushing his lips against hers and she resisted, trying to shove him, until she gave in, allowing herself to be touched again by him, to be loved by him, to be held by him. Her arms wrapped around his neck.

Karna moved her shawl, removing it, as he kissed her

on the neck and her collarbone, and on her breast, as they lay down on the hay.

And she giggled when she said: "The guards will wonder why we are here so late at night. We should..."

But Karna didn't care. He continued to kiss her. On her navel. And then on her thighs, finally removing his tunic, when her face contorted in a mix of pleasure and hope, as she touched his chest, and lingered her fingers over his scars.

"You didn't have so many of them earlier."

Karna nodded. He had faced a lot in the Himalayas. But for now, that didn't matter, as he went for her lips, and they locked in this passionate pool of love, of ecstasy and of achieving immortality in the land of mortals.

Their skin burnt against each other, they were sweating and they were moving with pace, with urgency but also naivety. They didn't know what they were doing, how they did it, they just knew they wanted to feel complete within themselves, they wanted to feel like the world had stopped, the god of time had been lenient and everything was moving according to them. Their eyes met, their legs intermingled and locked, naked, as he kissed her softly, feeling he would break her if he was too harsh, and she kissed him back and looked at him. Those golden eyes of his were reminiscent of the early sun she began to wake up for, after she fell in love with him.

"I don't know if we will have tomorrow, but we have tonight and I want to make the most of it," Karna said.

She smiled. There was melancholy swimming in her eyes, and she looked away. They lay there, naked, realising none the better...

That the horses which neighed earlier, were silent now.

Arjun was frozen.

His eyes shimmered under the silver light and it felt like he trickled pearls from his eyes. He was standing idle. Outside the stable. He had seen them. He had seen Panchali and Karna enter. But not exit. Not for a while.

And he could only wonder what was going on inside. But he had no idea—they were close. He wasn't aware.

This can't be happening to me. Not again.

Arjun lowered his gaze, and tightened his jaw. He had the bouquet of tulips he had managed to tear off from the roots, to present to her as a sign of affection, but he crumpled them in his hands and walked back.

To not turn his head again.

To forget this night ever existed.

As morning dawned, he looked confused.

He opened his eyes to find himself in the stable. Smiling, he remembered how the night was filled with passion and love. He was grinning and his hand, they went over to the side where Panchali was, but he was holding a tuft of hay and there was nothing. He turned to see she was gone.

And he realised, that even though she was with him, she wasn't. She was going to be betrothed to someone else and this overwhelming sadness crept onto him.

Yesterday was a dream. And this morning was his reality.

A reality that he had to accept.

For it was going to turn grim. Worse.

He had to leave for Anga. Duty called.

He knew what his purpose was—to defeat Jarasandha.

28

The day had gone quickly.

Karna was mostly preparing for the trip to Anga and it would take him five days to reach on a chariot driven by three horses. He hadn't seen Panchali and he didn't want to complicate matters further by going to her and confusing her more. If she wanted to be with him, she would. And that would be her decision, not out of any compulsion.

The king was kind enough to give him a chariot, and when Suyodhan had learnt of this, he came rushing to the courtyard, where Karna was packing his rucksacks and his saddlebags with his reed ones.

"You are leaving without troops," Suyodhan said, and Karna saw he was wearing a golden dhoti and nothing else. He did have a string just wrapped around his chest and his beard was thicker than usual. He looked like he had just taken an immersive bath.

"I am," Karna pushed his stuff inside, and patted his horse.

"Are you mad?"

"Why?"

"Father has sent the royal decree to Anga and so

forth everywhere. Jarasandha will know you'll be coming without a band. It won't take him a single night's gold to hire a bunch of assassins and kill you on your way."

"I can defend myself," Karna said, shrugging.

"You can, when you are prepared. Not when you are..." and Suyodhan in his momentary anger, tossed a rock that he had just grabbed from the ground, towards Karna.

Instantly, Karna grabbed it, without even turning and he looked at Suyodhan, with a grin on his face. "I'm *always* prepared."

Suyodhan shrugged, "Show off."

"Always."

"What is your plan?"

"And you are interested why?"

"Your actions would impact my reputation." Suyodhan came next to Karna, and they both stood tall and towering even though Karna was much taller. "My father has entrusted faith in you. The battle starts in the next couple of days. Have you thought of a plan?"

"He should have given me an army."

"You have thousand troops under Devi waiting for you. They are your people."

"Against three thousand troops of Jarasandha."

"You have the rebels too, who didn't join the military led by Devi. Talk to them. Convince them."

That was the idea.

"They might listen to you. You were born on their land."

Karna nodded. And then he paused, turned to his peer and said: "Thank you for announcing in front of everyone I was the king."

Suyodhan nodded. For his brusque exterior, he had soft lines and the gentle look of a sailor waiting for his seawater fish. "I told you I would try."

Karna smiled and bid goodbye to Suyodhan.

After he was done packing, he looked back at the palace, hoping for his father to come, to bid him farewell. But he didn't see him. And he was let down, surely. He felt frustrated too.

He pulled the rein and made a sound for the horses to move, the wooden wheels turning, as he began to manoeuvre the iron grilled gates of the palace...

When he heard a voice.

"Wait."

He turned around, and stopped to find an unlikely face bidding him farewell. It was the mother of Arjun—Kunti.

She was sweating and she had a small jar in her hand, which she had been carrying. He instantly hopped off the chariot and took the jar, so she could breathe. She was smiling at him, while exasperated.

"Rajmata Kunti, you shouldn't have," he kept the jar inside the chariot. "Should I get you some water?"

"No, no, just..." she nodded, her hair was wiry and she looked pale. "Have a safe journey."

"You didn't have to come."

"I am just...um..." she was coughing up words carefully, "I am just grateful that you forfeited the duel yesterday. It was kind of you."

"Of course. What is in the jar?"

"An apricot infused juice. Something I thought you would like."

"Oh."

They stood in silence. Looking at each other. Karna was confused that Kunti maa had come to see him off and felt grateful.

"Uh, so…I just wanted to say you have very nice earrings."

"Oh yes," Karna smiled, touching the kundalams. "It's a gift from my mother."

"Mother? Where did she get it?"

Karna wanted to say that she found it in the basket, in which he was found, but Kunti maa didn't need to know so many details. It was of no point to over share. "She got it from somewhere, I'm unaware where."

"Indeed." She swallowed a lump, growing paler, as if she caught his lie, as if she could see that Karna was hiding something. "I knew a man who had eyes like you."

"I hope he was a good man."

"He was. Very much so," Kunti maa lowered her gaze, playing with her fingers.

"I should leave."

"Yes, yes, please do so. Apologies for making you wait."

"No, no, of course not."

It was awkward. It was embarrassing and he was back on his chariot. Out of the palace, Kunti maa became a dot in the background, as he passed through the narrow streets of the city towards the outer flanks, passing the watchtowers.

As he reined in his horse, he began to think whether he should have got some soldiers to escort him. The roads could be treacherous and being a king, he had to be careful. Dhritarashtra, like Suyodhan, had offered him that, but he had declined flatly. He didn't want to attract unwanted attention towards himself. He knew if he went with a band, it would create whispers and it would lead to action. If he went quietly, with his cowl on and hidden in the shadows, and reached Malinipur in three days, it would be fine. He wouldn't be attacked. He'd be free.

But he had one stop to make in between.

He had to meet someone from his past.

Someone who could help him defeat Jarasandha.

Drona saw him leaving, a flash of anger and frustration growing in him. The boy was a problem and he knew he had to deal with him, down the road. How, was the question! Not only had he defied him in the past, but he had also humiliated Arjun at Rangbhoomi. Drona wouldn't have cared about people dying but he did mind that Karna saved Arjun's face.

He was staring out of the window, and gritting his teeth, as a morbid thought passed in his head:

I should have killed you when I had the chance.

But then, he turned. He had reached this window, because he and his guardsmen were searching for his cane.

Apparently, it had gone missing the previous night.

He limped across the corridor, wondering where it had disappeared.

With a grin, Karna pulled out an ornate silver and golden baton from the shadows of his cowl, revealing it to be a large cane.

He saw the stick and it made him laugh as he rode his chariot, thinking about how he had managed to steal it, in the dead of night before he had met Panchali.

I hope you can live without this, old man. Because you won't be seeing it again.

29

The sun died.

The two boys sat in the forest, cross-legged. Greasy. With mouths as foul as the woman opposite them. Barely wearing leaves and looking at them.

She had eyes of emerald, or even darker. Something that was close to being very much like the stones of Greek fire.

The two boys were very much like their mother. They loved her. She had taught them everything. She had knowledge beyond her years.

One of them had asked: "How do you know so much?"

And she said: "I was a courtier to a king. A mighty king. One of the last Rakshas lords, from the blood of Raavan. And he taught me everything."

For the two boys, history was fascinating and they always thought that the Rakshasas were extinct when Lord Ram and his men had vanquished them. But it was not true. Some survived. Some had the divine blood of Raavan, the worshipper of Shiva and they continued to rule the Vindhya mountain ranges for a while, tribal in nature, worshipping animals and scouring them, eating human flesh as they believed that true power came from the enemy's beating heart.

"Why are we here?" the sensible one asked.

The other boy was slow. He was weak with malnutrition. And he had a tongue, always lapping out of his mouth. And he was goofy. The sensible one had to always be with him; making sure he didn't do something stupid.

"Because your training is over and you are ready to go into the world. Out."

"No," the sensible one said. "We don't want to leave you."

"You won't. I'll be in your heart."

He looked confused. "But why did you teach us if you only were going to leave us?"

"To make my mark in someone's mind. To leave. I do not have many days left, but you do. You have an entire life ahead of you," she said.

Her lips were black and her heart and her skin were chalk white, but then she would put a strange powder on her face, extracted from the plant with which she used to wipe it around.

"You have one last job to do, though," she said.

"What?" the sensible one asked.

"The world is a scarring place and you were disbanded by your father because of your brother." And she laid out the knife in front. "*Kill him* and be free."

Jarasandha was watching from the chariot windows, the thoughts of his past as a child in the dark, damp rainforest of Magadha came blaring to him.

"What are you thinking about, your highness?" Gonanda asked. He was sitting by his side.

Jara bit his lips. *No one knows what I did after that.* "Nothing. Just worrying about the situation in Mathura."

Gonanda sighed and it was a deep one; a scarring, dark one. It had just been a few days after they had declared war against Dhritarashtra that they learnt of another problem that was brewing. In Mathura, which was ruled by his son-in-law—Kansa.

He was killed.

Brutally. Twisted neck. Contorted body. When the corpse was brought in front of Jarasandha, he knew only a vicious man could do it.

And he was told: "It's a boy. Not a man. His name is Krishna."

And that was it. He wasn't told more. His daughters wept on his shoulders, wearing a sari that was drenched in their tears. Kansa was married to both of them and Jara could feel their sadness. "I shall avenge him, my girls. Don't worry."

And that was what he was doing.

The chariot was taking them to *him*.

He lived fairly close by. But not in the capital. He was too dangerous to be in the city, so he was given a nice hut and a farm, and a fleet of people so he couldn't escape. He lived there. Always.

"Why do you need him?" Gonanda asked. "To be honest, he's a..."

Mess. I know. That's what we need now.

"I can't be in two places. Anga is a shorter battle. We just have to kill the bloody Devi out there and we will be done. Mathura could be a challenge. Apparently this Krishna lad has joined all the Yadu tribes and he's making his fortification there. We need to drive him out and who better than *him*," Jara said.

"I see."

"We need to be stronger than ever, Gonanda. Really strong," Jara sighed. If his wife Usha was here, she would have led instead of Jara going to *him*.

The chariot was finally reined in and halted, the wheels skid and they were on a patch of grass, after ascending the hills that grew a lot of bananas and oranges. He came out, his golden embroidered sandals stepping on the earth, while his long, crimson sherwani flapped over the long tunic he wore. His bangles shimmered and his orange dyed beard glowered.

He could see the hut in front and the guards patrolling. Behind him, behind the chariot were hundreds of soldiers, who were making sure he was safe.

He walked to one of the patrolling men and asked, "How has he been?"

"Your highness, he has just managed to kill two of our men till now. We had to shackle him." There was fear breathing in his eyes.

"All right, understandable." He looked at the door with a deep breath and walked towards it.

Let's meet Kaal.

When Jara entered the hut, the first thing he saw was a bald man, showing his back and sitting on the ground, worshipping a murti. It was a strange murti and Jara realised what it was—

It was the sculpture of Goddess Kali with her tongue out, lapping and lashing. There were paintings kept all around, or what he painted on. Kaal had a fascination with creating all sorts of designs with all sorts of colours and he had created...

Death. Destruction. Mayhem. Chaos.

Blood. Women were wrecked and men were killed. Children were burnt and there was no hope.

Kaal believed in that.

His skin, from the back, was torn apart, like someone had sliced through it, and it was stitched. He had a burnt patch on his head, sitting in the darkness of the room, with just a fire lamp throwing light on his head partially and his loose tunic and rags.

Gonanda was on his side and he stayed in the corner—afraid, he might attack.

"Kaal," Jara called out, "how have you been?"

There was no response.

Jara leaned against the wall as he said, "We need your help, Kaal. We need someone to lead my forces in Mathura. It's a long journey..." his eyes fell on the manacles, "I hope you will behave."

The man in front didn't say anything. Instead, he went to the side and it seemed like he was getting something. It was a piece of paper. A parchment of some kind, which he slipped towards Jara.

Jara was confused. He picked it up. It read:

Lord Kaal,

It is my pleasure to inform your supreme intellect that

there is some news. The blind king has made a sutaputr his commander of the army and interim king of Anga. His name is Karna and he's quite good at archery, at least from what I saw at Rangbhoomi. We have to be careful about him. Remember the dockyard attack? It could be him since such fine archery is possible by either Arjun or Karna and as far as I know...Arjun had been in Hastinapur for a long time.

And within that parchment, there was another. Jara raised his brows as he read further:

Lord Kaal,

Also, since the time we have returned from Champa, Devi and her raiding platoons are going to different forts of ours for supplies. She thinks it's safe. I believe it's the perfect time to kill her, create an ambush. There will be no ruler then.

Regards...

Jara was stunned by all the information Kaal possessed by just stationing his spies in different corners of the country. He looked up at the warrior in front, who came on his feet, the shackles clanging and creating noise; he had something in his hands. An iron mask. Made to fit his head. And he wore it like a helmet, covering his entire face except for his eyes and his nose.

And he turned.

The mask was placid and that was the scariest part about it. Emotionless. A monster lurking within.

The eyes were crimson red, looking back at Jara.

"You knew all of this and that is why...ah..." Jara understood, "that is why you killed my men. Because you wanted to find this Karna," he paused. "But I do not want you to go out and find this Karna. We don't know what he's capable of. I want you in Mathura."

Kaal walked further and Jara could see he was taller than him, much taller than him.

And then…he shook his head. *No.*

"Why?"

Kaal didn't say anything. He didn't have to. Because Mathura was just pure vengeance. It didn't hold any importance in terms of trade except for being a good port. But Anga was the future. With the share of Dhritarashtra's side of the city, he would be owning twice the amount of ships, using which then he could go and conduct foreign raids, since in Bharat, all of them were allied to the Kurus.

"Fine. Have it your way. But remember one thing, if you are not able to kill this Karna or Devi…I'll send you to Mathura and you deal with Krishna."

Kaal didn't say anything, but just nodded. And he snatched the parchment which included information about Devi's supply runs.

"Your highness, in all respect, who will raid Mathura then?" Gonanda desperately asked, as they walked outside the hut and towards their chariot.

"You," Jara said, shrugging.

"Me? But…"

"We won't attack Mathura at once. We will do it slowly. In waves. Each wave bigger than the last one. You start with the small one and by the time Kaal and I are done with Anga, I will send Kaal towards you and then come myself," Jara explained. "Anga will be over soon. If Kaal has set his mind to it, he will get me this land. I have never seen him this determined. Mathura will take time."

Gonanda didn't say anything. He was confused; worried too.

Jara had just made this strategy and he knew now how he would deal with this rat prince Karna. He had no idea who he was, but he was good at what he did.

"Have we no reports of any royal army movement in Anga?"

"The spies say none was heard. Just this morning, I received word. I wonder if Kaal's reports were correct."

"They are. That means our dear Karna is smart." Jara knew this tactic. This was what the Mlecchas would do. They would never move in a pack. That drew attention. They did it in pairs, less numbers. But how did he learn that from the Mlecchas? Was he a part of them? "I just need to know what he's thinking next."

While Kaal would be the brawn, Jara would be the brains to fight against Anga.

Let's see how long this Karna lasts with the power of two.

30

Before reaching Malinipur, Karna took two detours.

One to meet someone from the past…

And another, well that was far more important.

Karna battled rains and winds, rode on his chariot through narrow paths and wide lands, passing forests and deserted camps. He saw corpses everywhere; some feasted on by wolves, some rammed by the bandits. The very earth of Anga, as he had entered, had become strange. The smell in the air was of silver and sulphur, smoke from logwoods burning which left a strange metallic taste in his mouth. There was a massive amount of deforestation as the wood was used up by both sides, the conquerors. Because of that, he witnessed the hares and birds had died, of starvation and dehydration. The skies were stormy, while in the horizon, the sun was blanketed by thick, dense pollution from burning woods.

And finally, he reached the serpentine ravine, which once was the holy river, Ganga, but now had become just another water body.

He dismounted from his chariot and touched the water, dipping his hands into it. There was all sorts of garbage in it, thrown around.

And his heart succumbed deeply to turmoil.

This part of Anga, this part of Ganga, was important for him.

Very important.

Because this is where he was *found.*

30 years earlier…

Few months after the war with Jarasandha…

Radha knew he would not like it. But she still went with it.

While Adhirath was quite a practical person, she was religious. And here she was, at the banks of Ganga, early morning when the sun had just risen.

The water flowed seamlessly, with light, soft waves and thick reeds of plants grew around.

Radha had known that Adhirath was writing poetry at night till three and would be fast asleep for a while. Thus, she sneaked out with her soldiers, who had insisted on accompanying her.

"Your highness wouldn't be happy, but I still seek to be with you. Where you trespass is the land beyond our security, and we need men to protect you."

The Ganga river was in the outskirts of Malinipur and it was the only solace for Radha. Malinipur had been nothing like home for her. Even the palace she lived in felt icy cold. Her husband would sit for hours at home and would not work for there was nothing to do while all the power of the city was given to Senapati Vijaya, who worked for Dhritarashtra.

Her husband would leave for his job when he was called to drive his king around, but that was it. Even Satya, the great commander-in-chief, had become nothing but a manservant and a private bodyguard for Radha and Adhirath. He was a medium-sized man, with a snowy beard and deep, dark eyes, and hair that was cropped close to the head. A respected man, who had risen from the depths of the caste system to become a royal servant of arms.

A year had gone by and nothing had changed. Jarasandha still ruled Champa and Dhritarashtra ruled Malinipur. The lands had become restful now, ever since a truce was declared, which conveniently came quite soon. And now, they both ruled and enjoyed the bounties that they earned from Anga.

But while this was inevitable, Radha knew she could at least ask Ganga to give her an heir.

And this morning, she went to the banks to pray for it and wash her sins of her past karma away.

I feel all this happened because in my past life I must have been a ruthless warmonger, she thought.

She dipped her hands in the river and felt the chill, but she had to withstand it. She came on her feet and put her toes inside the water, slowly submerging her bottom half and going to the middle of the river. The waves grew strong, but the splashes of water were chilly across her body, making it numb.

Satya with his soldiers were waiting on the other side of the banks, away from her sight, as she wanted to repent alone. In isolation.

And if Adhirath found out, he would curse her for

being such an idiot and believing that the water which was used for making spices and minerals was also used to beget children.

But I have faith.

And with this, she took a dip, submerging her mouth, her chunni—making it all wet. When she pulled herself up, she felt this energy flowing through her, under the blanketed rays of the sun that gave her this insurmountable pleasure of warmth.

She took another dip. Her eyes closed, her nose blocked by her two fingers, she prayed to the river goddess to wash off her sins, and give her new hope…

When she heard it.

It was a slight snarl of a cry.

She pulled herself up from the waters and noticed the crying was no more deafening but more vibrant. Pushing through the wafts of water, she walked on the fertile soil and moved towards the cries and wails.

Is this happening for real? she asked herself.

Her eyes scanned the surrounding, until she found a bunch of thick, bamboo plants in the corner. Stuck in between, was a reed basket just floating over the algae.

She passed through those plants, grabbed hold of the basket and stared right into it. Covered in a rich, satin shawl was a young infant with a child-sized breastplate and kundalams on top of its chest.

She picked up the breastplate to examine it, to know where it could be from and she noticed it was made for a teenager. Even the kundalams must have belonged to a teenager, for they were meant for small ears.

"Someone abandoned you," she said, clutching the basket against her chest as the child no longer sobbed.

Could he be the child of an unmarried woman? That explains why he was abandoned.

She began to push the basket towards the bank when she noticed that the basket wouldn't move. It had been stuck elsewhere and her eyes wandered to know the reason, when she saw what was tugging along with her—

A crocodile.

Her heart skipped a beat and colour drained from her face. The crocodile had been concealed between the bamboo plants and thus she couldn't see it earlier. His serrated teeth were clinging on to the other handle of the basket.

She wanted to pull it away instantly and run for the land but she knew the crocodile would get hold of her.

I must save the child. I must...

She tried to slowly loosen the grip of the crocodile, who snarled in return, but was ready to leave it. She did it gradually, not alarming the creature when...

The crocodile instantly gnawed and masticated a part of the basket.

The infant cried and the crocodile opened its large mouth, ready to eat the baby.

"NO!" Radha screamed, her voice echoing through the entire area.

She pulled the half-broken basket towards her and the moment she did, the crocodile leapt for her and the infant.

A shadow passed over them and Radha saw Satya, coming out of nowhere and grabbing the crocodile by his mouth. He had lurched from the banks and on to the crocodile and was now trying to grab his sword.

Radha clutched the basket against her chest and

staggered to the bank, her breath uneven. She could feel the tension biting the chill that she was feeling from the cold as fear engulfed her. She wanted Satya to win; she shivered.

The crocodile moved its back and flung Satya on the other end, who tried to retain balance over the water. And when he did, the crocodile went for him.

Satya instantly moved to the other side, pulling his sword out, as water trickled from it.

The crocodile opened its mouth and rapidly bit through the water, through the air reaching towards Satya, when…

Radha flung a rock.

She had picked it up from the banks where now she and the child rested. The rock went with precision, at the speed of an arrow, smacking one of the crocodile's eyes.

And at that moment, Satya plunged the sword, deep inside the crocodile's mouth. The animal gave a snarl, rolling over and washing away with the river, which now was no more the colour blue.

Radha, in all the years of training for archery and precision of aim, was glad that the handwork she had put in hadn't gone to waste.

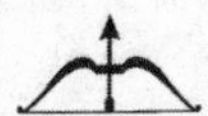

"Your highness, I hope you are fine?" Satya asked, yet again, while he massaged his wounds from the fight.

They were returning in their chariot, where the water-soaked Radha was cradling the basket in her arms.

"Yes, I am, Satya." A smile came on her face. "Yes, I am."

"You are happy, your highness. It doesn't feel like you were just attacked by a reptile," he chuckled.

Radha had almost forgotten about the ordeal. She could just see the child, the glistening kundalams and couldn't help but smile.

"I believe you won't be searching for his parents," he signalled over to the child.

"He was gifted to me by Goddess Ganga. Why should I? My karma has been cleared and now since he has come in my life, all the miseries will go away." She played with the infant's nose.

She knew she would have a lot of explanation to give to Adhirath but she also knew, he would be happy.

There was a new member coming in their family...

"I have thought of a name, Satya. Would you mind telling me how it is?"

The senani nodded, waiting. He was grinning too, for his queen was happy and was beaming, something he had never witnessed in his long years of serving.

"He's the first abandoned child in history to be adorned in gold and riches, so I thought of the perfect name," she smiled. "Vasusena, the boy who was born in wealth."

Present day...

Karna came on his feet and walked back to the chariot, sitting on it thoughtfully, mulling over the past.

The next destination was to meet his friend.

More like his mentor, though.

Someone who had withered in the passage of time, disappeared until Karna heard about him along his journey. To make sure, he had gone to see him until he had seen the man being caught and taken by the Nishadhs.

Why, of course, it was his old master and the commander-in-chief of his father Adhirath—Uncle Satya.

31

23 years earlier…

Vasu was eight years old, practicing archery with his guru.

"Not like this!" Uncle Satya scolded him, positioning his arm straight, while his legs were bent a little. "We have gone through this, child."

He grunted under his breath. He was distracted. The sun was high up, while the breeze smoothly touched his face and blew towards his earrings which dangled and shimmered under the rays. He had curls that flew in the back till the nape of his neck.

"If you want to impress your mother, you need to start working on your posture."

Vasu had remembered the day when he had seen his mother's trunk filled with instruments of archery and he had asked Uncle Satya about it, who in return said that before marriage, Radha used to perform feats of valour using her archery skills. But she stopped after marriage. It was not that her husband told her not to, but she just felt she had grown out of it.

And thus, Vasu wanted to show that he was following her footsteps, becoming as great an archer as she was once.

But that day was different and now, he wanted to just play with his friends.

"I don't think I'll ever be a good archer," Vasu sighed.

"Focus, boy!" Uncle Satya retorted.

Vasu instantly straightened and closed one of his eyes, while the arrow was strung up in the bow and pointed to the wooden bird in front of him.

"What do you see?" he asked.

Vasu was confused. He saw a bird made of cinnamon wood, but he knew it was a trick question. "I see um... um...erm..."

"What does your gut say?"

"I see a bird?" he instantly said it and waited for Uncle Satya to hit him with a stick, but he didn't do anything.

"Shoot," he calmly ordered Vasu.

And he did, with a single, bleak shot—the arrow went straight through the air and...

Hit the branch on which the wooden bird stood.

"Darn!" Vasu cursed under breath. "Why did I miss?"

"Because you weren't *seeing!*" He snatched the bow from him. "You need to focus on what you want to hit. Imagine, there will be a day when an enemy comes and how will you defend yourself?"

"I uh..." Vasu hadn't thought of it. He would only look forward to fun and games in the city streets.

Uncle Satya shook his head. He had a wispy, wise beard and he was Vasu's teacher, his guide and his guru for the time being while he was at his palace. "You must always feel the arrow. The arrow and the bow are a part of you. When you feel it, you will move with the arrow and towards your target. You will be there in the present. All right, boy?"

Vasu scratched his head. He had no clue what the old man was saying.

"Who is the greatest archer of all time?" Vasu asked. "Perhaps, he can teach me better, you know."

Uncle Satya chuckled, kneeling down. "There is Bhishma Pitamah who says he has mastered the art of the greatest weapon of all time—Brahmastra; there is Dronacharya, the martial arts guru. Tell you what, boy, when you grow older, you must seek out Dronacharya and learn from him, if you want to impress your mother." Vasu had heard about the famed Acharya, a guru of exceptional talent who had learnt the ways of warfare and advanced military arts through his time spent with Lord Parshuram, the sixth Avatar of Lord Vishnu. He was still considered to be alive and hidden in the depths of the Himalayas.

"Did you also learn from him?"

"Oh, I wish. He has a vetting process," Uncle Satya said. "And he only trains the royalty and you are royalty, the Prince of Anga."

Vasu felt his chest fill with pride and he beamed, his chubby cheeks creating two dimples. "Well, yes, I am."

Uncle Satya's silver-coloured eyes softened. "I know you came to me that day to learn archery because you had just learnt you were adopted."

Vasu didn't want to remember that day. It had been just a few months back and when he had learnt about it, he almost looked at his mother like an alien being. It took him time to accept that he was loved and he was their child, but still, he felt he was an outsider in the house.

And he knew, the only way for them to accept him, especially his mother, was to impress them—with his archery or with his poetry, to show that he was just like them. To show, *he* was their son, even though he was not their blood.

"But even if you aren't able to become an archer or a poet and goodness gracious, don't be the latter," Uncle Satya continued with a chuckle, "they will still love you. They love you for who you are, Vasu."

"It feels weird," he rubbed his elbows.

"I know. I was against the fact that she had to tell you. But she thought you must know. You are meant to know, otherwise she would take that choice away from you."

"Choice?"

"The choice to grow up and find your real mother. I'm sure one day you will." Uncle Satya ruffled his hair. "Who gave you these beautiful earrings and the breastplate that's kept in your room?"

He had never thought of going out of his comfortable home and searching for a woman who had abandoned him.

And he didn't want to. At least, for now.

"Go now, and enjoy with your friends," he patted Vasu's arm.

Vasu smiled sadly, moving for the gates and glaring back as Uncle Satya waved at him. He waved back.

I might have been abandoned then.

But I'm not abandoned anymore.

32

Present day...

Tataka forest, modern day south west Bihar...

If there is one community one must not venture into, it is the Nishadh community. Armed with the most ancient weapons and living in houses created on the top-most peepul trees or mangroves, these tribals had a way of talking to each other in signs. From hooting to clapping, they would make noises to communicate.

And Nishadh, which literally translates to the forest people, from huts to treehouses, to small empires, had grown considerably. Their entire life was managed in the woods and across the branches and vines. But they weren't as uncivilised as one would make them to be. They were quite smart, and were excellent hunters and fishermen. They would station their base close to the seas or the rivers, so they could have food from there.

And while most Nishadh tribes were peaceful and lived in seclusion from everyone, the one Karna was going to meet and the one in which Satya was captured—was the most dangerous.

Fuelled by rage and anger, driven by justice, this community of Nishadh were not peaceful but rebelled against the soldiers of Dhritarashtra and even Jarasandha.

And that's why, Karna was more than glad to meet them.

And they were too…on one condition.

As Karna reached the dense forest, he could hear the whistles and the claps.

Here they come.

With a cool attitude, Karna got up on his chariot and laid out his hand in front. He had no armour or weapon. He wanted to show them, he was no threat and except the greenery, the seagulls and the occasional baboons and lemurs who populated the forest—he didn't see anything.

Until they came.

With a poke.

A spear was jutting next to the back of his throat, a spear made of a simple, sharpened bark. The Nishadh had a habit of not using metal, iron, anything to do with advanced technologies. It was just not to their taste.

"Well, glad to meet you too."

Pushed and shoved ahead, Karna was besieged by dozens of spears next to him, while his hands were clasped by a hard bamboo string. He was told to walk further, until he reached a small clearing where an aqua blue lagoon was based, and there were treehouses, interconnected with bridges made of bamboo too. There were totems kept, who the Nishadh worshipped and there was a small shed where the murti of Rakshas Raavan was placed; according to the Nishadhs, he was their dharmaguru. Not evil.

By the looks of it, these people were quite primitive and they looked the part too. They didn't wear anything that was imported from the Greeks and Egyptians which the royalty wore. In fact, they were in leaves and loincloths and simple clothing, to cover the essential body parts. Some men and women, even children, walked naked, with brusque, dark-skinned bodies and charcoal-coloured hair.

The smell of fishes and chicken wafted in and a goat's cries as it was being beheaded could be heard, while he was pushed and walked on to the staircase that led to the top-most part of the treehouse, up in the skies, where the clouds could be felt and the air was chilly. People passed Karna, noticing a civilised man in tunics, watching him carefully as if he was an alien.

Karna even saw some of them sharpening their weapons and their reed bows, smaller than his, of course, but daggers too, not made of metal but wood.

The Nishadh had a history—apparently their great ancestor was King Vena, so evil and so horrendous in his actions that the goddess Bhumidevi had to come down and transform into a cow, go into hiding because Vena was hurting the earth he lived in by his atrociousness. A group of rishis came together and killed Vena, helping Bhumidevi.

While the modern Nishadhs don't care about the past, it was interesting for Karna to see how they were born out of hatred, greed, and evil.

As he came forward, he entered a hut and found himself in a nicely lit room, where a man sat. He looked a bit older than Karna, with a plastic smile, a wooden crown with flowers around it and a charred, scarred body. He had one eye, the other was made of marble, and he had piercings in his nipples, ears and nose.

"If it isn't my old friend, unclasp him," their chief said.

And the men who had brought Karna instantly did so, not realising that he was the chief's friend.

"You should really paint my picture here and paste it for them to know that I know you," Karna said, massaging his bruised wrist.

"Don't mind them. Have you brought it?" There was greed in the chief's eyes.

"Of course, as promised to you earlier," Karna said, as he came forward and presented the chief, who was of short built and meeker than chiefs usually were. "Here it is."

He handed him the cane which belonged to Dronacharya. Karna had hidden it under his tunic.

The chief, grabbed it instantly and began to hungrily look at it. "It's such a beauty, isn't it? Father Hiranyadhanu would be so proud if he was alive today. After all, that guru made a fool out of me. I can imagine him limping around in the halls like a fool now." He paused and gleefully ordered his men. "Get his reward."

The men agreed and they walked in the background, only to pull out a man who was bound on all sides, weak, and his hair all over his face. He looked like a hermit, and not like the sage and guru he once used to be.

Karna saw Uncle Satya and he couldn't help but feel sad for him. He didn't know how he had come to this. And what had led him, but he knew he would get his answer soon.

"Your Uncle Satya has been quite a nasty man to our land. And he would have gotten his head axed and rolled over on the muddy ground if it wasn't for you who had come to meet me. Be gone now," the chief ordered.

"I have a proposition," Karna said.

The chief raised his brows. "Indeed you have. Heard you went to the forest encroacher Dhritarashtra and begged for a crown."

"I didn't beg. They gave it to me."

"But they didn't give you an army. They want you to lose, isn't it?" the chief giggled.

"You can help me change that." Karna knew having the Nishadh community on his side would be smart. When Suyodhan said he had to look out for an army, he had little idea he could use the unorthodox ones, and not the ones you usually choose from.

"Oh, can I?" he came on his feet, and walked, and kept his thumbless hand on Karna's shoulder. "What proposition is this?"

Karna looked at the chief.

Of course, he knew the bloody bastard. He had met him back in Drona's Gurukul.

But this man never got close to Gurukul. He was never allowed because of his caste.

So he picked up all the teachings of Drona by eavesdropping, then he approached the great old master to tell him that he had learnt from him in secret. Drona was furious, but he knew this chief was good at archery and so, as *dakshina*, he asked him to cut off his thumb.

Why, of course, Karna stood in front of the Nishadh chief and king—

Eklavya.

33

The man had changed.

He was no more the man he knew; but a fiend of some kind.

Was it a mistake to take him in for the army against Jarasandha?

He wanted an asset but did he get a liability instead?

They both were in a hut given by Eklavya for the night, as they would leave for Malinipur the next day and meet Devi.

Like a scared puppy, Satya was in the corner, rubbing his nails together and clattering his teeth.

Karna had to go out and talk to Eklavya. The silverlight had come and the slight flute music from the natives were heard, the smell of robust chicken being cooked, as well as crabs and salmon. These people were celebrating for no reason and that was the life of a Nishadh. Even when the world would go up in fires, they wouldn't.

"Do you remember me?" Karna asked Satya.

The man didn't answer. His face was lowered and his bushy hair acted as a hood. He was blinking hard.

"I am Vasu," he said. "Remember me? I had gone to Dronacharya's Gurukul, the one you had suggested. God, what has happened to you?"

Satya looked up. He had those silver eyes, as he used to. "Boy," a gruff, hoarse tone came, "why did you save me?"

He speaks.

"Because I want your help."

"What help can I offer? I am good for nothing. You have made a wrong decision," Satya said.

Karna nodded. "Perhaps, or perhaps not. So you plan to run away?"

"Soon, as I leave this abyss. But why did you help me?"

"Do you not remember *me*?" he sounded frustrated.

"My past life doesn't matter. It was a dream."

"My mother was Radha. Your queen. You were a commander-in-chief, who taught me to be a warrior, before anyone else. You taught me archery…have you…?"

And he shot a look of contempt. "Radha…" he said, "Rajmata Radha. Yes. I see her face, but it's a blur. I remember…Vasu…oh, it's a blur. Lot of it is."

"I am Vasu."

"You are?"

Karna showed his kundalams. "Remember?"

"Ah, the earrings," he was trying hard to remember, "yes, yes, I can remember. But I leave when it's done."

"What did you do to grow contempt in the heart of Eklavya?"

He paused. He was thinking of that too. "I remember Radha." He responded, as if the question Karna had asked was not important. "Yes, I do. She was ill and we were worried. And then she withered, it was years back, seems like another life that I used to lead. Like an old lady, but she wasn't old. She had some sort of fever that got her. Oh, what a sad day it was."

Karna paused, pursing his lips. "What happened to you after that?"

"Vasu...Vasu..." his eyes narrowed. "You are the boy who left us to rot."

"I was at the Gurukul."

"You could have come for your mother." Satya came on his feet, stinking of puss and shit and dirt. "That's why."

"What why?"

He had come close now and was also crouching a bit, resembling someone who was absolutely intoxicated by some kind of a drug; his eyes were bloodshot, his mouth dripping saliva. "That is why I don't remember you," he paused. "You were a bad memory."

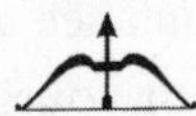

"I have to show you something," Eklavya said, as he moved out of the camp of the Nishadhs and on to a lonely path.

And unlike most chiefs or senior lords of the country, he walked alone. He had no guards, except for Karna.

"I don't see your men."

"You are here. I don't need anyone else," Eklavya said, as he walked with the cane of the guru he hated.

And yet, he used the cane. Karna knew, that no matter what and how much contempt Eklavya showed towards Drona, he still respected him.

Moonlight was beaming through the clouds. And there was a fog that moved like a serpent amidst the woods.

Karna was still confused about what Satya said back

at the quarters. The man seemed deranged and he almost lost hope in taking his help. *I should have not gone out of my way to get him out.* But he would still try. Never give up on anyone, he had learnt in the Himalayas.

"Is it true you met Lord Parshuram?" Eklavya asked.

Karna knew that being a part of the pact with Parshuram and learning from him, he could not reveal the truth or offer any kind of idea that would perpetuate something against Lord Parshuram. "You can say that."

"And he also exiled you?"

"Yes."

"What's with you and Gurukuls?" Eklavya turned, his dark skin gleaming under the moonlight. "Why do you have to be kicked out of it every time you enter?"

Karna shrugged. "I don't see a problem in me."

"Because you are full of yourself, that's why."

"See I like the condescending statements in the dark and I actually look forward to it in the day, but I would like to know if this is the only reason we are here."

His ruby ring flashed and then he showed, signalling something close to the plants and shrubs, "I am here to show you this."

Karna knelt down and looked at what was being pointed at—only to realise…

It was a hand.

A human hand!

Karna felt a tug of fright inside his throat, bile stuck that he was unable to swallow. "What is this?"

"What do you think it is?"

"I mean, why do you want to show me this? It's not awfully romantic, you know."

Eklavya rolled his eyes. "Your sharp-tongued attitude wouldn't get me anywhere. The reason why I'm showing you this is because if you want my army to fight against Jarasandha, you need to do me a favour."

Karna sighed. *I am not doing anything*, he thought. He had to try using words to find his way out of this and also get benefits. "You do realise by killing Jarasandha, you will not have people attacking your livelihood?"

"But that woman still would. What's her name? Devi. Yes. You have partnered up with Dhritarashtra and he's an even bigger problem to me."

"I am the king. I won't let him…"

"That's all in the air for me. How do I know? What is the guarantee? I do not believe in contracts and scrolls. After all, I am a savage, aren't I?" he mocked, the word that he often had been called by the so-called *civilised* people. "All I know is that if I spare few hundred men to your battle, I should know I have given them to someone who has done a favour for me. Otherwise, it'll look like I'm doing it for free and I don't do anything for free."

"I would give you the war loot. Fifty per cent?" Karna desperately asked.

"What would I do with war loot? Gold? Silver? Our community doesn't trade in your currency. We barter. We share. And we love. I am sure your people don't do that."

Great. More mockery.

Karna sighed, gritting his teeth.

Eklavya continued, "My men can be useful. They are vipers who will come at night and destroy Jarasandha from the back and all corners and what not. They will be less in number, but they will be effective. Smart. And believe me, I am only doing this favour because I know you. You keep your word, like this cane. I know you'll be a good king, but to be that, you need to help me."

Karna picked up the hand, without speaking or protesting further. He investigated the hand and he could see, it was viciously bitten. "What am I looking at?"

"A murder. By a creature of another world."

"Please don't start with your..."

"They are called weretigers," Eklavya snapped and Karna rolled his eyes, as they heard the trudge of the wing beats and the raven cawing. "Half man, half tiger. Awful beasts."

"How..." he couldn't swallow this stupidity. Karna knew that the Nishadh had a habit of believing in the supernatural, thus they also had a post for a sorcerer, a witch who would do rituals for them. They believed sickness was caused by the possession of ghosts, or *preta* in their terminology. It was all too much for him and he would have just bat his eyelids, but then it was someone's faith, so he thought better of it. "Okay, fine. So it's a weretiger. It's killing your men."

"He was one of my best. I left him here, because I was too afraid of him. The rest of his body—it's gone. Done, for good. Eaten by the weretiger."

Karna came on his feet, the severed, chewed up hand still grasped by him. "I see. And why is this weretiger killing your men?"

"Probably because he's hungry. A weretiger changes at night and they hunt for flesh."

"But why so close to your settlement?"

He shook his head, biting his lips nervously. "Well,

because he was one of us. A soldier of mine, who had gotten sick with a disease. Had red boils all over his face. We took him to the witch doctor and she gave him some medicine. Hypnotised him, performed magic on him, or something, I don't know. When he woke up, his boils were gone but he had changed. He was craving flesh and since he was one of us, we left him out, drove him away, but he came here and he began killing. None of my men were ready to murder him because he was one of them. We don't hunt one of us, by our own hands. And so I wonder, you are in need of help and you are the most brilliant archer of Bharat. Who better than you to defeat this creature?"

"So you tell the king of Anga to do it?"

Eklavya came closer and for a moment, Karna could see his eyes blink with excitement and the same naivety he had as a child—small and full of life until his thumb was cut off and he wasn't able to do the one thing he loved the most: archery. "Isn't the king's job to make sure his people are happy? We are unhappy with this murderer, *King Karna*." He spat the words with glee. "Would you do it?"

"Do I have a choice?"

"You can leave."

"But I need your men."

"And I need the head of that creature. We all have our desires," he smirked.

Karna nodded. "Fine, I'll do it. I'll hunt for him in the morning."

"Smart. At night he's..."

There was a roar which came from the woods. Like that of the tiger.

"Ah well, he has awakened. We should go back."

Karna wasn't prepared. He didn't have his weapons or his armour. He had to go back to his quarter and perhaps… perhaps he would also take Satya. Perhaps spending more time with him would change Satya's behaviour towards him, even though guilt was something Karna was carrying as he didn't return to his mother. To his dying mother, and for that he would always curse himself.

"I wanted to ask you something," Karna said.

"Yeah?"

"What did Satya do that you had to enslave him?"

Eklavya halted. "You don't know. Ah." He nodded. "Your so-called master from your early days peddles drugs. An extract of Somalata plants, he delivers and deals with. Sells to the highest bidder and earns a bit of coin in between."

Somalata? He had heard about the plant. They grew in the north and they could be highly toxic when overused or could give the best psychedelic experience when taken in moderate doses. But many lost their lives trying too. Somalata was used by the earlier gods, like Indra, who could even digest the toxicity but modern humans couldn't. And it was now banned everywhere.

"So you take him in for selling Somas? What's so special about that?"

He shook his head. "He was selling to children, Karna. He was selling to young, impressionable *children*."

34

22 years ago…

Vasu could finally show it.

This was his time. For one straight year, he had been practicing to show off to his mother his archery skills.

And his mother, father and little brother were waiting for him, while he was holding the reed bow in his hand looking at the target in front of him. It was an apple; behind him he could feel the presence of Uncle Satya.

Radha, was excitedly clapping and cheering for him, but Vasu was far from feeling normal.

He was nervous. Not because he wouldn't hit the target. It was fine if he couldn't, but then he would fail. And the idea of failing had really seized him. He was choking last night and was having an anxiety problem; it was like his breath had allowed itself to come in less numbers and he was feeling icy cold; his entire body succumbing to this swampy marshland. But now he felt better. Uncle Satya had told him to concentrate on his breathing and not focus on the failure, but only on the success.

If you put your mind to it, you will succeed.

But was it that easy? Just putting your mind to it?

He took a deep breath again, and fastened the arrow on his string, pointing it towards the target—when he realised, a knot of frustrating nervousness had formed inside his throat.

I'll fail. I'll fail. No.

Vasu was adopted.

He was...

I am a disowned child. By not making my mother proud, I will be disowned again. I will be castrated. They won't love me.

He was overthinking and it was getting to him so much that the tips of his fingers had got cold while his head had begun to ache.

Not now. I can't let uncertainty do this.

YOU ARE ADOPTED! YOU WERE THROWN IN THE RIVER BY YOUR REAL MOTHER, YOU GOOD FOR NOTHING...

He closed his eyes—his thoughts were not letting him concentrate. He had started practising archery to impress his mother and he looked at her again...she looked confused, but still ecstatic. She had hope in her eyes that her son would be an archer. A great one, something she wasn't able to be.

And then he shot the arrow.

Without thinking. Without patience.

And it landed away from the apple. Quite far.

There was silence in Vasu's surrounding, and he could feel a sense of deafness where all he heard was this loud sound of hoofbeats—when he fell on the ground.

I have failed her.

He was letting his anxiety get to him, when he saw his mother's shadow looming over him, and she was trying to call out to him. She was worried.

Sorry, mother. For not being your son.

Present day...

"Why are you taking me?" Satya called out from behind.

Karna had him in a long leash and he was pulling his old guru behind. And it was awkward for him to do so, because he still respected him a lot even though Satya had become a degenerate user of Soma and a dealer of it.

"That's why you can't remember me," Karna said, trampling his feet over on the crunched ground, as he had returned into the familiar territory of the so-called weretiger. "You are too intoxicated."

"Or perhaps, I do not want to remember you," Satya spat on the ground. "I need some green. Give me green. It's been a while..."

"Shut up," Karna stopped.

"What shut up? Who the..."

Karna had by then closed his eyes and breathed deep as he could and he began to concentrate. The surrounding, the chirping of the sparrows and the hissing of the wind. He wanted to feel something...a creature...

And then he heard it. It was of something chewing on a bone and serration.

"This way." Karna pulled the leash from Satya and they walked further, in between the hedges, where shrubs and plants were growing.

"I remember you, though," Satya grimaced and chuckled. "You are the one who was afraid of failure, isn't it? A boy, a wimp." He was laughing. "You had such panic attacks, ain't it?"

"Shut up," Karna sighed. He was already regretting bringing Satya here.

"How are you now, boy? Have you overcome that fear?"

Karna didn't answer. Perhaps, he still had it. Perhaps, he had overcome it. That was the thing about fear. You didn't know when it would grab you by the throat.

"What are we bloody hunting?" Satya sighed, bored.

"A tiger." That's what Karna thought it would be. It can't be a half man, half tiger. He recalled the severed hands, it was done in such a way that it definitely had to be an animal bite and the Nishadh thought it was a creature from another world.

"A tiger? Gah! What a filthy animal." And he began to tug Karna away. "I want to go back. You listening to me, boy? I want to go back and have myself some green."

Karna's hand was at the end of the leather leash and he looked up with frustration at his guru. "You aren't going anywhere."

"Who are you to say that?"

"I have rescued you."

Satya came forward, and stood next to Karna, shorter than him but still having the steel gaze and a filthy smell of rodents festering in his mouth.

"What became of you?" Karna was disgusted and he contorted his face into a pitiful frown.

"I became what the world made me," Satya spat. "A

man who was risen by the sweet Radha to be a commander, only to be plunged into darkness, when everything around him was drenched in blood and chaos. I became, boy, what my caste entitled me to be. I aspired to be a warrior, but I was a cobbler's son. And when I got free from the duties of the commander, I wasn't able to get myself some job so I found the green. The green is an escape and that's why the gods used it."

Karna impassively watched the wretched man, who had believed his lies, though one question still perturbed him. "Why did my father throw you out after mother's death?"

"Father…I don't remember…" he massaged his head.

"Adhirath," Karna reminded him.

"Yes, yes…the man had given up. Yes. He didn't need me. So he let me go, even though I didn't want to go. He said, he'll be going back to Hastinapur. Where is he now?"

Karna didn't respond; shaking his head. His father shouldn't have let go of Satya. And he began to tug him further, when Satya made him halt. "I won't go, boy!"

"Fine!" Karna exclaimed. "If you help me, I'll get you the bloody green."

Satya narrowed his gaze, licking his papery lips. "Indeed you would, boy. And you would also help me get a throne and some whores to lick my balls too, right? Stop making a fool out of me."

"You were selling to children!" Karna yelled. "Children! They can die, Satya. They can be killed by the substance. Why did you do it?"

He shrugged. "To earn a living, perhaps, boy? Or have you forgotten that with so many silver spoons in your mouth?"

"Silver spoons? I was born to a king who became a pawn. I grew up feeling isolated and abandoned, fearing the failure so much it affected my health, only to reach a Gurukul where I was thrown out, only to go to another Gurukul and get thrown out again. I was hated by everyone for my caste and the only woman I loved is forced to marry the one person I hate the most. So no, I wasn't born with a silver spoon," Karna's eyes raged with anger.

"Well, boy, no one said life was perfect. All we can do is stop feeling sorry about it."

It was clearly a jibe.

But this time, when Karna tugged, he didn't push back. In fact, he walked with him. And they did so, until they heard the scream and the agony of a growl and a roar. It was a mixture of a lot of things and Karna instantly pulled out his bow and arrow, with his sun gleaming armour, and he looking at the skies, and the tall trees around them.

"Why are you looking up if it's a tiger?" Satya asked.

And then Karna saw a shadow. Up high, sitting on the branches. But he couldn't see it properly.

Though he knew one thing from just looking at it.

"Because," Karna said, realising Eklavya was right all along, "it isn't a tiger."

35

Karna didn't hit it.

And it moved. As quick as it had come.

The creature didn't stop.

But it was looking at them. And it didn't attack. *It doesn't have feral instincts.*

Karna raised his brows, wondering, trying to understand what he was dealing with.

"That's not a tiger, boy. That's something else. What have you got me into? Will you get me killed?"

I need the Nishadh on my side, Karna reminded himself. *No room for failure.*

The little he could see of the shadow, he had seen that the creature had hard skin and had hair all over its body, with a face that resembled that of a tiger. But it was bipedal since it jumped from one tree to another, escaping.

"We need to trap it," Karna said. "It knows we are here to hunt it, so it'll be careful."

For a moment, Satya was quiet. And then he said, with a voice that didn't sound like someone who was craving intoxication, but someone with a strong, powerful, bullish tone: "What's the plan, boy?"

Traps.

He had learnt it during his time in Gurukul along with Dronacharya...to defeat an enemy, one must not just be all powerful and resilient but also be smart.

Karna knew the morning was in his favour, but he had to survive the night too, so he got himself and Satya to work.

They both began to cut down branches from the tree, and also bamboo sticks. Karna handed Satya a knife and they both began to create slivers of sticks and sharpen them.

And while they did it, Satya asked: "How do you know the creature will get caught in this?"

"Because we will lure it into it."

They managed by the evening to create fifty or so sharpened sticks that could be lethal.

They began to find a place which was more or less muddy and swampy in nature, where the sticks could be placed.

They plunged the sticks in the ground, then covered it with patches of grass and plants to conceal them. Once it was done, Karna grinned that they finally were able to create a circle of thorny traps that if the creature would step on—he would be instantly stabbed and collapse.

"It's smart, boy. And I hope the creature isn't smarter."

"If he's a creature, he won't see it."

If...

It could be a man too.

"What do we do now?"

"Wait for the moon to come," Karna said, as the sun

was dying and his favourite part of the day was getting over.

The fog was intense, and as they silently waited amidst the circle of thorns, they had their weapons ready. Satya had his knife and he sounded reluctant to be there, grumping and growling under his breath. Karna was quiet. His eyes were closed and he was listening to his breathing to control himself.

I have to succeed.

I have to fight the failure.

Karna noticed something—there was something in the bushes, and his arrow was brought out instantly and pointed towards it.

A raven cawed and burst through it, moving for the skies.

"I should have just gotten myself executed with an axe. Nice and painless. And not get eaten by whatever this beast is that we are hunting," Satya cried. "I am too young to die." The wrinkled, snowy-bearded, white-haired man said.

"Sure you are."

"I have begun to regain my memory..." he said, "... and I don't remember you being such a wisecrack when I used to know you before."

"Well, four years did me some good."

Satya couldn't help but chuckle. "Four years eh? Four years is a long time."

"Short, if your life's purpose is yet to be achieved."

And it was. He had a *promise* to keep.

"Why didn't you return?" Satya asked, this time with warmth in his voice.

"If I did, I wouldn't have been able to do what I was supposed to do."

"And what is that?"

Karna didn't respond. Until it was completed, he wouldn't tell anybody.

"Fine. But you could have come to your mother and then gone back?"

"Perhaps, or perhaps I would have given up and stayed at Anga. Lived my whole life like that and not kept the promise I was supposed to keep. Or perhaps I would have been smitten by grief. I knew, staying away…it made me cope with my mother's death."

"Radha would have hated you if she could hear those words right now."

Karna shook his head. He didn't want to speak about the dead. Their souls were at peace now.

And while here, they weren't.

The conversation was hampered, as the shadow, as quick as a whip began to walk, bipedal but faster than a human being, until it stopped…

The shadow turned its head at the trap and smelled it.

"It knows," Satya said. "It knows we laid a trap. Oh shit, we are dead."

And then it growled.

Karna's arrows were ready to strike.

But the shadow didn't touch its feet to the trap.

Instead, it roared and lurched.

The body moved, suspended in the air, and Karna

instantly rolled over, realising it had managed to get onto Satya.

Karna pulled his master from the leash he had tied himself to and towards him, missing the burly arms of the creature. Satya fell on the ground, while Karna shot an arrow.

It hit the creature on the back, who just roared and pulled the blade out.

Satya came on Karna's side, as Karna pulled out another set of arrows, this time three of them and he was ready. Even more so, than ordinarily.

But the mist around them slithered like a serpent, making it impossible for him to see. So he closed his eyes again, listening to the beats of the third set of footsteps when he told Satya: "Don't move. I'm listening."

And as he was told, Satya stopped and he could only hear one set of footsteps. Moving. Calculating.

He took a deep breath and Karna pointed the arrow in a direction in the mist he couldn't see, but he knew it was the right direction.

I got you.

Through the mist, the creature leapt. Splitting through the fog and the cloudiness of the surrounding. Its mouth opened. Its hand and legs pointed towards Karna.

And he shot it.

The three arrows plunged into the creature's chest, smacking him back and with force throwing him down, as the creature began to growl.

Karna came forward, his eyes setting on what he had just killed.

And he realised, it was not what he had expected.

It was a human. It was a *he*. But it was wearing the skin of a tiger all over his body, as if he was part of it and his eyes were blood red, his skin was withering now and he had boils all over his body.

Satya came on the side of Karna and they both watched the man dressed like a tiger king, groaning in pain.

"This is not a creature from another world."

"No, but he looks like someone," Karna narrowed his gaze.

And before he could do anything, the man leapt from the ground and towards Satya and they both rolled down towards the thorny traps.

Karna slipped and fell, as his arm was tightened around the leash and he got tugged.

Satya punched the man and rolled over, as they were trying to come close to the thorns and the blades they had jutted in the ground.

Karna had lost his bow and arrow and he was trying to pull himself back, but Satya was already in the duel and he could feel a sharpening pain in the leg, as each tug made him moan. Karna could feel the stress and the tension building in him, as he shouted at his guru: "Lead him to the..."

And before he could say, there was a loud, gushy sound of a blade going through multiple ties, against the flesh, piercing through it deeply and there it was. The darkness shrouded as he realised, Satya was killed...

Or was he?

In front of him, he saw the body of the man-tiger spread over the thorns. He could also see Satya had managed to miss the thorns and had saved himself from the trap he had himself created.

They both smiled at each other.

The so-called weretiger was dead, and as Karna came forward to see the creature himself, he saw the ring that the creature wore.

It was ruby.

And the one thing he knew about Nishadh customs was that the family wore the same ring and ornaments.

The ruby apparently...

Karna raised his brows. This just got even more complicated.

"I believe we are done now," Satya said. "Boy," he slapped Karna's back. "Good job."

"Yeah, but I need to ask one more thing to Eklavya."

"And what would that be?"

Karna looked at his guru and said: "Why would a son want to kill his own father?"

36

Karna dropped the corpse in front of the natives.

All circled around the body, and watched it in awe—some of them poking, with others hissing that it was not a monster. It was human.

And then Karna turned to look up where the treehouses were lined and he saw Eklavya, standing close to the railings and looking at him with a lethal gaze.

Karna and Satya walked, and as they did, Karna used his knife to break the bond between them.

"You are free to leave," Karna said to Satya, and the old man was confused.

"Just like that?"

"I can't force anyone to be part of my mission to stop Jarasandha. If you feel you have it in you, then join me, but behave. You cannot be dealing anymore. But if you can't, I wish to not see you when I'm out of Eklavya's hut."

The rain had begun to prick and the natives scampered across with giant leaves covering their heads.

Satya was dripping wet, confused. "You are making a big mistake, thinking you can take on Jarasandha."

"Why is that?"

"He's a really smart foe, boy." The man was speaking with clarity now, probably because he wasn't intoxicated anymore.

"But you can help me fight him. You know the people of this land better than anyone else. While I ventured across Bharat, it was you who stayed here and I need your experience in knowing who is our ally and who is not," Karna said.

"I'm just a nobody," he shrugged.

"Then so be it," Karna sighed, bowing to his guru. "It was nice being with you again. I felt nostalgic. Good day."

And he left his master, his guru, behind as he walked to Eklavya, ready to ask him some very tough questions.

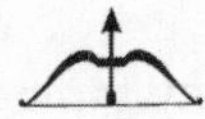

Karna entered the hut, and he was tired. He felt exhausted, as if someone had beaten him up. He had been travelling and hadn't got peaceful sleep. And now he had battled a raving lunatic, and was injured with bruises and wounds. But seeing Eklavya, all flustered and sitting on his throne, was what made Karna smile.

"You'll get five hundred of my men. Not the best lot, but effective. Take them and make sure they return to their families in one piece," Eklavya said, ordering his men to also do the needful.

Five hundred would be less, but Karna knew that the Nishadhs weren't whom you used in a straight terrain battle. You used them with strategy and mindful thinking.

"You aren't happy that I killed him," Karna noted.

"Of course I am," Eklavya said with a defeated face.

It was of remorse; frustration. "I knew when I was hiring you, you would kill him. It had to be..." he whispered to himself, "it had to be done."

"Yes." Karna looked at the guards around Eklavya. There were almost five of them, in such a hut. "Should I ask in front of them or you'll ask them to leave?"

Eklavya paused; clenching his jaw and then he stomped his cane, and the men left instantly. He leaned back and said: "Say what you have to."

"Why?"

"Just that?"

"Yes."

"I..." he shook his head, "it's tough to explain."

"Try me."

"Well," he nodded, "my father was an ambitious man, more ambitious than someone who lived like a tribal. Like me. Like you see around. Except me, none of them are so educated. I was, because I eavesdropped. So anyway, back to the point. My father was ambitious and he wanted me to be taught by the royalty's guru. He wanted me to be a king soon and he had already begun building blocks of my kingdom, in the far east where the land was unoccupied and we could have created a new world for ourselves. Anyway, he wanted me to impress Drona, and make him feel I'm the best and I *was* the best, on par with you and Arjun. He wanted me to fight in armies, rule lands for the royalty and come back and rule this kingdom when he would pass away."

"And then Drona did the unthinkable."

"Indeed," tears began to fall from his eyes, "and I lost my archery and my training wasn't complete either.

Without my archery, I was nothing but a fool. I had lost my identity. But I knew I would reclaim it, unlike my father who saw his prodigious son lose the very thing he knew he would be best at. His dreams were destroyed. Now I was his...well...ordinary child. And he was angry at Drona, but angrier at himself for driving me to the guru. He took that guilt and let it affect him. It started slow, the disease, this mental thing, and it began to corrode him until we took him to a witch-doctor who made it worse by giving him medicines that would make him burn with rage, cannibalistic. She made him think he was a tiger."

He shook his head. "I realised she was doing it to usurp my power, by making my dad look like a threat, someone possessed; and to make everyone feel that I would bring the same fate to the tribe. You know how our kind is. They believe any shit you tell them, as long as it's outside their ordinary thinking. She did it to bring forth her son and so I caught her before that, and I killed her. And her son." His eyes raged and he was no longer a sad, poor soul but a vengeful, vicious man. "And before anyone could know it was my father, I announced that he had passed away, while I exiled this creature who once was my father. Soon, my father began to kill my men and I knew I had to do something about it. I couldn't have sent just anyone because they would know it was my father... until I just saw how he looked like now. He was no more identifiable." He chuckled morbidly to himself. "I should have just let some of my men kill him, might as well have saved that favour for some other time and saved my five hundred men."

"They won't die," Karna promised. "They are doing the right thing for their nation."

"We don't believe in the idea of nations."

"You stand on the ground of one. So better believe it," Karna paused. "And I am sorry for your loss. You did the right thing and I hope that Drona one day realises the consequences of his actions—they transcend through time and space."

Eklavya nodded. "Thank you. You know, you are not a bad man."

"Why did you think I was?"

"Because," Eklavya came on his feet and strolled towards Karna, "You are a very dangerous man, Karna. I happen to believe that dangerous men have dangerous ideals."

"My ideal is not at all..."

Eklavya cut him off and said, "Let's hope. Let's hope it doesn't make you lose everything in the process of getting what you want."

"How will I lose everything if my purpose is everything?"

Eklavya arched his brows. And shrugged, with a grin.

"Oh also," Karna said, before leaving, "I will require that blueprint of that medicine, the one that witch-doctor made which made your father cannibalistic."

"Why?"

Karna smiled. "I have just got an idea."

As Karna came out of the tent, with thoughts brimming in his mind, he looked down to find the empty, rainy clearing of the settlement, and no one was there, probably because of the weather.

But he did see someone. With a leaf to cover himself.

It was Satya.

He didn't leave.

Karna grinned.

Well, I suppose it wasn't so bad coming here, after all.

37

Devi knew she lived in a man's world.

But she made a pretty good place in it—one way or another.

She was a tall, broad woman with almond-coloured skin, rich and with sheen, having one side of her hair grazed while another was in tufts of braids and designs. Her eyes were underlined heavily with kohl, her body inked with designs made by colourful needles being pierced, created a dotted design. It was all over her body.

The roads to Champa were barren and empty. There were open fields and a sense of isolation and loneliness. At night, about a hundred of her men raided the local village close to Champa for a supply run—she knew she was too old for it herself.

Even though she was fruitfully young, almost in her early thirties, she was tired of the bloodshed.

But she knew, her field days weren't over out of compulsion but out of choice. She liked the battle; the uncertainty, the war.

They reached the village and as they arrived, they went in with torches and arrow-ready men, waiting to pounce and strike, but nothing was there except for corpses strewn across the field.

This was just another village in Champa, laden with violence created by Jarasandha. And by now, she had gotten used to it. The numb feeling she had faced during the earlier supply runs was gone now.

"Aren't we worse than Jarasandha?" A voice came from one side.

And a mare appeared, holding a young girl with a beautiful, exotic smile, eyes that were narrow and gleaming, and hair that was cut and fashioned till her long neck.

"In what way?" she asked Manvee.

"By stealing from the dead."

"What we steal is given to the living." She referred to her kingdom in Malinipur—a five hundred acre fortress, with large stadiums, forts, castles and watchtowers. "Our men toil every day and I believe what Jarasandha has left behind is what we can give to our people."

"We are beggars," Manvee said. She was her second-in-command, even though scrutiny was met with when it came to her, as she was a woman. "Scavengers." But it didn't hurt Devi. She knew it came from a good place, as Manvee was a good woman, a heart made of gold, and selfless, which was in stark contrast to the ruthlessness that Devi projected.

Devi argued that if Manvee was a woman, then so was she, but then Devi didn't look like the traditional woman. And she had told the council, 'You don't look like traditional men, but cocksuckers.' Now, they were old and grumpy and they fought, but Devi had blessings from Dhritarashtra and thus she carried the flags, even on the back of her saddle; the iron pole with the saffron flag with an elephant drawn on it was waving.

"What village is this for?" Manvee asked.

"It was a shipbuilding and trading one. Though, how does it matter?"

"Why did he kill all of them?"

"So no one could tell how they built their ships and what went into it. There's no evidence left."

Manvee's face contorted into a panicky frown. "Then he should have not reigned from Champa."

"He did, because he couldn't be in the territory where his enemies were, on the same terrain. It could lead to great disadvantage, strategically."

Manvee nodded. And they made their way, her men searching the places, and huts, and breaking through doors.

Devi looked around, feeling safe here. "We camp here," she ordered. "And we bury the dead with respect."

Devi had told her men to burn the corpses far away from the village to not get unwarranted attention from someone they didn't want it from.

And so they did. Some of the men went to cremate the bodies, while some went to hunt for the night and made bonfires to cook.

Devi sat with Manvee for a while, until she went to the hut that was cleaned for her and washed herself with water from a jar. A small carpet was laid out on which she would sleep. Her arms and legs were wrapped in bruises underneath the bandages. She had leopard skin all over her body and bear fur, acting as her kneepads and elbowpads, while a large cowl made of animal fat was over her, as a cape.

She drew it down and closed the doors behind her, when Manvee entered.

Devi sat on her chair and sighed. "I don't feel so good."

"Why is that?" Manvee asked.

"Probably because a cunt is coming to take my place," Devi growled under her breath. She had taken control of Malinipur, for a long time now.

After Senapati Vijaya had died.

"Isn't he the prince?"

"An ousted prince who somehow found the liking of the king," Devi struggled, a goblet of wine was slipping from her fingers. "Politics is not my thing, girl."

"I know. You are more of a brawny one," Manvee giggled, and she came and sat across Devi's lap, kissing her on the cheek and then on her drunken mouth. "You smell of cherry."

"The men will see."

"Let them have the view."

"They'll tell the king."

"Let him come here to see the view."

"For a small person you are quite a joust, woman," Devi grinned.

She and Manvee had been lovers for a while now. It had been a year perhaps, since they confessed their feelings of attraction and bedded each other. It was a strange flurry of excitement, of hope between them.

"He will make you the senani of his palace," Manvee said.

"What if he doesn't? What if he kicks me out?"

"That is...if he wins against Jarasandha," she winked.

"Politics? You mean I should let him die and continue the crusades as it is?"

"He can have an *accident*," Manvee grinned.

Devi clenched her jaws. She wasn't sure how she felt about that; killing someone in cold blood. After all, she had committed hundreds of murders, but only the guilty were killed, not someone who was on her side. It would be quite risky to kill a king. She raised her brows and shook her head. "There are a few things I am sure about and one is that I cannot bend my morals."

"But didn't you already?"

She was bringing up the past.

"It was just that one time."

"Sure it was," Manvee said, and she kissed her mouth with all the determination and passion she could gather and so did Devi, pressing her thighs and wrapping her arms around Manvee. "Or..." she pulled back, "you can do something better."

"And what is that?"

"Asamaka," she said.

That was where Manvee was from. The southern kingdoms, which were scattered lands and had no autonomy like the north did.

"Let's go there," she said.

"And do what?" Devi asked.

"Live peacefully. Away from this."

"You mean leave what I'm good at?"

"We will live a good life. I know a place. It's an ashram. We can take refuge, build a hut and create a farm. Soon we will have a life."

Of what worth? Of what meaning?

Devi questioned herself and she didn't know the answer to it. But perhaps Manvee was right. Perhaps, there could be a life beyond this. Beyond all this chaos and blood.

"We can think about it," she said, with a smirk.

Manvee grinned. "Really?"

"Yeah."

"You are amazing," and then Manvee grabbed her by the neck and pulled her in for a kiss.

And they kissed for long, enough for them to feel good enough to go to bed, forgetting the chaos, forgetting the sounds that were coming from outside and the trumpets being blown, Devi had lost her senses and that was the reason it happened...

The walls burst and broke, as a figure with an iron mask entered. The bricks were torn apart by the figure's entry and the first thing he did was grab Manvee by the neck and twisted it, in a split second.

It happened so fast that Devi couldn't process it at first.

She saw the figure with the iron mask holding Manvee like a swan with its neck broken and her eyes welled up with tears. Behind him, from where he had come, she saw her men being killed.

It was a bloody ambush.

The iron-masked man tossed Manvee in a corner—towering over her and she saw the face. It was placid. Like the iron mask, it had no emotion painted over it.

Devi could hear her men dying and see Manvee's lifeless body lying in the corner, as if she didn't matter at all...

It can't end so soon.

Devi didn't have her weapon on her and she tried to kick the giant man, but he was going for her throat, unaffected by her kicks.

And then she shoved his hand away by kicking it, until he got angry and he brought his arm against Devi, when she dodged it...

And he broke another wall of the hut. The ceiling was beginning to crumble.

He has too much strength.

He pulled his hand out, and while he was doing it, Devi made a run for it.

As fast as she could, escaping the hut and moving in the dead of the night, she saw her men were the new victims of this town. Those who didn't die were either going to or were fleeing.

She saw one man, struggling with another on top of him, in black clothes pushing the sword over him. She knew she couldn't let one of her soldiers die when she could do something about it.

And with a grieving heart, she rushed and yelled and scowled, shouldering the enemy and shoving him on the ground, while she helped the man.

"Leave and warn the ones who went to bury the dead."

The man nodded and scurried.

She decided to leave when she saw the towering figure was standing behind her. And then he pulled out an axe and brought it next to her, but luckily she dodged it.

She tripped and fell, as her men were weakening even more and she had no backup. The fires had raged, and the orange flames were close and she could see the axe was coming closer, almost against her beating heart...

When she kicked the figure in his groin. The figure yelped in pain and knelt down, dropping the axe, as she grabbed the axe herself and moved for his head.

"This is for Manvee."

And the iron-masked man looked up, as Devi brought the axe against his iron skull. For a moment, she thought the figure was dead, until he pulled the axe and looked at it, as if it did nothing.

I should leave now.

Even Jarasandha's men with their half moon black flags were moving towards her now.

She was chased, her feet hurting, her breath shaking and trembling until she found one of her mares. It belonged to Manvee and she grabbed it, heading for the roads up ahead.

She rode and the two horses followed, while the man in the iron mask stayed there. He didn't use a horse. He was too big for one.

So she didn't look back. She was sweating and crying and had none of her men with her.

Did they just attack my people?

But Manvee...she's dead...

Her chest was hurting and she was feeling pain like she had never felt before. She realised there were no hooves following her anymore and the cold-hearted man in the iron mask was now becoming a dot.

But the magnitude of his presence still remained enormous.

38

Twenty years earlier…

In Girviraj, Magadha, modern day Bihar…

Jara got high on the Soma.

He had been taking it for a while now. And he couldn't hold it anymore, the way his wife Usha wanted him to. He had tried and since his daughters three years back had left him, he saw no point of not continuing with his addiction.

When he drank Soma, he felt the visuals and the energy kicking in and his head would enter a trance-like zone.

But today, he had taken it for a reason.

That was, to fight off the enemy in front of him.

Roaring at him, with thick, brown mane and a golden, uproarious body—it was a lion. And a big one.

All of Jara's ministers, his soldiers, his people were in the circle of the large menacing fight that was about to happen.

The lion was being pulled back by Jara's men.

Jara signalled his men to leave the lion. And so they did, the manacles breaking, the chains shattering as the lion began to run towards Jara. It was an empty, sandy field where the civilians and the spectators were watching from an elevated stage, so they didn't become the victim of the lion.

This was supposed to be for entertainment. This was supposed to be for *his* entertainment.

The Somas had kicked in and he could feel the anger, the emotions—everything just dissolving and making him tougher and more agile.

He had a breastplate and gauntlets and kneepads and a helmet. But the whip that he held in his hand was the one which would be his weapon; his solace.

The moment the lion came galloping and lurched towards him…

Jara rolled over on the other side. The lion was taken by surprise and roared again. They both looked at each other with respect, as they began to circle around each other—their eyes locking, their faces impassive. Jara waited for the lion to attack which it did.

He could hear its roar.

Jara didn't wait. He didn't have the patience. And the moment he leapt forward…

He felt he was transported into the desert. And in front of him, there was the lion but he had a human torso and a human body but with a lion's head.

"Shree Vishnu avatar," Jara grinned. "Meet the mahabhakt of Mahadev. OM NAMAH SHIVAYE!"

His trance was showing him that he was fighting something else altogether.

He approached the lion-man and attacked him with his scrounge. The lion-man deflected it with his claws, grabbed Jara by the throat and pushed him down on the ground.

Grimacing, Jara dodged, his heartbeat increasing as he pulled himself up and attacked the lion-man from behind. The hybrid got pushed back, and Jara brought down the scrounge around his neck and began to choke him.

The lion-man screamed in agony, then pulled himself up on his toes and slithered away like a rodent.

He leapt at Jara and began to bite through his armour… chewing on the bronze and the Chandravanshi elephant symbol that it had.

Jara staggered back, trying to get away from the fangs. He rolled over on the desert again and he could see he was wounded in the chest.

But he felt no pain. Soma did that. It would make you numb to any pain.

The lion-man came forward, his claws glowing, his chest glistening when…

Jara left his leash and punched the lion deep in his chest.

The ferocity of the punch was so strong that the lion man fell back on the ground, the sand splitting into two; dust swirled poetically.

Jara blinked. And with each blink, he realised, he had returned to reality. The sombre, disappointing reality where the lion was lying unconscious after the punch and all his people were screaming in joy. He was bleeding from the chest, but he didn't care.

He lifted his hands as he spoke, albeit in a slurry tone: "We have introduced a new form of entertainment. From around the world, we shall call the best fighters and the wrestlers and they wouldn't just wrestle or fight with a human but with animals—from bears to elephants…

and this sort of practice shall bring us joy and unity and display the prowess the Magadh kingdom is popular for. And this fight with the lion was just a taste of blood, for what is to come in the future." He grinned. In reality, he wanted to establish entertainment tax and steal from the ministers who made money on the side.

He knew there was another market through this form of entertainment—gambling. Many rich men would gamble their fortunes and he could earn profits from it.

He turned towards his partner in crime, Kalyavan of Ionia, ancient name for Greeks. He was a dark-skinned man, and he was clapping furiously, greed and ferocity clearly visible in his eyes.

"King Kalyavan of the Greek empire has brought us his finest fighter from the island of Essos," he introduced the Yavana, the Indianised name for the Greeks, "who shall begin this grand celebration of entertainment with the first fight. You can start betting on him, whether he will win or not."

Kalyavan came forward. He looked brutish. Honey coloured eyes and a slim mouth with a lanky frame. He wore multi-coloured robes as he entered the middle of the field with a fighter that was eight feet tall and was wearing a loincloth, having giant-like features. The unconscious lion, by then, was dragged from the field.

"This is an opportunity for the Greeks and the Indians to shake hands," Kalyavan smiled. "My father was from here, but he married a foreigner. Ever since, I have lived in the islands of the east, I missed my homeland. But…" he thumped Jara on the back, "King Jarasandha of Magadh has promised me a home here and what better way to show the interest of the Greeks and Indians united together than over a form of sport—which is wrestling." He paused. "It was very kind of King Jarasandha to show off his skills as a wrestler against the mighty lion and just like Heracles from my mother's land, he defeated it like an ant."

The ministers, the nobles, and the other allied kings of Magadh were there. Even Bana was there, eating his apple, sitting on a pedestal, smiling. Kans, from Mathura, with his daughters was supposed to be here, but he had fallen ill and Jara had understood this matter.

"I welcome you Brutus," Kalyavan introduced his first fighter, who raised his hands. "He will fight the grizzly bear of the north."

Jara saw the nobles and the kings were writing down names, whether Brutus would win against the animal or not. And they were throwing coins.

Jara shared a glance with Kalyavan.

Easy money.

But then, his eyes fell on the farthest corner of the wrestling arena—and she was there. His wife. Usha.

And she did not look happy.

"You don't have to worry!" Jara exclaimed, as they entered their private chambers and he washed his hands with water from a basin. "This is just a way to form an alliance with the Greeks."

"To start gambling?" Usha was on the bed, sitting at the edge of it. "What's next, Jara? Murders? Kidnappings?"

He clenched his jaw. "You are being hysterical."

"The Greeks have a nomadic approach. We don't have that. Kalyavan only came to you because you agreed to dirty your hands in this so-called wrestling sport, oh the poor animals." She raised her brows. "And then he convinced you to fight the lion, to show that the king was openly promoting this sport."

Jara shrugged. "I volunteered."

"And you took the bloody Soma."

Jara noticed the icy glare of his wife. "I did, yes. I have been taking it for a while."

"I feel you don't even care about the promise you made when our daughters were born."

"I do. But they are in good hands. It shouldn't matter to us anymore. As for me, I am free," Jara smiled. "Come on, my dear, there's nothing to worry about here. I am under control from the Soma."

He tried to come close to her and forcibly embraced her even though she tried pushing him away. But then she relented.

"That's good," he smiled.

"You always say you have it under control. But you don't," she said. "That happened the last time too when you hurt me..."

Jara didn't hear the rest. He didn't want to remind himself of his own actions in an intoxicated state. It was like when he was high on Soma, he didn't want to be bothered by the outside world, or external problems. She had cribbed; screamed at him. Jara was a tough man. He just wanted to push her. But that push resulted in a shoving so hard, she fell against the wall. He tried to help her, but then she slapped him on the face. He got very angry and the vision of his brother appeared in front of him and he slapped her back. Then began to choke her to the point...

Jara sighed. The memories had returned.

"I won't do that again, I promise."

"I can't be here," she said.

"What?" He pulled back to see whether she was being serious or not.

"I can't be here, Jara. I am...uh...I am building a learning centre for Rudra Veena and will be teaching children how to play it," she said, referring to her favourite musical instrument that she loved to play when she was distressed or even to just pass her time.

"Where?"

"Champa," she looked up. "There's a nice place. I can find myself happiness there."

"For how long?"

"Till your business with Kalyavan and your constant fixes with Soma are done." She came on her feet, not locking eyes with him. "I hope I will be allowed."

Jara knew she didn't need his permission, and yet she asked for it. Jara didn't have to say anything, but just nod. He couldn't let go of the business deals with Kalyavan just like that. He had been making sure the army of Greeks would be in his support, so he could use them in need, if ever Kuru planned a major strike against them.

When she was about to go, Jara said: "Take care of yourself."

"No," she shook her head, "Jara, you take care of yourself. I want to be with the man who first came to my balcony and used to throw a rose every day till the time I accepted his marriage proposal. I want to be with the man who built Shivmurtis in each part of his kingdom, to show his love for Mahadev. I want to be with the man who was kind to animals and created hospices for birds. I want to be with a saint, not a killer and a slaughterer."

"I'm a king, Usha," he said, to make her understand and justify all of his actions.

"It doesn't mean you have to be a piece of shit, Jara."

And then she left.

Along with his heart.

39

Jara remembered that day.

It was the day he had lost himself. It was the day she was gone from his life.

What he didn't know was that it was also the last time he would see her.

I shouldn't have done what I did. It's my fault.

Jara should have quit Soma. Intoxication was not more important than Usha herself.

And Kalyavan...

The Greek still had relations with Jara, but Jara had stopped the menacing animal fights. He had kept his word and agreed with Usha.

He looked out of the window, in the early morning, when his skin was still sensitive and the light was strong. He looked out at the palace preparing for the battle. Elephants had worn their armour, and so had the soldiers, thousands in number. Spears and swords were getting sharpened on whetstone, while the priests had come to give the blessings of Lord Shiva.

Om Namah Shivaye...

He closed his eyes.

All his life, he had tried to do what was best for his nation. For his kingdom.

And at what cost?

Everything.

He shook his head with regret and with pain.

I could have saved you, Usha.

But no.

He had never told the truth behind his wife's death. He had never told anyone, even his daughters who had begged and cried to him to do so. He just knew that the death was personal to him and it was his own fault.

"Jara," he heard a faint whistle of a sound, like music to his ears.

He turned and saw her.

She was in the shadows and he could see her silhouette. She was crying; whimpering.

"You are here," he smiled.

"Jara," she said again, there was pain in her voice.

"I knew you would come. Whenever I drink..." he looked at his empty goblet which had the sapphire coloured Soma liquid in its most pure, intoxicating form. "I see you. Darling, I apologise. I apologise for not being there. I love you. I want to keep drinking until I die and see you again. I want to redeem myself for not being there for you when you needed me."

"Jara..." she said again, coming out of the shadows and revealing the marks of a noose around her neck. "It was *you* who killed me."

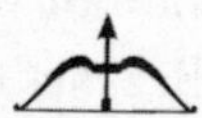

Devi sat frustrated, in her quarters.

She was shivering and a shawl was wrapped around her. Her soldiers had gone back to the camp, many in number to fight back, but the reports had come that no one was present except the corpses of her men.

Manvee is dead…

She tried to fight back tears but burst out anyway, for the third time. Her cheeks were sticky, her mouth was sour and she had the option to have the grape wine, but she chose not to. She wasn't in the mood.

While she stewed in her thoughts, her men waited for her to give them further instructions—she did know what the best course of action was. And that was to…

Fight back. Revolt. Have the battle of all times. Get killed and kill them. Devi wanted to avenge Manvee, no matter what.

And she had waited for the famed prince for too long.

She came on her feet and threw away the shawl, moving for the door and onto the balcony where her men stood. The night was foggy but she could still see the inside of her fort, where there was a small fish market, soldiers in abundance, sitting and talking or practicing. She could see the targets with arrows pointed at them, while stables were being cleaned with horses being fed and washed. Kids of the soldiers' families ran amok. She turned to see the city of Malinipur, which was all around her, with the fort right at the centre.

Malinipur wasn't the most advanced in its heyday. In fact, it was quite a collection of villages and two-storeyed brick or sand buildings. Bazaars and small markets alike, ashrams and temples, mango trees, with narrow roads and adjacent hills.

I was sold here. In the city. A young, orphan girl exposed to a greedy man of filth.

Senapati Vijaya had grown to like Devi when she was young, a girl without a name, and he had named her Devi. He had wanted to marry her when she was just eight years old. It was not the best of times, Devi realised, to be married to an old grunt of a man like him.

"Listen all," she said, "I have news to bear."

Her soldiers got down and began to form a cluster, underneath the balcony, looking up at her. Most didn't like her because of her gender, but they still respected her for who she was. A warrior, who was born on their soil unlike Senapati Vijaya who was a foreigner for them. The Angan pride was a big thing here and she was devastated how Jara had broken that pride, by creating a massacre.

"We have had a bad supply run as you all know, and we are just a week from the battle to begin. The last report our runner had given was that Jarasandha was already preparing for the war and the camps were in the process of being built. They took one of the old watch towers, fifty miles from the Champa river. They are doing it now. Getting it prepared. But we can do something about it. Attack when only some of the soldiers have arrived to build the camp. We can plunder their resources too..."

And her words were cut off with the fort doors being opened.

Devi and all her men, the people who were living inside, looked down at the door.

"HE'S HERE!" The gatekeeper who were at the gate towers shouted loudly. "HE'S HERE!"

Devi sighed, as she allowed the men to open the doors.

My luck.

"He has a fleet of people, general."

Fleet of people? The last message she had received was that he was coming alone to avoid detection.

What is he up to?

"Are they armed?" Devi shouted at the gatekeeper.

"They are more than just armed. They are the Nishadhs."

Everyone gasped at hearing the term.

Their sworn enemies!

Ever since Devi had controlled the landscape, she had been cutting down timber, but the Nishadhs hated that their land was being used for greed and profit.

"Steady your arms. I believe our prince has sided with the enemies before he has even come here."

Karna knew bringing the Nishadhs to the doorstep of the city fort was a big problem. But he knew that he could explain it to them.

Entering the city was a problem too, but he showed the scroll of Dhritarashtra at the city gates and they allowed him in. He didn't bring all the Nishadhs with him. Some camped outside the city and were told to stay silent and speak when necessary.

But he brought some, to show Devi that this was how he was going to win the battle. If he had brought all of them, they would be considered a threat and would attack. But less numbers wouldn't cause that same panic.

Team up two of the enemies together.

"Just to put it out there," Satya said, as the gates were beginning to open and Karna's heart was thumping, "this is a very bad decision."

"What would you have suggested, master?"

"Probably not tell them and use the Nishadhs in secret."

"If the soldiers learnt that, they wouldn't follow me. They'd brand me as a lying king. Do you want that?"

"It's a big *if* and they wouldn't have known."

Karna shook his head. He was a fair man. And he had to be fair to his own people, his Angan military.

He turned his head, to find a tall, broad woman exit the gates to see Karna and Satya. While Satya grinned and flirtatiously waved at her, she watched the Nishadh in their leaf loincloths, their tribal colours and outfit, carrying bamboo string bows and wooden arrows.

"I believe you are Devi," Karna said, and he dismounted. "I am Karna, the king of Anga. Or the interim king. However you want to look at it."

The woman didn't say anything. She looked hurt, as if she had lost someone recently of grave importance. "Why have you brought them?"

"Because I allied with Eklavya to fight Jarasandha."

"That was the stupidest thing to do. Jarasandha's army is a bunch of tried warriors. They are not even properly trained," she said, gesturing to the tribals behind him.

"It doesn't matter. I don't need them in terrain battle."

"This is a bad idea. Them being here can lead to bad attitude among my men," Devi said.

"You mean *my* men," Karna corrected her.

She frowned, and arched her brows. "Of course, *your* highness." She mockingly said.

"Then I feel that you should really not question my judgment," Karna said. "I have come here to do what is necessary, in whatever way, and my men have to adjust."

He called out to Braj, the Nishadh headman of the group Eklavya had sent. He was a short man like his chief, and he had hair across his cheeks but not on his chin.

"I have brought him because I want my men and Braj to be friends again. It's a sour topic, but it has to be done."

Devi reluctantly nodded. "Fine, bring them in and...I feel you will talk to the soldiers yourself."

"Of course."

"Then please, come."

She clapped and the gates were opened wide.

Karna saw his people; his men. The flags with white elephants drawn on them, but they had lost the Angan sun emblem which they used to carry, as Adhirath's ancestors were Suryadev worshippers. But he entered, along with Braj and Satya.

Knowing fully well, that it could easily end pretty badly for him.

40

Before Karna could even go upstairs and drink perhaps a glass of wine, the fight had begun.

After all the bowing and the introductions by Devi, where she basically said she had given the reins to Karna now, the soldiers had agreed and were motivated. But soon, issues arose when Karna was ascending the stairs to talk to Devi and Satya in private, Braj and his men started quarreling, that quarrelling led to a fight between the soldiers and everyone soon caught on, with Karna forcing them to stay apart. And thus, Braj was told to stay in one corner of the fort, where they would not be hassled or harassed racially like the soldiers would usually do by calling them the natives of the forest or primitives like apes.

By the time it was over, Karna went to Devi's quarters which would be his eventually, and sat down, while he drank the wine he was offered by the servants and ate some food. He was famished. He asked the servants to feed Braj and his men too, but cut and slicked jackfruits.

Hearing all of this, Devi snorted and rolled up her arms against her chest defensively.

"I hear you are not happy," Karna said.

"It's just strange to feed the men who we have been fighting for so long."

"The Nishadhs aren't our enemy. They retaliated because you took their land. Wouldn't you, if you were in their place?"

Devi didn't respond, but grunted yet again.

"You must understand, General, that I don't plan to take your place," Karna said, leaning back on his cot now. The room was dimly lit and it smelled of lavender incense where the agarbatti was glowing in different corners. "You have been with these men and I like that. I was just teasing you outside. But I want your cooperation. I want your men to side with the Nishadhs."

"They won't fight with the Nishadhs on their side. They won't trust them."

"I know they won't. But you'll have to convince them," Karna said.

Devi nodded.

"Now you need to tell me..." he kept the goblet down and with a fiery rub of his two hands he asked, "...what the situation is right now."

And she did.

It took her hours to explain what she had gotten on board, what else was there, how she lost her second-in-command as well as about the iron-masked man, who could be the enemy's secret weapon. She even displayed a map in front of him, to show where Jara would be tentatively planning to settle his war camp and pointed at where they should.

After hearing all of it, Satya was the one who had spoken: "Jara has chosen the Champa river because frankly he would use it some way or another to attack."

"Who is he?" Devi asked.

"My second-in-command," Karna grinned.

"Well, it's nice to meet you, lady," Satya winked at her.

"He stinks," Devi growled.

"Yes, that's my aphrodisiac, right there, baby," Satya chuckled, but she didn't.

"Matters on hand, you are wrong, old man," Devi said. "He won't attack from there because the Champa tides are unreliable. You see, the land for the war he has chosen does in fact, contains a lot of terrain too..." she pointed on the map where the blue colour was less and brown was dominant. "Also, Jarasandha isn't a fan of using boats as a way to act."

"But if we station our camps close to Champa, we could be at risk of a guerrilla attack coming from the direction of the river, in case he does?" Karna asked.

"It is a hypothesis," she replied, "but what I have learnt about Jarasandha in past endeavours is that he is not a big fan of guerrilla warfare. He comes in a grand manner, because he's all-powerful and he wants to show that, so we can use Champa as a base for the camp. That's my suggestion."

Satya disputed that; shaking his head.

Karna nodded. "Fine. You know Jarasandha better. I hope you are right. But just in case, we should station a few miles away from the river so even if there is an attack, the damage is less."

Karna saw her smile a little. He couldn't afford to

antagonise her instantly, because she held the soldiers, she knew them and their names. For them, he was a foreigner for now. A king with no crown.

"Let's move to another problem. We don't have enough men," Karna announced. "How do we solve that?"

"We have conscripted a few more people but many aren't coming," Devi said.

"Because they don't want to die," Satya shrugged. "I have a solution, your highness, if you want to listen."

Karna nodded.

"On my journey to do what I do," Satya said, coming on his feet and dramatically explaining, "I had come across a watchtower. It was an old one, but quite effective. It was hidden, close to a lake where I was dealing..." He paused.

"Dealing what?" Devi asked.

"None of your concern, lady," Satya winked again. "But you see, I was doing that and I happened to see these people. The watchtower had more than a thousand slaves working and the ones they were working under were Jarasandha."

"So what's the big deal?" Devi shrugged.

"No. The slaves, you see, were ex-Angan military. The ones who instead of using swords to cut flesh, were using swords to cut timber. It's a timber-making watchtower and it stays hidden. I was dealing with one of the soldiers of Jarasandha there, so I noticed and it piqued my curiosity."

"Where is it?" Karna raised his brows.

"Close to Champa, but also not in it."

"Why have they not killed them?" Devi asked.

"Because they are honourable men, and good muscle

to do this job. And frankly, Jarasandha wouldn't want anyone to discover this, because this is where he still makes money from," Satya said. "I got to know through happenstance. But we can use it to our advantage."

Devi didn't look convinced. It sounded too good to be true. But perhaps, it was a gold mine, ready to be snatched.

"Do you think they will work with us if we free them?" Karna asked.

"I can try. After all, I used to be what Devi is now," Satya grinned. "I've spoken too much and now I must quench my sore throat with some alcohol."

And he did that, as he finished talking, while Karna saw Devi getting nervous and confused. Karna didn't know whether it was a good idea himself, but it was worth a try.

"Rather than doing all of this, I have a better idea," Devi said. "Why wait for one week? Let's just attack what they are building right now."

"My dear," Satya scoffed, "this is Jarasandha. If you attack him now, he will hit back bigger. And he will not stop. While Anga has no structure or form, he has had it for a long time now. So no, until we are fully prepared to do so, anything else is a foolish endeavour."

Karna nodded. "I agree with him." He came on his feet and patted Satya on the shoulder, as he ordered Devi: "Send some runners to the place Satya tells you to. Let me know the first-hand account of what they see. If Jarasandha has not reined his people back from the watchtower, we attack it fast and we attack it effectively."

"What if the soldiers don't side with you?" Devi asked, gritting her teeth, angry at her idea being rejected.

"Then I will make peace with the idea that I have saved veterans and my people," Karna sighed. "We are fighting a mammoth, a giant amongst men. He has many soldiers. I know we have the possibility of losing, but I also know that in the process of losing, I want to save the leftover lives he has chosen not to kill."

Karna could see a bit of respect flash in Devi's eyes but it lasted only for a moment and then went off.

"Fine. Will inform and update you, your highness. I'll relieve you now from your…"

"No, please," Karna grabbed his weed bags and so did Satya. "This is your room. I am sure, I'll find another quarter for myself."

"But this is the biggest one."

"I don't care," Karna said. "Thank you."

And he left the confused Devi, who was a bit bewildered by his charitable attitude, but also frustrated by his way of making decisions.

Karna walked out, as Satya went downstairs to drink more at the winery. Karna looked at his men from the balcony and called out: "I need to speak to you all."

A hundred or so soldiers gathered; those who weren't there and in different forts, would know and hear about it later from these men.

He could feel the footsteps behind him, of Devi, who was listening as well.

"My name is Vasusena. I was born in Malinipur. Right here. I grew up here. I saw the world from here until I went to learn from Dronacharya and then from Parshuram. I am an archer, and a man who doesn't care about regality. I'm one of you. I fight with you. I win with you and lose with you. As a child, when this city was taken over by the usurpers, I promised myself that I would reign over it and here I am to do just that. You are my people, my blood, and this is our soil. We want these usurpers to end their reign. If not fully…" he looked at Devi, "at least partially. And we should fight blood for blood, for our people have shed blood in Champa. It's a ghost town now. And I do not plan to venture there until I avenge all those souls by killing the man who had caused it. Jarasandha shall meet his end. Not in my hands, but *our* hands," Karna roared, and everyone hooted, raising their arms. He could see the soldiers were grinning, they were happy. It was a rousing speech, but it had to now be executed.

This is the beginning of the end. Or of another beginning.

I'll know soon.

41

Satya was not a changed man.

He just knew that when he had remembered the face of the little boy, he felt something in his chest. It was like a warm, nostalgic feeling and he knew for certain he had to do something about the boy.

As his mind stopped being blurry, he got more clarity: he had to help the boy. The very one who would have panic attacks as a child, because he was not living up to the expectations of the world.

He had changed tremendously.

Unfortunately Satya hadn't.

As the night descended, so did he from the fort and into the narrow lanes of the city of Malinipur which looked like a poverty-stricken world of disease and dirt. But it was good for him, because he would find his escapism right here.

He walked around, asking for it, while keeping his cowl to cover his head. He didn't want anyone to know that the king's second-in-command was strolling the city streets like this. And though the guards at the fort asked for permission to walk with him, he disallowed them.

The fireflies zigzagged in the night and the ravens

perched from the arched buildings, while the cobblestone lanes and the dripping sound of water from the drainage pipes could be heard.

Malinipur wasn't like this, once upon a time. Four years ago, it wasn't this horrific.

If this place had turned like this, he could only imagine how Champa would be. Before the usurpers like Dhritarashtra and Jarasandha had arrived, Anga was a small but beautiful land with cherries and gooseberries growing all over and known for its beautiful architecture. The days were longer and the nights were young.

Not anymore, unfortunately.

He asked around for grass, until he happened to meet a man who agreed to sell him some. The man was stinking, but it was no trouble.

"Come with me." He crookedly walked and made them follow.

The guards of the city were flocking around, with their spears and shields, while they walked inside a small lane and then further down, where there was a small house with its door open.

Satya entered and he immediately recognised the smell of some fish that was being cooked. He stroked his beard and saw a sickly woman, perhaps the man's wife.

The man on the other hand, asked him to follow further, but seeing the wife Satya felt something strange in his stomach. The man finally took him inside a room where a small boy, barely eight or nine years old, came up to him.

"Give him," the man said.

The boy nodded and from his pocket, he took out the leaves and handed them to Satya.

Satya saw that the boy was sickly like his mother, but he had innocent eyes. For him, it was just leaves, he didn't know they were intoxicants. Satya felt another twist in his belly.

And he dropped more coins than he was supposed to.

The man begged and was grateful, hugging him. Satya nodded.

And left. With a heavy heart.

As he was coming out, Satya was welcomed by two guards.

"What are you doing here?"

"Who are you?"

Satya didn't utter a word. He was confused. Should he show his face? Should he not? But then, they didn't give him a chance as they grabbed him and tried searching him. In the process of doing that, his face became visible.

And their faces went pale.

"It's the new king's second-in-command," one guard said to another, and they instantly let him go. "Sorry, sir. We had no knowledge. Sorry sir." They bowed before him.

Satya had leaves in his hands and they were visible. The guards looked at his hands, and they could have arrested him, but they didn't. They just kept bowing and apologising.

They did however have a certain sense of disappointment flashing in their eyes.

"It's all right. On with your duty."

And they did so, as they whispered amongst themselves.

Satya looked at the leaves in his hand and looked back at the lane. And he couldn't feel less guilty. Few days back, he had given the leaves to children and he had felt worse than ever, when he came back to his senses.

Now he had everything. He had stature. He had money. He had weapons. But he was old, though it didn't matter.

He crushed the leaves in the palm of his hand and walked back to the fort.

Without his cowl on anymore.

42

23 years earlier…

On his way to Champa, Jara could feel something.

Something dreadful.

The world wasn't behaving the way it was supposed to. Omens came in abundance. Jara noticed the ravens first. They flew around. They puckered on every direction he took. They perched on the cedar trees and watched him and his men move to Champa.

Jara was bringing more than fifty soldiers along with him. Like any king should, while travelling from one place to another.

Magpies flew around in the sky too. And the rodents and maggots were seen slithering on the muddy ground. The storm had passed, but the skies were turbulent, bursting with energy.

And that was the time, when they saw—

A horseman and his horse, both laid on the ground, wearing a breastplate with the elephant symbol on it. He was riddled with arrows in the back and his face was drenched in mud. He had a scroll lying next to him.

Jara dismounted from his chariot, carefully making

sure his crown wasn't tipped off. He knelt next to the corpse and picked up the scroll. His senani, watched from the back.

Jara opened the scroll and it said: *WE HAVE BEEN ATTACKED! SAVE US!*

He clenched his jaw. "Commander, let's hasten our horses. We have to quicken our pace." With a heavy heart, he sat on a horse rather than in his chariot and made his way. As fast as he could. He didn't want to delay. He only hoped everything would be fine. He knew this was a bad sign, but hope caressed the crevices of his heart.

As they neared Champa, Jara saw the large fortress of the city. It was built like a miniature version of Hastinapur. It had watchtowers and castles inside it; bazaars flourishing with excitement and vitality. But he noticed something odd.

The gates were broken down. His men were sprawled dead. In a bloody mess.

As he entered the gates, all the people, the citizens were hiding from Jara; he was confused as to what had happened, what really led to his soldiers' death. Their corpses rotted in every lane.

"This explains why they weren't responding to our letters," his senani said. "I thought they didn't get the mail or something else happened. But…we were attacked. And even the messenger couldn't come on time."

There were a few citizens out in the market, but they were afraid. They were holding on to their loved ones; their children. There were beggars and saints. There were gurus and there were sadhus. There were merchants and there were goldsmiths. They all were petrified.

Jara went near a child. He was holding a small basket in his hand which had loaves of bread, but blood was splattered over it.

"What happened here, boy?" he asked.

The boy blinked. He looked nervous; and he should be. His usurper had just asked a question.

"They came...they came at night."

"Who?"

"The people. Rebelled!" he whispered. He was disheveled; dirt was all over his face.

Jara sighed deeply.

No.

"They retaliated, your highness," his senani said, who was on another black stallion. "For you were taxing them and making them work."

Jara had sanctioned that.

But for some reason, he didn't feel the attack was a retaliation. It was strategic. Very well planned. A guerrilla attack which happened at night. Took everyone by surprise.

"Did anyone know Usha would be staying here?"

"We kept it discreet, your highness."

Apparently it wasn't discreet enough.

Jara rode towards the kul which the school was. Her school. His men, the remaining alive ones from Champa were taken to be nursed and asked questions. His senani handled everything, checked how many soldiers they had left in Champa; while Jara raced towards the school.

Champa wasn't brutally attacked. Only the soldiers were killed. Many of the citizens on the other hand, were still revolting, while some others hid.

Jara was lucky that he came in time to actually create a stronghold and his senani had already sent ravens to Magadh, to bring reinforcements in. One more day and the Kurus would have come and established their dominance over Champa.

How luck works, Jara could only wonder.

As he neared the school, he saw it was a large royal place with a chestnut shed and a cedar tree right next to it.

He dismounted from the horse and began moving towards the school when his eyes fell on the tree. It was weird. There was a twig that was lopsidedly hanging in a very strange direction and as he came closer, he saw it wasn't a twig at all.

It was a person—hung from the branch of the tree.

And around the person, there were many kids, small children who were trying really hard to get the person out of the tree.

Jara came forward, looking closely as he knelt on the ground and screamed. He couldn't even contemplate what had happened or get teary eyed at what he saw right in front of him—she was there.

Hung like a wooden toy.

Usha was pale. Veins were popping out. Her eyes were open. Her neck had a bamboo rope that had been tied to the top branch by these scoundrels, these madmen.

Jara couldn't believe he was seeing this image.

The children looked back at him and they went quiet.

"Why didn't you take her off?" he asked. "WHY?" He screamed at the children.

On top of the branch from which she hung, more ravens perched.

"Sir, we—we—we tried to help Usha aunty but she's too heavy. We aren't tall enough. We asked for help but no one wants to help as she's the queen and they don't want the blame on themselves." One of the kids came forward, the older one, who replied.

Jara felt numb. And he began beating the ground, as dust began to swirl. There was an ache. He couldn't even say goodbye. He couldn't tell her how he felt.

And then he looked at the children.

She came because of you all.

She came because she wanted to train you.

You are the reason she has died.

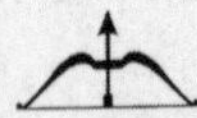

Jara was tall enough to pick her body and bring her to his shoulders and then into his arms. She was cold; ice cold. Tears began to stream down his face. He didn't know what he would say to his daughters. He didn't know who would tell him to stop drinking Soma, to be a better person. He didn't know who would say "I love you" to him again and would mean it.

He just didn't know anything anymore.

His senani had reached close to him by now and as the others saw him, their faces went pale.

Not because of the dead queen in Jara's hands.

But because of the pile of corpses of the children Jara had just *slaughtered*.

Flies were beginning to swarm over them.

But Jara didn't care. He put her on his horse and mounted on it.

"Your highness, Rajmata Usha...the people killed her?" the senani asked.

Jara clenched his jaw. And then he saw all the people who had revolted against him, being put forth by his men. They were all tied up and they were angry and frustrated by his rule and exploitation of the trade.

"Champa is mine!" Jara roared through tears. "Kill them all." He ordered his men. "Kill their wives. Rape them and murder their boys and sell their little girls to brothels."

And he finally saw the flash of fear in the rebels' eyes, who realised their actions would hurt their family.

"You saw my kindness," Jara announced. "Now you will see my wrath."

43

Present day...

Jara had to remove the thoughts of the past and focus on the present.

They were in the middle of the road, moving for Champa river and he was in his chariot. And then they had camped. More than three thousand soldiers were here, while close to five thousand had gone with Gonanda to Mathura to usurp that faster. It was how it worked.

Jara wanted to finish with this boy Karna and move on. He was waiting for the good news.

At night, he drank Soma and rested. And in the morning, he was welcomed with thoughts regarding his wife. Usha was there and he could picture her in Kasi, when he had first seen her—the vibrant girl, who had lost her brother to Soma. And now, before he could show her that he was better than that, he was corrupted and went back to it. The irony was, that it was Soma that would bring him to her.

But the visuals of his wife were frightening. His eyes would flash and he would be stricken by the noose around her neck. She was murdered by the rebels and in response, he killed each one of them when he left Champa. No one was spared, for the blood of his wife was shed in Champa.

He thought about his mother too. The one who had told him to kill his brother and then herself. It was a strange request.

What he did though, was something out of proportion.

That day was as black as mother's black tongue.

But he carried her name.

And while his thoughts were raging, he saw the shadow of his tent growing bigger and the man who appeared outside was large like a giant. Then he saw the tent flaps open and his guards didn't say anything, for it was…

Kaal.

He was in a burnt up tunic, with wounds across his body, but he didn't care about it much. The iron mask was still on him.

"The attack on Devi happened a few days back. Where were you?"

Kaal didn't say anything.

"Is there any point to even discuss anything with you? You won't utter a word," Jara growled, with red eyes.

Kaal brought forth a parchment.

On which, it was written:

Saw a man around the watchtower, my lord. I believe the new king has already started eyeing us. Wonder how he found out about us. Tell us how to proceed further?

The watchtower was a prized, hidden location. He couldn't let them have it. But why would they want it? Jara's interest was piqued. It was hidden in the rainforest, away from the shenanigans of the city. And it was where they were cutting timber and loading them up, which in huge quantities would go by the river Champa on a ferry and reach the territory of Magadh. But the specialty was that they were not using their men, but hardworking veterans to do their work.

"The battle hasn't even started and they are attacking my base. Though the question is, how did they know about it?" Jara asked himself and Kaal's breathing intensified under the metal mask. "Do you think we have a spy amongst us? But…no, I don't think so," he paused. "How is it that you have such a good network of people without uttering a word, while here I struggle?" he chuckled to himself.

And then Kaal asked, his voice heavy and metallic underneath and he spoke for the first time in many years, "I'm going there."

Jara was surprised, but then perhaps he was speaking because it was only him and Kaal. No one else.

"Fine," Jara leaned forward. "But I have an idea. Care to listen?"

If he didn't want to, he would have left.

But Kaal didn't.

And so Jara told him his plan.

44

When Karna reached with a hundred men to the watchtower, along with Devi and Satya, they realised there were no patrols.

He was on horseback and was wearing his golden armour, which glinted in the dead of the night. He could smell the apples and mangoes, as the gushing ravine crawled inside the thick woods, like a serpent.

"It's quiet. Very quiet," Satya said. He had cleaned himself up, by trimming his beard and his hair. "Doesn't feel good."

"They may have reined the people in," Devi suggested positively.

"Or they know we are here."

"How would they?" Devi raised his brows.

They rode further, while their men were behind.

Karna was impassively watching the roads ahead, only to see there were no further patrols as well. And when they came close to the sand-made fort, which was quite high in size and width, Karna saw the fire torches were out—no light came from the fort.

Strange.

"Are you sure this was the one?" Karna asked Satya, who was himself perplexed.

"Indeed, I am," Satya sighed. "I think Jarasandha knows."

Karna still ordered his men to do a perimeter search of anyone suspicious, which they did. And once it was over, his men with the stallions came and said: "Your highness, I see no one."

"No one?"

Karna was met with a negative shake of the head. "So it's an empty watchtower? But still, let's see."

Devi and Satya nodded and rode further through the forest and across the shrubs, entering the watchtower that was corroded by the greenery around them too.

As they entered, Karna could see it was empty. And he felt it had been empty for a long time. He could also feel the watchful, suspicious gaze of Devi towards Satya, who might have been thinking that Satya was making a fool of them and had led them right in the middle of an ambush.

But Karna knew better. The old man would never do that.

"Search for supplies, but guard the gates. We have to be on our toes," Karna ordered his men, as Devi stayed behind for the order to be executed.

Let's search.

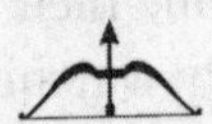

He opened doors with his bow still held up high, to make sure the room was empty.

But it was really empty. His men were ransacking cartons, jars and boxes to see if anyone was left. But none was.

"It's a ghost town," he told Satya, who agreed with him.

Karna felt it was a wasted effort after countless doors were opened, until he saw a door partially open. And from inside it an orange light came.

He opened it and went downstairs, slowly moving with an arrow strung on the bow, Satya behind him with a sword.

And he saw burnt logs, hung on the walls, lighting up the place and large cages inside which he could spot multiple shadows.

Karna came closer and realised that those shadows had a face and they were tired, exhausted men, gagged with their hands tied behind them, so they couldn't escape or move. There were hundreds of cages and in each cage, there were multiple men.

"They kept them here. They left them here," Satya said. "But why?"

"Let's untie them and ask."

Karna went to one of the cages and knocked down the metal lock to open it and let out the men, who instantly rushed out. Karna pulled down their gags.

"What happened to you?" he asked, while Satya had been opening other cages and ordered men from upstairs to get there and help further.

"Thank you, sir. They came two days back and gagged us all. That's about it. We don't know anything else."

"Do you know they all left you here to starve?" Karna asked.

"We heard footsteps upstairs though, yesterday. They were still loading up timber and they were going on about their day. But they didn't feed us for days and...." The man looked weak.

Karna patted him on the arm. "You'll be taken care of now."

He saw hundreds of men getting free and hugging each other, and he couldn't help but smile.

Why leave them like this?

Was that the plan? To make them sick by starving them, so I can't use them?

But many still managed to look fit enough.

Perhaps I won't get an answer.

And he was wrong. Definitely wrong.

As he came upstairs, Devi saw an influx of men behind him, just scurrying like rats and gathering themselves around in a huge circle. They were all happy and Devi couldn't help but feel joyful about it as well.

"It was an easy mission," she told Karna.

Who was not satisfied.

"Perhaps," he sighed. "But we should leave now. Let's not wait..."

And his eyes looked up at the dark, starless sky which had a beacon of light, that was growing.

And it grew. More. And more.

Until it got closer, far closer than he had anticipated, only to realise it was a big ball of fire...

That was moving towards them!

45

I should have guessed, it won't be that easy.

Karna instantly shoved Devi aside, and pushed himself further, hurtling towards the corner, as the ball of fire crashed on the ground, killing some of his men in the process. For a while, he could not understand or speak, his mind moving in different directions and his heartbeat was ruthlessly fast.

What is going on?

"Fall back, fall back," he heard Devi call out to his men...

And then another ball of fire came. Straight into the ground. They were thrice the size of a chariot wheel and they were smelling of strange ingredients.

He sighed, taking deep breaths, as he prepared to run, while his men moved out with the slaves who they had just rescued.

And then another.

Until he saw that the back gate of the watchtower was shut and the only gate that was open had a group of men, hundreds of them, with the half-moon symbol drawn on their black armour walking towards them.

And right in the front, he saw the man Devi had mentioned.

The iron-masked man. He was standing tall and with one firm shove of his finger, he ordered his men to shoot arrows.

"Shields!" Karna yelled to his men.

He pulled out his own shield and lifted it up in the sky, as arrows rained on them hitting their iron shields. He began to scamper and walk towards Satya, who was doing the same, while the corpses of his men were laying all around, and the slaves with no weapons or armour were scurrying around running for their lives.

"You need to find a way to open the backdoor," Karna ordered Satya.

"But how? That's a bloody iron gate, boy!"

Karna knew that. He was afraid, until he heard the swishing sounds of more arrows smacking his people, as their throats were pierced. The iron-masked man was close, and he was taking his time to reach, as if he knew as soon as he got his hands on Karna—he would kill him.

"Use the…" he looked at the balls of fire that were approaching. "Roll them over."

"What do you mean roll them over?"

"Take sheets of cloth lying around and roll it over. This path is shaped like a slope and with a push it'll roll and break the backdoor," Karna said.

Satya understood the idea. "That's sweet."

"I know. I'll try to hold them back, while you try."

"Good luck, boy."

And Satya got busy, ordering the slaves to help him with Karna's plan.

Karna concentrated on the iron-masked man now, and his soldiers who were getting closer were already in combat with Devi and her men. Fire and fury was all around them, and a clanging sound could be heard...

Karna took out long arrows and aimed at the men. He was quick, and moving at a rapid pace, he shot down one man after another.

He had almost had a good run, until he felt an arm grab him...

And he felt the pressure on his neck, as he was held by the throat and suspended in the air, realising he was grabbed by none other than...

The iron-masked man.

The iron-mask was strange and emotionless, as he looked at Karna, for a moment with amusement, before he was plunged to the ground. With a quick fist aimed at his face, he moved his arm...

Karna pulled out the arrow at the right time and without wasting a moment, stabbed the man in the eye, who groaned loudly under the metal mask and moved back. As he shuffled to the corner and fell, he felt a flurry of arrows hit his breastplate that stuck there, but didn't injure him. Another soldier appeared and was about to stab him with a sword, but Karna kicked him between the legs and quickly pulled out another arrow from the quiver, shooting the man in the face.

Karna came on his feet, thinking his nightmare was over, when he saw Satya had managed to break apart the back doors with the fireballs. The slaves were escaping behind Satya...and Karna turned to see Devi who, along with her men, was still battling with her long javelin.

"Fall back! Leave!"

Devi nodded, until her eyes fell on the iron-masked

man who was still recovering from the stabbed eye. And her face grew red with temper. Without listening to Karna's orders, like the rest of his men did, she went further and began to hit the iron-masked man on the head and on the face, with the javelin, repeatedly until he pulled out his axe and with a quick cut, slashed her waist.

"You fucking filthy animal!" she yelled.

She fell back, and groaned.

Karna yelled, as he pulled out several arrows and quickly began to hit the incoming soldiers on his way, and towards the iron-masked man, who was picking Devi up, emotionlessly like one picks up a toy.

"Leave her alone!" Karna shot another arrow, and it went and hit the bullseye, smacking the iron-masked man right on his nose...

He fell back and hit the ground.

Karna grabbed the bleeding Devi and asked, "Can you do it? Will you be able to walk?"

She had gone pale for a second but nodded.

"Let's leave then."

Devi was brutally bleeding from the torso and she was holding on to her wound, hoping it won't get worse. She didn't even have the energy to pick up her weapon, her javelin. Karna was helping her. She was surprised to see how nice he was, but he also took her position, made her feel small and...

As they staggered towards the back gate, where their horses were waiting, she turned back to see the iron-masked man pulling out the arrow from his nose and standing dauntingly silent, walking towards them.

More so, an archer had arrived and was aiming at Karna's head.

She wanted to warn him. She should. That was the right thing to do.

But if he dies, I'll benefit.

The thought of what Manvee had told her came to her mind.

He can have an accident.

The archer was going for the head.

And Devi took too much time to think, even though he had saved her, even though she should not do so. Even though, he had been nice to her...

"Arrow! Dodge!" she heard Satya cry loudly.

And as the arrow was released, Karna dodged, as he was told.

But he didn't notice that Devi had seen it coming.

"Come," he made her sit on the stallion, while he sat on another one. Most of their men had escaped, and those who couldn't were flayed on the ground—dead.

Devi turned towards the iron-masked man, who had now walked close to them.

"Does he not bloody die?" Karna asked. "Is he even human?"

The iron-masked man had his axe in his hand, and his men were left behind, but Karna shot further arrows, as their horses took off. The arrows didn't hurt the man, but it was enough to push him further behind, till he became a dot, just like he had before.

I couldn't kill him.

She had let her emotions take the most of her and that was not usual, but she did. But that was not the regret. The regret was that she was prepared to get a man killed just because he had taken her place.

She felt guilt and regret.

How could I think like this?

But then, he did take her place. She saw her crimson hands, bloody as her wound was gushing, and she leaned forward on the horse, closing her eyes.

But if he had died, I would have taken his stead.

Would that be a good thing?

46

Karna hadn't rested, but his men did.

They had lost a lot tonight, and morning had broken. Water was served, and so was food. The slaves were given different clothes to wear and were made to sit in front of the bonfire.

Devi was tended to by the bhisak, who was stitching up her axe wound.

And Karna...

He felt he hadn't slept in years. He wanted to go to his room and just fall on his cot, but he had one important matter to discuss. They were in the common hall of the fort, which was a large spacious area, enough to seat a thousand men. Sunlight beamed from the open window spaces, while more food was being served to them, and even wine.

The sun was up and most people were sleeping. He awakened them by saying, "I hope you all are done for the night. A new day has risen." There were hundreds of men, all clobbered, sitting on the floor.

Satya was there though, and he was feeling grumpy, not his usual self and Karna couldn't help but feel, he needed some of that dry humour right now, which he wasn't getting.

"I have a few words to speak," Karna said, and the men nodded. They were all frowning or grinning. It was dependent on their mood. "We have lost a few men, to save you all. We had learnt you were treated unfairly by the soldiers of Jarasandha."

And most men in the group spat on the ground on hearing his name.

"He's evil!" someone even shouted.

"I'm sure. He must be," Karna said. "I don't know if you know me, but I am the recent king of Anga. I have just been handed the crown but I do not wear it because we have not won against the bad guys. And to fulfil that purpose, I come here asking for your support."

They were all uncertain. Some were afraid too. And they had every right to be. What Karna had witnessed the previous day was chaotic violence. Jarasandha had played them. But he underestimated them and they were able to escape. And his weapon...that iron-masked man, the invincible creature of darkness, was a hybrid of his own. And yet, Karna had the audacity to ask for help.

"You are hundreds in number and I would need your help. We are short on people when it comes to soldiers. We don't have them."

There was another pause. None of them were speaking. And he lowered his gaze, until one person stood up.

"Your highness, I would love to beat the asses of at least some of those bastards."

Karna grinned. "Thank you."

"You saved me and I am in debt, your highness."

And then another rose.

While they were rising, Karna was counting and

realising that many slaves had joined him. By the end, he had enough men on his side, but many also didn't join. "For those who have volunteered, you will be paid handsomely and given food and you will be sent to your families."

"We don't have one. The only family we have is our soil."

"Then I believe you should kiss it, worship it," Karna smiled.

They all grinned.

Karna looked at the ones who weren't ready to join and they were quite a large number as well. "I know fighting for me could be another sort of slavery for you all, but it isn't. It's an honour. Instead of manacles, you'll receive swords and shields. Instead of abuses, you'll receive respect from those poor farmers and villagers of Anga who toiled every day to pay taxes for us to be here. If we don't fight for them, we are worse than our enemies. But I understand your plight."

No one else responded. They were still adamant.

Karna nodded. "Thank you all." And the ones who did join, bowed to him. As Karna departed, Satya followed him.

"What should we do with the ones who didn't join?" Satya asked. "They are quite a big number."

"Yes, they are," Karna sighed. "I have an idea."

"And that is?"

They were far from the common halls that had gone busy again, with people talking to each other now.

"I want *you* to convince them," Karna smirked.

"And how do you want me to do that?"

"Well, we can't force them to join us. But we can play tricks," Karna shrugged, showing his cunning side. "Set them free, and get our men to kidnap them and take them somewhere, until another set of our men go and save them. Then they will feel indebted and happily join us."

Satya raised his brows. "You really want to fool them?"

"We need all arms on our side," Karna said. "And I'm ready to do anything for that."

Satya chuckled. "Boy!"

"Yes."

"I wish your father was like this."

"What do you mean?"

"Clever. You are one clever bastard while your father was always honourable, someone who would always play by the rules, wouldn't bend. I hope you win the war."

Karna smiled at the old man. Master Satya was a unique person and he had taught him all this while to be honourable, but Karna had travelled enough to know that being honourable sometimes could get you killed. You could be good, but also do bad things on the side if you were to keep up with the world.

The sun was up and he had to go. He hadn't performed his adulations to Suryadev yet and it was from there that he got his power, his energy.

"I hope your words are the predictions of the future," he said. "I hope that very much."

Devi had awakened to the kisses of Manvee, when her dreams became a nightmare. She hissed out the puff of air she was holding in, wounded, with her torso stitched and her face smeared with Ayurvedic medicines. She stayed on her cot, frustrated for a while, her eyes gazing at the window from which light appeared, until she heard a knock and saw her least favourite person.

Karna.

He stood there, with his hands clasped in front, looking innocent; concerned, even. She had thought about him, about not killing him or making it look like an accident. She could give him a chance, especially since she should be indebted to him. But she had gone mute the last time, and her tongue was forced to not say anything. It was a strange occurrence. She felt guilty, and now she knew she wouldn't do it again.

"How are you doing?" He asked, and he didn't look like he had come from a battle.

"Fine," she grunted.

"Then not so good," Karna sighed. "I wanted to talk to you about something."

"And I thought you were worried," she snarkily responded.

He smirked. The kind of smirk which she hated. He had that attitude of a boy who was spoilt, and yet at times, he showed he could be responsible too. She didn't know what to feel about him—whether she should like him, hate him, or respect him.

"I am. And that's why I am here."

"Is this a lecture?"

"It is," he straightforwardly said, as he came closer and sat down next to her cot. "Five."

"Five?"

"Yes."

"What five?"

"Five men," he began, "were killed because we didn't fall back because you happened to jump on that iron-masked man out of your own personal vendetta. I lost five men over your recklessness."

Devi clenched her jaw. *So this was it.*

"You want to make me feel bad about it?" she didn't lock eyes with him.

"I want you to feel responsible."

She growled. "Your highness, you are quite a piece of work. For someone who has just arrived on the scene, you are lecturing me about caring for my men. I have been doing that ever since Vijaya died."

"I know," he nodded. "Your husband. It's mighty brave of you to take over after he had a heart attack."

"Yes, he did."

"He was quite an old man, I know," Karna nodded. "But as far as I've heard, he didn't have a heart problem." And he sharply looked at Devi, with an accusatory glance. "One can wonder what happened to him, but perhaps the veterans of the fort can provide certain explanations."

"You think I murdered my husband?" she said through clenched teeth.

"Even if you did, it doesn't matter," he shrugged. "He was a vicious man. I know because I was a child when he took over Anga and he used to take little girls to his room and they wouldn't return to the streets after that. You are one of the few who fought his onslaughts and for that I have immense respect."

Well take your respect and shove it up yourself, your highness.

She controlled her anger.

"But I know you are an emotional person. Manvee was an important asset to your rule and her death was unfortunate. But you cannot...and will not..." he looked directly at her, his voice a tad more forceful, "...risk the lives of my men for your personal crusade. You understand me?"

Devi wanted to shout and rip his face apart. But she stayed silent. And also forced a smile, a reluctant one.

Karna smiled back. It was a plastic one; no remorse that he just threatened his general.

And then he left.

Devi knew she should be indebted to him.

But it's his loss, he saved me. Now I will make sure I let that accident happen, just like the one Vijaya had.

47

Jarasandha hated many people in this world.

But he didn't hate anyone as much as he did Vrishni.

While he had been travelling to the banks of Champa, they were camping every night. Since it was a large group, they had to station themselves when the moon would greet them, and the mutton would be roasted and drinks would be served. Jara knew travelling with soldiers and establishing a war camp was a task of its own and required a lot of money and time—and he didn't have that much.

And so in one of his camps, when he was busy strategising with his commanders and his captains, as to how they would fight the enemy—Jara was visited by her.

She had come to the camp's entrance and was wearing a long gown, with a hood over her head to hide her purple lips and maroon eyes.

When she said her name was Vrishni, the guards asked Jara who immediately was struck by a cold shiver that ran down his spine.

How did she know?

He allowed her to come towards his tent and dispersed his men so it could be just him and her.

She took off the hood and he saw a beautiful woman

with an enchanting smile, but he knew she was a vicious one. She had long nails and they were painted red.

"How are you?" she asked.

"What are you doing here?" Jara was curt. His hair was all over the place and his beard was longer than usual.

"I heard my boy's plea," she sharply said. "Where is he?"

"He has been quite unsuccessful at what he's doing nowadays," Jara said. "He's not able to catch my bloody enemies and he's making a fool of himself."

"Perhaps he met his match."

"Karna? Bah! I doubt," Jara shrugged.

"Take me to my boy," she sounded ruthless.

"I am the king. You can't order me around," Jara said.

"Because of me, he is who he is."

"You have turned him into a brute. He was not like that always."

She was walking around a table on which grapes, apples and some mangoes were kept. There was a goblet and a jar of Soma too. And she dipped her finger into it and tasted it. "Indeed, you have succumbed yourself to the addiction of the Soma," she paused, thoughtfully. "You know, it comes from the plant *Ephedra Sinica* which is grown in a foreign land and north of here as well... or what we call the Somalata plant in general. The drink is extracted and some say if it's drunk with purity in your heart, it can make you immortal. What *you* are drinking here is the adulterated version of the plant since Bharatvashi have a tendency of adulterating every natural thing in the world."

And she would say that, because she was a foreigner.

"Have you come here to give me a lesson?" Jara asked. "On the history of Soma?" He knew that she had a fair knowledge of it. In fact, she was a practitioner of Soma and a woman of science, often considered a witch by the natives. She knew what to mix and what not to mix with Soma.

"I have come here to help my boy," Vrishni clenched her teeth. "One of his men came to meet me."

"His men? They are my men."

She grinned. "You have no power in what he does and who follows him, Jara. He's a man of his own world. He only serves you because he is not the diplomat you are. That is what makes both of you a really tough team to beat. But I believe this Karna boy is ruining your plan."

Jara wanted to abuse her. But he refrained. Because few years back, when Kaal was not the daunting personality he was today, he was a very weak child and Jara with great difficulty found Vrishni who was young too. She treated him and she gave him a drink, which made him indestructible, energetic, and his pain was no longer painful. He would be immune to any hurt, and he would grow larger and broader than everyone else. He would become a warrior. But seeing this, Jara tested the same drink on others and it didn't work. They had gone mad and killed themselves or killed others. That's why Vrishni was always close to Kaal. He was her only successful experiment. Perhaps it was because of his blood, or the composition of his body…but it made him more resilient and tougher after the drink.

"I'll take you to him," he said.

Kaal was in another tent, on a rock slab, lying down. Naked. His entire body was visible except his face, on which he was wearing the iron mask, even now. His entire body had amassed wounds and bruises.

He was unconscious.

Vrishni came in and began to touch Kaal's scarred body, worried and concerned, while Jara stood in the corner. And then she looked up.

"He was badly wounded last time," she remarked.

"I know."

She sighed. And then from the rucksack that she was carrying, she pulled out vials and a goblet and began to mix things.

"I forgot what you add," Jara said, casually walking towards her, his hands at his back.

"Soma, some parasites..." she smirked, "...it's a combination of death and deadliness. Why do you ask?"

"Because I was thinking of..."

"Don't even think about it," she sharply cut him off. "You might be a king, but you don't have the same blood as Kaal. He's..." she looked at her boy. "He's special. You are not."

Jara narrowed his gaze as he grabbed her by the shoulder and clenched his fists on her skin. She instantly felt weaker and meek. "You are not allowed to speak to me like that. I am your king."

Vrishni came close to him and looked into his eyes. "Is it the Soma that's making you enraged? Why are you drinking now? Because you have gone weak again. Thinking about your wife. About your brother," she chuckled. "Are you remembering the time your mother asked you to kill your brother? And you did. You actually did."

Jara shoved her away. He had told Vrishni all of this in a moment of weakness, and he regretted it. "You don't know anything about my brother. You don't know what I did."

"I know you murdered him in cold blood and then you murdered your mother."

"I killed him," Jara said. "But not the way you think I did." It was his guilt. It was getting to him again. He had done a lot of things that were questionable. He had murdered children and women and destroyed families. He was evil in every sense, and yet he had a justification for all of it.

"Just like you killed your wife?"

He shouldn't have told her all of that, but she had hypnotised him. She had told him that through hypnosis he could redeem himself but it was a malicious trick to make him confess his deepest guilt and his subjective truth.

Jara didn't say anything until she was ready with the goblet. She went to Kaal and was taking off his mask, when Jara grabbed her hand.

"Don't you dare touch the mask. No one is allowed to see him. Not even me."

"How will he drink?" she asked.

Jara poked Kaal on the shoulder and then patted him on the face. He heard a groan.

"Pull up your mask," Jara ordered.

And Kaal did, as Jara slipped him the Soma, with only half his face showing. He drank until the goblet was empty. The groans were fine, and he would rest now.

Jara patted him. "You'll be okay." And then he turned to Vrishni. "Get lost now."

"I plan to stay here," she smiled wickedly.

"Cunt, you..." and Jara felt Kaal's hands over him, just grabbing him by the wrist and Jara looked to see Kaal, whose eyes were watching him. His nose was broken and so was the rest of his face, but his eyes still had the pale light left. "Fine," Jara sighed. He had to listen to Kaal, otherwise he wouldn't do his bidding.

"You stay."

And then he looked at Kaal, who was staring back at him. "You and your spies are not doing really well, man. And I am tired of it. Twice. You lost twice. Now let me handle it for you."

"Do you have a plan?" Vrishni asked casually.

"You don't have to know," Jara responded with venom in his tone.

But yes.

He did.

He did have a plan.

48

Karna dreamt of *her*.

He could feel her beside him. He could feel her olive skin, her chestnut hair and her eyes like a pair of almonds, but she smelt of gooseberries and spoke in lullabies. When she touched him, he would feel a current run down his spine. He dreamt of all of her, until his mind wavered and spiralled, as he began to feel he was back in the snow. From where he had learnt. But no. This snow wasn't the snow from the Himalayas, but downstream, where he had met *them*.

It was them, in their animal furs, yellow skins and golden hair. They would speak in a foreign tongue and behave differently. They had advanced shields and swords made of bronze instead of iron. And they were a tough, beautiful lot. Blue eyes, even.

He woke up with a jolt, sweating like a pig, his face pale and drenched.

Someone was knocking on the door. He was feeling lazy and exhausted, but he came on his feet and his hair was all over the place. He went to the door and opened it to find Satya who didn't have his beard anymore except for a thick, bushy moustache that fell on each corner of his mouth, though he still had his matted hair.

"We have a visitor, boy," he said.

"What kind of visitor?"

"Apparently, they know you."

Karna shrugged, opening the door and walking back to drink some water from a jar. "So what? Since I have the crown, people would know of me."

"No, boy. They *know* you."

He stopped drinking and held the jar tightly, as he took a deep breath and turned his head. "What do you mean?"

"It's an emissary."

"From?"

"The Mlecchas," he said. "Now, boy, I want to know what kind of things you were dealing in with the bloody Mlecchas."

Was it a coincidence that he just had a dream about it?

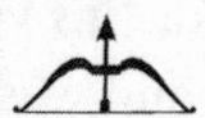

Mlecchas, technically speaking, was a term used by the natives of Bharat towards "foreigners". But not the kind of foreigners who came for tourism or trade. No. They were the ones who continued to stay here and exploit the resources of Bharat through every means possible. They were barbaric and nomadic, very much like the Rakshasas. But they were beautiful and they had created their own cult of sorts. They would station themselves in the north, for there were less kingdoms there due to the heavy snowstorms.

Karna knew what kind of foreigners would be meeting him now, as he sat on his two knees, waiting for them in the meeting hall. The music was blaring in the corner, and he didn't have his throne, for now. It wasn't built in the fort. He did not want to build it himself either as he hadn't become a proper king yet. He promised himself, he would dive into these aspects of vanity when he would be crowned and repeated the smritis from the pandit, making him a king no one could dispose.

He saw the hall doors opening and his guards escorting the emissary, who happened to be two people.

One was a dark-haired woman, barely old enough to be there and another was a golden-haired man. They both had crystal blue eyes, light in colour and they were fairer than any native of Bharat, almost chalk white.

Karna noticed the girl. He knew her. He could feel he knew her, and when she smiled, he noticed her dimples and his eyes brightened.

"Shanaya," he grinned, "it's you."

She had braided hair and was wearing an armour and she looked...different. She was a young girl, the daughter of the captain.

"How are you, Vasu?"

"Well...I've been better."

He knew these Mlecchas were Ionians from the land of Ionia, though in Bharatvarsh they were called Yavanas. It was a different way of calling them Greek. But they also had the blood of Bharatvarsh running in them and Karna knew why. Shanaya, for instance, was the daughter of a Greek father and a Bharatvashi mother. The reason, the Ionians were placed here was because of Kalyavan, the Black Greek who had partnerships with Jarasandha. Kalyavan was himself half-Greek and a native of Bharat, and he had many like that around him.

But Kalyavan was a ruthless, crazy man who was imbued with too much power and thus many captains of his with their own troops escaped his clutches and became nomadic.

Shanaya was a part of one of those groups since her father was Captain Archimedes, a one-eyed soldier to Kalyavan, who had more than two thousand people at his disposal.

Why are they here though?

"My name is Rhode, your highness," the golden-haired man said, old as a bird, but still had his dye on. "And since you know Shanaya, no introduction is needed."

"By coming here you have put yourself at great risk. Mlecchas aren't the most respected of the lot," Karna warned with a cheeky smile and he saw Shanaya who was grinning back at his snide humour. "But my men are forgiving and forgetful. So tell me, what can I do for you?"

"Indeed, we are not respected because we are deserters of the Black Greek and he has bounties on us. Our names were forged wrongfully and we became the otherworldly creatures to the natives," Rhode sighed. "Anyhow, Bharat till now has been kind to us when it comes to nature, not humans. Except for you. Captain Archimedes remembers you, and thus, when he learnt you had become the king, he sent me here."

"For what?"

"For an alliance, of course."

Karna raised his brows and couldn't help but chuckle. "What do you mean, alliance?"

Shanaya spoke, snapping him: "Vasu, the man you fought is a common enemy. He has sided with the Black

Greek and the Black Greek now has forces against Mathura. We are extending our support to Krishna as well, and we thought why not you."

"In fact, it was Shanaya's decision," Rhode added and she blushed.

"Well," she shrugged.

Karna remembered Shanaya as a young girl when he had met her before. She was small and mousy and she would show him her collection of flowers. She loved collecting them, he remembered, and Karna felt she always had a crush on him, but then she was a child and he never took her seriously.

"Interesting. So you have come all the way to tell me this?"

"And to make you meet the captain," Rhode said. "He has come here from the north and he's stationed a few miles from Malinipur. He reminisces about how you used to dream to be a king and he's proud of you."

It must be more than that. Something far more sinister.

Karna knew that Archimedes might be a good man, but he was a clever one. And if he has sent Shanaya and Rhode, there must be some ulterior motive he couldn't think of. "What do you want in return? Money? Citizenship in the kingdom I'll make?"

"We do not strive for petty things," Rhode said. "And I am just an emissary. It is not my jurisdiction to say what we need. But I can assure you Captain Archimedes has something to ask of you for this favour."

"Favour?"

Rhode licked his lips. His voice sorely lethal. "It is no secret, your highness, that you lack in infrastructure as well as an army. Isn't it true that the battle is just a few days away and your men are not high in number? Mlecchas might be considered evil, but they are fighters and strongmen."

Essentially what Karna heard was: *You need us. We don't need you.*

"Fine. You shall be staying in the quarters. Let me think about it and I'll tell you by the evening."

He shared one glance with Shanaya who nodded in return. She wasn't happy with his tone, but she shouldn't be. Putting Mlecchas in the army, at the forefront was in the strictest sense…royal suicide. Since they were criminals by the royal order. They were supposed to be put in prison on sight.

Devi was going to say…

"No," she was flustered, her face red and full of anger. "Your highness, respectfully," she said through gritted teeth, "you first bring in the forest bandits, now you bring in the foreign bandits. Do you really want to win this war by breaking every rule and precedent our nation has strived for?"

They were in Karna's quarters, and he was leaning against the wall, his arms crossed and his muscles tightened, while Satya on the other hand, was picking his teeth.

"War has no rules, general," Karna said, remembering the *promise* he had made when he was really small and he had to fulfill that *promise* in whatever way possible.

"In all fairness, we don't have enough men. We still don't. Almost three thousand of Jarasandha's warriors are going to be destroying us. We have to bend the rules to win."

Devi shook her head. "Maharaja Dhritarashtra won't be happy."

"He has given me the autonomy to take whatever decision I want."

"In the realm of..."

Karna shook his head. "We have to meet Archimedes. I know him, Devi. He is a sinister man, no doubt but he has taught me a lot. And he helped me reach and meet Parshuram. If not for him, I would have died with frozen balls in the north."

She sighed, exasperated. "You are alienating your own men, your highness. They might feel that siding with criminals, will make you a criminal."

"A king," Satya began once he was done picking his teeth, "doesn't have to be loved. He has to be respected. If we win the war, by hook or crook, the soldiers won't give two rat's ass about who we sided with. I know the Mlecchas are criminals, but they are criminals because they didn't side with the empire who enjoyed the lust of violence. Kalyavan is a crazy man and just because of Jarasandha, he holds a portion of Bharat to himself and has the right to call his men deserters—whoever doesn't support him in his cause for violence. So from where I sit, we are siding with the good lot."

Karna nodded. He had learnt that quite a long time back. "Let's do it then," he said.

Devi wasn't convinced. She looked frustrated that her words were not taken seriously, and Karna came forward, putting his hands on her shoulder as he said: "If you want, you can leave. You don't have to be part of all of this. And I will understand. But if you believe in me as a king, you stay here."

Devi blinked. He didn't know what she was thinking, but they were deep thoughts of conflict. "Fine. Let's see."

"Hurray," Satya added, bored, "now we can…"

They heard someone knocking on the door.

Karna casually walked to the door and opened it to see a young man who bowed and handed him a scroll. The man, he noticed, was younger than any other soldier. He would barely be eighteen and he had a nose like a swine, with big nostrils. "What's your name, kid?"

"Shantanu, sir."

"Ah," Karna smiled, "do you know Shantanu was the ancestor of Hastinapur? Once a king of it."

"Yes sir, my mother named me after him."

Karna didn't know if a soldier down the road would be named after Karna. But he could hope for that. "You are relieved."

Shantanu bowed again and left.

Karna opened the scroll and read it. Satya and Devi were quarreling about something else, when he said: "We have a situation." His skin was pale.

"What would that be?" Satya asked.

"Well…" Karna said. "Jarasandha wants to meet me."

49

Karna was packing and his chariot was being readied. He had passed on the duties of the king to Devi for now as Karna and Satya would venture into the hidden Greek territory. While he still had apprehensions, he had to clear it anyhow, down the road.

He was wearing his breastplate and hanging his bow around the shoulder, with a quiver dangling on his back, when he heard a voice:

"I always wondered why you were called Karna."

It was a faint, familiar one and he turned to see Shanaya with her oceanic blue eyes, smiling at him. She was leaning against the door.

"It means to 'to obey'," he said.

"And is it better than Vasu?"

He shrugged. "That's only for the ones who know me well."

"So you are saying, I know you well?" she was teasing him.

"Yes, of course. Your father was of great assistance to me," Karna smiled back.

"To obey," she walked playfully to him. "Were you an obedient student? I know you people have Gurukuls. Were you obedient there?"

Karna thought. Was he? He didn't respond to her clearly. "To a certain level, yes. But not for everything. If I was asked to murder, I wouldn't. If I was asked to steal, I wouldn't."

"So you stick by your ethics?"

"Yes."

"I wonder what your Guru thought of this."

And he did wonder about it himself. Meanwhile, they were prepared and he decided to leave on a chariot, bidding farewell to his people and moving along with his men and the Greeks, with Rhode and Shanaya. He couldn't help but travel down the passage of time to where he used to be.

Four years back.

In Gurukul.

50

Four years earlier…

Ujjanak…

It was his first year. A dreadful year, one could say.

Gurukul had been the best time of his life and he had learnt a lot, but he had also faced a lot of issues with the Pandavas as well as the Kauravas.

And the only time he would practice and learn would be early mornings, after presenting his adulations to Suryadev. He was at the cliff, touching the light and immersing in it, when he heard footsteps behind him and he instantly turned to face an old man, walking with a cane.

Drona was grinning, and didn't even fidget as Vasu pulled down his bow and smiled back at his guruji.

"You are a fast learner. You have learnt more from me in this one year than most others could," he said.

Vasu nodded humbly. "Whatever you say, guruji, I will do."

"I like that phrase," he smiled. "Whatever you say. It's a heavy statement, you make."

"But isn't that what a student does when his guru asks for a *dakshina*?"

"He does," Drona patted him on the back. "I am glad you listened to me and you practiced in the morning. The mornings are for you and the thunder is for Arjun. You both are the greatest archers this world will see, mark my words."

Vasu smiled. The words were tough but being compared with his rival did light the fire inside him.

"I want to rename you. I want to call you Karna. To obey. To listen. You have been always a boy who did everything that was asked of him. You broke through merit and so forth," Drona hugged him.

"Karna…" Vasu said the name to himself. *It sounded nice.* "But my name was given by my mother."

"You are also Radheya, named after your mother. But the name is not important, the reason behind it is. Why you are called what you are called is far more important. You understand me, child?"

Vasu nodded diligently.

"Good. The year is ending, and your training is complete. Have you thought of what I would ask as dakshina?"

He shook his head.

"Think about it. And don't be like Eklavya."

Vasu asked, "Why did you make him cut his thumb?"

"Because he's an eavesdropper. If he would have come and asked for my teaching, I would have gladly allowed, but he eavesdropped and listened to everything. I don't care if he was Nishadh as long as he was good at what he did, but stealing from an acharya is a crime to the gods," Drona explained.

Vasu nodded. He knew why Drona was saying all of this. He had been feeling numb about how everyone called him 'driver' and 'sarthi' and 'suta'. The words were meant to be derogatory and it would hurt him tremendously. It was only Drona who was kind to him and make him stand up against them. Drona also asked him to associate himself with a god, to get his blessings in abundance. Suryadev wasn't Karna's choice, but he was always blessed by the god of sun since birth, starting from his breastplate to him feeling the warmth when it came to mornings.

"Yes, guruji. I won't."

Karna, ever since then, had called himself by the name that was given to him and he made sure other people followed it.

He was in the ashram, where he and Suyodhan were lying down. None of the other Kauravas or Pandavas or the other royalty were there. The ashram had many cubicles and each one was devoted to someone or the other.

Suyodhan was trying to sleep, but his eyes were wide open, with dark circles around them. He had a weak, thin body, but he was good with a mace.

"What are you thinking about?"

"Today they didn't attack me," he said, in this utterly mechanical tone.

"The Pandavas?"

"Yes," he shivered, his words were icy cold.

"You need to stop getting scared. They love to tease you."

"Drowning me in a lake isn't teasing, Vasu. It's downright threatening."

"I know," he tried to cheer him up. "I have a new name. I am called Karna from today."

"Karna?" He raised his brows. "One of my brothers' name is Karna too."

He frowned. "But he won't be as popular as Suryaputr Karna."

"Stop being so pompous all the time."

And they both chuckled.

Karna sighed. His friend, Suyodhan, was the only person in Gurukul he talked to. He also talked to Suyodhan's two blood brothers, but they were never really conversational with Karna. For them, he was just a driver. But Suyodhan never cared, even though he was the oldest of the royals. He was himself stuck in the wrong place, where he was continually traumatised and harassed.

Karna, for some reason, never faced the brunt even though he should have. The only thing he got was that he was continuously called the sutaputr every day.

The nightingale sang, and Karna said, "You sleep, I won't. Okay?"

Suyodhan sighed. "But what if..."

"Don't worry. I'll be on the lookout."

Suyodhan swallowed a nervous lump and nodded his head. "Are you sure?" He shivered a bit, his cheeks sucked inward and his nostrils flaring.

"Yes, I am sure."

"Okay."

He closed his eyes. And as he did, Karna went to the door of the ashram where the curtain hung and he looked outside, making sure no one entered. After a while, he could hear the snores of his friend and he smiled to himself.

He could sleep, but he didn't want Suyodhan to feel he went back on his word. So he remained like that, for a long time, his thoughts drawing to his childhood days, his parents, his young stepbrother and Panchali. He missed Panchali. He had thought he would go and meet her once everything was over. Once everything was done for. When he would graduate and become a warrior like a Kshtriya.

I will ask for your hand in marriage.

He didn't know whether she liked him or not though. She was just a very sweet person, who had always treated him like a friend. *Perhaps just a friend...*

The thought made him morose.

And while his thoughts were drifting, he felt drowsy and was slumbering after a while.

It was a bit later, when he awoke to silent screams when he turned to see a shadow looming over Suyodhan. That shadow was continuously beating and punching Suyodhan on the head. He heard the giggles as well. And he rubbed his eyes to find that Suyodhan's head was wrapped in the blanket and he was being punched and kicked by the shadow.

Karna didn't take a moment's notice, but launched himself at the shadow, only to realise it was quite big and he was tossed to the corner, slamming against the wall.

"Sutaputr, stay away from this."

And the shadow disappeared, along with the shadow's friends, who were two in number and as his eyes were clearing up he saw it was none other than Bheem.

He clenched his jaw and went to help Suyodhan, who was crying and whimpering with wounds over his body and his face.

"YOU TOLD ME YOU WON'T SLEEP!" he exclaimed, crying.

And Karna hugged him instantly.

"It's okay…it's okay. I am sorry…"

And Suyodhan fought back, but the two boys remained in an embrace.

Karna realised this couldn't keep continuing. He saw that the light was returning in the background of the ashram and he heard the final words of Suyodhan, who said:

"*Something has to be done about this.*"

51

In the last week of the first year of Gurukul, Karna was standing in a large assembly of people consisting of all the royalty of Bharatvarsh.

They were dozens in number, all standing with their straight backs and their fierce weapons.

He didn't care about watching others but Suyodhan, who was on his side, and was looking relieved. Relieved at the idea that he would be back home, in his mother's arm and away from the problems he had been facing here. Drona had been a partial guru, if not to Karna, then to Suyodhan since he favoured the Pandavas. Arjun was his prodigy, he was the son he never had.

Even though he had one, but someone who just learnt on the side.

Drona, with his cane, was standing on a large rocky pedestal, that overlooked all the hundreds of students and he was beaming with hope. He had a snowy beard and his hair was cut short.

"When you had come here, all of you, I was surprised and overwhelmed whether I would have the audacity to help you all. But you were such brilliant students, you made my teaching easy. From making you all learn horse riding, to sword fighting, to archery to wrestling, to learning about our history, mythology, culture, religion, and learning the smritis and the vedas, we have come here together…where we are at the beginning of another three years of journey. But what is that one thing we have left to do?"

"Dakshina!" someone yelled. "We have to give dakshina before the first year ends, the fee."

Karna saw who it was, and he had never seen that boy, to which Suyodhan nudged and said: "That's the other Karna."

And Karna couldn't help but frown. Suyodhan was just teasing him and he knew that.

"I am sure you are happy we are leaving this place for some time," Karna whispered to his friend.

"Yes, I am. But when we return, I have one task to complete."

"And that is?"

Suyodhan didn't respond. His face was impassive.

And so Karna listened to Drona:

"Now you all might wonder what is that dakshina? What would I ask for, from you all?" He shrugged. "What I believe I should ask from any student. Undying loyalty. Loyalty towards me and what I say, no matter what. And when the dakshina is paid off, you all will be free to go."

Karna waited for the task to be given, as Drona continued:

"I used to have a friend. And he betrayed me. He betrayed the words that he clung on to. I want you all to exact vengeance on the one who betrayed me. And in return, I want none of you to utter a word about it. It would be a secret and the dakshina would be paid."

It didn't sound right, Karna thought. It felt selfish for a guru to make a student do whatever he wished, even if it didn't make any sense. But he saw all the students with their diligent faces agreeing to Drona and nodding.

"That friend of mine has a kingdom, and that kingdom is important to me because half of it belongs to me, by his word that was given to me long back. I want that half. And to get that half, I want this private army of mine to do that for me."

But we are your students, not your army.

It almost felt like Drona was preparing these kids not for Bharat, but for himself, to complete this deed.

Suyodhan whispered: "Great, some action."

"Don't you think it's wrong?"

"Well, little rebel, it doesn't matter. As law says, you have to do what the guru asks for while paying dakshina since he taught you for four years, otherwise you will be branded as...well...not someone you might want to be branded as. Even Eklavya gave off his thumb to not be on the wrong side of the law and he was a Nishadh."

Karna clenched his jaw. He was warming up to the idea, until Drona's story took a familiar turn. In fact, it had been familiar. He had heard it a long time ago. Many years...but where?

He arched his brows, as Drona continued and made him recognise the source from where he had heard of it:

"I want you all to attack my old friend and the king of Panchal—Draupad."

And at that moment, Karna's blood ran cold.

But...Panchali?

52

Present day...

Karna realised they were travelling to the edges of Malinipur.

The world was blanketed in shadows and they travelled with their garrison across ridges and cliffs, and ascending to the pathway where their armour clanged and clicked, their swords dangling from their sheaths and their hoof beats making quiet, urgent noises. It looked different, the vast emptiness, the hills with green vegetation, the sly whispers amongst the soldiers as to whether this was not an ambush.

Karna initially was on his chariot, but then he chose to ride a horse, along with Shanaya and Satya, who were moving by his side. He carried his bow on his shoulder, his thoughts raging back to his time with Drona and how he had ordered everyone to attack the woman he liked; or loved even. Arjun had agreed and so had everyone else, probably because it was dakshina. But Karna hadn't cared.

I should focus on the present.

His eyes darted, as they trampled across the forest,

moving in high speed. They had camped for the night and soothing music was being played. Shanaya had tried talking to him, but he had politely smiled at her and left for his tent.

The next day, as they travelled around the hills and moved for the marshland where Archimedes was supposed to be, he saw Shanaya stopping her horse, reining it and walking towards a flower.

"We cannot delay any further," Karna stopped and so did his men.

But Shanaya was busy admiring the beauty of the flower. It was a yellow one, with red streaks.

"What is it?" Karna asked.

"A Ganges primrose, quite exotic in nature," she smiled. "I never thought they grow on this side of the land."

Karna smiled to himself, seeing her childish fascination. As she sat back on the horse, the entire garrison moved further into the marshland, with a distant murmur of the river in the background. The skies were grey, almost rainy.

"We are close," she said.

"We better be," Satya was on the other side, growling. "My ass is sore."

Shanaya frowned and whispered to Karna, "Is it appropriate for a man like him to talk like this?"

Karna shrugged. "You have to get used to it, I suppose."

"I wanted to ask you something," Shanaya prodded.

Karna's eyes were hawk-like and he saw the marshland, patches of grass growing around the lake, and rows of trees. It all looked very dull.

"Yes."

"You remember when you had come to my father's camp in the North, I had asked you, if you have someone back home? A girl perhaps?"

Karna nodded, "Yes, I do." He was defiant.

"You told me there is this girl, Panchali. Did you wed her?"

Karna narrowed his gaze. He had spoken a lot, out of pomposity, but life often puts you in a different direction. "No, I didn't. She's supposed to marry someone else."

"I see. I am sorry."

"It's all right. I feel I am born to live alone."

Shanaya forced a smile, and Karna moved his horse further ahead, ignoring the pensive glare he received from Shanaya.

The rain had throttled and so it was clear. The landscape in front was misty and dark, but it was not dark enough to not see what was happening.

Fire. Cries.

There were people fighting and Karna reined his horse, and observed that there were two sets of people, one set in animal pelt and the other in crimson armour, battling each other with their irons and metals.

"Father has been attacked," Shanaya cried in a panic.

At that, Rhode ordered his men to move further and before Karna could stop Shanaya, they had gone ahead.

Karna's army waited for him to react and he was curious as to what was going on. Men with their boots sunk in the lake water, some fighting on marshes and hanging from vines and jumping inside the deep water, there were all kinds. The rain was not doing much, and it was all over the place, with thousands of soldiers fighting.

"Should we enter?" Satya asked, nearing his mare to Karna's. "Losing soldiers when we need them can be risky. Let them fight their battle and we can wait till it is over."

Karna mulled, "I have learnt one thing. I might lose soldiers, but I gain a lot out of goodwill. But if I gain less soldiers now, I will lose a lot of soldiers. I have to invest in loss, in order to gain."

"You talk like a merchant of pig shit, you know that."

Karna grinned and ordered his men to flank forward and assemble their gear and move into the battle. Though not much was clear, he could see his men enter and fight for the Mlecchas.

He remained there, static as he heard the battle cries. He told the rest of his men to wait with Satya, as he dismounted and prepared to go forward himself.

"Have you gone mad risking your life for a Mleccha?"

"It doesn't matter who they are. I have to help."

"You are valuable to Anga. You cannot risk yourself over an attack on an outsider."

"It matters to me."

Karna raced ahead, his arrows slung on the bow, as he moved into the battlefield and he could feel the mist, the rain, the volley of fire arrows, yells and scowls. They were all over the place and overwhelming for a moment, as he entered and skid further. He began to roll over, shoot arrows at the red ones, moving quickly until he felt someone slam him against his shoulder, throwing him in the mud.

Karna came on his feet to see the soldier in front of him with a hammer in his hand. With a quick shove, the hammer came towards him. Rolling over, he quickly lunged at the man by shooting an arrow at his head and the man succumbed wondering where the attack had come from.

I must search for Shanaya.

In all the mayhem and chaos, as the rain splattered down and the grey skies belched, he could taste the salt of the blood in his mouth. He licked it and moved further ahead, shooting arrows like only he could, almost all of them going through the helmets, or their necks, before killing them.

His eyes searched for the little girl who had grown big now, but he couldn't find her. She had disappeared and the crimson armoured men he noticed were foreigners. They looked Greek. When one of them came towards him…

He was grabbed by the throat and drowned in water, and he could see the image of the man, with less clarity… he was confused and gasping for breath.

And then the grip loosened and he saw the man who was shoving him down—*die*.

Karna pulled himself out of the water, his armour and his dhoti drenched, as he took the air in and realised the value of it.

"Are you okay?" he heard the voice and turned to see Shanaya, who pulled out the revolving dagger from the man. She had a sword, and a dagger.

"I was searching for you."

"To help me? I don't need help," she laughed.

Another soldier came from behind; she contorted her

frame and twisted, slashing the guts out of the soldier and plunging her blade into his throat.

His heartbeat was racing and being part of the battle, he always let the adrenaline roll. He tried to get up, but felt his legs weaken, and Shanaya helped him, when two soldiers approached her.

With a quick reflex, he shot two arrows towards them—both piercing their foreheads and shoving them down on the ground.

"Show-off," she grinned.

Karna smiled back. He could feel he was having trouble breathing for some reason and it was really getting to him.

Is it my panic attacks?

"Who are they?" he asked, trying to distract himself.

"Kalyavan's men. Apparently, they were following us..." another soldier came, and she slashed his throat in an instance again.

"You have been trained well."

"I aim to impress," she sniggered. "Are you okay?"

"No, I am just..."

Karna had faced this quite often and it happened when he was in a stressful position. His thoughts began to clobber together and he was unable to breathe.

"You'll be fine. Don't worry. You should not have joined."

"No, it's okay."

His legs were weak. *I'm having an attack. But why?* It was not failure he was afraid of right now, but then these attacks come and go, they sometimes had no reason behind them.

"You need to fight it," she whispered to him.

"I know."

"No! Karna, focus on your breathing."

"Yes!"

I often do in the morning, but there's no light. It's rain and thunder…

"Focus on your breathing…"

He could hear her voice and then he felt darkness descend, as he fell down on the ground.

53

Karna woke up with a jolt.

But he wasn't dreaming. He had bandages tied all over his body, but he was here, in a tent perhaps. And when he did wake up, he woke up the shadow in front of him, who instantly went for him and asked:

"Are you okay?"

It was Shanaya.

He blinked. Confused. "What happened?"

"It's over. Calm down. We have defeated them." She smiled, running her fingers through his hair and calming him.

"Why are you here?"

"I was worried. I hope you don't mind, I slept on the other side of the tent, so don't worry."

Karna clenched his jaw. He didn't like how Shanaya was trying to be so nice and get close, but then he should be grateful.

"What happened to you back there?"

Karna shook his head. "I have these...attacks since I was a child. It happens when I think I am losing," he paused. "I thought I had it under control, but it's just..."

"Because you hate losing?" she asked.

"Yes," he sighed. "I always considered myself a failure."

"Then perhaps you should be proud about it."

"What do you mean?"

"It takes a great deal to be a failure," she chuckled, her hair was let loose and he saw her black hair, like a ravine flowing down her back, with her aquiline nose and her definite jaw. "One has to *try* different things to be a failure."

"It's not a good feeling."

"More than failure, it's the fear that eats you, Vasu," she said. "We all fail. I believe that's a part of life."

And that's something I have not accepted till now.

"I know. You must think of me as not a king anymore. Who falls during a battle?"

"You came to help. That's what matters more than whether you win or lose." She paused, as her eyes drew towards his naked chest. "There are these perennial flowers like tulips, which when grown, fall down and then they rise up again. Year after year, they bloom and fall and then bloom again. But what doesn't change about them is their beauty, their scent. It remains forever. One should not worry about falling, but it's the rising up that's the important part," she sighed. "You should focus on your breathing. I know it'll work magic on you."

I know. I try.

"When you are ready, meet my father. He's eager to have a conversation with you." She smiled and then she moved for the door, when he said:

"Shanaya?"

"Yeah?"

"What happened to the little girl who thought the

world had ended because she lost her mother to the armies of Kalyavan?"

She smiled. "She's right here, Vasu. She never went anywhere."

Karna nodded. He recalled how she would weep when he had met her earlier, and she wanted to take revenge against Kalyavan for her mother's death, but now she seemed at peace.

She left him and he remained there. Quiet.

I should meet Archimedes.

Karna moved out of the tent and he saw that to the east of the marshland, where they had been fighting, this camp was established along the forest lines, using the foliage as a cover against the rain. More than thousand or so soldiers were there, lined up till the horizon and they were all feasting in different corners, drinking. He saw Satya dancing with a terracotta jar on his head, and when Satya saw him, he scampered to meet his king.

"Boy, you would have died."

"It wasn't the attack from the Greeks which made me blackout."

"Then?"

"It was my own personal problem." He was feeling guilty and most of all, weak. He didn't want to feel that way.

"Great. Just what we need during the battle of our lives. A king who has a problem."

Karna rolled his eyes at the snide comments he had

begun to expect from Satya. "You know, an old second-in-command is also not much of a help."

"Who dared to call you old?"

"How many did we lose though?" Karna's voice turned serious.

"One, perhaps two. Not much. The Mlecchas handled their enemies pretty well."

Karna shrugged, as he heard the voice behind them: "Karna!"

He turned hearing his name, and so did Satya, to find a middle-aged man with a golden beard and long black hair which was tied in two braids, wearing heavy armour and carrying two axes on each side of his girdle.

The braids were enough to tell Karna who he was.

"Archimedes," he said. "How are you?"

They embraced each other.

"Come have a drink with me," he said.

Karna nodded, his eyes falling on Shanaya's pensive glare from afar, and he smiled at her softly; she smiled back.

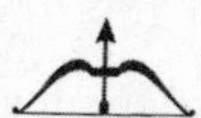

They sat inside their tents. Rhode was there too, and Archimedes handed him a goblet of wine and then immersed himself in a deep, uninhibited drinking session.

"I knew this would happen," he said, tossing the goblet to the side.

He saw the tent was empty except for stacks of paper, rucksacks, weapons and dimly lit torches.

"And what would that be?"

"The attack. Kalyavan has been on my heels for a while now. He thinks I shall exact revenge for what happened with my wife." He had a foreign, exotic accent. "But alas, I came here, out in the open from my northern forts, because I had to meet you, brother," he patted Karna on the shoulder. "You have done good for yourself."

Karna humbly smiled. "Thank you for helping me when it was needed."

"When I saw you, you were a helpless, frozen to your cockers boy. Now look at you, a crown on your head and regality flowing from your words."

"I'm still an interim king."

"Bah, the politics don't matter to me. What does though, is I have come here, exposed myself because I want you and me to participate together."

"You want to fight with me?"

"Kalyavan's only ally is Jarasandha. Let's kill him," he grinned. "You and me. And Kalyavan will be weak and from there, he's mine."

"Why do you want to side with a king who has such a small army?"

"Because you will give me legitimacy."

Ah, there it is.

Karna grinned. "Legitimacy? Why do you want that? Aren't you happy in the north?"

"Someday, I want to move down, where I can be safe. And Anga is a good place to live, down the road. Partnering up with you will mean I would have to not worry since I'll be branded as a king's ally." He paused, leaning closer, smelling of mutton. "You should understand, Dhritarashtra, the Maharaja of Bharat, doesn't care about me. He just branded me a traitor and a criminal because Jarasandha did. But if I am with you, I'll be legitimate."

Karna could see the desperation in the Greek man's eyes. He knew he was in a place to negotiate. "But that would harm my reputation."

"I know. To side with the Mlecchas. And you are right. It would. But how in the Hades wrath does it matter to you? You are a king!"

"You have to be pardoned by the Maharaja."

"You are the king!" he exclaimed. "The Maharaja has no rule in your stead."

"But I am still his vassal until he gives me the reins.'

Technically speaking, Karna knew he could have the Mlecchas on his side as conscripted mercenaries in the books. Dhritarashtra wouldn't say anything, except get a bit angry about the entire thing. But Karna wouldn't be breaking the rules, as long as the Mlecchas behaved well.

But, he was still a vassal.

"You know, I happened to meet a politician of your race, recently. Quite smart he was. And he told me a bit about your rules and regulations," he chuckled. "You have a few loopholes in this argument. If I may, can I address them?"

Karna leaned back. Raising his brow, he glanced at Rhode, who was just a silent spectator. "Of course."

"An interim king who is an acting king can also make the Mlecchas legitimate till the time he is the ruler. He doesn't need to have a pardon or is in need of it."

"Yes, but if I am not full ruler, your pardon can be revoked."

"I like to gamble on sure things. And I know you are a sure thing, kid."

"But even for this, you have to..." and he paused, his blood running cold.

So this was it. This was the plan all along. That is why...

"You have to marry," Karna sighed. "Yes, so that's why you had sent Shanaya, didn't you?"

Cheekily, Archimedes grinned. "You catch on fast, kid."

And that is why Shanaya asked about Panchali...she was making sure I was not married.

"But..." *I love someone else.*

"Think about it, kid. You will be gifted with two thousand soldiers, fighters, berserkers and crazy men who will die for you. Do you really want to say that 'but'?"

Karna hesitated. The temptation was strong.

He could win then.

He surely could. But he had something more important to talk to Shanaya about. He had to do it, if he was to take such a decision for her.

He said, "I would like to meet her, before I make a decision."

He was given the privacy and the time to think about it, and while he hadn't told Satya, he knew he would find opposition. But the idea of getting an army tenfold in size compared to what they had and finally be able to take Jarasandha head on, would be possible now. But was it the right thing to do?

Not just to his people, but to...Panchali?

She was clear about not being with Karna. She had told him she was destined to marry Arjun, then why bother? But still, his heart ached for her.

And his mind raced back to the day when he had left Gurukul, breaking protocol, he had escaped to meet her and warn her that Drona was coming to attack them.

How *that* had unfolded though was not what he had expected.

54

Four years back…

Panchal Kingdom, Kampilya

The Panchal Kingdom had its capital in Kampilya which was on the southern side, but regardless of that, the Himalayas stretched across the horizon in the background with its frosty tips, looming like giants. The river Charmanwati was in the south and the forest Naimisha to the east. They were surrounded by Matsya and Surasena and Kuru to the west. It was densely forested and had occasional snowfall too.

And the entire kingdom was divided into two berths, with the northern kingdom being on the lower end of the plain, less developed and not used properly. The Panchal didn't have trade points and naval supremacy was a far-fetched thought for them, but they were strong in creating all sorts of jewellery, ornaments, knitting modern clothes and the manufacturing buildings. Panchal was for the merchants.

It was a vibrant kingdom, with beautiful golden, ornamental palaces. They were hardly attacked, as they were well-protected from all sides and nestled nicely. The Ganges flew from here as well, and it divided the northern part of Panchal like it always had a habit of doing with most kingdoms.

Karna had reached by then and had informed Panchali who was happy to see him, but not happy at the news. And they were now inside the common halls of the kingdom where Panchali's mother and father were sitting on their throne, while the audience was divided on each side, and soldiers were present in light-coloured armour.

Panchali's mother was Kokila Devi who was a short woman, but her eyes were razor sharp, just like her daughter's. And Draupad was a funny, lanky man with a straight face and a meek look about him. Panchali was sitting alongside them, almost too concerned.

"So you are saying that Guru Drona is going to attack my place over a petty promise I made as a child?" Draupad clarified.

Karna could hear the audience gossiping and giggling at this stupidity.

"Yes, your highness."

"Weren't you part of his Gurukul?"

"Yes, your highness."

"How do I know this is not some scheme by him?"

Karna felt a bitter cold and before he could defend himself, Panchali adjusting her ornamental dress said: "Father I vouch for him. Vasu won't lie."

"Indeed, you sutaputr have smitten my daughter. Child, how many times have I told you to not be in the presence of such low-lives? He's a driver's son. He's a liar. He could be lying right now."

Karna felt like punching the king, but he refrained for Panchali's sake.

"I know him father," Panchali sternly added. "Trust me."

"And trust I shall," Draupad leaned forward, clearly bored. "So what do you want me to do with this information now, boy?"

Karna was confused. He knew he had to tell Draupad, but he had no idea what else could be done. "Strengthen your defences?"

"By the rule of law, I am a vassal to Maharaja Dhritarashtra. I won't be harmed by the likes of Guru Drona, who is under Dhritarashtra. So you can stop worrying about it and stop bringing me these bogus claims," he laughed. "And even if he does attack, my men can fight a bunch of spoilt untrained kids."

He was too pompous for his own good. Karna knew he could, but they weren't untrained. In the first year itself, the Pandavas especially had shown quite a number of advancements.

"And what's more surprising is that my own Dhrishtadyumna hasn't come to warn me, but a peasant like you has?" he referred to the boy who was diligently listening to Drona.

"I broke the rules, that's why. Your son won't. He will join the cause to destroy you because the rule is to follow what your guru asks for as dakshina."

And many did.

"That's true. And I love my son for that. He follows the rule and he's not like you. A rebel?"

Karna looked up. Clenching his jaw. He had only come

because he couldn't risk Panchali's safety. If in crossfire, this ended badly for her—he wouldn't be able to accept it.

"Let them come," Draupad said. "We will see. And once he does, and if we fight, I shall hand you over to him as someone who broke rules and should be banished."

"What..."

But before he could react, the guards had come around, clasping him and shoving him down on the ground.

"FATHER!" He heard Panchali's voice...

But it was too late.

He was already being dragged by the men towards the prison cells, the anger in his heart reflecting on his face and the feeling of utter betrayal coursing through him.

Karna was punching the hard, concrete walls till his fist began to bleed and then he began to smack his head against it.

Not only did I risk my entire training in Gurukul for THIS, this stupid man is risking...

And his thoughts got interrupted when he heard... loud cries. Shouts. Yells.

Karna instantly propelled himself to the top of the jail cell, grabbing the railing and he could only see the roads, but the footsteps—people were running helter skelter and scampering...

Until a soldier came and fell down straight in front of the grill, his lifeless face only meters away. Karna shoved himself back, hurling down on the ground and feeling a sudden coldness seep through his skin. He felt a narrow lump in his throat and swallowed it, until he heard footsteps. Loud footsteps! And he found a shadow creeping up to his prison door...

Only to open.

And the shadow revealed itself to be the familiar, beautiful Panchali, who was all worried, and sweating.

"I disguised myself and came here, stole the bloody key from the warden," she said. "I am so sorry, Vasu. It's all my fault..."

"No, no..."

The sound of an explosion snapped between their conversation and they both got frightened, only to hold each other's arms together.

"You need to escape," she said. "Leave now."

"But what about you?"

"All the women are assembling at the eastern watchtower and we will be fine. But I had to come before you get into a worse problem. I almost feel bad luck follows you."

Karna raised his brows. "Tell me about it."

"Yeah. I can't believe that old man convinced my brother also to get involved in this plan. But then, he was always someone who followed the rules. You are the special kind, aren't you? You go against what the world does."

"I just don't follow orders blindly, especially if my loved ones are under threat."

At that, she smiled; a warm, sweet smile. "I wish I could spend more time with you, Vasu. We have lots to talk about. I hope father solves this..." the cries grew even more intense. "But if you ever are here, close to it, please do come. We shall meet."

He smiled.

"I'll leave now," she said. "Take care of yourself, Vasu."

There was a sense of elation, a flutter of excitement in his stomach.

Screw the bloody gods, let me just do it.

And before she could leave, he grabbed her arm and pulled her towards him, planting his lips on hers and kissed her, as hard as he could. A smile creased her face as she pulled back; she was looking at him in a different light, with a different expression.

"I had to do it," he expressed.

"You are..." she chuckled. "You are something."

"Well, that's one compliment."

"Now, leave!"

And Karna did. He didn't wait around.

But could he really?

55

Drona thrusted his cane on the muddy ground, as he waited patiently for the palace in front of him to collapse.

And then he walked further, on the main roads of the city, where the corpses were lined, with a blank expression on his face.

Truth be told, he had always had a limp, but he was also someone who didn't care much about it. He could live without the cane, but it just gave him a threatening presence when he held it in his hands.

Drona walked further, as he saw his students battling the soldiers with ease. They were quick, young and agile. Freshly trained.

Drona also knew that by the excuse of a dakshina and its primitive rules that had been concocted a long time back by other rishis, he was able to manipulate them well. Dhritarashtra might be angry, but let him be. Drona could always tell him that he was doing what he did in the realm of law. His students were paying their dakshina. And he was not a part of it directly even though he strategised it. Also, Panchal was a young kingdom, a vassal sure, but something the Maharaja won't be worried about, if it turned into ashes one day. It was about an ill-forgotten promise, and a promise in Bharat made to a friend had to be kept—no matter what. Maharaja believed in that, even though he had a way of skidding around promises.

And there was another reason. A reason of investment, that Drona had thought of giving to the Maharaja if asked.

And the reason was walking with him. The young lad, carrying his bow and arrow—shooting.

No. It wasn't Arjun. But it was his own son, who had the shape of a mani inked on his forehead.

"Drauni," he called his son, "this is going to be yours."

"Yes, father."

He stood outside the burning palace, and soon saw his students—Arjun's bow and arrow pointed at Draupad, while Bheem was dragging Draupad by the throat and bringing him forth in front of Drona's feet.

He was wounded and was whimpering as he touched Drona's feet.

Drona instead put his cane over Draupad's back and said, "This is for not keeping your promise."

"It was a childish…"

"No. It wasn't. Not for me. I came here, begging to you with my son for my half and you shooed me away. And so, your action has led to this and so many of your men are now dying."

"Wha—what do you want?" he said, and he looked up, blood spurting from his mouth.

"I want my half," he signalled to the hills. "The northern part of Panchal. My son, Ashwatthama, shall rule that."

"Take it," he said desperately and joined his hands. "I do not want it."

Elation grabbed hold of him. His plan had worked.

"But Dhritarashtra shall hear of this..."

Drona pressed his cane harder and heard a loud moan. "That's another thing. If you want your women to live, you won't utter a word to him."

"But...but...he will hear of it."

"Deny it then. It doesn't matter. It's as if nothing happened."

"But word will get out."

"As long as you deny it, it's not real. Otherwise, my dear Arjun shall go up to the towers and murder your daughter."

There was a flash of worry in Arjun's eyes, Drona noticed. He didn't want to do it and why would he? He loved her. But Drona was his guru and if a choice had to be made, he would have to choose his guru, not some harlot he had a simple fancy for.

"Fine, fine. I will."

"Ashwatthama will be good for Northern Panchal. He shall grow the armoury and make me proud. Northern Panchal will be a military zone."

"Yes, yes," Draupad begged.

"Good."

And then the king of Panchal looked up and said, "How is it that you were able to conspire and influence my own son against me...but not the weakling sutaputr? How?"

Sutaputr...

Drona knew that Karna had to lead this battle, but just before leaving he had disappeared. Even Suyodhan didn't know where he was and that was odd. He was probably under the impression that he would come around here to help him later…Drona hadn't paid much heed for his eye was on the kingdom. But after hearing this, worry crossed his heart.

"What do you mean?"

"He came here to warn us that you all were coming."

"Karna…my Karna?" A stab of betrayal plunged in Drona's heart and he could almost feel his legs weaken.

"How is it that you were able to…"

"Where is he?"

"Here. In prison."

Because he's not as weak as you think he is.

He's quite the opposite.

Drona looked up at Arjun with his grey eyes, who was listening to this conversation quietly, when Drona said: "Find him."

Arjun nodded.

56

Karna had no weapons.

And as he was escaping, moving towards the valley where the river was flowing, rocks were hurtling down the hills from where he had come, his eyes fluttered in the direction of the shadow behind him. It moved and zapped quickly, as he turned to see who it was:

Arjun.

"Guruji told me to find you," he said, his bow and arrow pointed towards Karna. "But he never said I had to find you *alive*."

"You don't have to do this."

"You defied him."

"For Panchali," Karna said.

"You think that's the right answer?"

"I did what you should have done."

He shot an arrow, but it missed Karna and went past his ears, plunging on the earth.

"This was done on purpose," Arjun gritted his teeth. "I did what was necessary, what my guru wanted."

Karna shrugged. "Then you are an idiot. Drona used you for his selfish purpose."

"Perhaps, but that is what following a guru means.

Even in darkness, even in blindness, one has to follow him."

"Well then, I'm not a blind sheep."

The moonlight slivered and it shone over them. The frogs croaked and the owls flapped in the background. He was close to the hills and his feet were ready to pounce away, to go where he didn't know.

"And I don't listen to what the sheepherder wants me to do," Karna added.

"You work on your emotions. This shall be the end of you then. Remember always," he strung another arrow, "you will lose because of this. Only the smart and cunning wins in this world."

"Then it's not a world worth living in."

Karna didn't wait. He rolled over, grabbing a pair of rocks and began to aim at Arjun, throwing it towards his face.

One of them hit him and Karna leapt on Arjun, lurching over him.

They both fell on the ground and rolled over, as Arjun punched Karna and he hit back.

Karna felt he was on the defensive end, as he was plummeted and pushed by the bow and towards the other side as Arjun pulled out an arrow from his quiver and instantly shot his right arm.

A searing pain shot through his arm, as he fell on the ground.

"Let me...go." He tried to pull the arrow out of his thick flesh, but Arjun didn't give him the opportunity.

Two more arrows were shot. One at the knee. One more at another shoulder and Karna fell down; breathing shallow breaths, hurt.

Arjun towered over him as he kicked him in the stomach.

"It's not a fair fight!" Karna yelled.

And Arjun stopped. "You are right. But does it matter?"

And he hit him again on the face.

By then, Karna was bleeding and his vision was blurry. He remained there, as Arjun said, "Remember this day. You have been given a second life because of me."

Karna sighed, not saying anything as his jaw was hurting and bleeding, the salty taste permeated the inside of his mouth. He looked at another shadow appearing and he heard the cane's sound coming, closing in. And the blurry vision became a tad bit clearer, when he saw the full face of Drona, who looked disappointed, hurt. It said: *You were my child and you broke my heart.*

"You are not what I thought you would be. You are a rebel. But you are just misled. I shall heal you."

"But guruji!" Arjun cried. "He broke the rules. He should be thrown out. He hasn't given you dakshina and to be in your Gurukul, one has to pay the fee."

"And he shall," Drona came on his feet. "But not now."

Not now...

And his vision turned blank, darkness enveloping him, like an uncomfortable blanket he wasn't so fond of.

57

Present day...

Karna waited for Shanaya in a dark room, tracing his fingertips around a goblet of wine, mulling over what was happening.

Before talking to Satya, before talking to anyone else, he had to talk to her. She deserved that respect. To hear the truth. To know it under each breath.

And before he knew, she entered, looking graceful as ever in her grey gown and her hair tightly wound up in a bun. She had scars to show, but she was proud of them. Her blue eyes were deep, dark and intense, her face was oval, and her skin shone.

She stood there in silence.

Karna looked at her in quite a different way than he usually did. For she was a kid to him always, but now she would be his wife—if he allowed it, of course. The fire crackled in the hearth and the embers moved like fireflies in the dimly lit tent.

"Did you know about it?" he asked.

Shanaya nodded. "I should have told you, Vasu. I'm sorry."

Karna clenched his jaw. He wasn't angry with her, but then, they were brought under the pretense of an alliance—only it would be of a martial kind. But kings did that. They married dozens of women for their empires.

"Do you want to?" he asked her quietly.

"The question is—do you want to? Ally yourself to a Mleccha."

I don't care. But the world does.

He sighed. "You should know something about me. And if you are okay with it, then only can we talk about it further."

"And that is?"

"I won't be able to ever love you," he said, walking up to her, leaving his goblet behind and locking his eyes with hers. "And I respect you enough to tell you that to your face. You are a beautiful woman and you deserve someone who loves you. Marrying me will mean marrying someone whose heart belongs to someone else."

Shanaya remained stoic; impassive. "Is it the same woman you talked about?"

"Yes."

"But isn't she marrying…"

"I know," he nodded. "But that doesn't change how I feel about her. She might love a hundred men after me, but I can't. It's just not how I function."

Shanaya nodded. "I see. So you wanted to be honest?"

"Yes. You deserve that. And even after hearing this, if you want to marry me, so be it. I'm okay with it then."

He didn't know what she was thinking. But she remained quiet. There was silence between them, an unspoken tremor.

"Then I am marrying for my people. Not because I have loved you since the first time I set eyes on you," Shanaya said.

"You were a child, girl!" Karna blurted.

"I was. But I am not anymore and you are right. You might love someone else, but I love you. And I think that's a curse one lives with," she said. "Are you done?"

Karna paused. *She's hurt.* But she had every right to be that. "Yes, I am."

"Good. If you want, we can start the ceremony."

Karna nodded. And she left. She didn't smile or grin the way she used to. She was just sad and he felt worse than before. He knew speaking the truth would free him, but then he didn't want to hurt others.

What truth is any good when it breaks people's hearts?

He wished he was like Drona or Arjun. Corrupt from the heart. Ready to change.

He shook his head. Perhaps he would win the battle against Jarasandha.

But he felt he was defeated today.

58

Meanwhile in Hastinapur…

Arjun was walking with purpose to the lion's den.

That's what he called his guru's quarters. His guru had received an entire fort for himself, where his soldiers stayed, as did his favourite weapons.

He went through the halls and towards the courtyard, where there stood a fountain.

He saw his Guruji, all poised and practicing. Even in old age, Drona didn't let his limp get in the way. He was practicing in front of a hay target, shooting arrows. His veins were popping out and his beard was glowing like the winter snow. Guards circled around the fort, keeping a watch on their prized guru, while Ashwatthama was in Panchal, where he was building factories to sell weapons.

Arjun hadn't been feeling too good for the last couple of days. While his wound had healed, he was a bit frustrated. Karna's entry at Rangbhoomi was a disappointment. Not only that, Karna got Panchali for himself too. He hadn't talked to her after that, but if he did that would break his heart even further.

How could he tell her that all he did was to impress

her. Arjun was born talented but he knew the drive, the passion, was because of Panchali. He wanted to be fit as a ruler and a warrior for her.

When he had helped his guru take control of Panchal, in the couple of weeks that followed, Draupad had shown a fascination towards Arjun. He had liked him because he had shown strength when others couldn't. Draupad had a way with things—he would believe that the true strength should be with Panchali.

But if her heart was with someone else, what good was it?

Bah.

Or perhaps he was a warrior not for her but for himself. He was just putting the blame on her. He didn't know much. He just knew that whenever he was practicing archery, he would feel good about it only when Panchali was around to see him.

"Arjun, my dear son," Drona said, without even glancing back at him, "I ask and you come."

"Of course, guruji."

"Even after Gurukul has ended, you show discipline," Drona turned and limped towards him. "You show respect towards me. It's very rare."

Arjun smiled. "Of course, a guru is a guru, and it's not subjective to the location."

"Indeed. What are you doing nowadays?"

Mulling.

"Practicing, guruji."

"You know what I hate, son?"

"What?"

"I hate opportunists," he seethed, with poison in his

words. "I hate those who come and like to take things away from others. Selfish, greedy. I hate greed, you know."

"Yes, guruji."

"Do you think Karna is an opportunist?"

Arjun didn't have to think about it. He knew the answer already. "Yes, he is."

"Do you know, I happened to investigate and learnt that the attack on Vijaya dock was conducted by a very skilled archer, wearing a sun symbol. My spy informed me that the villagers saw that symbol. Now who could that be?"

A chill ran down his spine. "It was Karna?" He couldn't believe it. He played all of them.

"Yes. He has used his talents against the empire and for that he must get the worst punishment."

"Treason?"

"No," Drona shrugged, "Dhritarashtra has a problem. He used to be smart, but now he's just emotional. Probably because he wants to connect with his children, which he couldn't earlier. He listens to his son. And we don't have enough proof. The evidence can also be considered coincidental since anyone can be wearing the sun symbol, it is a symbol from Kunti Kingdom. I don't want Rajmata Kunti to face the brunt of it. After all, she's your mother."

Arjun nodded. His mother Kunti was from a kingdom which worshipped the sun and Suryadev, thus had their emblem on their armour. "So what do you want me to do?"

Drona squared in front of Arjun. "I want you to find him."

"And do what?"

He didn't have to say.

"You want me to murder him?" Arjun was surprised.

"But it should look like an accident," he shrugged. "We must do something, or he'll be a greater threat to you down the road."

It didn't sit well with him, just like the time against Panchal. It felt immoral; wrong. But he couldn't question his guruji. That was the law.

"But he has an army now. He's a king…"

While I'm a pauper.

"I know. And because of that," Drona clapped his hands and a soldier arrived, bringing a scroll, glancing at it, "I happen to be in touch with Jarasandha, our rival. He is a bad man, but a diplomatic one. We have a mutual interest—to eradicate Karna."

"But isn't that going against the king himself?"

"No." He put his firm hands over Arjun's shoulder, his hypnotic grey eyes looking at his student. "You need to realise—the moment Karna is eradicated, I shall vouch for you to Dhritarashtra and you shall lead the battle against Jarasandha. Let that stupid king think that I'm betraying my king. He doesn't know I have ulterior motives."

The idea of being a commander to Anga forces fascinated him, even for just leading an army. After all, he had just graduated and wanted to face a ton of action.

"All right, guruji, as you say," he bowed in front of Drona, who returned it with a thin, parasitic, feverish smile from the corner of his lips.

Suyodhan was planning to meet Guru Drona, in hopes of reworking on his old technique of attacking with a mace, when he happened to catch a glimpse of Arjun entering the scene. He hid in the shadows. Arjun looked determined, and Suyodhan followed, hiding behind one of the pillars to hear the conversation between Drona and Arjun.

And he was glad that he did.

For it chilled him to the bone.

They were siding with Jarasandha, to defeat Karna. I must tell father.

He was glad he had come today. Perhaps some divine power brought him here. If Karna fails or dies, his father would not have the same trust that he had on Suyodhan, that he had grown to have on him.

I should meet him.

His mother and father were having a feast in the garden area, where the flowers were blossoming and plants in pots were hung from the beautiful branches around them. Both Dhritarashtra and Gandhari were guided by the servants to eat, until Suyodhan, shoving everyone away, walked inside the scene and bowed.

"Father!"

The blind king turned. "Your mother and I are having an important lunch. Some personal time. I hope this can wait, son."

"No, it can't father."

The king sighed and turned towards him. "Go on."

Suyodhan narrated the entire event he had secretly

witnessed and the king silently listened. He didn't show any expression, but when Suyodhan was done, he said: "Politics is always the virus that grows in an empire and kills it."

"You must imprison Drona and stop Arjun," Suyodhan suggested.

"Imprison? Have you lost your mind, son? He's too valuable to be imprisoned. He's an acharya, a respected man. Don't you think I know about you and him attacking Draupad? My men are everywhere but I stay silent because he's too valuable and he has never hurt me personally or my family. And I know by this action, he plans to eradicate Karna, not me. So I have no threat."

Suyodhan couldn't believe his father's words. "But... but..."

"Listen, Karna is...well...he's just someone to put some brunt on Jarasandha. The moment I feel it's the right time, I shall come in and destroy Jarasandha or make an ally out of him again. We'll see. What's the saying? If you want to win a war, send your idiots first. Let them make some damage and then bring out the soldiers."

"But I thought you believed in him," Suyodhan felt betrayed; angry at his father.

"I do, of course, I do, my son." The king smiled. "But he's expendable. My army isn't. Why do you think I don't support him by giving him my soldiers? Because I want Jarasandha to waste his time on him and when he's weary and bored and tired, I can come in. That's what I did with Karna's father. And it worked. These petty battles should not worry you. You concentrate on your studies."

He clenched his jaw.

"And also for Drona, let him do what he wants. If Karna dies, we will have someone else in his place. I mean, they are replaceable."

"But what Drona is doing is wrong."

"Perhaps. But then who are we to judge what's right or wrong?"

Suyodhan got up, deciding to leave, forcing himself not to utter ill words to his father, when Dhritarashtra said: "Son," his voice had softened, "I know you are angry at me. But this is how a war fucntions. And as for Drona's plan—Karna will always face opposition not just from his enemies but from his allies too. A good king knows how to fight both battles. If he's as good as you say he is, let him deal with it. If he comes out a winner, it will be us who'll be clapping for him, being happy for him. But for now, his battle is *his* battle. Not yours. Not mine."

Suyodhan didn't respond. And walked away, knowing fully well in his heart that he would be leaving for Anga to warn Karna and support his friend.

59

Devi knew how she murdered her abuser, her husband—Senapati Vijaya.

It was a form of aconite she had gotten from a travelling witch doctor. The witch had said it was a powerful poison, also called wolfsbane. One drop of it could wreck havoc in the membranes of cardiac and neural cells.

She had planned it well. She wanted to show it was an actual heart attack; after all, Vijaya was growing old. He couldn't even jog or walk upstairs. She would feed him red meat, something that would slow his heart and he would begin to have chest pains, accompanied by slow breathing. It was a patient process, until she dropped the poison. She had kept it in his drink and had gone out to hunt a boar. When she returned, she showed everyone how devastated she was. But under the smeared kohl and red cheeks and red eyes, was triumph over abuse.

And she had smiled. In silence. In loneliness.

Devi didn't know whether she would feel guilty about it. Perhaps she won't. But she was ruthless and everyone who would come in her way—would die. As she plotted the demise of Karna, she heard the commotion outside. She opened the door to see a bunch of men quarrelling with each other. It was the Nishadhs and her men, and they were fighting. Punching. Kicking, each other.

"Stop it all of you," she scowled.

She saw someone coming towards her quarters and realised it was the pig-faced Shantanu. His head was lowered. "May I talk to you, general?"

"Yes."

They went inside and she sat on her cot, while she listened to the man.

"It has been three days King Karna has been gone and we have a plea, general. We are not happy with how the king is doing. We accepted him as our own, but then he brought in these outsiders."

Devi nodded. "I know, I understand."

"Do you plan to make him understand?"

"I hear you, soldier. Now go and cook some broth for your comrades," she ordered and the soldier nodded.

Devi sighed. Her men were becoming hostile towards her, but she was thinking from Karna's perspective. Perhaps to win, you needed to make other people happy. The Nishadhs were a temporary solution, so she knew they would go away once the war was over.

But still...I have to kill him. His ideas are problematic.

And then she would take over. She guffawed at that thought.

Right then, there was a sudden knock on the door, yet again. She allowed the person to come in, who entered all frantic and said: "General, there are Mlecchas organising camps and building them close to the Nishadhs. Our entire kingdom is surrounded by our enemies!"

What? Mlecchas?

"How are they allowed to camp?"

"The king, general. He has returned with thousands of Mleccha soldiers."

As Karna entered, he was met with silence.

He noticed no smile. Not even an acknowledging nod. No one was happy about how he had brought the Greeks along with him.

Just like before, he had brought a small band of Greeks inside, with Shanaya by his side. The fort was silent, and Satya who was riding his mare along with Karna said:

"And I thought wenches will dance and trumpets will blare when we come. I wonder what happened to their enthusiasm."

Karna grimaced. He knew this would happen. But not to this degree. His own men were frightened. And they should be. They were surrounded by the people they had been fighting for so long. But now was the time to make them understand why he was doing it.

He looked up; locking eyes with Devi, who showed callousness instead of emotions. She remained quiet and seemed done for the day. Her eyes lowered and her lips pursed. She was not happy.

But I'm not here to make people happy I'm here to win a bloody war.

Karna saw each person's face, crossing them on his horse and moving swiftly to the staircase. He dismounted and he could see his people; confused and alienated. The Greeks were guffawing and grinning. They were the animal fur-wearing warmongers, who liked to stay in the forefront. Archimedes didn't accompany them, for he would do it once the war was over and a part of Anga had been carved out.

Karna came upstairs, from where he planned to give the speech, as the ground beneath him was filled with people. Even the citizens were peeking and peering from the corners. They were waiting to find out what the new development was.

"I have returned from my meeting with the Mleccha king, Archimedes. A foreigner," and he could feel the careful, silent gaze of Shanaya, walking around Karna and standing next to him.

Devi, for that matter, was in the corner, not speaking at all, her arms tightened.

"We will win this war with them. The Mlecchas were kind enough to extend their support to us. Now, we know they have not been the most trustworthy in the past, but they are good people. I have had brief encounters with them, when I was struggling to reach where I am today."

All silence.

"The Mlecchas and I have come to a decision to ally with a marital contract. My wife," he held her hands and raised it, "we have married. And you should know that it is important for all of us to realise that we are all in this together. I would like to hold a feast tonight, for you to all get to know each other. My second-in-command, Satya, will organise it. I do not want fights. I do not want quarrels. I want you to all come in one place and see the purpose—of a free Anga. Free of Jarasandha. Of Dhritarashtra. And with that purpose in your mind, befriend your new brothers and your new sisters." He paused. "We will win this war. No matter what. Just like I was born in an Anga ruled by usurpers, I don't want hundreds of children being born right now, to be born in that city. I want them to be free when they are out of the womb. Keep that in mind."

Everyone was unconvinced but he looked at Satya, to begin preparations for the feast. And then he looked at Devi.

It was time to talk.

60

Karna was slumped in his chair thoughtfully, and was being studied by Devi's lethal gaze.

Shanaya was in the corner, crossing her arms. Satya wasn't there, busy as always.

"Is she going to be here in every meeting now?" Devi asked.

"Yes. She's a good warrior. We can take her inputs," Karna replied sternly.

"Great," Devi sighed. "So what next? Partner up with Jarasandha to fight Jarasandha, your highness?"

Karna narrowed his gaze. "Your tone is not appreciated, general."

Devi clenched her jaw.

Karna looked at Shanaya who had a mousy face right now, perhaps frustrated, a tad bit exhausted from the journey.

"We have to discuss something important," Karna said. "Something more important than the current scene at the kingdom."

"The people are not happy," Devi said. "And your decisions will be met with bad repercussions, I warn you."

"Perhaps," Karna shrugged, "but my worry is more

linear. It is the idea of what'll happen when Jarasandha comes. He has given us a scroll, to meet in the middle."

Devi paused and nodded. "Yes. And you plan to reject it?"

"No. I plan to go. I want to hear what he says. What's the latest movement report of his army?"

"He has reached the banks of Champa and his army awaits. We will dispatch troops as well from tonight onwards," Devi responded mechanically. She had memorised the details. "It would be wrong to say he doesn't know about your recent alliances."

"I'm sure he does. And I want him to know. He should be afraid," Karna stood up.

"If he tells you to ally against Dhritarashtra, it is my moral duty to report to him, you know that, right?" Devi said.

"We need to be smart," he said. "I have an idea."

"And what idea would that be?"

You'll know.

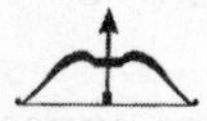

Karna went into the quarters along with Shanaya and they closed the door behind them. They had sent the scroll for a meet up, hopefully by tomorrow or day after, and the sound of festivities was in the background. Shanaya went and changed her clothes with the help of handmaidens, behind the curtain, while Karna stayed and was glumly glancing out the window, where he could hear the Greeks celebrating and some of the Angan soldiers too.

Perhaps they won't understand why he was doing

it. It was a team-building exercise for him. Putting two different sects and given alcohol, even enemies could become friends.

He turned to see Shanaya, who was in her sleeping gown, looking ethereal, with the pale moonlight glistening on her and her black hair, glimmering. She came closer and smiled. "What are you looking at?"

"You have become beautiful as you have grown up."

"Oh, I see. Thank you very much," she chuckled. "That's a very *friendly* compliment."

"Don't push it," Karna chuckled.

"Well, you were the one who said you love only one person."

"And I still do. But I don't see why I can't compliment someone else. Especially my wife."

She grinned. He could see sadness behind her eyes. And he wanted to make her feel good. She was…sad. Well, anyone would be.

"What have you always wanted to do?" he asked.

"I've wanted to always fight in a war," she said. "Die with my men."

"That doesn't sound so appealing."

"It isn't. Because since my childhood, I have seen castrations, ostracising, blood and mayhem. That's what I want to die in. The world is not worth living if you don't die in a grand manner." She spoke with the pride, which he had often seen in Greek people. "What about you?"

"I have a *promise* I made a long time back. Once it's complete, I do not know. I've never thought about it." And before she could ask him what the promise was, he deferred the topic and said: "I hope your men will fit right here."

"Of course they will. Give them a target and they will fight," she chuckled. "Also, I wanted to ask you. Are you sure about me participating in your plan?"

"Doing what?" he said.

"You know."

He nodded. "You are capable."

She shrugged, "I try."

"And you shall succeed. Just be careful."

"You too."

The plan was simple, but effective. Devi was shocked, when she heard it and when he had told Satya, he had just said: "I pray to the god of cunt to bless you with the wisdom that you sorely missed out on." Four years had left him with a bit of a vocabulary, Karna realised.

But it was all right.

For he knew, the meeting with Jarasandha was the beginning or...*the end.*

61

A place was decided.

It was quite an ordinary place. An undulating plain where nothing grew, except for patches of grass. The silver light of the night was beaming on it. One couldn't see much.

And that was the point.

There was no scope of a secret attack. Or an assassination. Since it was a plain field, there were no trees and one could not string an arrow from the top of a branch or hide under the shrubs.

It was a very safe place and two kings meeting each other need to do it in such a place.

It was customary for kings to meet beforehand, before the battle, as a way to find a middle ground. If no middle ground was found, they would return to their camps and the battle would begin. They wouldn't have too many with them, just enough to guard them in a circle and their food would be tested by testers, and there would be music.

Thus, when Karna arrived, Jarasandha was already prepared. He was already seated and was feasting on grapes and apricots.

Karna appeared, and sat down, after he dismounted

from the horse, staring at Jarasandha. He had changed. Karna had heard about how he looked, but he had never seen him up close. He had never noticed how his beard was orangish and he had a cleft on his lips, and no moustache. His hair was cropped and he had wrinkles on his face.

"Finally, after hearing so much about the famed king of Anga," he said, lying down on a carpet, under the moonlight and grinning like a jester, "it is nice to meet you, love."

Karna sighed. He forced a smile. He never understood this thing—between the kings. Why would anyone want to do it? They were going to fight each other and they wanted to meet before that. Why?

But he refrained. And he continued smiling at this vicious man.

"You called me and I am here."

"You brought a healthy amount of soldiers," he looked at them. "Are you afraid I might attack?"

"One can never be too sure."

He shrugged. "If I had to attack, love, I would have done it a long time ago. But I don't care. I have been seeing your developments..." he got excited and with determination looked at him, "what you have been doing. Anga was in a dire state. Malinipur had no men. And when I had waged war against it, I knew it would take me less than an hour to take everything. But seeing you going around the bloody globe to find soldiers for yourself was inspiring. First, you teamed up with the Nishadhs, then the Mlecchas, and only then you attacked me. Before the battle commenced. I should have declared a war on that day itself, but I didn't. Because you showed me something far more superior than a petty battle."

Karna waited. There was something more; his breastplate on which the sun symbol was made, glistened.

"You showed me you have power. You have the strength to fight your odds. You have the strength to do the impossible," he grinned. "And that is something I look for in a king."

"I feel an offer is coming."

"And you have foresight too!" He chuckled. "Yes there is. As you know the truce of Anga was between me and Dhritarashtra. I give you a choice to partner up with me. To fight against the Maharaja and rule Hastinapur together. What say?"

"I am not that strong…"

"You are. You have already amassed a lot of army for yourself."

"Yes, I have," he proudly nodded.

"Yes, you have, indeed," his grin grew wider. "Right now, you are an interim, someone who doesn't have a place. Dhritarashtra can come and take it and you would have no choice. What will you do then?"

He had not thought about it. He wasn't sure himself and his face remained impassive; clenched.

"I wouldn't do that. Under me, you are already a king, not an interim. And you help me take over the crown. Initially, I wanted to defeat you but it's wiser to have you as an ally than an enemy."

Karna nodded. "Indeed."

"Are you a Kshtriya?"

"No."

"Well, you surely are one. Don't you dare lie."

Karna closed his eyes. And he couldn't help but laugh. Jarasandha laughed with him, and he poured some wine for Karna, who drank with him.

"Cheers. But what are you laughing about?" Jara asked.

"I am just surprised how the tables turn. We are going to battle in just a couple of days and look at us—trying to find a middle ground now."

Jara nodded. "That's how politics works, love."

"But there's one thing," Karna said, as he looked behind Jara to check the iron-masked man wasn't present among his soldiers. "You didn't know me. I mean before all of this."

"Should I have?"

"Well, you displaced my father from the throne," he said.

"Adhirath?" He was piqued with interest. "You are the son of Adhirath. Wow, I am shocked. He has surely been blessed with the right progeny. But so did your ally Dhritarashtra. Come on, love, I mean you can't hold that against me."

"I know I can't. And you are right. But you did something worse," Karna nodded to himself.

"What do you mean?"

"I don't know if you remember," Karna said. "This was after you took over Champa and I was just born. I was quite ill at the time. My parents were trying to find a bhisak. And I was…well you did something."

"What did I do?"

He paused. "You killed my mother."

62

22 years earlier…

By the time they reached the closest village in the outskirts of Anga, it had begun to rain.

Spurts of water just smacked on the ground, muddying the roads and the houses, made of red clay walls and wicker windows. They all were huts, just one put after another, with lanes in between where the beggars hid under scorched shawls from the rain.

Radha had her chunni covered over the basket, to deflect the rain, but the basket was drenched even then. She couldn't let more water seep into the child's body.

Adhirath reined the chariot in the middle, but there was no sign of life.

"Everyone has gone inside because of the rain."

She could smell the coconut trees that were shaking hard in the background of the village and cornfields were being plucked out of the ground due to the wind. She could hear the rain, the gusts of wind and the howls of the wolves from afar, as if they had heard of what Radha had done to one of their kind.

And then her eyes fell on the horror, that her dear husband missed.

She let out a silent scream, as she whispered: "It's not because of the rain."

"What?"

With wet arms she signalled over to the walls, showing Adhirath why all of the citizens were inside.

On a few hut walls—men and women and children were nailed with their backs to the road, their buttocks red and their skin torn apart as if with a blade. Maggots and rodents feasted on the corpses. With their blood, it was smeared in Sanskrit: *Shudr will die first.* Shudra, according to the varna system, were considered low castes and pollutants of the society, even though Radha and Adhirath didn't believe in that nonsense.

"Who would do this...?" Adhirath let out a horrible gasp.

The rain had intensified.

"Let's leave from here," he said.

"No. We don't have time. We need to find the bhisak here," she replied.

Adhirath, clenching his jaw, nodded.

"Fine. Let's start knocking on doors."

By the fifth hut, they had almost given up hope.

They were drenched. The child was already wet by now, despite the draped chunni. Few responded to the knocks but they shooed away the couple. Some were just petrified and whispered: "Run or he will catch you."

Or...

"He is here."

No one would tell, who it was. But Radha didn't care. She had to find the bhisak.

She knocked on the next door and began slamming it until a woman with curly white hair opened it partially. She had a long cloth wrapped across her meek body.

"I need to find the village doctor," Radha said, panting.

"You are not supposed to be here," she said. "You are not safe. Leave."

"I want the bloody doctor!" She showed the child. "He's ill."

"And he'll be dead if he's anywhere here in this village."

And she began to close the door when instantly Radha put her foot in between. "You either tell me or I shall rip your tongue out, woman!"

She broadened her eyes in shock and looked down at the child. "He sits at the hill, a hut close to the peepal tree." And then she closed her door on them.

Radha shared a hopeful glance with her husband and then they both looked at the ascending hilltop, which was small and easy to trudge up. That was where the huge basilisk of a tree with a canopy as big as several homes clubbed together, vines hanging like an old woman's wrinkled hands, stood. Silently. Creepily. They also found the hut, where they were supposed to go.

Without further delay, they ascended. Along the way, she pulled the chunni to look at the child. It seemed like he wasn't breathing.

Please stay alive. Please!

She looked up at the skies. "Suryadev, you guided me to him. Don't let him die."

Of course she knew, there wouldn't be any verbal

answer but there was a reply indeed, since when she reached the hilltop, the rain had stopped but the sun was yet to come out.

Anything is better than nothing, she thought.

The gods truly want this boy to be alive.

Adhirath knocked on the door, while Radha waited behind him. She continued to praise Suryadev for his guidance.

After a while, the door opened.

And an old bearded man stood in front of them with a saffron angavastram around his hip. A mala made of miniature conch shells dangled from his neck. He was hunched.

"I'm just a humble bhisak. I'm a Brahmin," he clarified, as if he thought they were one of those who had killed those Shudras. "I'm not your enemy."

"We are not here to harm you. We are not those killers or any part of their group," she clarified. "We are here because of the baby…he's ill…he was umm…" and then she stopped, biting her lips, as she glanced at the exhausted Adhirath. "Please help us…we have nowhere else to go."

The doctor blinked at them and then with a shrug, opened the door wide. "Come in."

With a smile on their lips, Radha and Adhirath did so, when they heard something in the back. From far, the hooves of black stallions hitting the wet ground was audible. Yells and scowls were heard from down the hill. The stallions were huge in size and Radha had seen these kinds in Angadesh. They were direct imports from Persia and were more powerful than ordinary Indian horses. And they only belonged to the royalty.

"He's here," the bhisak shivered.

"Who is he?" Radha asked, stepping inside the hut.

The bhisak mumbled under his breath, uttering that dreadful name:

"Jarasandha."

63

"What happened here?" Radha asked, as the bhisak treated the child.

"What usually happens when Jarasandha arrives. Chaos and unnecessary slaughter," he responded, as he began to touch the nerves and feel the child by the throat, the chest and the legs and then pumped some air in the chest, to push out the water inside, which trickled out from the sides of the infant's pale lips. "He has swallowed saline water and he was exposed to cold weather for a long time. It's almost a…a…miracle, he is alive. He is breathing but very slowly."

Radha nodded. *One hell of a miracle it was.* She thought. She was on a stool while Adhirath was drinking water from a terracotta jug.

"I'll just make a concoction," the bhisak went to his table and pulled out tulsi flowers from a jar, some black and long pepper, ginger powder and honey—he began to mix with a pestle and mortar, made of copper. "I am not sure whether it'll work but I can try."

"Why is Jarasandha harming innocent villagers?" Radha asked again, intrigued, while she kept peering from the window to see if any Persian stallion could be seen around.

None so far.

Fear dictated her actions.

She knew time was of utmost urgency as Jarasandha and his men would at anytime find her and her husband with the child.

"You saw the corpses?" the doctor asked.

"Yes," Radha nodded.

"Those are the men who rebelled. Jarasandha's men detected good corn production in this village's farms. He faced a…uh…rebellion of sorts from the farmers when he tried to take over the farms. He nailed them all because they were all shudras. Bloody mongrel! No other caste—be it a vaishya, kshtriya or a brahmin—of this village spoke up. They were silent. Quiet. As if the shudras' lives didn't matter," the bhisak continued. "He searches for more low class, but to be honest, he doesn't care which caste it is. He just uses it as a reason to kill people. He just wants what he wants and he gives out these flimsy reasons. Whoever opposes him, automatically becomes a shudra since shudras can be killed and no one is likely to protest for them. They are, in the strictest terms, nobodies. And who cries for a nobody?"

Radha gritted her teeth. She wasn't aware about this part of Jarasandha's character. She glanced at Adhirath who had his pesky chest up high and his moustache glistening under the candles inside the hut.

"Guruji," he began, "you must know that we cannot afford to give you anything in kind. We have coins but we know the bhisak doesn't take monetary transactions."

"It's all right," the doctor shrugged. "It's a child. I'm more than happy to help him," he paused. "Is it your child?" he asked.

Radha said, "Yes."

"Okay," the bhisak nodded.

He had made the paste, moving towards the infant, and with it he slowly he began to slip it inside the infant's mouth, but he spat it out.

"Help me," he told Radha.

She came on her feet, coming close to the child.

"Hold the baby," the bhisak said.

She nodded, holding him awkwardly. She didn't know how to cradle him in her arms as she was a nervous wreck, but the bhisak positioned her arms in the correct way, with the head of the child on her right arm, while the left arm acted as a platform for his back.

"Feed it to him," the bhisak said.

"Why me?" She was shivering and she was nervous. She had never held a child in her life, in her arms like this.

"Because a child will never refuse anything that his mother gives."

She nodded, taking the paste in her pinky finger and putting it close to the icy lips of the infant. His lips brushed across her skin and they were so soft, so cold. And then slowly she could feel the gums and the tongue just lapping up the sour tasting paste. Very slowly.

"Give me more."

And she did it again, the gums and tongue moved quicker this time and she liked the tickling sensation on her skin. A smile forming on her lips.

"It feels nice," she muttered and she saw Adhirath, who came to stand next to her and hugged her sideways with his hands on her shoulder. "The way he does it, like just nibbling on it, like a…like a…squirrel." She chuckled at her husband, unable to believe that tears had formed in her eyes. "He seems better."

"You should leave," the bhisak interrupted. "Jarasandha will be coming any moment and you would become his victims. If he gets to know you are Sutas, you will be nailed just like the others."

Radha nodded. So did Adhirath. "If we keep giving him the paste, will he be fine?"

"Hardly," the bhisak said. "He will be a little weak. I would suggest you leave the infant here and run for your lives. I can tend to him in patience and you can return when things calm down."

"What if Jarasandha comes?" Adhirath asked.

"I'll hide the boy. What else?"

Radha couldn't believe that this idea was even proposed. "I can't leave my child like this. Not when there is a mongrel around."

"He's safer with me more than with you. Also, he needs his medication. The paste I gave is just a preliminary measure. He needs sun, lots of sun to get some energy. And as of now, I see no bloody sun. It's damp," the bhisak said, peering from the window where the clouds were roaring. "You both cross the corn fields and ignore the corpses. Reach the Ganga river and hopefully at the bank, there will be an abandoned fisherman's boat since Jarasandha even managed to kill the fishermen and fisherwomen. If you return to your vehicle, Jarasandha will know. Take the boat and run for your lives. Perhaps in a few weeks you can return to check up on the boy and I'm sure he will be fine."

Adhirath turned to Radha, showing his back to the

bhisak. “He has a point, my love. We can be safe for now and return later for the boy.”

Radha glared at him and even though she wanted to slap him for agreeing to this idea, it made sense. So much sense, that she was conflicted. “What if…what if he’s hurt? What if…”

“He’ll be safe here,” Adhirath patted on her shoulder.

And with bile stuck inside her throat, every cell in her body screaming *NO*—she said:

“Fine.”

64

Radha had reached the corn fields when doubt began to shadow her judgment.

It hung like an amulet in front of her, just acting as an instrument of morality. She didn't want to leave the child for selfish reasons, and yet she knew it was the right thing to do.

"Will he be fine?" she asked for what felt like the hundredth time.

"He will be, my love. Don't worry."

The skies were favourable now, even though there was a sliver of grey overcasting. Seagulls fluttered above their heads. Radha trampled on the weeds which made a crunching sound, as she passed inside the corn field whose plants were double her height. They were well hidden from the outside world.

"My gut says we shouldn't leave him behind," she said.

Adhirath had been holding her hand, and he pressed it harder. She felt he was about to shoot her down, but instead he trusted her. "You are always right about these things. Why do you feel that way?"

"I don't know. Just intuition."

There was a short chuckle from his end.

"What?" she arched her brows.

"My mother used to have that too whenever I would go out to play with the kids. We would climb hills and race to the top. One can get hurt, in all the hastiness. She would know I was hurt even before I was and when I did, she would wash my wounds," he smiled to himself. "She called it a mother's intuition," he paused. "He needs his medicines but. How will you assure that? If we take the boat to Champa," he referred to the capital of Angadesh, where they lived and the only land which was untouched by Jarasandha, "it'll take us a few hours and it could potentially risk the child's life."

Radha shook her head. "I'm sure he will be fine. I have trust."

"But why?"

"What?" she was dumbfounded by the question.

"Why?" he asked again.

She looked down, at their hands which were tightly clasped and she said, recalling her past: "I was five when I was lost in a fair. I tried finding my mother for the longest time, but I never got to her, until a priest helped me and we found her. When my mother saw me, she was shocked to see I was with a priest."

He was taken aback. "You mean..."

"Yes, she never really knew I had vanished for hours. She didn't care." Tears fell down her cheeks and she wiped them away. "The reason why I never wanted to be a mother was because I never understood what a mother's role is in a child's life. They are potential destroyers of the child, just like how my mother scarred me. I was also afraid I might end up like my mother. But after I married you, things were different. I realised I can be better and I tried a lot to have a child until Vasu was gifted to us by Ganga mata," she paused. "I don't want to leave my child like how my mother did. I want to have him. In my arms. For as long as I can."

Adhirath grabbed her by the cheeks and kissed both of them. "You are nothing like her."

She nodded, shaking by the jaw, feeling numb at her knees.

Adhirath had a clenched jaw, and he just stared at her with rigidity. "You have always been an emotional fool. And that's why I love you. Let's go."

"No," she put her hand on his chest, "you leave and get the boat. I'll get our child. Then we are leaving."

A sense of elation burst in her eyes.

"Yes, we are, my love. Yes we are." And she kissed him hard on the lips, before heading for the bhisak's hut.

By the time she reached, she regretted her decision and was grateful she was there.

Yards away from the hut was the peepal tree, where the bhisak was being hung from. A stool was kept underneath, so he could rest his feet on it.

Around his suspended body, which struggled over the stool were five individuals, all with bronze armour and iron swords.

Except for one.

He stood in the middle, Radha noticed. Shorter than most, neckless, but had a dyed orange beard which hid his insecurity of having no throat. He had a cleft on his upper lip, bulgy eyes like that of a frog's and short, curly hair, black as charcoal. He had a wrestler's body, tight muscles, broad chest and thick thighs over which he wore a dhoti. A mani dangled in the form of an amulet. A lapis lazuli ring on his pinky finger. The most distinctive part about the man was his inked jewellery. There was a process of *gudna* where with needle dipped in ink, a beautiful design was created on your skin and acted as an ornament.

But her attention was directed back to the bhisak who was alive for now. With a loud scream, she said to the monsters: "LEAVE HIM!"

They all turned.

The inked man came forward, with a malicious smile. There was something unsettling about him, Radha could feel it. As if adharm has taken a new birth and appeared in person.

"And who might you be, love?"

She didn't say anything. Frozen. She didn't even have her knife with her while all these men were carrying some sort of a blade except the inked man. He had a scourge—a kind of a whip with mini-blades attached to it.

"Let's start with me then, if you are shy," he continued. "I'm Jara. King Jara. And these are my men."

A shiver ran down her spine.

No. I was right. The baby is unsafe.

But where is he?

The bhisak in between all the struggles as he tried to free his neck from the noose said, "Leave, girl. Leave!"

"You know her?" Jara turned back to the old man. "Oh wait, hold on there. You are the newcomers to my village. It was your chariot out there, right? It belongs to Adhirath, the failure of a king. My men told me about the chariot, you see. Your people are the worst. Me and your king Dhritarashtra, we made an alliance, but your people still rebel and because of you…" He shrugged with a lethal, grievous expression, as he walked to the bhisak.

"The doctor is a Brahmin. Why are you killing him?" Radha asked, with clenched fist.

"Any man who assists a low caste is a low caste himself," Jara said. "Had to interrogate a few villagers to know that a couple was trying to find a doctor."

"You are crazy," she said.

"I'm told that often," Jara sniggered and his laugh was this coughing, wheezing sound. All his men laughed along with him.

He was a Chandravanshi, who were the royal bloodline, supposed descendants of the moon-god Chandra, thus they worshipped the moon. They were valiant, but here Jara…he defied everything the Chandravanshis stood for.

"Where's your husband, bitch?" he asked.

Radha didn't say anything.

"Ugh fine, bore me. I might as well do something fun." And then he pushed the stool on which the bhisak was standing.

He began to choke and in his final flurry of redness he screamed: "BABY…UNDER…TABLE!"

Jara and all his men had their attention on the bhisak and when he said that, they got alarmed. Jara turned to Radha. "Baby?"

That was when Radha made a swerve and sprinted towards the hut. Jara did so himself, as his men were dumbstruck as to what had just happened.

Radha, beating through the fire that rose in her chest, numbness cascading inside her body, raced to the door of the hut and leapt inside.

Jara wasn't too far behind her, but Radha with a quick swerve kicked the door close on him. Jara fell back, rolling over as she hurtled herself at the door and with a bamboo string that was lopsidedly hanging from the corner of the door, tied it from all sides, so Jara couldn't enter.

"You can't escape from me, bitch. You can't," she heard Jara's voice.

Radha instantly went for the table and threw it over to see the child was in the same basket as she had left him, with the shawl on top of him. She left the basket and took the child in her hand and cradled it, grabbing hold of the earrings too, but not the breastplate, the *kavach*. He wasn't so cold as earlier, but he also wasn't opening his eyes.

Radha began to measure her options. There was only one exit and that was guarded by Jara.

She hugged the child against her chest, tears in her eyes, as she wondered, what she could do right now.

Suryadev, you have been protecting this child for so long...please do it again.

There was no response. Panting, she looked at the windows to see what Jara was up to, but instead she saw no one.

Has he left?

But she was too quick to think that, as the next moment she felt warm. She smelled smoke. She heard the crackling of the wood.

Arching her brows, she realised what it was.

Fire.

FIRE!!!

By the time, he had appeared in front of her, she was hyperventilating—then he brought out a knife.

He pulled it out and attacked, stabbing her, when she felt a certain pang and fell forward, rolling downwards.

She realised the pain was going to stay with her for a while.

For how long, she had no idea.

She rolled over, as she could feel everything blurring. But she knew she had to make a run for the boat. Where Adhirath was waiting...

65

Present day...

"Ever since that fateful day, my mother has gone through excruciating pain where you stabbed her. Initially, we thought it could be cured, but it was poison. The slow kind. And then over the years, the pain throbbed, made it worse. She took medicines, but nothing worked. She continued to hold on to her smile, but the fever continued to get heavy on her, perhaps the gods were merciful on some days, but barring that she was in constant pain until the end when she was..." He paused, taking a deep, slow breath. "She knew and I knew and everyone knew that death was imminent, but it was prolonged—the pain. The only reason she stayed with the pain was for me and my brother."

He looked up at the pale Jarasandha, on whom realisation had just dawned.

He wanted to say something but he coughed. He asked the musicians playing in a corner to stop and he eyed Karna. "So *that's why.*"

"I was born in Anga but it was not what you usurped that drives me to kill you. My intense desire to kill you stems from the fact that you tortured my mother her whole living life," he came on his feet.

"You don't have to do this," Jara said. "You don't have to leave. Become an ally to me. Let bygones be bygones."

"That's easy for you to say."

He narrowed his gaze "Trust me, it isn't. Anga stole my wife from me."

Karna nodded. "I grieve for her then. But I firmly believe in the idea of karma."

"How dare you say that?"

Karna smiled. "I'm going to kill you, your highness. It's just a matter of time."

And he walked to the horse that was waiting for him.

He didn't wait much longer, but the grape in Jara's mouth remained static. He was confused and alarmed. Karna's horse neighed and as the sun had begun to rise, he left.

And he never looked back.

Jara felt an extreme amount of hatred for himself and towards the new fool.

He thinks he can fight me. He wants a war. I'll give him a war.

Jara was on his chariot, already drunk with rage and looking straight at the camp. His camp. It was miles away from the banks of Champa, and it was littered with hundreds of camps and bonfires and even a watchtower where his scouts were positioned. They were looking through their spyglasses and watching from afar, to notice any movement.

He had entered and before he could talk to his captains about the battle plans, he realised the commotion that had taken place.

People were running. The nurses and the bhisaks' tents were on fire. Lots of oil drums were ripped apart, as well as the food trunks and water supplies.

Jara saw his soldiers were sprinting towards the back end of the camps, and he raced there too, in exhaustion and in anticipation, to figure out what had just happened.

He reached the southern part, where he found a familiar figure standing with her white, pale gown and her loose, curled hair.

Vrishni.

"What happened?" he squared next to her.

"Attack. A silent one."

And in front of her, lay the waste—camps burnt, lots of food and water reserves destroyed, even the armouries that he carried were smashed to bits, and horses stabbed to death. The stables were burnt, it was all mayhem. The backside of the war camp was always the less protected area and anyone who's attacking is aware that it's also the most vulnerable.

But no one does, as the war camp emerges in vast territory. And at the front, everyone was well-equipped. But the southern part was dedicated to cattle and livestock for food and also the water turbines. Everything stayed there and was the lifeblood of the entire war camp, as the battle raged for days. They couldn't keep going back and forth from the city to the camp, so they brought the necessities with them.

Though the necessities weren't here now.

"Who was it?" he asked her and he shouldn't have asked her, but she was closest to him and his captains were busy reprimanding others.

"The Nishadhs, though led by a Greek apparently, according to the reports," she shrugged. "You were played by the boy, Jara. Be careful."

Jara instantly showed a surge of anger and he wanted to grab her neck and pin her down, but relented. Kaal would get angry. He sighed. "How did he come from behind?"

"One can only hope we find out this answer."

Jara moved away from her, and went to one of the captains, asking him, "Have we lost men?"

"They were only knocked down, your highness. In fact, it's uncanny for them to attack like this. They didn't kill any one of our men, but destroyed all of our supplies."

They want to deplete my resources.

Jara cursed. "If we begin the war, it'll be stupidity. He wants me to incite the war."

"Perhaps, your highness."

"But I won't. How much time will it take for us to bring back more supplies from the city?"

The captain looked afraid and scatterbrained. The question bugged him as they both knew the war would be indefinitely delayed, no matter how much man-power they used.

"Ugh, fine. Just bring the leftover supplies from the south to the east of the camp. Keep it under good watch."

"All right, your highness. Though I have a feeling, he won't be attacking us like this again."

One can never be sure.

The sun had risen and the orange flares were on Jara's face, which had livened up. He knew he had been played and Vrishni was right, but by that time, his eyes fell over the watchtower where his guards were drumming hard and blowing their horns.

The captain went pale. "*Your highness...*" He gasped.

It was a war signal.

The battle had begun. But...

I was wrong. He didn't want me to start the war.

He is bringing the war to me!

66

The arrow in the sky looked like a beacon of hope.

Except it wasn't.

It was the damnation of a soldier, as it pierced through the armour and went through the flesh—the fire that burnt, the pain that it caused, left the soldier on the ground, crushed, with dirt all over the man's face.

And over his body, ran hundreds of feet.

Or perhaps even more.

They moved on horses, on elephants and on chariots, as the two sides of the war met and clashed and crashed brutally, with swords flinging. The infantry of both sides of the battle was in the forefront, while the cavalry with its horses were swinging their long spears and stabbing each other's enemies. They were ramming the shields and breaking their armours, helmets toppled and skulls were crushed. It was absolute chaos. Absolute bloody chaos, with crimson pools forming under the orange sun that was glistening over them, giving them warmth in the icy land of the dead.

The archers were at the back and they were dipping their arrows in oil, lighting them up and shooting them across the sky that ignited and crashed against the enemy arrows, the reeds were broken and their splinters spilled on the ground, showering over the unsuspecting soldiers.

Satya wasn't supposed to be a part of the war. It didn't make sense to be here. Not now. He was on the ground, far at the back, ordering his men to shoot the arrows and letting the archers butcher the people.

As it happened, another set of arrows came from Jara's men and he put his shield up, as the cascading arrows smashed against the shield.

He ordered another set of men to cover the eastern flank, attacking Jara from the side, as he gazed across the horizon to see if he could find Jara, but he wasn't there.

Of course he wouldn't be.

He was the bloody king. He would sit in his tent and order his captains to do his dirty work. But Satya glanced at Karna's horse. He looked ordinary, rather than a king. Humility showed on his face and he had a helmet on, ornate and golden in colour, with his thick beard that had mangled and grown more than it was supposed to. His entire chest was covered with the breastplate and he seemed like any other soldier.

But that was the plan.

The soldiers, if they found the king, would corner him, and thus the king had to be hidden when he fought. So he succeeded without even letting anyone know.

Karna went into the battle, leaving behind the horse and moving ahead with the help of his archery. Satya used to have that sense of impatience and virility once upon a time.

But he was an old man now.

He brushed through the handlebar moustache that had grown on each side of his mouth, as he ordered the men further…

When he saw.

A young boy, a soldier of his infantry, was lying dead. And so were many others.

Something stopped him from going in the battle but… he could hear the words: *Captain! Captain!* Someone was shouting but he could only imagine the comfort of the drug Soma. How warm it was. How it would feel and give him euphoria but also help him lose his head and forget about the world.

But seeing his men die like that, it was important for him to do something. Far more important to be here, than to be in a selfish world one creates for themselves.

And so he did.

He dismounted, a sword in his hand as he moved further and each step of his caused a tremor on the ground. He came close, his bones shivering, but courage was planted in his heart. Fight for Anga! Fight for Anga! He would repeat the words as he slashed the incoming soldiers, deflected a volley of fire arrows with his shield and moved another sword against the man, when he was parried and shoved away, his shield snatched.

And before the enemy could attack him, out of nowhere a horse just smacked the opponent on the face and ran over him.

For a moment, Satya was confused and derailed, but he caught his wits.

Soma…Soma…

His thoughts went there, sweeping in a direction...

I can't be here.

And he skid further away, his heart beating ruthlessly. But not out of fear, as he scampered away from the thick of the action, but out of guilt.

Shanaya fought for her people.

And it wasn't the people she associated herself with—the Angans were not the ones who she fought for. It was the Greeks.

If Karna would have married her and loved her, she would have felt all of this belonged to her. But it didn't. It belonged to only him and she was helping him fight for her father, Archimedes. She had a good relationship with him and humour was a big part of it, but when it came to the battlefield, one had to be selfish.

That's what her father always said.

And she was in the thick of the battle; one of the very few ladies in the battlefield, but she still made an impact.

She knew amidst the arrow thrashing and the loud yells, shrieks, the shields falling—there was Devi too. She was in the far corner.

Shanaya had a hammer for a weapon, as well as a shield for herself and with it, she was moving towards anybody that she could find—and she would slam it against the enemy. Her Greek comrades were close to her and they had created their own little circle of death, formed out of spears.

"RAIN OF FIRE!" Shanaya yelled.

And they all held up their shields, as another volley just slammed on their shields and they covered it well.

"MOVE IN!" she ordered again.

And the circle continued further, until it dispersed as an elephant feet came in between, smashing them on the ground, and Shanaya leapt away, as most of her men were crushed under the large feet on which Jara's mahout sat.

Gritting her teeth she moved for the elephant and began to smack its feet. As she did, the elephant loudly shrieked and made a sound of trumpets that would haunt her and lifted its two feet before crashing them on the ground, killing people from his own side as well as hers.

She narrowly escaped, as she fell in one corner, when Shanaya saw an Angan soldier, who was on the ground, begging her for help as an enemy constantly struck him with a sword...

When she looked the other way and moved for the Greek soldier, who had lost his leg as she grabbed him by the shoulders and brought him away, moving back to the camp to fend for him and nurse him.

Battles were not at all organised.

They were all over the place.

And Karna had never been in one. But here he was, and he felt guilty. He should have been more prepared. Five minutes into the battle, he had already fallen from the horse and on the ground, he was confused, devastated and horrified.

He could feel a knife was planted on his breastplate

and he had no idea how it came about. It was pierced right there, and he pulled it out.

He did bring a sword along, for safety's sake, as well as a shield that was on the back where his crimson cape was flowing. His breastplate gleamed as he began to use his arrows, shooting anyone who came in front of him.

A soldier appeared next to him and he propelled his sword and swung it across his chest. It made him fall on the ground.

Karna brought out four arrows, as he saw four soldiers coming towards him, and with one stroke of his bow, he shot all four together, in the head.

And before Karna could get comfortable and control his heavy breathing, he felt a tug in his throat that was making him lose control; as he was having trouble inhaling, worse happened.

He felt a searing pain, as a hand grabbed him from behind and smacked him on the ground like a puppet. He took a bit of time to come on his feet, as he turned around and saw a large axe moving towards him, when he rolled over and pulled out his arrow, shooting it at the enemy's face.

But the arrow just made a clanging noise, and bounced off the iron.

Oh no, it's him.

He saw the iron-masked man, as he circled around him, while Karna gained his momentum and stood up, feeling the lightness of his quiver and realising—he had only a few arrows left on him.

The iron-masked man looked bigger and scarier for some reason, and he propelled himself further against

Karna, who dodged him narrowly and launched a quick shot at the nape of his neck, which stung him.

But that didn't stop the iron-masked man, who instantly swung the axe carving it inside Karna's chest as he fell back. The iron-masked man came forward and brought his big arms across Karna's throat and began to choke him when Karna smacked him on the throat, with a punch, on which he choked and Karna rolled back, shooting another arrow...

Not at him, but at the incoming enemy behind, who were going for a silent attack on him.

The tug in his throat still remained, as he saw the iron-masked man bringing the axe and then swinging it across Karna's face, which he deflected, but it slashed through his arm and he felt an excruciating pain vibrating through his entire body.

For a moment, he was dizzy as he was unable to breathe too.

I'm a failure.

Even though he didn't want that thought to overpower him, it was there and he licked his lips and concentrated on battling the man in front of him...

When suddenly a shadow jumped over the iron-masked man and grabbed him by the throat.

Karna didn't have to see to know it was none other than Devi who was on him, holding him by the throat, as Karna brought out the last arrow and went for another shot...

Aiming at the eye socket which was visible through the mask.

And it flew across the muddy field, moving for the iron-masked man's face...

But he grabbed it in between and used that arrow to stab Devi in the arm, who didn't loosen her grip even though she was crying and shrieking.

"I'LL KILL YOU!"

But the iron-masked man grabbed her head and shoved her on the ground. He went for a punch, which she blocked with her armour and Karna came forward, grabbing the nearest fallen spear and stabbing him in the gut.

The iron-masked man bled and was confused, before he pulled it out.

"FALL BACK! FALL BACK!" Karna heard his captains calling out.

"We need to leave," he said to Devi, who nodded.

She didn't attack the iron-masked man, who remained there and didn't attack as Karna's men were pulling back and so were Jara's. Even though he could have attacked, the iron-masked man continued to look at them as Devi and Karna began to slide into the background.

"Thank you," he said. "I would have died if it wasn't for you."

Devi walked beside him, holding on to her slashed wound, and responded: "It's nothing personal. You saved me. I saved you. We are even."

And with a roll of her eyes, she moved ahead, while Karna rushed to the camp.

In confusion, he saw his men bringing other wounded or dead soldiers. The battlefield in front of them was closing up and it lay scattered with bodies. The war camps would now assign Chandalas to go and grab corpses for cremation.

But in these battles, one didn't know *who* won.

From where he stood though, and seeing his army almost cut and sacked in the middle of the ground—he realised he had lost.

67

Jara had been studying the landscape from the comfort of his tent. He even had his scouters who had returned to him and narrated how the battle had unfolded. As long as the conclusion was in his favour, he was glad.

The battle for now had been won by them, because it was Karna's side of the army that had fallen back and he was grinning at the triumph, even though tomorrow would be another day.

He had ordered his men to stand guard for the night, in case there was an attack, while the ones who were wounded were either sent back or were being nursed back to health. And the ones who survived were showered with wenches, wine and food as they were filled and fattened up for they did a good job. Long rows of tables and chairs were placed and his soldiers had food, while some of them just rested. Hundreds of them were ordering their cheese, their wines and their roast. Chickens and goats were being cut to be cooked and served.

Even Jara, for that matter, was cherishing the moment. He had a long chat with his captains who told him that tomorrow would be their day and it would take less than three days for the entire battle to be over.

He congratulated them and asked them to feast, when he saw the wounded and unharmed Kaal enter and glance at him. Jara would have congratulated him for breaking down Karna's weapon—his hand—but Vrishni was around him like a dog on a leash.

Jara was glad that Vrishni was the one who gave Kaal the mighty powers he now possessed but she was also his damnation.

Jara entered his tent, followed by Kaal and Vrishni, who were standing solemnly.

Jara took a moment to sip his wine and lie down on the cushions and with a wide grin, he said: "Now the boy knows who he's dealing with."

"Yes, you have shown him," Vrishni said, circling the silent, dormant Kaal.

"So, what do you need? Why are you here?"

"I shared something with Kaal. Something that stuck out like a thorn and I thought I should share it with you, once he said that it makes sense."

"He *said*?" Jara guffawed. "After you made him into this creature, he has stopped speaking. He has become..."

"A soldier," Vrishni completed the sentence and Kaal with wounded eyes, watched Jara. "You don't have to worry about what he has become. He still loves me. He's my boy. But you need to start realising that Karna is a formidable enemy and not some kid you can just throw off."

"And why do you say that?"

Vrishni came in front and her voice was almost like a whisper, while her necklace gleamed: "Didn't it strike you as strange that he attacked a portion of your supplies but left a large amount of food and wine, not hurting it at all?"

"He must have been in a hurry. They saw the first thing they attacked."

"And yet the wine caskets were untouched."

By the third eye of Lord Shiva, she can't even let me enjoy my winnings.

"What are you implying?"

"That this battle he started was a ploy."

"What do you mean?" Jara came on his feet, eyes narrowing, anger surging.

"It was to make you feel that you had won and you would celebrate and drink those bloody caskets of wine, and also to distract you from having this thought, which he succeeded in, as you were busy in battle, but I had the time to think."

"You mean he poisoned them?"

"Perhaps."

"Bah! That sounds preposterous..."

And then they heard it. A soldier appeared without even a notice inside the tent and with a sweaty forehead said: "Your highness...something is happening..."

"What?"

"The soldiers...they are having a stroke!"

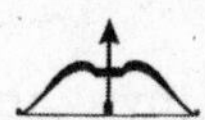

Jara, Kaal and Vrishni rushed to the feast where earlier music was being played, but now only silence prevailed, as hundreds of soldiers were having a stroke, foaming at their mouth and contorting.

What is happening?

He ordered the soldier next to him, who had come to inform him: “Check all the outposts of the camp. Is it happening with them too?”

“Yes, your highness.” And he rushed off leaving a trail of smoke behind.

Jara remained there, as the bhisaks and the nurses arrived at the scene and tried to check out the problem, while he remained static. The wine was poisoned. Of course, Vrishni was right. And as he turned to the sorceress, she was already busy checking the eyes of one of the victims, who was foaming.

“I have seen this before,” she said.

“What do you mean?”

“From where I come,” she began, “this is one of the teachings of *Maya*.” She talked about the Rakshas magic which was less of sorcery and more of a science. After all, she was a Rakshasi and looked more civilised than her male counterparts, but the myths of the Rakshas have been going on forever and they weren’t as primitive as they were thought to be. Their knowledge in science and other studies led them to cut down humans and test on them, and thus they were called cannibals. “It’s a way to really cut down your enemy’s offence.”

“Hows’ that?”

“By making the enemy’s army a bunch of raging monsters. Creatures. Cannibals. There’s a certain parasite—*toxoplasma gondii*—which kind of manipulates the cognitive way of looking at things and makes the person…well in simplest terms…crazy. He didn’t poison them. He just turned your men against you!”

And when she said it, one of the men just stood up and with bloodshot eyes moved for Jara, when Kaal came in between and stabbed the man's head, who then fell on the ground.

"And if you hypnotise them..." she said, "...into believing they are a particular cannibal like a weretiger or a pisach, you would have a formidable enemy who will think that way. But the question is, how did he get access to it? From another Rakshasi, of course."

"How does it matter?" Jara shrugged. "Kaal, kill all of those present here. Stab them."

"NO!" shrieked Vrishni. "I can reverse it. Just give me some time. Kaal, my boy, bind them, as many as you can."

"Will you be able to cure them?"

"Yes," she confidently said. "But you better hope that kid doesn't attack you because your army is next to dead."

"I have some left. I will..." he gritted his teeth. *He wants me to surrender but I shall not.*

Jara ordered the remaining soldiers to go to the infirmary and get the wounded to help them too as they had lost a large number of soldiers in a very short amount of time. And while he saw Vrishni going through different potions and pastes, he realised that her coming here did work in his favour, in some way or the other.

And he was glad. But also horrified, that Karna had played him again. Jara couldn't be so stupid and he smacked his forehead in frustration, and turned to leave for his camp, while his men gathered their wits, when he saw a hooded shadow standing in front of him.

He had come out of nowhere, like a silent spectator amidst the running and the clashing of the people around them.

Then he took off the hood before Jara could ask him, he saw the long locks of hair just dancing on his shoulders, with sharp, stormy grey eyes like that of the clouds and a definite, handsome face. A nose-ring, on a sharp nose.

"Who are you?" Jara asked. For some reason, he felt familiar but he couldn't place the figure.

"I believe he has really nicked all of you," the boy chuckled; barely Karna's age, perhaps even younger.

"You come here to my camp," Jara walked to the boy, who was slender in frame, not burly like the famed wrestler, "and you insult me. Identify yourself."

He pulled out a scroll and Jara snatched it from him, his back turned to the boy as he read it, noticing the familiar words. "Ah, I see. I was not thinking of entertaining this because I thought I would win."

"But he stumped you," the boy said. "I can help.'

"You know, it makes me wonder, why should I trust you?" Jara asked.

He smiled. A slimy smile. "Because we have a mutual friend and an enemy."

"What do you have in mind?" Jara asked.

"An ambush," he said.

Jara narrowed his gaze. "I see."

And before he could say anything further, he heard the gurgles of a man reaching out for him, to grab him and eat him, when the boy brought his bow and arrow, and shot it in the skull, tearing apart the eyes and the brain, scattering them on the ground. It was inches away from Jara and if he had just been a little towards the left, Jara's head would have gone with it.

"Nice aim," he shrugged. "We are having a bit of a team morale crisis going on right now."

"Never thought Karna could peg all of you like this."

Beats me too, kid.

But he was smart. And Jara had to be smarter than him. He had to stop underestimating his enemy.

"Do you drink wine?"

"Sure."

"Good." Jara came forward and smiled. "It's nice to finally meet you, Prince Arjun of Hastinapur."

Arjun smiled. "Not so nice. Since we have a mutual problem."

And Jara could only wonder what it was.

68

The hooves slammed against the ground, in the windy night.

Suyodhan had the reins of leather in his hand and he was leaning forward on his stallion, as he made his way through the path which would lead to Karna, and Malinipur. He had left the comfort of his home in the darkness and had escaped. He didn't let anyone, not even his men, follow him. He went quickly as his absence would be met with dismay and worry, especially by his mother—he had to reach Karna, and tell him what was going on.

His beard and his hair were being caressed by the wind, and the hoofbeats were the only noise in the otherwise silent forest.

Suyodhan kept glancing behind, to see if he was being followed. That there was no ambush in these woods, even though they were dark. He didn't carry his mace, but a meagre sword along with him, as a mace would slow down his horse.

Come on. Fast!

He had camped in between, sometimes in the wood, at other times in the villages and towns that he would come across. He was dependent on the niceness of the humans, who were shockingly sweet to a stranger like him, giving him curd and rice to eat. They didn't know he was the prince and the heir to Hastinapur and Suyodhan knew that when he would return to the safety of his kingdom, he would shower those who had helped him with wealth.

As the hours went by, his eyes were getting droopy and his face was growing slack, when he saw something in front of him and tugged on his reins as the horse neighed in the dead of night, the crickets croaked and the owls watched with round eyes, as to what happened.

Suyodhan saw the shadow was lying on the ground and could hear a weeping sound. He dismounted and found a young girl, who was slain with her guts spilled out, her face pale and she was crying like anyone in her condition would. Her eyes met his and she reached out to him with her crimson fingers:

"Help me…help me…"

Suyodhan rushed towards her, leaning down, to see the stab wound, and realised she was beyond help. She was surviving on her last few breaths and her flesh was smeared.

"Who did this to you?"

'"They…"

"Who are *they*?"

"You need…to…leave," she whispered to him.

"What?"

"It's all…a…"

And before she could finish, he heard it. There were footsteps and hoof beats, and instantly, he unsheathed his sword and deflected the blade that was coming towards him—when Suyodhan shoved him behind and he found soldiers...

Black-armoured soldiers. Jara's men.

Suyodhan realised they were on their horses, and some were on foot.

Suyodhan didn't waste any time. He quickly dashed around, missing and dodging people, as he raced to his horse and grabbed it—moving forward, the horse unleashed itself.

He was on his way, determined to escape his captors when he found two horses moving towards him. They were pointing their bows and arrows to shoot at him from every direction, but Suyodhan was manoeuvering his stallion from left to right, dashing and clashing on the ground, until he finally reached a turn, shifted position and moved for the ravine. The horse galloped across it, until it had caught on to him on the side, and Suyodhan was shocked by it, as the guard was almost reaching for him—using his blade against him. Suyodhan parried and dodged, until he unsheathed his own sword and deflected the blade, swinging it across the captor's head, slicing it.

The headless horseman fell from the horse, as the other horsemen brought out their arrows and shot continuously until one hit Suyodhan on the back; he felt a piercing pain, searing into his flesh as he lost control of his leash and fell over, and the horse continued to gallop further aimlessly.

Suyodhan groaned, feeling a kind of pain he had not felt in a while, as he pulled out the arrows and yelled.

And while he did it, the hoof beats reached closer and

he noticed they had surrounded him—almost two or three by then, and they were pointing their bows at him.

Great. So much for saving Karna.

Shoved in the corner of the iron cage, and bound to the grills, stripped naked with his cock lying flat, his eyes pale and scars across his body—Suyodhan was tortured and fed rat shit in his prison, in the war camp of Jarasandha. He had been trying to push and prod the iron chains that bound him, but it wouldn't work, plus he was surrounded by an army. He had been here a day or so.

Suyodhan grunted and growled under his breath.

They must have been keeping a check on the roads. And I looked suspicious.

People didn't know Karna as much as they knew Suyodhan; he had the face of a regal lord and his beard was prominently the most beautiful beard of Hastinapur.

Suyodhan waited, as he took deep breaths, feeling the frustration of being unable to do anything, feeling helpless, when he glanced at the shadows appearing as he heard:

"As you said," one voice spoke, more adult and mature, "he was on the way, so we apprehended him. Cut up a village girl to deceive him."

"You shouldn't have done that," another young voice that was stern.

"The methods are mine," the adult voice said.

And Suyodhan saw the shadows taking form, as he found it to be Jara and none other than...Arjun. The betrayer.

Arjun glanced at Suyodhan, with a keen flash of an eye and asked Jara: "May I have some time with him?"

"Of course. But after that, we need to discuss our plans."

Arjun, with a little embarrassment, nodded. Jara grinned at Suyodhan: "Your father would be very afraid now. I'm not letting you go ever and I shall ask for the world in return for you now. All thanks to this boy," he slapped Arjun's back, who was flustered at the moment.

Jara left. And Arjun and Suyodhan stood in silence where Suyodhan could feel he was in the corner of the camp, where a lot of commotion was happening. It was dark. Quite dark, in this part of the camp.

"How did you know I would come?" Suyodhan asked.

"I am an archer. I have eyes like an eagle. I caught your shadow," Arjun said. "But I knew I had to deal with you outside, where you would be more vulnerable."

"What you are doing is wrong," Suyodhan said, grunting.

Arjun remained impassive.

"You can go back. Rectify it. You do not have to side with the enemy."

Arjun didn't say anything yet again. He was quiet.

"It's because of her isn't it?" Suyodhan clenched his jaw. "I have learnt one thing in life, brother, and that is not to define your life being influenced by someone. What you should do is not for anyone else, but for yourself. Not out of haste, but out of importance."

"Says the person who was about to kill Bheem at Rangbhoomi."

"That was different."

Arjun smirked. "Everything is about perspective, I feel."

Suyodhan shook his head. "Your jealousy when it comes to Karna will lead you to worse things. Be better than Bheem or anyone else. Be a better person."

"And what good would it do, if I did that?"

"You'll always win, even if you lose. Because you won't compromise on your integrity."

There was a flash of conflict.

"All your life," Suyodhan began, "you have been controlled by your feelings towards Panchali or your undying loyalty towards your guru who continues to misuse you," he paused. "Have your own identity, Arjun."

Arjun nodded. He didn't look convinced. "If it was coming from a place of love, and not desperation to live, I would have listened. But Suyodhan, you are a cruel, vicious man who never saw the ills of your own ways and you deserve every bit of what you are going through."

Arjun left and went back to the shadows.

Suyodhan yelled and shouted, but to no avail, and he remained there until tears fell down his eyes. His words weren't impactful even though, what Arjun didn't know was that it had come from a place of love, right from the heart.

69

Devi was looking at the infirmary, watching hundreds of her men cobbled up in a small space, as their wounds were continuously being treated.

For the infirmary, her army had managed to create a large dome-shaped tent made of linen, stretching over other small tents, as they all knew it would be used a lot. Corpses from the battle were brought from the field and were given off to the Chandalas who had come to cremate them. The rest of the weapons were being sharpened. Arrows were being crafted. They were all busy, in their own worlds.

Devi's eyes fell on the rows of corpses being carried by the hunch-backed Chandalas and she felt a pang of guilt for losing so many people in battle.

She herself was badly injured, and her entire body was hurting. She decided to leave for her tent, when her attention shifted to a young, familiar boy on the ground with a bandaged head, lying down and moaning in pain.

She walked up to him and saw his cherubic pig face. Shantanu.

"How are you doing?" She knelt down next to him, her dhoti creasing.

"Not good, general."

She patted him on the shoulder, "You did well out there."

"Why is it that we plan for so long but the battle lasts for only minutes?"

"Because every minute out there is like an hour," she sighed. "Hope you feel better," she was getting up to leave, when Shantanu held her by the arm.

"General?"

Devi was perplexed by this sudden gesture. "Yes?"

"Before the battle, me and some men, we were thinking of..." he clenched his jaw. "Executing his highness."

Devi contorted her face. "That's treason and you can go to jail."

"Better than being ruled by a disloyal ruler who has no touch with his people."

"This will lead to more problems," Devi said, even though she wanted the same thing.

"But general, I am telling you this because we don't know when it'll happen, but it might. We are still planning. As I said, it will only take a minute to execute and it is important we do it. I am telling you this, general, because we want you on our side during this mission. It is of importance."

She clenched her jaw. "I'll let you know."

And she walked back, outside the infirmary, with thoughts running through her mind. She wanted to do it, but she was afraid she would be stabbed. And what promise would a lad like Shantanu stick to? For all she knew, he would betray her and put the blame on her. And because of her gender, she would be branded a heretic and paraded as a witch who took down the king. She had to tread carefully, but first she had to know what she would be doing because she was still in a dilemma.

A battle went on on the field, and another went on inside her mind.

Karna was impassively walking towards his tent, his jaw clenched with anger. He had just had a long conversation with his captains and they had told him about everything that their scouts or they had seen during the battle. And while they had lost men, quite a number of them, they would have had more casualties if they hadn't fallen back. And now Jara was severely wounded by the army and Karna's men, after some rest, would prepare their positions and hoist themselves up.

He had decided the next battle wouldn't be so disorganised but would be planned in a way that would include the execution of the strategic vyuha formations.

But his mind was weary and indifferent.

Karna went for the tent and opened it to find it empty, except for the manservants who were cleaning the tables and his cot. He ignored it and moved around, while his men behind him moved too, and his eyes darted to none other than the one he was trying to find—

His wife.

She was sitting along with her Greek friends and sharing a laugh. She still had her armour on and had bruises and cuts all over, her hair braided, but she looked like a different person. As she saw Karna, she turned her head and grinned at him:

"I believe it went..."

Karna didn't pay attention and grabbed her by the arm and took her to a side.

"What is wrong with you?" Shanaya asked.

Karna saw her glimmering eyes. "So this is how you take your revenge."

"I am not taking anything."

"You left our man behind."

"It was just a few of them," she shoved her hand away from him, "and I thought someone would get him."

"You need to be there for your people, Shanaya."

The girl, who didn't look so helpful and nice anymore, just grimaced. "I am. *My* people."

"You don't have to do this. I can't be out there wondering if you are just there for the Greeks."

"But they are my blood, *my* men. You aren't."

"You did a great job in burning their supplies and poisoning their food, and I thoroughly congratulate you for that. I wouldn't have been able to do it with you. But if you want to be more than just simple muscle for a king, you need to start caring for those who are not your blood."

She was hurt. He could see it and he was being rude with her, but he was angry and he wanted to vent. It was important for her to know that what she did was a mistake and must not be repeated.

He grabbed her by the shoulder, patting it, tracing his fingers on her arms and comforting her, as she lowered her gaze. "I am sorry. I was just...I know why you feel alienated from my people. It's because of me. I am sorry I couldn't love you...rather I can't love you. It is a curse I have to live with, but if you choose to do this, I can't let you go on the field again."

"It's not because you wouldn't return my love. I am not childish," she scoffed. "It's because you won't even *try*."

For a moment, Karna was speechless. He lowered his gaze too, loosening his grip over Shanaya.

"All my life I have had been surrounded by warriors—berserkers who had nothing to do but were just filled with anger and frustration and rage. I saw only that and I grew up inheriting that. When I was young, barely fifteen years old, I met a boy. And he was kind to me. Affectionate. He taught me archery and he showed me that there was more to this world than just hatred. There was love too. I know you didn't want me to fancy you, but it was inevitable. With you, I felt a tug and I continued to feel a tug, unable to hold on to the hate part of me until I met you again and I realised why I loved you in the first place. You exhibit hope in this world, that perhaps this world might get better one day, just perhaps. All the shit you went through, and you still continued to be a good person," she sighed. "But I do not determine my actions on such emotions. What happened on the battlefield, your highness," she said in a metallic tone now, "was an error on my part and I apologise for that. I clearly thought saving my kind was more important and I was wrong. I have to save both. Because I can't let your lack of love towards me dictate me into being emotional on the field."

Karna didn't say anything further. He was quiet and he let the silence reign, before Shanaya shrugged.

"You are a good person," Karna said and he leaned forward, kissing her on the forehead.

He hugged her, but he didn't get any in return so he remained silent, until he heard a cough from behind, and they both turned to see it was a messenger waiting.

"Your highness, there's a letter."

"From?" Karna asked.

"It says Arjun. He says he has Suyodhan in his custody and if you want to save him, you have to come and meet him alone."

Arjun? Suyodhan? Where did they come from?

Karna asked, "Where?"

"There's a long stretch of forest, here in Tataka."

This is not going according to the plan.

70

Karna entered the war tent, which was his other quarter where the map and the wooden figurines were spread on a platform. Devi and Satya had already reached. Karna saw them clearly for the first time after the war. They looked stricken by wounds. Satya was paler than before and his handlebar moustache was wet with sweat.

Devi was standing and she looked exhausted too. They were discussing strategy when they saw Karna and Shanaya.

"We have a problem," Karna said and he looked at the scroll in front of them, removing the figurines.

"Suyodhan?" Satya grimaced. "Oh what shit is this?"

"Arjun is playing with us," Karna said. "We need to do something."

"We don't have to do anything," Shanaya added. "As I told you, he's not your problem. Let Dhritarashtra handle it."

"But how did they come in the picture?" Devi asked. "This is a war between you and Jarasandha."

"He must have teamed up with Jarasandha, or perhaps Jarasandha must have convinced him," Karna said. "The problem is that Arjun himself would get into trouble by doing that."

"From whatever I know about Jarasandha," Devi added, "this is his plan. To distract you from the battle. He knows you are being smart with him, so he's using your old companions against you. It could also mean an ambush."

"It *is* an ambush," Satya nodded. "And I'm sure, boy, you aren't foolish enough to go ahead knowing this threat."

Karna was pertrubed, as he went for the nearest chair and sat on it, leaning back. He was worried about his friend, his helper. He clenched his jaw and lowered his gaze, thoughtfully mulling things over and humming at the same time, in a loose grey tunic and white dhoti, his kundalams dangling from his ears.

"So, as my inner council, what do you propose?" Karna asked quietly. "We don't do anything?"

"We can dispatch a squad," Satya suggested.

Shanaya came forward and put her hand on him. "I can go and help him, Vasu."

Karna knew the slightest error would be a problem here, and he couldn't risk Suyodhan bearing the brunt of it. Not just out of friendship but also because it would sour his relationship with Dhritarashtra as Suyodhan was the wall between Karna and the Maharaja, who made sure the dark side of the great king didn't harm a small king like Karna. It was a strategic decision to secure Suyodhan.

"It will lead to further complications. I can't risk it," Karna shook his head. "I'll go."

"You are doing exactly what he wants you to do," Satya scowled. "Don't let this battle go in vain. This is the second day and we can launch a strike by evening, leading to a good triumph on our side, if you fight along with us."

"I am not the only capable fighter here. You have Shanaya. She can lead the Greek and Nishadh squads, while Devi could be the commander-in-chief. Do the Mandala Vyuha," he ordered. "And let everyone know that I am commanding it." It was the kind of formation that would have the commander in front, with the cavalry on each eastern and western front, followed by infantry and drummers that would be leading the pack of soldiers in a solid formation.

"But you won't be here," Devi was confused.

"I know."

He took off his kundalams and handed them to his general, while reaching for his breastplate from the back of his room and giving it to her. "You wear it and fool everyone by making them believe it's me. The Mandala Vyuha will show it's me and in war, no one really notices the intricacies of the face. And you lead all of them, while I go and stop Arjun."

Devi was awestruck, gasping, and her face opened as she saw the kundalams, like shiny golden orbs glimmering under the torchlight. The belief Karna had in her, he had explicitly shown. "But why confuse the enemy?"

"To make them think I didn't take the bait. To irk them. They will attack us thinking the king is not here but when they'll see an illusion of the king, they will be taken aback."

"This is a death wish," Shanaya flared her nostrils. "Not only are you going into danger's mouth, you are also going without your armor."

Satya, by then, had no response.

Karna knew he would take some of his men with him. “I am sorry. But I shall return and if I don’t, Devi shall complete the mission.” And he squared up next to his general, who was still confused, her eyes tearing up as he hugged her and said, “I am sorry I threatened you the last time. Be careful and lead the men well.”

Karna glanced at Shanaya, who was not even locking eyes with him, and he was dismayed. He wanted to see her face once before leaving, before going in the dark, going into the ambush, but he had trust in Arjun, even though he was a reckless boy.

He had trust—that he could be understood.

71

Arjun was sharpening his arrows with a cleft of a dagger and made them pointier than before. And while he had been here for a day, he had not interacted with anyone and remained silent. Quiet. Kept to himself.

Thoughts about what Suyodhan had said to him had begun to impact him and he was really feeling conflicted. He knew what he did was dictated by his guru's orders and his love for Panchali. But was it right? Was he being the right person by doing this? Drona might say yes, but then something was pricking his conscience.

I have to be diligent in my decisions. I have to follow my guru, at all cost.

"You are here," he heard a voice.

And he looked up to see a woman in a grey gown, with shiny eyes which had a sheen, and he found her irises to be like that of a cat. She blinked and smiled.

"You are the bhisak."

"Far from it. You are going to ambush Karna," she noted. "For that, I have something for you. Follow me."

Arjun was dumbstruck by what was happening, but he walked behind her, passing by the soldiers who were filled in the infirmary, while many were on the ground.

And few of them were alive and taking care of others. The illness still persisted, but it had gone mild, and they weren't rageful and blind anymore, but rather just struck with fever. Arjun could only wonder how one might stand up after such an incisive attack.

"You fancy archery?"

"Yes."

"Good. I've just the right thing for you then." She smiled and Arjun couldn't help but smile back.

They reached her tent, and he found the inside held lots of transparent tubes, porcelain jars and little boxes made of wood, which had some liquid in them. She had leaves of all kinds, separated and kept on the table. And the smell of the room was atrocious, but Arjun ignored it.

"You are a Rakshasi. What sorcery have you built here?" Arjun asked. He had heard about the Rakshas as who would eat humans but she didn't look like a cannibal at all.

She came forward to the table and brought a jar with a purplish liquid simmering inside over a light fire that she had created. She showed it to Arjun.

"I have something for you. It is *Atropa belladonna*, also known as a Nightshade. A deadly poison that can paralyse anyone hit with it. Just take your arrow and dip the end to it, but I would suggest wear a pair of gloves when you do, otherwise you might end up hurting yourself," she warned, with a diligent nod. "It has atropine that makes you paralyse whatever you hit. It's a rare plant and thus not used in battle to a large degree, but if you are isolating Karna from his army, it's good to use it on him. He would slowly die from it."

Arjun knew his rivalry would one day end up in bloodshed, but he never believed it would reach here. Where he would be a cold-blooded murderer of his rival. It did pinch his conscience but he sighed deeply. "That's interesting."

"It is." She took one arrow from his hanging quiver and dipped it in the liquid. Then she whistled for a soldier, and stabbed him with the arrow. The soldier fell down in shock, cursing her and began to shake, unable to move his leg and crying out loud. "Oh don't cry like an infant. I'll build you a new leg." She rolled her eyes and then glanced at Arjun. "Impressed?"

"You didn't have to do that."

"You are soft for a soldier," she growled.

"Why is a Rakshasi helping the king of Magadha?"

"Because we have a mutual friend who I care deeply about," she said. "And he has requested me for his help in this, as Karna has really befuddled him in the battle."

Really? Is he that good?

Arjun saw the man was still crying and he grieved for him, but he took the jar of poison in his hands and under his arm, as he carefully placed it for balance.

"If you are a good archer, you won't have to worry. The poison will do the work. So, are you a good archer?"

Arjun smirked. *Clearly she hasn't heard about me.*

The sun was hidden behind the greenish sky; the entire mood of the scenery was drenched in a greenish tint. A storm was brewing as the leaves were moving in the opposite direction from what Karna was doing.

He had his bow and arrow, and he had two men behind him, as he gazed back at the Tataka forest where the scroll had told him to be in. But it was dead silent, except the sound of the breeze.

He walked further, as he saw the dense and dark forest, the bushes were larger than usual and the trees were improperly lined.

Why did he call me here?

Karna carefully walked inside, his eye darting everywhere like a hawk, watching, the two men with their unsheathed swords in their palms, ready to strike at the next interference. The path was undulated, going up and down, and it had different levels of plateaus, a river that was coursing, and the wind was cool, tracing his clothes like a salve.

Karna pulled out his weapon, stringing his arrow, and closed his eyes.

Come on. Where are you?

And then his concentrated hearing led him to feel the sound of *something*. He couldn't make out what, but he moved carefully, until he was close to the origin of the sound.

He was right there in the middle of the clearing, and fifty yards away from him he saw the bound Suyodhan. Who was laid flat, on the ground, and his eyes were closed and he was either crying or snoring. Karna couldn't make out but he was making a sound.

"Your highness! We found him!" The soldiers behind him got excited and decided to move, when Karna narrowed his gaze.

"No!" he exclaimed, but it was too late.

A shiny beacon appeared and it lunged right next to Karna, smacking his soldier in the arm. The soldier fell down, his arms paralysed. And another set of arrows, which came out of nowhere went further, attacking the other soldier, leading him to fall down too.

The arrow had plunged inside the thick skull of the soldier and his mouth and his eyes stopped functioning.

Karna instantly took cover behind a tree, trying to glance carefully from there whether he was able to see Arjun—but he was nowhere. He glanced again at his soldiers and they were all near dead. They were weeping, but they were unable to move wherever they were hit.

What is he attacking me with?

Karna realised that it was not an ambush by Jarasandha's army. No.

It was an ambush by his old rival—Arjun.

72

Devi felt different in the armour she wore, as she rode into the battlefield with thousands of soldiers behind her.

She had initially been reluctant to wear this armour, but she was forced by Satya, as this was the only way to fool the enemies.

And so she grabbed the breastplate and was on her way to do the deed.

The formation was what Karna had suggested and she could see her army was surging from all directions, in comparison to Jara, who had no planned formation.

I shall win this one.

Devi had hated Karna for a while now, but this sudden step of being selfless and giving her the reins was what she didn't expect from him. And for some reason, deep down, she wanted to make him proud by completing what he had asked her to.

The enemy on the opposite flanks were silent and looking at her in hundreds. They all looked confused, as Karna had predicted. They wanted answers, but none was given, as they saw the shiny breastplate and the kundalams from afar.

Her vertebrae hurt, as she rode on the chariot, which

made the creaking and the rolling sound, her eyes darted in front, as she shouted at her archers, behind her on horseback, to shoot the arrows against the fiery arrows that were coming towards them.

She had grabbed hold of the shield and blocked the rain-fire, as she lurched, letting the chariot crash against her enemies.

She pierced the crowd and with her blade, began to cut her enemies down. Her body was flexing and moving fast, while the enemies were moving and lashing towards her, only to realise she was a woman and getting shocked by her appearance; getting deceived.

She deflected, parried and rolled on the ground, her eyes darted at the onslaught of weapons towards her, as she fought back, with her shield, shoving it across the enemy soldiers and plunging her blade into their thick chests.

Another came from behind her, and said: “I HAVE GOT YOU, KING!”

But she toppled him over, and stabbed him in the face. The two enemies moved in front and she dodged until a blade struck her breastplate and made a resounding retaliating sound; she then fought back with a quick swift attack across the throat, cutting the soldier down, while she shoved the other soldier with the shield until an incoming arrow hit him in the eye socket.

She was a bit confused, sprays of blood over her face, as the adrenaline of the war was getting to her and she yelled. She could hear her men yell too.

And she felt she would win, as did the men around her, as her enemies had begun to scamper.

Except for one.

The iron-masked man.

Jara had gotten himself a pair of dice that he had found in his travelling trunk and in anxiety, he had been scrubbing them together. Unlike last time, he was standing close to the battlefield, where there was a large tent, shadowing the stormy weather, his eyes on the war that was taking place, when he saw a scout running across the desert field and falling on the ground.

"Your highness, Karna is here."

What?

"He's here, your highness."

For a moment, Jara was confused. *But he should have been lured out of the battle and to Arjun, to save Suyodhan. That was the plan anyway.*

"Are you sure?"

"Many have witnessed the breastplate."

Jara clenched his jaw. "Indeed, but did you see him use a bow and arrow?"

The messenger looked confused; half-closed eyes, with dirt over his face. "I think he was using a sword."

Got him.

"It's not him," Jara smiled, as his captains covered each side of Jara.

"But why would he try to fool us?" one of the captains asked.

"To make us fall back. To make us think that he didn't take the bait," Jara said. "He knows we are weak right now in strength and that we attacked him again because he was not here, and was taking the bait. So he gave us the illusion of being here, to confuse and shock us, even instill fear in us," he laughed. "But he thought of me as a fool. He was wrong."

He pulled his hands at the back, the dice in his hands shuffling hard, as he threw them on the ground, and the number that came was three.

Three.

"You know what you have to do," he told the captains, grinning at the counteractive plan that he had conceived.

The iron-masked man brought his axe forward and Devi, rolled on her side, as it plunged on the ground. She quickly went for a swift attack to his torso, but only managed to scar him.

And then, he brought his burly arms to Devi and smacked her on the face and she was tossed on the ground; a bit bewildered and confused.

She tried to come on her feet and was trying to reach for the fallen shield, as her leg was grabbed by him and she was lifted midair, suspended, before being thrown on the rusted, dry land, as the desert sand smoked and puffed.

She coughed loudly as a numb sensation ran through her entire body, a pain that was unbearable.

She still tried to reach for her sword, when he pressed his legs on to Devi's legs and she felt such a surging pain, that she yelled loudly. But as she was being pulled, she grabbed the sword and made a quick slash against his throat.

He sprayed blood, as he left her mid-way, and was pulled back as she fell on the ground, limping and bleeding from everywhere. Her eyes, with bloodlust, looked at the iron-masked man who was by now holding his bloody throat, and had fallen on the ground.

She limped to him and was ready to plunge her sword.

"This is for Manvee." She was about to remove his iron mask, when she saw the lower half of the mask. It seemed quite familiar as if she knew this face...

Then she noticed the skies were like glowing ember in colour, becoming fiery with every moment...

Catapults!

The balls of fire crashed against the ground, rolling over her soldiers, even the ones who had their shields on, as they crushed, burned and crumpled them.

She yelled loudly. And then she saw another set of fireballs...a total of three reaching for her, when she felt a pull taking her away from the iron-masked man, who was still on his knees.

The impact confused her, but she looked at Kaal, who was now limping away from her side of the battle, moving back.

She could have easily lunged at him, but that would mean...more waste of time...more deaths.

I can't let that be repeated.

"FALL BACK! FALL BACK! RETREAT!" she yelled and her men instantly lifted their shields and began to move towards their camp.

Devi stood there, with a broken leg, as she saw her men, being saved by her decision and moving in a secured perimeter form the catapulted iron balls.

She also happened to gaze at the iron-masked man, who was disappearing within his squads and factions, who had also pulled back. He disappeared in the mist, in the darkness, along with her thirst for vengeance.

73

Karna remained behind the tree.

"You don't have to do this," he shouted.

But there was no response.

And so he turned to see if there was anyone else—any shadow...

An arrow zapped almost inches away from him.

Karna pulled himself back and fell on the ground, hiding in between the grass, which were rather tall in height. His eyes were up on the tall trees, but he couldn't see anything.

He must be camouflaged well.

Karna began to drag his body against the ground, amidst the shrubs and the tall grass. His breath was frantic. He was counting each drag that he took, his eyes clearly watching the northern side, so he could see if an arrow was coming towards him.

The breeze had tightened and the shrubs, along with him, had begun to move and he was becoming a tad bit visible.

I need to find another cover.

And just when he thought that—

An arrow zapped past him!

He rolled over, as the arrow smacked on the ground, swirling dust, as he grabbed hold of his legs and made a run for the rock, skidding as fleets of poison-drenched arrows lunged towards him. He somersaulted on the ground to find cover and took a deep breath to calm his senses.

He had been in fights. He was in a battle. But he never imagined an invisible enemy like Arjun could be so threatening.

He looked at Suyodhan, who was a bit close now, and he grinned to himself.

"Do you think by killing me..." Karna began, "you are getting your chances higher with Panchali? I don't think you know one thing. She chose you, Arjun. She chose you. She never chose me..." and his voice trailed off, seeing the image of Panchali in front and wondering why he loved a woman who didn't accept him, who didn't wait for him and an image of Shanaya came in his mind. "She loved me, of course, but she chose you for marriage. I haven't brought her here because she refused to come. Do you understand? Do you think by killing me you'll be able to face her? You'll be the man who killed the man she loved. Will you be able to wake up every day and be able to face yourself?" Karna stated. "You wouldn't let this hamper your morality. I'm sure your ethics wouldn't allow someone like me to get killed, someone who your lover loves. I know somewhere between this rivalry of ours, you are a good person. You are just misguided."

There was a pause. He couldn't hear anything. Anything that might impact him, and he went down in prone pose again and began to move with his elbows on the ground.

Arjun was still invisible.

And then…

It happened…

Two simultaneous arrows went for him.

Karna rolled over, pulling out his bow and arrow, and shooting instantly back from where it had come, as he skid further and moved for another rock, dragging himself to a tree.

"Have you forgotten how it was like? I had woken up early. Before dawn, and I had gone out to practice when I had seen you. You were practicing all night. And both of us drowsily smiled at each other and talked about archery, exchanged notes. It was like any other day and we should have fought because we were on opposite sides of the team. But at that time, we had no one around, and so we just behaved not like rivals, but like acquaintances—just two good students of archery. Do you remember that day?"

His breathing had intensified.

"I knew that day I was not talking to someone who just chose archery because he was gifted. I realised that day that I was not talking to a prodigy, with a gift, but a hardworking boy who wanted to do right by his talents. Who wanted to better himself," Karna said, pulling an arrow on his bow. "I truly feel you are a born archer, Arjun. I do," he paused, realising that his words…they were coming out of genuineness and honesty. "But you became a *great* archer by hardwork and sheer determination and only someone who truly loves this craft can do that. And because of this amazing gift of yours, you take it lightly. You think you do this because of some girl, but you are wrong."

Karna saw Suyodhan. He was close. He had to grab him and make a move. But Suyodhan was heavy and his thoughts were running fast. "You do this because you love it but you are just too afraid to say it. You feel putting the weight of this gift of archery and your work towards it on someone else, will make it less of a burden...well, someone as talented as you is afraid, at the end of the day. To be not a..."

An arrow smacked against the branch of the tree and went past its trunk, just inches away from Karna's eye, as he withdrew.

Wrong words! Wrong words!

"Drona wanted to take over the kingdom for his son Ashwatthama," Karna said, finally, as he realised he had to come out with the truth.

And with it, he stepped out of the cover his hands up as he tossed his weapon on the side.

"If you want to kill me, kill me," he said, walking up to Suyodhan, one step a time. "But you must hear me out. Drona took the kingdom for his son, to give him a place because the Maharaja was clearly not going to give Ashwatthama anything. He's no royal blood, so Drona took it for his son. That is why he attacked Draupad. It was not because he was wrong. And I know you are here because of him," he said. "He must have asked you to disperse with me and said he would give you my position. Well, I suppose you are wrong there too. He won't."

Karna had reached closer to Suyodhan, who was lying wasted on the ground, all battered and wounded—tortured to the extent that he would need several days of rest even if he was rescued.

"He'll give it to Ashwatthama," Karna said. "No matter how much he treats you like his son, Arjun, you are not his son. Ashwatthama is."

Karna paused. Waiting for a response. But he only saw tall, giant trees in front of him. "At the end, you have to make a decision. About what to do now. Is killing a good option, or being the better person? It's quite easy to raise a bow and shoot an arrow, but it's the most difficult thing to let go. Of your vices. Of your..." he paused, realising that he himself had led an entire battle against Jarasandha for revenge. Was it right? He didn't know. "Be yourself, Arjun. Strive for individuality and try not be influenced by the wrongdoers. One day you might be guided by the right person, but it is not today."

Karna went to grab hold of Suyodhan and he lifted him on his back. "I'm going to turn and leave now," he loudly declared. "But I just want to say something which I never have..." he almost teared up, "...no matter how much we hate each other, I will respect you as an archer more than anything. And one day we might have a duel, but again...today is not that day. Today is the day I kill Jarasandha. Our fight is saved for the future. Sooner or later, I don't know when, but it will happen."

And Karna moved ahead, with the heavy Suyodhan on his back, moving for his stallion.

And there was no arrow flung towards him, except one that slammed next to Karna's feet.

But he knew it was not an attack. It was to bid Karna farewell.

Because I know he never misses an open target.

As he saw the two figures disappearing, he waited till twilight inside the darkness of the foliage and then he leapt from the branches and on to the floor. He looked at the poison drenched arrows and he threw the quiver away.

Arjun didn't know why he stopped. Karna spoke a lot and he heard everything, but he didn't know what held him back. Was it the fact that Panchali left Karna for him or was it Drona's true reasons? But Karna wasn't lying. He might be a bitter rival, but he was an honest man. And that was one thing that continued to ride on him.

Silently across the river, he walked with his hands behind until he reached his reined horse and mounted on it, looking into the clearing which opened to a new horizon. Night had begun to descend and the last light of the day was shining on him. It was the light of a thunder, a clap of the rumbling sounds as if his divine father Indra had just bestowed his blessings on him.

Not strength.

But wisdom, to see things with more clarity.

74

"We lost."

That was the first thing Karna heard when he returned with Suyodhan hanging like a lifeless corpse on his saddle.

But he didn't want to hear anything else. He knew his men had lost today, but he ordered them to take Suyodhan to the bhisak, while he made his way to someone special; someone important. Someone he didn't care about, but he should have.

Karna raced across people and across his captains who were approaching him to discuss something. He happened to see Satya talking to the troops while drinking glasses of wine, and Devi was about to reach for him, limping and handing back his breastplate—

"You did good," he said.

"No, we lost. The catapults…"

"It doesn't matter. Tomorrow is another day and we shall fight again," Karna smiled. "Keep the breastplate for now. I have to go somewhere."

Devi struggled to smile; and the frustration and anger that she had towards him early on, wasn't displayed as much as he was used to seeing in her. And Karna realised that to have a happy inner council, one had to make them feel useful, productive. It was a tactic to be a leader.

He went inside his tent to see Shanaya lying there, her back towards him, and he leapt on the bed, slowly tracing his fingers across her skin. She was in a red gown and she turned to look at him, almost astonished.

"I was worried," she was taken aback.

Karna smiled. "And that's why you were sleeping away to glory?"

"Well, I was *reasonably* worried," she grinned back. "I knew you would return."

"You have trust in me."

"Of course."

Karna watched her eyes with candid urgency. "I am sorry I was such a bastard earlier. You were right. I didn't even try. And here you are, leaving everything behind, fighting a crusade that isn't yours, or mine. You are one of the few women I have met in my life, but you make me feel like I don't need to meet anyone else."

"Are you...*flirting*?"

"Yes, unabashedly."

Karna didn't wait. He bent forward and locked lips with her, as she took him in his arms. He felt her fingers slowly moving across his scalp, as they both were passionately immersed in the moment.

And even though Karna could see flashes of Panchali coming in front of him, he realised it was okay. Because in his heart, he still loved her, but he had finally begun the long journey of loving Shanaya.

Suyodhan was feverish as he lay in one corner of the tent, on a cot, looking pale, dark circles under his baggy eyes. As he opened his eyes, he saw a shadow in front of him, with a reflection of the torchlight and the smell of ayurvedic creams which carried an aroma of the forest.

He saw the shadow become a person, and he found Karna, who was now kneeling down, while on one side of him, was a bald bhisak in a saffron dhoti, mixing the paste.

"Where am I?"

"At my camp."

"What...what happened?"

"You don't have to worry," Karna said.

"You rescued...you rescued..." words were crawling out of him in a wrong fashion, but he was still comprehending things, "you rescued me, didn't you?"

Karna didn't have to respond.

"I am sorry," he said. "I had come to warn you but I was apprehended and ambushed. I am sorry...did Arjun..."

"I handled him."

"He's—he's dead?"

Karna shook his head. "You'll be fine. I would like to send you back to Hastinapur, as soon as possible. The Maharaja shouldn't feel I am risking his son's life."

"Ye-yes..." he sighed, he was still getting images of different parts of his life, but one in particular, "I am sorry."

"It's okay, you didn't know."

"No, not for that." He sighed, sweat trickling from his forehead, as he could feel the pressure points of his body. "I let you take the fall."

"Oh."

"I know I wasn't in your debt, but I was." He began to whimper and tear up, and he didn't want to feel this way, but he was. The guilt. "Drona had accepted you even though you didn't give him the dakshina. He still went with it because you were special, until I rolled you into a bigger problem."

"It's not a problem..."

"It was! I was the one who poisoned Bheem, not you!" He screamed in agony and the veins popped out of his forehead. "I was so frustrated of him, I had to do it and so I did and when Bheem survived, he said he was poisoned and everyone knew it was me. I was the server of his food on that day but you...you took the fall and you were charged with conspiracy of murder against royalty and you were exiled."

Suyodhan watched the placid expressions on Karna's face, as he was listening to him. "If it wasn't for Drona's discretion, you would have been in jail, but I begged him not to say anything to the Maharaja. He agreed and he knew it was me, but he still put the blame on you, to humiliate you. Perhaps he wasn't giving you a second chance. Perhaps it was him just waiting for an opportunity to make you feel heartbroken, to backstab you, to humiliate you. And he did."

Karna nodded. "Yes. And as I told you, you don't owe me anything."

"I owe you my life, my friend. You saved me." And he raised his arm, weakly which Karna took, and then they both shook it.

Shantanu was supposed to assassinate him. Him and the other defectors of Karna's regime, had planned that, but seeing the royal prince of Hastinapur here, and wounded... ooh...that sounded more treacherous and twisted.

And so he walked in the dead of night, seeing the soldier in front of him, one of his allies.

And he said: "Are you ready? It's a long journey."

"Yes."

"Make sure you inform clearly," he said, and gave out a grunting sound, as he coughed and spat. Shantanu looked young and small, but he wasn't. He was quite old, but his face was eternally youthful. And he had hated Karna for a while. In the beginning he was in awe of the archer lord, but soon he had witnessed his rule, and how he brought the enemies inside—he was the kind of ruler who had hired the people who were behind Shantanu's brother's death. He was a soldier too and he had met his end at the hands of the Mlecchas, if not this particular section, the other one. But it didn't matter, they were all the same.

"Yes."

Shantanu handed him a piece of Suyodhan's clothing as proof. And smiled. The mare went off, as he thought to himself: *The king must know that his son is here in a camp which is consistently losing, harmed because of Karna's poor decision-making.*

And he smiled wider. Getting him off the throne was far better than killing the king.

75

The fire burnt in between as the inner council sat around it.

It was chilly tonight, and they all were covered in furs and blankets, under the stormy sky. Some sat around the fire, just like Karna, Satya, Devi and Shanaya.

They were discussing their future plans.

"We cannot resist more attacks like this," Devi said, leaning forward, her hardened voice gleaning. "The catapults were terribly surprising and effective against us. I know on both sides men have lost lives, but I firmly believe we need to do something."

"And what would you suggest?" Karna said, a blanket over him, his golden eyes, deep and sharp.

Satya had a goblet clutched in his fingers, as he snapped in between: "I would suggest the battle should be over now. Losing more men is not something we can afford, boy."

"So, give up?" Karna shrugged. "I don't think so." He glanced at Shanaya who was quiet, and her lips were pursed, as she sat next to him.

"I have another idea," Devi rose from her seat, rubbing her arms. "Why don't I give in to him?"

"What do you mean?" Karna arched his brows.

"The woman has gone mad. It's finally happened!" clapped Satya.

"No, no," Devi shook her head. "I pretend that I have changed sides and want to help him; give him some fake strategy of yours and learn their next attack and escape."

"What if you are not able to escape?" Shanaya asked.

"Then I send a raven or a pigeon, I don't know, but something that'll get the information out."

Karna clenched his jaw. "Spying, is it?"

Devi nodded.

"And what is the guarantee that he won't kill you on sight?" Satya chuckled.

"No guarantee, but I believe we should take risks. We won't ever know what he's planning next. And I'm sure Karna's bag of tricks is finishing. We can't win a war with a bunch of guerrilla tactics. We might win a battle, but not the war. For a war, we should know what the enemy is doing, what he's thinking," Devi explained.

The idea seemed jarring and scary to Karna. What were the chances Devi would turn against him? But thinking ill of people irked him. He shouldn't, of course, as Devi had changed and done well for him. "All right," he said. "But general, I feel if you get caught there, you have a plan."

"Yes. I'll kill myself before being tortured to reveal our strategies."

Karna nodded. "Good."

Satya and Shanaya looked at each other incredulously that Karna endorsed suicide, but it clearly showed that the nation's well-being was far more important to him than a person's life by now.

"You must start preparing to leave. Go unarmed, and go with a white flag, so they know you come in peace. And I shouldn't say this, but sever some heads of our fallen soldiers and take them with you, so he knows you defected from my camp by killing my men," Karna instructed, and with a determined face Devi nodded, as Shanaya and Satya looked on in shock, at his gruesome technique. "But keep a lookout for the exits and escape routes when you can, even if you don't learn anything much. Jarasandha is smart and he will try to find loopholes in your story so give a convincing one, as to why you left my side.

"I can think of many convincing tales," Devi grinned.

Oh, she jokes as well.

"Great."

And she left for the preparations.

Shanaya, Satya and Karna sat in silence, until Satya said: "I believe we are making a grave mistake continuing this war."

"Are you saying this out of the fear that you will lose?" Karna asked.

"What do you mean?"

"Your men, under you, they saw the fear in you on the battlefield. You are afraid of venturing out on the field, and it's understandable. But do not put other people's moral—"

"Boy, I was part of wars and battles before you were born," Satya came on his feet, with sharp anger in his eyes. "All my life I wanted to die protecting this land until I realised it was not worth it. Until I realised that these drugs are my life and you gave me hope that I can still do what I love. But it's tough. You can't just switch from one to another. Now I fear death. I don't look forward to it." He saw the fright and impassiveness just lingering in his irises. "And I don't fear death for just myself, but for others too…for you, for your wife, for everyone on the field."

With that, he left.

Karna raised his brows and he wanted to say something, but he felt flustered and embarrassed. "This man," he finally said to Shanaya, as he felt her hands slowly reaching out to him and holding him tight, "he was my idol when I was growing up, endorsing wars and bloodshed. Never thought he would speak like that. Do you think he's right?"

"About wars being pointless?"

"Yes."

"I feel the pursuit for a nation and its development is far superior than what an old drunkard says," Shanaya said.

Karna chuckled. And so did she.

By the next morning, Devi had prepared her stallion to leave and she was feeling a tug in her throat and a knot in her stomach—it was fear and this confusion of what would happen. She was going into the lion's den and she would face a lot of challenges, but it was important for her people.

But just before leaving, she had to do something. She had to meet someone. It was important. Briskly walking across the camp and passing the stables, the kitchen and rmary, she came to the large tent where food was distributed, and soldiers, without their pads and their armoury, sat cobbled together, having their rice and curd, served on pieces of large coconut leaves.

Devi passed across hundreds of soldiers, to find Shantanu who was having a frolic discussion with his friends.

"Soldier, a word please?"

Shantanu nervously left the food and came up on his feet, isolating himself from the group, as they stood away from everyone in silence.

"Yes, general?"

"I would like to inform you that assassination of the king or even plotting is conspiracy for murder and you will be put on trial and hanged at the earliest. Do you understand?"

He was taken aback. "But general, I thought you…"

Perhaps earlier. But Karna should be given a fair chance.

"It doesn't matter what I think. You need to realise that one word to the king, and you would have no life. But since you have not done anything and you speak only words, I am letting you go."

"But general, why?

"Also I know from the logbooks that an unofficial rider has left in the last few days for Hastinapur. Now one might wonder why that is." She stepped closer, towering over the small boy. "I hope for your sake that no one from Hastinapur comes, and if they do…you shall be staked."

Fear lingered in his eyes. "General, I have heard you are leaving for a spy mission. Best of luck."

She left, shrugging, walking back to her mare, thinking that the look she got right before leaving, clearly meant: *I hope you don't return from there.*

76

Karna woke up with a jolt.

It was early morning and he had gone for a stroll up to the tallest peak where he could perform his adulations to Suryadev, and by the time he returned, he had begun to feel the iciness on his fingertips and his heartbeat oscillating from bad to worse. Soon, he reached for his bed where Shanaya was sleeping and crashed on it. Usually he felt good when he returned from his prayers to his divine god, but today it was the opposite.

He had taken a nap and dreamt of failure. Of rejection. Of being a constant disappointment. Until he woke up, drenched in his own sweat.

"Are you okay?" a voice came from his side, and the owner of it was stroking her fingers across his naked chest.

"Yeah, I'm just...I don't know."

"Are you stressed out about failing again?"

He paused. "Shouldn't I be?"

"We won't fail."

"How do you know?" He looked directly at her, and their eyes locked. She pursed her lips and planted a kiss on his cheeks. "Because we will make it."

"And if we don't?" His voice was frantic. "I can't lose, Shanaya. I can't. I have to win. No matter what."

"This undying attitude to winning is what is causing this big stress on your health. In this condition, you won't be able to win anyhow."

"I don't know…I just…" he said, worriedly. "I have to get rid of Jarasandha, I have to take back Anga. I have to do everything in my power."

"And if you aren't able to do it, there's another day. There's another time. Just because you fail, doesn't mean you can't get up again."

"I have been trying to get up ever since this battle has started. No matter how I bloody attack Jarasandha, he comes back up and uses his army. I almost feel I have even lost Devi, and I have lost my people who hate me for choosing foreigners," he growled.

"You have a weapon you haven't used."

"That is?"

"Brahmastra."

He was shivering, he realised, and she grabbed a blanket and wrapped him with it, making him sit and he calmly put his head on her lap. He stared blankly; his eyes shimmering and face gaunt. He had managed to cut his beard off with a dagger the previous night, as it had begun to itch, and the bathing facility at war camps wasn't the best.

She began to run her fingers across his scalp and his hair. "I always liked your hair."

Karna didn't say anything.

She tried distracting him. "I was always curious about what happened after you met us. My father helped you reach the top of the Himalayas. Did you find what you were looking for? Did you find the mythical Parshuram?

I know you aren't allowed to divulge the details of Brahmastra, but are you going to use it?"

"Y-yes, I did meet him but Brahmastra…it's more complicated than you think."

"Okay. How was he like but? Parshuram?"

"He gave me the bow."

"Really?"

"Yes. It's made of hard wood and it's much more durable than an ordinary one."

He paused. His mind racing back to the time when he had reached the temple, up in the hill, which was in the midst of the icy fields where a little town was bustling.

But it wasn't like any other village out there.

77

Three years ago...

Karna had finally reached.

His eyes were drawn to the place which was supposedly where Lord Parshuram lived and breathed. The immortal, who had seen the world when it was not like that, it was before this time and he would live to see the future as well. Karna was in awe, wondering how he would be like, and he had been drawing up designs as to how he might look like, but none would compare to what he would witness.

From the outside, the land in front of him looked simple. The villagers weren't too worried and they were on their daily business with their yaks, sheep and cows. The snow was thick here, as Karna with his horse, came forward to the gates; an exciting rage beating in his chest.

If it wasn't for Archimedes, he wouldn't have been here. Spending time with the Mlecchas was indeed an enriching experience, especially since he happened to learn a lot about guerrilla warfare, about how they use heavy armoury rather than light ones, and about how one could be invisible.

Karna had wanted to be invisible since he knew he

was going to be blamed for conspiracy of murder against Bheem even though he hadn't done anything. But none of the royalty chased him and that bothered him. He could understand why Suyodhan did what he did, but he didn't understand why Suyodhan felt all right to pass the blame on to Karna. He remained quiet, when Karna brought it up. He didn't even say it was a joint effort.

But Karna did what he had to do for his friend, and perhaps one day he might even make him repay for his silence.

For now, a smile was on his face, as he reached and entered the village, moving across men and women who were busy in their own worlds. He wanted to ask whether they knew where he could find Parshuram. Until he found a large idol of someone with matted hair, wearing leopard skin and carrying an axe right in the middle of the village. He was in awe of it, and he continued to look at it for a while, until he heard a voice:

"Made from granite, it is."

He turned to see a young man, relatively young, though much older than Karna, with the same matted hair and leopard skin over him. But he had a long stick that he scrounged the ground with and he walked calmly along with Karna.

"Are you...why are you..."

He was confused. Was this Lord Parshuram? No, he was too lanky and thin, and not broad like the idol.

"Who are you?"

"You are a warrior," said the man. "Saw you from a distant mile and I knew it was you. You have been asking about us..." his hand went over Karna's breastplate.

"Indeed, the symbol of Kunti Kingdom. Are you from there? Why do you seek my presence?"

"I am…I am not. I actually received this from my mother."

"Mother, you say," the man had piercing golden eyes. "And who's your mother?"

"Radha."

The man came forward with his stick, and Karna almost toppled on the ground. A shivering light flashed in front of him, as the man said: "Why do you seek me?"

"Are you Lord Parshuram?"

He had a warm grin on his face. "Walk with me, student."

Karna was almost glad that he was called a student, but he scampered and did as he was told, while the mysterious man took him uphill from the village, where a small temple rested. Karna saw, to his surprise, that the temple was on the cliff, close to a hundred feet in height where a blizzard could come and wipe them away, but they didn't fear anything. From here, the entire village looked beautiful, even the green and brown lands below, and the tallest mountain peaks of Bharatvarsh looked divine.

The temple had little huts around it, cobbled together, and there he saw a lot of men with matted hair and leopard skin, just like the mysterious man. And they were all practicing sword fighting or archery or javelin throw, even martial arts and hand-to-hand combat.

In fact, Karna turned to see the long rocky peaks, from where the matted hair men were climbing, and had long ropes and a hook, climbing the ledges, perhaps reaching the ridges too.

"What is this?"

"Parshuram," he said. "Named after our ancestor. Our father."

"Father?"

"Our teacher, more like it."

"But…isn't Lord Parshuram one person…"

He chuckled. "Lord Parshuram has been dead for over a hundred years or more than that."

What?

"I am his pupil. And so are all of them."

Karna walked inside the temple, and he was made to sit down and was given a bowl of broth. The insides of the temple had no furniture but just rugs on which you had to sit, while candles burnt around them. It was very peaceful and silent.

"You leave behind your tracks quite recklessly," the man said. "A simple trip down the town, and I happened to hear a young, muscular boy with a shield and a bow, searching for Parshuram."

"And you were waiting for me?"

"Of course."

"Why is that?"

"Because of the breastplate," his eyes were shining.

"Breastplate?"

"I used to know someone who used to wear that . But alas, we are always open to educating the youth of this country without anything in return. You have come to learn from us, haven't you?"

Karna nodded, his knees on the ground, surprised how simple all of it was. "Yes, guruji."

"We train young warriors from all over the land because we firmly believe in the idea of Lord Parshuram who wanted to eradicate the land from the evil Kshtriyas. And as you can see, we are corrupted by the land and all the people here…their thirst for power has made them greedy. We cannot attack these Kshtriyas but we can, of course, train those who can." He paused. "Our kind taught one of our pupils, a long time ago. Drona was his name and instead of fighting the Kshtriyas, he ended up joining them," he scoffed.

He couldn't believe all of this. Karna thought travelling here would be tough but convincing the guru to teach him, would be tougher. But the man in front of him and the hot broth he was sipping were enough to make him feel at home.

"Have you graduated from a Gurukul?" There was a sharp edge to the tone.

Karna bit his lip. "No, I have not." *But I have trained in it.*

"Good, because we do not allow students from the Gurukul which are under the lands of Kshtriyas. The north is specifically Kshtriya-free. Now, a tough question, student," he looked down, his eyes carefully watching Karna, as if he was studying his each movement to detect any lies. "Are you a Kshtriya or are you a Brahmin? Because I'll know. Sooner or later."

Karna bit his lip again. He knew if he lied, he would get in and if he said the truth, he would be sent back.

But he nodded.

"Yes, guruji," he said. "I'm a Brahmin."

78

Present day...

"So there is no Lord Parshuram?" Shanaya asked, with delight and confusion.

"Yes," Karna smiled. "There are multiple followers of him."

"But why do they stay the way they do?"

"They continue to live by the teachings of Lord Parshuram, the prime martial arts guru of warfare."

"But what do they do with the knowledge?"

Karna shrugged. "Keep it for the day when the world will need another eradication of a Kshtriya like Lord Parshuram did the first time."

"And you are not supposed to reveal that Lord Parshuram is not alive?"

"It's a secret," he looked at her. "And I told you. If someone kills me, it's your fault."

They chuckled. Karna continued to rest on her thighs, when he asked her, "I think I shouldn't have sent Devi out in the open like this. Jara will know it's a trap."

"I think that idea of bringing the severed heads is clever. It gives the idea that she's ready to be out there.

And also, everyone knows that Devi wasn't too happy when you came to rule over her men and her. So, that, I feel will be good enough to convince Jara."

Karna nodded, "I hope you are right. But thank you. By sharing my story, I feel better. Though not altogether. I just don't know what I'll do if I fail."

"You try again, silly. That's what you do."

He smiled, and when he got closer to plant a kiss on her, he heard the sirens and the drums and trumpets. They both looked at each other in confusion and Karna slipped off his bed, and walked to the window of the tent, to see what the commotion was all about. Since his tent was up on the hill, he was able to see from afar, hundreds of men with banners and flags along with them, and they all were in fur coats, while their flags were coral green in colour. And no one stopped them from entering. For very good reasons.

Shanaya shared a glance with Karna as she said: "What is my father doing here?"

Karna would have offered drinks or brought more fruit plates in front of Archimedes, but the man solemnly sat opposite Karna, holding Shanaya's hand, kissing it and looking at her softly. He had a thick bun of hair, tied in a ponytail, with kohl-dark eyes and a long, wiry, tied-up beard.

"How is everything, my dear sunflower?" he asked.

Shanaya weakly smiled. "Everything is great."

"Good."

Karna was quiet. They were in the tent, while more Greek soldiers had appeared, creating unwanted resentment amongst people. He felt the eyes of his sponsor and father-in-law, Archimedes, and with cool, calm eyes watched him back.

"You know why I am here?" he asked.

"Enlighten me."

"I'm here because your exploits of Jarasandha are echoing across miles," he said. "And they are not favourable towards you."

He closed his eyes in defeat. *I knew this was going to happen.* He felt a tug in his throat and his breathing intensified.

Breathe slowly. And calmly, he spoke to himself.

"I gamble on winners and apparently I was wrong. You are losing my men and I am not liking it."

"Father," Shanaya began but Archimedes lifted his arm to silence her, "I would suggest, my sunflower, that you leave. It's between us."

Shanaya clenched her jaw and nodded. With a soft touch on his shoulders, Shanaya left and Karna felt frailer, but he had broadened his chest to show he was not weak. "So, do you have anything to say?" Archimedes asked.

"Yes," Karna nodded. "What has *he* promised you?"

Archimedes arched his brows. "What do you mean?"

"He got to you, didn't he?"

Archimedes was quiet. And then he burst out in a roaring chuckle.

"I should have never trusted you," Karna shook his head. "People were right about foreigners. They are backstabbers. I thought it was a stereotype. But it's true what they say about stereotypes. There is a reason why stereotypes exist, because they're usually true."

"He promised me citizenship in his newfoundland," Archimedes broke out.

"And you agreed?"

"He is winning, boy," Archimedes shrugged. "What do you want me to do? Stay silent and trust all on you."

"Well, that's why you made a martial alliance. That's the reason—"

He raised his fingers. "And because of that, I didn't attack you. Jarasandha wanted me to attack you but I said my daughter is in love with you and so, I'll do the next best thing."

No.

"I'll take back my army."

"You can't..." he tightened his fist. "I am close to winning..."

He shook his head. "And if you do, I'll be prouder, but I am not a gambler. I only bet on sure things and right now Jarasandha is winning."

"How do you think Shanaya will react to your decision? She will be hurt."

"She's too young to understand politics. But you understand. She will shout, cry, but let her be. It's for her survival because..."

Karna added, "She will be safe when Jarasandha will attack me." He was already losing hope and his breathing was growing heavier than before. The majority of the army was of course the Greeks. And they played a big role. Without them, he would be left with some Angan soldiers who already didn't like him and the Nishadhs, who were quite small in number to go into the battlefield.

"Yes, and then he shall marry her, after he kills you."

Karna nodded. "So do what you have to do and get lost from my camp."

Archimedes chuckled. "Kid, you'll realise why I did what I did one day. It's all about survival," he came on his feet and patted him on the shoulder.

"He is with the Black Greek," Karna said, quietly. "He has partnered up with Kalyavan, who killed your wife."

"I know, and that is why I gave you the benefit of the doubt that you'll win, but when I saw how many soldiers you lost..." he paused, "I had to side with the enemy."

Archimedes patted him on the shoulder. "Take care of my daughter while this lasts."

Once he disappeared, Karna exhaled a deep breath and he felt all the anguish and the frustration of being a failure. He knew he would become like his father; cornered from everywhere with nowhere left to go.

I don't know what I did wrong.

Karna stayed in the tent for hours. He had heard the loud yells and shrieks of Shanaya and soon he could hear footsteps, and hoof beats, leaving the camp. He remained frozen where he was and then he felt Shanaya's presence and her constant apology—how she didn't know anything about it, and she could never believe her father would do something like this.

Karna stayed the way he was, and didn't speak much, because he couldn't. He could see in the reflection of the sunlight that beamed in the tent—a shadow of his father and how much of a failure he was.

He told me we were not meant to be kings. I thought... He was right.

"It's all right," Karna said to Shanaya, "it's not your fault."

He held her hands and tried to show that he was being strong. He walked out of the tent, and looked at the people. All of them were scattered, they were looking at Karna and he could see a major chunk of the people had already left...

He could also see Satya who was shaking his head. He should have explained but with a choke in his voice, he walked to the old man and whispered, while all eyes were on him:

"Protect Shanaya. She will be under threat by the soldiers as she's Greek. Get your most trusted men to do so."

"But boy, I told you..."

"I know. Archimedes should not have been trusted," Karna said. "But we need to plan our next move. We need to do a headcount and see how many can come, and then we need to find a way to win this war..." and when he said the following words, he felt stupid, but somewhere he knew that was the path he had to follow—"without *fighting* the war."

79

"We have won," Jara announced, sitting on the long, wooden pedestal.

And everyone loudly cheered.

There was a cluster of men, half of them still in the infirmary, but many were alive and they all were grinning.

"Today we celebrate. Tomorrow we attack," he arched his brows. "And end this for good. Slowly, we will take over Anga and begin the expansion of our kingdom. Do not forget this is just the beginning for us. Karna was a thorn on our side, and now once we have Anga, Dhritarashtra cannot do anything, because by the rules of war—he has lost, and even though he has armies, he will not be able to stop us," Jara smiled.

And then he stepped down from the pedestal, with a quick move, he heard the clapping and the applause, as the men hugged each other and drank together. Jara couldn't help but smile, as he walked inside the tent, to find Vrishni and Kaal, who were talking to each other where Vrishni was doing more of the conversation.

"You need to stop coming to my personal room," Jara warned.

"I see you have made your men happy," Vrishni said,

in her long, grey gown just gracefully tracing the ground. "But I feel Karna will not give up."

"After the deal with Archimedes, we shouldn't care," Jara chuckled.

By signing that treaty, he had risked his relationship with Kalyavan, who was practically Archimedes' enemy, but he knew Kalyavan would understand why he did it. And once all of this was over, who was to say that they would continue the treaty with Archimedes?

Jara couldn't help but mull over the fact that Arjun was unsuccessful and his deal with Drona fell through, but it was all right as Jara should have known better than to rely on the Kuru's shrewdness. They had none except for the sinister Dhritarashtra, who he knew would now come and save the day. Try to create another treaty, give him more in return, but Jara wouldn't listen this time.

"How are the infected men?" Jara asked Vrishni.

"They are healing."

"But we need to attack tomorrow. It's the end of it." He had the map spread out on a round table, where the markings were made, from where they would attack and where they would not.

"Do you think this path is the right one?" Vrishni asked.

"Yes," Jara filled his goblet, and sipped from it. "Kaal will lead it and finally put an end to this stupidity. I have to focus on Mathura then. Gonanda says that Krishna has been difficult and he's shrewder than Karna, so we just have to see how much more."

Vrishni remained unconvinced. A contorted frown on her face.

"What?" Jara chuckled. "Karna was a suta. You can't expect a Kshtriya's job from a suta. He can't lead his men," he paused. "What more can happen to him..."

His voice trailed off as he felt a fourth person in the room and he turned to see a soldier.

"Your highness, there is a new development."

"Oh," Jara grinned, "and what would that be?"

"Karna's general is here and she wishes to speak to you. She has defected," the soldier said.

And Jara turned to face Vrishni and Kaal; both of them impassive, but he couldn't help but snort another laugh.

Devi was led inside, with her hands clasped behind, while the heads of her soldiers were brought along. As she entered the deep maroon tent, she smelled the strong fragrance of grapes that infiltrated her nostrils and her eyes were drawn towards a man with a dyed beard, who lay on the sofa, with his arms and legs spread apart. He had a triumphant grin on his face. He shooed off his soldiers, who dropped the heads beside Devi and left.

The man, Jara, she could clearly identify, because of his orange beard and the cleft over his upper lip—glanced at the heads and narrowed his eyes. "So you murdered your men and you brought it as proof?"

"Yes," Devi quietly said, a surge of anger in her eyes, but she had to play it calm and cool.

"Indeed. So the obvious question in the room," he asked, "Why have you left him?"

"Because he took my place."

"And you think after winning over him, I'll give you that place."

"I just want to rule Malinipur, that's it."

"Indeed. And what would you give me in return?"

"His next step."

Jara snorted a laugh. "And why do I need his next strategy when I already have defeated him?"

Devi's blood ran cold.

"The Greeks have pulled out after my treaty with Archimedes and I don't think Karna is capable of fighting anymore," Jara stood up, and Devi couldn't help but want to cry her eyes out, as she had no idea this was happening.

Jara walked to her and smelled her, and looked directly at her. "Why do I need you? You haven't still told me that."

"Because..." she felt him too close and then she turned back, her hands still clasped, when she saw a shadow lingering behind her and it was the...

Iron-masked man, towering over her!

They had cornered her.

"You should tell us, why we need you, otherwise..." Jara was inches away and he smelled of wine and dirt, "your head shall be sent back to Karna."

"He...he..." Devi pursed her lips, her back against the iron-masked man, "he is trained by Lord Parshuram..."

"So?" Jara raised his brows.

"And because of that he possesses the knowledge of Brahmastra."

At that, Jara's eyes started shrivelling and he went cold. "What did you just say?"

"He knows how to create a Brahmastra," she said.

"And you know how powerful it is. He can decimate your entire army and you as well."

"Fuck!" Jara growled, pulling himself back and throwing away the goblet. "Are you lying to me, woman?"

"No...no...why would I?"

"Kaal," he said, "take this wench away from me. Let me think for tonight."

Devi felt strong burly arms grab her by the shoulders and shove her out of the tent, as she was pushed and prodded by the man who killed Manvee.

80

Karna knew he would be enraged. He never thought it would be *this* much.

He had brought the captains and their seconds-in-command in one common hall, and he stood up on the pedestal as they were raining questions at him…

"We should have never trusted the Mlecchas! Because of you, we will lose our land!"

"Calm down," Karna said. "I have a few ideas…"

"WE DON'T NEED YOUR IDEAS!" his soldiers shouted.

He nervously glanced at Satya and Shanaya who were quiet and in one corner of the room.

"We cannot follow a king who has lost like this," some others muttered.

Things were all over the place. After the Mlecchas had left, Karna received multiple opportunities to have dialogue with his lesser commands, who were unhappy. And who would give up on the battle and leave.

"We won't fight for you anymore!" more of them shouted.

"And you shouldn't. You should fight for Anga…."

"No we shan't!"

Karna gritted his teeth. "Then you all shall be labelled deserters and executed on sight." When he said it, he realised it came out of frustration and he shouldn't have threatened his own men, who were already spitting fire at him, but he realised these words frightened them and they were silenced.

Sometimes it's important to be rude, to shut the naysayers up.

But he didn't like that silence, because he wanted people to follow him not because they feared he would do something to them, but because they liked him.

Not all leaders need to be liked.

"Now, I have a few ideas," Karna began.

But nowhere in the group, could he feel that anyone cared. They were forced to be here.

"Satya will share them with you," Karna continued, feeling glum. "If anyone has a problem, they can meet me later in private."

Karna left, but with a heaviness in his heart. In his mind, he went back in time, his memories stirring, to the moment when he had a conversation with his guru, Parshuram, where he learnt about the Brahmastra.

His one last hope.

Two years earlier...

"You are doing well!" his guru, Rambhadra, said.

Karna was sweating and even in the bitter cold, he felt warm. He had been practicing his sword fighting and archery since morning, and his feet had nearly frozen in the snow, but every day when the sun would come out, he would get his heat and energy from it and he would stand at the edge of the cliff and give his adulations. It was his way.

"You must learn climbing," Rambhadra said, and handed him a hook and a rope.

"But I already practiced for the entire day."

"I don't care."

Karna should have realised that he would be asked to do that. And along with his master, they began climbing the hill, the hook stabbing into the crust as he pulled himself upward. This exercise was for strength, vitality and balance, as the hook, if given too much pressure, could throw him off guard. He saw Rambhadra, as he cleanly and easily pulled himself up the hill.

"How do you do it?" he asked, almost shouting, as the winds had turned harsher by then and he felt the chills he hadn't been feeling before.

"I have been doing this several years before you, boy. Let us reach the ridge which is on top and we can sit down."

Karna nodded, pulling himself further. He had been practicing like this for one year, in different forms. What he had learnt from Dronacharya, he felt he learnt ten times more here. But of course, it was based on a lie. Everything was. He had not told his master that he was not a Brahmin and at one point, his master had told him:

"You don't fight like a Brahmin. Brahmins, in general, have no knowledge of warfare when they come here, but you are swift with your bow and clean with your sword."

And to that Karna had to say he was taught as a child by his teacher, in his early years. But his master wasn't too satisfied with that answer.

Karna felt he had tugged further and he reached the ridge Rambhadra had mentioned. He clasped and held on to the ledge when he almost tripped but was grabbed by Rambhadra who held him tightly.

"Careful!" He pulled Karna up and put him on the ridge.

Karna could feel his breathing tighten, as he leaned further and moved towards the cliff and looked at the snowy world beneath him. The winds were harsher, but his master Rambhādra just joined his hands and looked up with a smile.

"You have been doing well, son," he said.

"Thank you."

"But the namaskar you do for Suryadev, where have you learnt it from?"

Karna didn't know how to answer that. "It's umm…I always connected to the sun."

"You should. It's the best natural source of energy out there," he smiled, sitting on the cliff, cross-legged.

"Guruji, I want to know about the Brahmastra."

Rambhadra didn't respond. He was quiet, and he continued to look at the scenery.

"Guruji?" he called out again.

"I have heard you. But I do not want to listen to you," Rambhadra said. "Brahmastra is a knowledge only few must possess."

"Why?"

"Because only a few are capable of possessing it."

Karna didn't understand these riddles. In the past one year, he had tried to learn about the Brahmastra in one way or the other, but he couldn't find anything substantial even after all the spying he had done.

"When Brahmastra is used," he said, "it can end worlds if it is used by the force of evil. If it is used by the force of good, it will gain and grow the world and make it beautiful." He again spoke in riddles and Karna was feeling a pang of anger as a result. "And it should only be used when you have no other options left."

"But I feel I am ready to know of it. Ready to gain the knowledge."

"You think you know, but you don't," Rambhadra said.

Karna pursed his lips and sat beside his master. They remained in silence, only to hear the vultures squawk up high in the sky as they continued to admire the beauty around them, when Karna said: "You told me you knew someone with my breastplate. A year back."

"Yes," his eyes softened.

"Tell me who it was."

Rambhadra tightened his fist. "A life I lived in the past."

Oh. Karna was always curious about this, because he was told he had come with this armour and anyone who might know of this armour would also know whose son he truly was—since he was abandoned in the Ganga river. "Who was it, master?"

"Back then, I was like you. Young. Feverish with delight. And I was a worshipper of the sun, under the great sage Durvasa, when I happened to meet a young girl, younger than me…we fell in love, but things didn't go well, a priest can't fall in love so I was thrown out and I found refuge here and became an ascetic…" Rambhadra shook his head. "She had that armour, the one you wear, but then it's very common for someone from that Kingdom."

Karna tightened his jaw. "Did she have a child?"

Guruji looked sideways. "How do you know?"

Karna wanted to say that there could be a possibility he might be her son and the elation of joining those dots was making him anxious—but there could also be a possibility that he was wrong. And that his hopes were getting unnecessarily high due to his constant need to find his real parents.

Perhaps I am wrong.

"What was her name?" he still asked, out of curiosity.

Rambhadra was quizzical about the fact, about how interested Karna was. But he still simply stated: "Kunti. Her name was Kunti."

81

Devi was put inside her own tent, and there were guards outside, to make sure she didn't escape. Her arms were tied at the back, and she was kept in isolation, as thoughts began to corrode her mind. She had thought of telling them about the Brahmastra, but she felt guilty now as it would make Jara do something about it.

I should have said something else.

But she had no time. She had to find out their next action plan, and thus, she pulled out a small pocketknife which she had concealed in the back of her dhoti. And she began to tear apart the bamboo string. They should have checked her, but they didn't.

Her mind raced towards the news of the Mlecchas. They betrayed them as she had expected and she wanted to knock some sense into Karna, but she had no idea. She had to know what they were going for, and thus sneaking out was an option.

She had, in his tent, seen some papers and a map.

And she had to tiptoe towards it.

With the knife, she began to cut through the fabric of the tent, and then slowly peered outside to see if there was anyone who would be out there to spot her. But there was no one and she went prone, dragging herself out of the tent and onto the ground, as she made her move towards the tent.

It was the dead of night and already a day had gone by since she had arrived. Not a lot of soldiers were present, and she had to control her breathing as she was moving towards the tent. She rolled over in the mud, and could see the entire camp—there were people and just like her, looked ordinary, just like their camp. And she realised they were not evil, just following orders and their king. They were no different from her own men.

Devi staggered across the tent, and saw the insides of it. There were no guards, surprisingly, and she was glad momentarily, but that also made her sense something was fishy. *Why weren't they here?* But she came on her foot and in the shadows, walked to the round table where the maps and all were kept, her eyes drew to the diagrams and she realised the attack was...

From the lake.

They were using boats to go and attack from behind, really ending this.

But I had told him that this won't happen.

She hit her head, realising how a long time ago, she had mentioned this to Karna and how she was so sure. But now...her hopes crashed. And then she heard something—people were shouting: "SHE HAS ESCAPED! BEAT THE DRUMS!"

Devi cursed under her breath and grabbing hold of the maps, rolling them up, she walked further to the back of the tent trying to flee....

When a hand burst through the fabric and grabbed

her by the throat. Devi began to choke and a pain went through her neck, as she was thrown on the ground, her jaw smacking against it. She began to profusely bleed, as the figure in front of her tore through the fabric. And revealed itself.

The iron-masked man. The so-called Kaal.

With emotionless, pale eyes he watched her, blankly.

She had a pocketknife in her hand and as his hand went forward to hurl her, she stabbed it in his palm, and he pulled back, slowly pulling the blade out and looking at her placidly.

"Don't even try," she heard a voice.

Devi turned to face the one in front of the tent.

It was Jara.

"He can't be killed. I don't know what he has become. But he can't be killed easily because we have numbed the pain nerves inside of him, so he's devoid of any pain in general," Jara sighed. "On the other hand, you are quite courageous. Sneaking up like that."

Devi noticed how Kaal just stood as a wall in front, and didn't even bother to touch her as if he had no rage inside of him that Devi had attacked him.

Does he even feel things?

Jara's snarky eyes went over to Devi's hands where she held the maps. "Ah, I see. Stealing war information. Never thought Karna would degrade to such sly acts. But he's a boy. What else can I expect? You know what, let me show you something. Why don't you come with me?"

Devi, even if she wanted to, couldn't leave as Kaal pushed her in front, and she walked, gritting her teeth, following Jara.

He managed to make her take a trip around his camp and spoke about how Karna was a fool, and he was a suta, and that because of him so many people were dead. He should have just allied with Jara and he wouldn't have faced the brunt. By the time his long speech was over, Devi realised where he had taken her.

It was at the Champa River with its momentous water, where hundreds of boats were being prepared by armoured men carrying blades and bow.

Hundreds of logs burnt on each end of the reed boats.

"You should see what we will do," Jara said. "And this is the final attack which Karna has no clue about. Poor man. He shouldn't have left this place without any security."

Devi cursed, biting her teeth. *I made him do it. And now, because of me, he will face the brunt of it.* She felt so stupid and she also realised that no matter how angry she had been at Karna, his ideas were always brilliant while she was just not ready to lead.

And because of this mistake, he would lose. Because of *her.*

"Why are you showing me this?" she asked.

"Because," he smiled, "a dying person should know what will happen to her side of the war."

"Dying?" she was confused.

And then, a hand grabbed her by the throat...and darkness enveloped her.

82

Guide me, Suryadev.

He had lifted both his hands up in a namaskar, while one leg was on top of another and closed his eyes, as he worshipped the sun in front of him. He was at the top of the hill, and his camp was on the downslope.

The sun had just risen, and this was the time for him to learn what he could do in these pressing times, when he was terribly losing. Hated by everyone except for a select few.

Guide me, Suryadev.

He called to the sun god again; he could feel the heat empowering him and the strength that he wanted to be bestowed with coming towards him. He smiled to himself until it became apparent that he was hearing some noises. A lot of sounds. His eyes drew back to his camp, and he could see what the commotion was about.

And he rushed like the wind, because what he saw was his camp getting attacked.

His breath was harsh and shallow. His chest was hurting…

Where did they come from?

He could hear the trumpets blaring, but it was too late

as the black-armoured men had begun to cascade down with swords and spears.

Karna was bare-chested and wearing a golden-orangish dhoti. He had no weapon on him, and his Vijaya bow was in his tent.

I need to reach for it.

He found the soldiers coming towards him, as they killed a few of his men. He took a pause to look at them, with a smirk. And then cooly he directed them to come towards him.

As one soldier appeared in front of him, he instantly dodged the jab of the sword and twisted the soldier's hand to drop the blade, which he then grabbed to plunge in the back of his neck. Two more soldiers came and he parried and dodged, rolled and stabbed his way through them.

He looked at the sword, which was shiny with blood, as he left them and moved further to find all his soldiers fighting back against the black-armoured soldiers.

But he continued to make his move towards his tent, and any soldier who came in front of him...he deflected the blade and stabbed them.

He was seeing corpses that were flayed, of not just his men, but of the women from the camp, the doctors and so forth, and the kitchen staff, even young kids, and it made his heart break. He could hear the loud sounds permeating in the background with the clashing of the swords and the yells and screams and rivers of blood spurted on the ground like the river Ganga.

He reached the tent, and as he did, he tripped over someone. His eyes flew back at what he tripped on, and it fell over a familiar figure.

He knew the man. He was stabbed and brutally masticated, his armour broken and bent.

Shantanu.

He had disappointed his young soldier and he just lowered his gaze, feeling guilty as he scampered further and moved to the camp, opening his trunk, his eyes gazing around the tent to find Shanaya…

But she wasn't there.

The stupid woman must already be fighting.

But he was also proud about this stupidity of hers, as he opened the trunk and pulled out his quiver made of pigskin, and he wore it across his naked chest. And then, out of it, he pulled out the longbow—Vijaya—which was shaped in a way rays of sunshine are shaped. And he grabbed it tightly.

This is it.

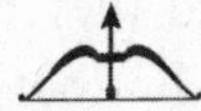

Satya was having a hard time getting a grip on reality. He had his sword. He had his breastplate and he had oiled his long moustache that fell on both sides of his face, but he was not ready. Something was stopping him.

I can just run. I can just leave everything. We have already lost. But…

The thoughts of Soma came and provided warmth to him, and he wanted to get that feeling again…this was a fruitless endeavour, this was of no use…

I should run…

But then his thoughts went back to the time he was the commander to Adhirath, and he had begun to manifest his dreams into reality when he saw the young boy he used to train; with earnest eyes of gold, a face which spoke of curiosity. The man in him had changed, but Karna hadn't. He had remained the same. And he had become more determined.

I don't know if I can die for Anga. But I know I should die for Karna.

With a grip on his sword, he moved out of the tent and the first thing he did was—slash the first soldier who appeared in front of him. Arrows flew at him, and he pulled the shield from behind, deflecting them instantly.

"COME ON!" he yelled.

And so they did. Satya found a new swordsman who appeared and he hurled his shield against the man and pushed him on the ground, with a sword coming after that, stabbing him.

Another appeared and they instantly tried to plunge the blade in his armour, but Satya turned and deflected, using his shield to knock the soldier on the face.

His eyes, meanwhile, had fallen on Shanaya, who had her hammer and was thrashing anyone who came in front of her, while behind her he saw there were mothers and children; probably the nurses and their sons they had brought along with them. He was always against the idea of children being at the camp. He also saw Shanaya was protecting the Angans, as she was pushing them inside the infirmary and locking the door.

Satya moved further, briskly walking towards her, as he had his shield on top, deflecting the arrows that were coming her way. He saw a soldier approaching, mud splitting as he shoved him away, and tossed him in the corner with his shield, and another appeared as he lunged at him and severed his head.

He had forgotten by the time he had reached Shanaya, how many he had killed but he was panting and was not hurt yet.

"We need to escape," Satya said.

"No, we can win this," she resisted determinedly. "The men who attacked are few in number. We just have to hold for long...and I need to protect the infirmary. All the women and children are here."

"Fine, I'm here with you too then."

Shanaya smiled. She patted him on the shoulder.

And then their warm exchanges took a pause, as their eyes fell on the one they sorely wanted to avoid.

With an axe, standing like a giant in between, was none other than...the iron-masked man. They both had heard a lot about him, and he had been here, there... around everywhere.

"I'll deal with him," Satya said. "Fucking moron."

And as the axe came towards him, he blocked it with his shield. It was a heavy attack, and he rolled over, whipping his moustache away as he went further and sharply shoved the blade towards the iron-masked man who deflected it with ease. He was playing it cool as well, as the world around Satya was crumbling with soldiers just falling like a pack of cards and dying, and fires from most of their tents growing.

"You know what your problem is?" Satya said. "You just have too much of an ugly face that you have to hide it behind that iron mask."

Kaal didn't say anything. He just picked up the axe in

his hand and lunged at Satya, who deflected and turned around, stabbing Kaal in the spine. The giant fell down, with a loud thud, but no yelp from his mouth emerged, as if it didn't hurt him even a little.

"You might be a big guy, but I used to be the commander of..."

And then Kaal swung his axe across Satya's legs, ripping them apart from joint to joint. Satya could feel the pain, as he watched his legs seperated from him, falling on the ground, clasping for his shield and sword.

He began to cry instantly realising he had lost his legs and he could feel his end coming.

He looked up to see the pale Shanaya who was making her way to him, when Satya stopped her, showing her his hands, his eyes pale, asking her to stop, realising he did what he did for Karna and for...

He turned around to see the feet of the iron-masked man coming towards his face...

The head burst like pulp.

Karna, for a moment, felt his heart stop and his limbs grow weaker as he saw his master—his guru from the past—beaten and battered, converted into a shapeless mess.

"NO!" he yelled, screaming out of his lungs and he even saw Shanaya who was crying, as she fought the soldiers.

The iron-masked man just pressed over Satya's pulped head as if it was a squashed orange.

"I'LL KILL YOU!" Karna didn't wait.

He darted towards the iron-masked man and with a quick shove, he shouldered him hard against the chest. The iron-masked man almost fell, as he brought two arrows out and rocketed towards the man's neck, stabbing him in the throat.

The iron-masked man took some time, but he pulled out the arrows from his throat and broke them into pieces with his bare hands.

His mask. That's his weakness. That's why he wears it.

Karna was plotting until the iron-masked man swung his axe towards him and he dodged, rolling back as he shot another arrow in the back to confuse the iron-masked man, who looked back to see where the arrow went for a split second...

And Karna needed not more than that.

He somersaulted in the air, as he grabbed hold of the mask, and climbing on top of the iron-masked man, he began to pull it apart. But the man tried holding on to it...until he lost his balance and fell on the ground, with Karna on top, both bathed in the dirt and spirals of dust. A searing pain went through his body as he continued to pull the mask up, and finally...

He did it.

Locks of his hair fell open to reveal the face, and the iron-masked man pushed him away as he came on the ground, grabbing his axe quickly.

He wasn't wearing a mask for the reasons I thought he was.

He was familiar. Quite familiar, and he was fuming.

He swung his axe repeatedly against Karna, who began

to move backward, and struggle and square off. And as he continued to do so, anger erupted in him worse than before, when a shadow lurched on him from behind and Karna saw it was his wife—Shanaya. She stabbed him in the head with the dagger, while Karna brought down his two arrows and said:

"You won't be missed by anyone."

And he shot the two arrows from his longbow and they went straight into the man's eyes—both of them, plunging deep into the sockets, making him blind...and he fell back. Shanaya used that moment to jump and stood next to Karna.

Karna, for surety, scampered and checked the corpse of the iron-masked man and saw he was placid like his mask, with no movement.

He's dead. Finally.

He pulled out the arrows from his eyes and plunged it again—deeper, so his skull and his brain would be mashed. "I will not..."

Shanaya hugged Karna, and they both wept for Satya, as they saw the man who had helped them was dead but so was his killer. He looked around, surveying the fact that the black-armoured soldiers were mostly dead and his men had survived, while many, after seeing the iron-masked men's fate had escaped from Jara's army.

"Did we win?" he asked.

"Perhaps, this one," Shanaya said.

Karna sighed. "We need to meet Jarasandha."

"And do what?"

"Finish this once and for all." He had also begun to wonder whether Suyodhan was fine, as he was lying on the bed all this while, sleeping and resting, far away from all of this. He wished his friend was here, but he had been brutally tortured earlier by Jarasandha. "And also learn one thing which he never told anyone."

Karna's eyes went over to the iron-masked man.

"What?" Shanaya asked.

He looked at the iron-masked man, who had quite a familiar face—of Jara, with the abnormalities of the body and his tongue...which was out, since his jaw was smaller than Jarasandha's, but other than that—he looked similar.

"That he had a twin."

83

When Jara dreamt, he dreamt of the day he had killed his brother.

But that's what the *lie* was.

His brother, since childhood, was ridiculed for his tongue and his lower jaw, and he used to be bullied for being slow. Jara was the only one who loved him, until his father banished his brother and so with him, Jara left too. And soon, he found his mother in the forest, the Rakshasi who had said to him:

"I'll teach you what your father should have."

She trained both the boys in all warfare and strategies and by the end, she became both a guru but a mother for them. They didn't want to leave, until his mother told him:

"Kill your brother."

Jara was confused. "Why?"

"Because he will be your deterrent. All your life. He will be what'll pull you back. Your love for him is so great that if he dies—you shall crumble. And thus, no one should have his blood other than you."

It made him fear more, and then while his brother who loved to play with dice was rolling them on the floor, Jara had brought the rock and he was ready to smack it, tears streaming from his eyes...

When he stopped, as his brother unknowingly looked back and just smiled. "Rock..." he said. "Rock..."

"No..." Jara grimaced. "I can't..." and he tossed the rock aside and hugged him. "I know people will make you my weakness if they see you. And thus, from today my brother shall no longer be considered alive. You shall be hidden in the shadows for as long as possible."

And from the iron and metal, Jara had created a mask for him, giving him a new face.

When he returned to his mother, he had his own blood, and gave it to her, which she saw and laughed.

"Good. Now kill me. My purpose is over," she said, and presented a knife.

"What do you mean?"

"I have no need to live in this world and the fact you will shed my blood, shall make my spirit be with you," the Rakshasi said.

Jara held the knife and he looked at it for a while, unable to understand, when he heard a choking stutter and looked up, his eyes contracting in shock, as his brother Kaal just smacked a huge rock on their mother's head, with the mask now on his face. And behind the mask, Jara could hear the sobs.

"Mother wanted to separate us. No one can separate us."

Jara smiled, hugging him. And they both stood on the blood of the woman who made them from two—into one.

When Jara had returned, he had returned with an iron-masked man, but as years went by, Kaal's intelligence didn't grow and he grew weaker, feeble, until he was attacked by Jara's many enemies. He was on his deathbed when Jara found a Rakshasi, who gave him... *something*.

Little knowing, that it was going to turn him into a monster.

Jara had woken up. His eyes were silent. And he could feel his breathing had softened. For some reason, he knew something was wrong. As if a part of him had died. And he didn't know why he felt that way.

With a jolt, he woke up and wearing just a dhoti, he walked out of the tent, his muscled body looking grand for his age. As Jara moved out, he saw people—injured ones, returning from the ambush. And he found his captain being taken by two men from both ends, who stopped in front of Jara.

"What happened?"

"We damaged them immensely, your highness," the captain was gushing blood. "But we lost many of our men too, especially Kaal."

"You lost...Kaal...?"

"Yes."

Jara couldn't recognise the emotion he was feeling. He just looked at the captain placidly and then nodded, letting him off. He sighed, he wanted to feel things; anger, rage, but all he could feel was...numbness. He looked up, across the camp, his eyes meeting Vrishni who had a soldier next to her, telling her the news, and she had the same shocked expression on her face.

And he knew he wanted answers.

"I hope you are going to fucking massacre the boy," Vrishni said, the moment she entered his tent. "I so hope that. Otherwise I'll rain fire over him."

"Calm down. In war, deaths happen," he said, but of course, he didn't mean it. Some deaths to some people are more personal than the rest.

"He was my boy…"

"He was your experiment," Jara shot up. "Stop treating him as if you are his mother. You are not."

"He needed…"

"He was your pig to be tested," Jara said. "And nothing else. Which makes me wonder, why did he die?"

"He wasn't invincible. He just couldn't feel pain and his physicality was mutated. What I heard was, that his eyes were plucked out with the arrows that belonged to that archer king." Vrishni came forward and thumped her fist on the table that was in between them, her eyes bloodshot. "He was attacked in the brain and revealed to the world."

"Have the men brought his body back?"

"Yes."

Jara nodded. "Have you seen it?"

"I plan to."

"You won't," Jara said, knowing fully well he was going to let no one know that behind that mask was his brother.

"But…"

"I know you will want to experiment on him again. And I won't allow that…"

Vrishni raised her voice, but Jara just put his hand forward. "Nothing out of you. And out of respect for

Kaal, I won't banish you, otherwise you would have been out by now. Get comfortable as long as we are here, which won't be for long."

She wanted to protest further, but she didn't try in front of the king. She knew his wrath would hurt her. "What do you plan to do?"

"Well," he sighed knowing well enough it would lead to controversy and criticism, "I am going to surrender… for a *price*."

84

Karna wiped the blood from his bow, with a piece of cloth.

While Shanaya made sure everyone was fine at the camp and was sending off the children and the women away for now, Karna knew the war was over. The job was done. He had lost.

He sat there in the corner of his room, and continued to wipe it. He no longer had the problem of breathlessness. In fact, it had vanished when he realised that there was no fear of failure, because he had already failed. He had led so many of them to their deaths. He instigated a war for his selfish motives to get the crown; otherwise everything was peaceful.

To achieve Anga and fulfil the *promise* he ended up becoming the bad man. The one you would tell stories about; of a rejected, and an arrogant man.

The door briskly opened behind him, and he knew it was Shanaya. He didn't want to turn, until he heard a manly voice say to him: "I heard."

He knew that voice.

"Suyodhan," Karna breathed, "how do you feel?"

"Worse. I should have been there to save them."

"No. This is not your battle. This is mine. And there is nothing left. Your father made a big mistake and so did you by putting your faith in me."

"Well," Suyodhan's shadow lingered behind him, "it's all right. We all lose."

"No. I lost my uncle...I lost my men...their respect, I lost my ally and I don't even know where my commander is..." he shook his head, realising he shouldn't have sent Devi out in the open. He should have not made such a bad decision. "Your father is on his way, as the scouters have told me. I am sure he has come to do what he did years back with my father."

"But this time, I'll be here. I'll request him for an army. It was wrong of him to just send you off without any back-up," Suyodhan said. "It's not over. You have damaged Jarasandha beyond repair as well."

"Because he fights majorly in Mathura," Karna said.

"If you ever want to succeed in life, my friend, you need to grow up and stop feeling sorry for yourself because no one...and I mean no one...gives a shit how much you tried and didn't succeed. If you don't, you get up and do it again. And then again. And again!" he exclaimed, stomping his feet. "Let me convince my father for a partnership. He will give his army and I will help you this time."

Karna solemnly turned towards Suyodhan, who had a bandaged upper arm, but he had arched brows and looked determined. "You are a good person."

"I am not fishing for compliments here," he chuckled.

Karna planted a small smile on his face and there was

silence between them, until it was broken by a loud shout: "MESSAGE!"

"It's General Devi's horse!" a soldier cried out of happiness.

Karna stood squared with Suyodhan and Shanaya, as he held looked ahead and saw the dipping sun. The crop fields grazed and fluttered from the storm, and a group of his men cobbled with him in the front, as the horse rode towards them.

How did she escape...?

The horse rode and he could clearly see her shadow above it...and her head...

It *fell.*

His heart drowned and Shanaya clasped his hands tighter, while the men around him gasped. The headless body of Devi collapsed from the stallion, who began to move faster and halted in front of Karna. Devi remained there, headless.

And all the elation they had felt at just the previous moment, was now gone. It just...vanished.

They decapitated her.

He instantly rushed to her and found her headless body, as her men stayed behind in shock and confusion. He skid across the ground and looked at her; tears streaming down his eyes as he began to beat the ground and weep, while Suyodhan's hands came over his shoulder.

No. It can't be.

When blood is shed, it drenches everyone around it.

With one step of his, innocent people had died.

"He's going to pay for it!" Shanaya screamed.

But Karna's soul was already defeated. He had given up. He wanted to ask *how* but his mouth was sour and stale, when Suyodhan said: "There's something in her pocket." And he knelt down, to take it out.

It was a scroll.

"It's from Jarasandha," Suyodhan said, and already it sounded like a threat.

"Read it out to me," Karna whispered, his eyes still puffy and red.

"He wants to..." Suyodhan's eyes went up. "He will *surrender*."

"What?" Karna looked up at his friend.

"But there's a condition," Suyodhan added. "He wants to wrestle you in the middle of the battlefield. And if he wins, he takes Anga. And if he doesn't—he will surrender and leave and not touch Anga. It's a king's promise."

Karna couldn't believe his ears. *Wrestle?* "It must be a trick."

"It makes sense," Shanaya said from one corner, her curly hair whipping with the brisk wind. "Father always said Jara was a big fan of wrestling. He has been a wrestler, born as one, like you were with archery. He wants to humiliate you."

Of course.

"Hasn't he already?"

"No. This is personal," Suyodhan said.

Yes. I killed his brother. And just like him, he wants to pop my eyes out with his thumbs.

"Then we can't accept it," Suyodhan tore the scroll. "Karna has little to no knowledge about wrestling.

Father arrives tomorrow, we can still win it without these theatrics," he paused. "And with their help, Karna can use the Brahmastra as well."

Karna was silent. He didn't want to take a decision. He came on his feet and ordered his men to take away the corpse, as he walked with Shanaya. He looked weak for a big man, fragile like a flower.

"We shall see tomorrow what the Maharaja says," Karna said to Shanaya and Suyodhan, who had become glad, in these morbid times. "But today, we mourn. We perform our *antyeshi*. Cremate the dead. And pay our respects."

They both nodded. Karna pursed his lips. He wanted to use the Brahmastra, and perhaps if he accepted the deal he would have to use it.

It was time.

85

One year earlier...

"I want to learn Brahmasta, guruji!" he exclaimed and his voice was direct.

Karna had been here for two years now and he could feel he had changed and become a better person, a better warrior. Now, he wanted to know the ultimate truth.

"You must practice for more years," Rambhadra drank from his flask calmly as if the words didn't matter.

They were in the dining studio of the temple; a calm, serene place where they were eating food.

"But why?"

"Because to learn about the Brahmastra, one must be at peace. Your emotions are too much. Your emotions will get the best of you."

"But I am patient!" he exclaimed, realising he just contradicted the statement and he bit his lips in the process. "I suppose I get it. But is there a way to prove that I have the power to get the Brahmastra?"

"Perhaps. There is a Rakshas den. When your training is complete, I shall show you."

Karna felt he had learnt everything. What else was left? And thus he asked that.

"The very fact that you ask this, shows you are not ready for it...or perhaps, you are. You are talented. We can see with the den."

"Then let me attack it. I will prove myself to you by defeating the Rakshas here."

Rambhadra narrowed his gaze. "Your soul is of a Kshtriya, crying out for war and battle. A Brahmin studies, is patient and waits. He doesn't let the rage for battle win over him. He plans his attacks."

"But I am not a..." he didn't want to lie again. So he sighed, as he went for the door of the temple, and he decided to take a deep breath, keeping his wrath aside which he had gotten tired of. In front of him, he saw a lot of temple priests had gathered in their leopard skin cloths and matted hair, looking ahead at something. "What is happening, guruji?"

Rambhadra by then, had reached close to him, standing toe to toe with Karna. "Indeed, the worst has happened."

"And that is?"

"Kiratas. Mountain bandits," he said.

Karna saw what he was pointing at. Lots of dots across the ridge and shoulder of the hills, people were climbing down and up from their grappling hooks and were stealing from the village ahead.

"And as martial artists, you don't do anything about it?" Karna cried.

Rambhadra chuckled. "We are Brahmins, boy. We do what we do only for the sanctity of what Lord Parshuram stood for."

"But the villagers..."

"They just steal. There is no bloodshed."

"But it's their food being stolen and their livelihood… they'll starve."

"We feed them."

He cursed under his breath, as he noticed how a young village woman was crying as a huge basket of rice was grabbed by the Kiratas who all were in bear-skins, dark-skinned, with some kind of green or teal paint over their forehead.

"This is wrong."

"Nothing is wrong in this world, boy. All that matters is the rule of the nature. The nature of a bandit is to steal, and the nature of the villager is to grow more to eat. That is the vicious cycle of violence that has continued on this earth for the longest time."

"But what if you break it?"

"By killing them, you mean? Bah, if you do that, aren't you practicing violence yourself?"

But he knew he had to be a better person than just following the rules. He knew not following the rules and rebelling had always gotten him into trouble, but Karna didn't listen. He went to grab his Vijaya, which was a longbow, his feather-tinted arrows, and he was on his way, his hook blade on his girdle, dangling from it.

All the priests were angry. Frustrated. He could see them arching, but he didn't care, when he was grabbed by the hand and he realised it was Rambhadra.

"If you leave, I won't be able to protect you," he said, with concern.

But Karna didn't listen. He had to help the people.

And he slipped out his master's hands from his and said: "You are right about the cycle of violence. And perhaps one has to stop the violence even if it sacrifices ego, but that's not me. I would fight violence with violence till the end of my days if I think that's the right thing to do."

Rambhadra didn't say anything as Karna lurched forward and moved in breakneck speed.

When blood is shed, it drenches everyone around it. The words echoed, but he ignored them.

By the time he had reached, only three were there and, with stolen goods they were climbing up the hill and would escape from the ridges.

I have to stop them before they escape.

He began rolling up the hook blade, which he tossed across the sky and it thrust itself into the snow crust.

He began to pull himself up then, as he tied it against his girdle. Now, it had become tight and he had his bow in his hand, ready to strike.

He aimed the bow, by the time he reached, he found himself looking at the hand which held the rice bag. He shot it across the Kirata's hand, who had not suspected him till then and it hit him, stabbing him, as he loosened the grip from the hook blade of his and fell down.

While Karna didn't catch him, he grabbed hold of the rice bag, and clung to it while the man fell from the mountain shoulders and on to the ground, dying on the spot.

This got the attention of the two other Kiratas who hissed and signalled each other to move faster. They had been moving on the right, diagonally, and towards a small ledge, from where they wanted to escape.

Karna began to dangle harshly from his hook and moved from left to right, until he gained momentum, reaching closer to the two Kiratas. He flung himself towards them, grabbing on to one from the back. Quickly, Karna pulled out his arrow and stabbed him on his arm. The Kirata yelled, while another tried to shoot him with the bow, and one of them…

Sharply stabbed Karna in the arm. He yelled loudly, but he managed to overpower the Kirata who fell, but Karna didn't, as he hooked himself again.

He instantly made a run towards the last one, who was close to escaping, when he jumped against the rocky, snowy slab, pushing himself in mid-air, his hook loosening and breaking apart—but he used his perfect vision to hurt the last Kirata—

And his body contorted, almost flying, as his bow aimed towards the bandit, shooting the last arrow, into his head. More food fell from him, and he crashed…

While Karna had no ground in between and he was…

Falling…

He could feel the ground approaching and he knew he was going to die. He struggled with the hook blade and threw it across the hill to thrust it in, but he missed.

Help me, Suryadev.

And he tried again, almost metres away from the ground, until the hook grabbed onto the snow crust and he felt a jerk, as he pulled himself up and saved himself from dying in the nick of time.

He continued to grin, as people around him were

clapping and bowing down and thanking him for eliminating the bandits.

Karna looked up at the priests, who had come to see the spectacle and their eyes were all adamantly watching him.

But they were not looks of comfort, instead they looked furious.

86

Present day...

Karna was hesitant to enter the tent.

Just like that, with Dhritarashtra's army, almost five thousand men had approached and gathered around his camp, like a fortified structure. They were heavier and bulkier than most soldiers of Karna. The towers were filled and Karna felt small—and humiliated. He could imagine how his father would have felt like when it had happened to him. In fact, now his father was here too, bringing the king on his favourite chariot.

He was nudged by Shanaya, who held his hands and smiled at him. Her black hair shone, and his eyes teared, as he nodded and let go of her palm and entered the tent.

Dhritarashtra was sitting on the carpet, sipping from his goblet like always, as Suyodhan was whispering in his ears; he looked desperate and earnest, probably convincing his father to help Karna further.

"You are here!" the blind king announced. "Please sit down."

Karna did so, as he noticed there were three guards in the room with golden masks and turbans on, hiding their faces and looking straight. Dhritarashtra was well protected—always.

He looked at the Maharaja who had his pale, white eyes staring at him and even though he was blind, his irises pierced into Karna's soul.

"I don't want to beat around the bush. So I'll just say it," he said. "You put my son's life at risk but you also saved him. Your men hate you since one of your men only came to Hastinapur to tell me to pull you away. And…you lost. Jarasandha won."

"The battle is not over."

"Oh please, look at your men. They hate you. Not only did you side with the corrupt, you ended up making them lose the battle even then. That's just being a poor king."

It stung him like a bee. The words. They were true.

"Now Jarasandha has concocted a silly deal of wrestling with you. I don't understand why. Perhaps you hurt him pretty bad because he doesn't do these things." *I killed his brother. I deserve his hate, but he deserves mine too*. "Now, my dear son is still being a good son and a good friend to you, and you are lucky he's here. I am ready to give my army at your disposal which I didn't in the beginning and help you win the war."

For a moment, Karna's blood froze. *Really? After all of this?*

But then he didn't smile because he knew there was something more to it—some *condition* which would be unfavourable to him.

"But in return what do you want?" Karna asked.

"Your kingdom, of course," he smiled. "Unlike last time, I wouldn't make the mistake of partnering up with

Jarasandha. He was a thorn in my plans and I thought he would be an ally. But declaring a war on us was a pretty unwise decision on his part, so I shall do what I told you to complete. But of course, your kingdom goes away, your throne goes away. Anga is no more yours. And it becomes mine." The smile continued to be on his face, and it was a snide, pathetic one.

Karna paused, as Suyodhan with an earnest voice said: "Vasu, it's a good plan. I know you wanted the throne, but if father leaves, whatever is left of Anga goes away too. At least, under father you can still rule as a commander."

"Of course. A post shall be assigned to you... for formality purposes," Dhritarashtra added the last comment like a joke, as a *favour* to Karna.

Karna could understand why Suyodhan would do this; convince him to give up. But his mind raced back to the *promise* he had made, and he knew for sure that he would rather die fulfilling it than give in to the offers of seditious kings.

"What if I win this battle myself?" Karna asked, looking up.

Suyodhan instantly went for a shake of his head, but Dhritarashtra couldn't help but chuckle. "And how do you propose that to happen?"

"I will do what I have to," Karna said.

"Really? *Really*?" Dhritarashtra turned to his son who was defiant and had lost hope. "Your friend is quite a stubborn soul. A very poor king though. You are risking everything...your life and your men's life and of course, your Mleccha wife, who stayed here while her kind betrayed you."

"I know. But I'm willing to take that chance," Karna said. "If I win, your highness, I choose to then not just give up the timber production percentage but also have no affiliation with your crown. *If* I win, that is."

"No fealty?" he raised his brows. "My, my, renegotiating a deal now. All right," he nodded in an instant. "Why do you want the timber production to go away? You want it all for your pocket?"

"No, I had made a promise to a friend," Karna recalled Eklavya. "I do not want to destroy nature. Anga has already been devastated enough."

"Ah, a true, honourable man. Sad, that most of them wither away quickly. Heroes don't live long, my dear Karna," the blind king said.

"But as long as they live, it is worth every moment."

The Maharaja was quiet. And then he turned to Suyodhan. "I believe we should leave then. Karna has a job to do; fight the impossible fight." He came on his feet and so did Karna, bowing before his Maharaja. "Remember one thing Karna, if you are going to fight this war, then I should provide you with some insight—your men..." he smiled, "they hate you because you haven't showed them you are the *king* and you have to prove to them why they should not hate you. I believe, if they see what you are truly capable of...I am sure they will like you."

Karna continued to watch the blind king and nodded, as he left, with the aid of Suyodhan who couldn't but feel sad about the time that was going to come next.

87

Karna, as he went out of the stable, decided to move for his tent, plans hatching in his mind. He had to finally accept the wrestling duel with Jarasandha, but he also had to be smart.

What to do?

He had taken on an impossible task.

As he walked, his eyes lay on his father at the stable, cleaning a horse, like a...driver. The chariot was golden and ornate, but more rusty from the last time he had seen it. Still, it stood, imposing.

His father glanced at him and met Karna's eye. He awkwardly stood, amidst the roars of people who were walking around him. He had a rotund frame, and his thick moustache was oiled with his hair combed at the back.

Karna came forward, and Adhirath embraced him. Anger is fire amidst family, but it dies as quickly as it rises. They held the embrace for long and Karna began to cry on his shoulders.

"I am sorry. You were right," Karna said.

"You don't have to be."

"I did...I was so foolsih."

"You are a smart boy. Don't you say that."

"I worked on this, forever…learning…and…I don't know where I went wrong," Karna said. "I didn't even go to my mother's antyeshi, I should have been there, but it was the promise…"

"Who made you promise?" Adhirath asked, clinging on to his son.

Karna paused. He had known that he would not tell anyone until he succeeds, but he didn't even know if he would now. And he wanted to have that satisfaction of knowing he told it to someone, especially someone who was the most important to him.

"Mother," he said, and his father's face was buried in his shoulder. "Mother had told me when I was twelve years old, I should do everything in my power to get Anga back, because I was the rightful heir. She wanted Anga to be free. And she said, even if you tried to stop me, to not give up. Learn. Learn. Learn. Just continue learning and return with a prepared plan, and I did but I still lost."

He paused.

"Perhaps you were right. I am just not made for it. I should have been like Shon, I should have just not listened to mother…"

"No, *I* was wrong, Vasu." Adhirath pulled him back, arching his brows. "I thought about what you said earlier. I was wrong. Not you. Not anyone else. I was wrong in not fighting back Jarasandha thirty years ago. I was wrong in believing that you couldn't do it. And you can."

"How but?"

"When you had come to meet me that time, you had the fire in you of becoming a *king*," he smiled. "You were too enveloped in your vanity. You liked the crown and the regality of all these things...and I thought you had lost yourself. That you had become the very thing that all these kings were. In the process of following your mother's promise, you got happy about other things, materialistic things." He teared up as well. "But remember son. Don't be a king. Be a *leader*. And your men...they will follow. I was never one. But I see it in you."

Karna looked stunned. *Of course. I was always fond of the position, but I forgot what I had to become in the first place. I had to free Anga and that was more important to me than being merely a king.*

"I rejected Dhritarashtra."

Adhirath smiled. And Karna smiled back.

"That is a good decision. A decision thirty years in the making, but a good one indeed," Adhirath said and chuckled. "Do you have a plan?"

Karna nodded. "Yes, I think so."

"And if you fail?"

Karna knew that if someone would have asked him before, he would have choked up.

But not now.

Because he realised being anxious about things was natural, but one could not let it overpower oneself and the fight against anxiety was a long one, but you had to fight every day.

"If I fail, father..." Karna smiled. "I will try again. And then again. Until I succeed."

88

Karna knew he would be doing extraordinary things in the process of defending his empire, but he never thought he would have to wrestle for it.

He was always average at it. And had no reasonable understanding of it. And while archery was more his wheelhouse, he knew he was on the backfoot with Jarasandha, the most famous malla yoddha of Bharat, who had built training grounds dedicated to Hanuman and Lord Shiva.

Karna wore his *langot*, with his hair tied back so it wouldn't hinder his wrestling. He was ordained in sand, and his hands were dirty and soiled.

This was it. This was going to be his end or beginning...

"Are you sure?" Shanaya was by his side, sitting close, her sword dangling from her girdle.

"Yes."

"You don't have to do it."

"I know. But I need to do it. The men under me should know and should follow me and if I stay on the backfoot, if I stay in the corner and order around, they will never look at me as a leader," Karna said.

"All right. And do you want me to go about what we discussed?"

Karna nodded. "Yes. Be careful though."

"I don't think the plan will work."

But Karna understood human psychology. "It will, if *you* do it."

"Fine. I'll work my charms," she grinned and kissed him full on the lips. "I know we have lost a lot but we will work it out. We are in this together, all right?"

"Yes, I know," he smiled.

And she left, to execute one part of the plan as he wanted.

Now, it was time for the speech.

Jara was getting prepared.

Even though it had been sometime now that he hadn't wrestled, he still missed every ounce of it. In the middle of his camp, Karna was preparing after the announcement that he had accepted his scroll, with disdain and hurt, since his general was sent back to him headless. He knew his idea would be accepted, and thus he prepared. He had a round club which he was manoeuvring, while sand was put on his naked body, his hair was greased.

The middle of the battlefield was cleaned, all the corpses removed, and ghee was poured on it, to make it softer for the wrestlers.

He turned on his side while he practiced for the wrestling match, when he saw Vrishni who was moving with a vial of powder, which she carried in her hands.

"I have prepared this for you," she said, without any emotion.

She had not been talking to Jara for a while now after he had stopped her from seeing Kaal's body. Anger had surged in her eyes and she continued to be silent, until now.

"What is this?" Jara asked.

"A powder that'll blind him and you can defeat him easily and kill him," she said. "Just sprinkle it along with sand, in one of your attacks."

"Wench," he chortled, "you really think I would bow down to these theatrics? Malla yuddha is a game of honour. I can't bastardise it with these tricks. Karna was my br...umm...Kaal's killer," he corrected, "but he didn't dishonour my request even though I incited him. He took it, did what a wrestler would. And I will give him an honourable death, with my arms around his neck, but not by cheating. By doing the right thing."

For a moment, Vrishni was surprised. And then she grabbed the vial tightly in her fist and left.

Jara sniggered and his eyes drew to the battlefield.

Let's begin.

Karna could hear the trumpets and it was his time to leave, but before that, he stood in a position which would be higher than others, so everyone could witness him.

"When I came here," he began, "I was sceptical. People wanted a new ruler," he saw hundreds of his men, who were going to desert him soon. Some had packed their bags to scamper too. He didn't see Shanaya because she had left to do something important. Suyodhan didn't stay back. He was forced by his father to leave with him on the condition that he would put the offer for Karna. "A new king. General Devi was a good substitute and she would have been a fine queen if I had to pass my helm to someone. But unfortunately she has passed. And we all grieve for her. As you all stand, I have hopes for a greater future. One where people are free here. From everything. And from everyone. It was unfair for me to bring the outsiders, to bring the Mlecchas and the Nishadhs..." and he looked at his small band of Nishadh army. "But havent' they done good for us? The Nishadhs infiltrated and poisoned Jara's men. The Mlecchas fought with us until they left, realising we were defeated. And I know they abandoned us, but didn't Shanaya help your wives, your sons during times of conflict?"

They all looked at them with a little bit of confusion but also reverence.

"I don't stand here as a king anymore. If I go out there and lose, you won't have a king," Karna said. "I stand as one of you and I know many of you want to leave and you are free to go. All of you. I won't stop anyone. I won't call you deserters and I won't put a bounty on you even if I survive. But if we win this, by not your handwork anymore, but by your faith in me, and in Anga—then stay. Stay for the earth you stand on," he paused. "I wasn't much of a leader to you all. But I promise Anga will be so much better than it was ever before. Because this is not just my land. It's our land. And to make it a better Anga, I will take the first step of defeating the tyrant who has killed our people for so long. I will do it with my own hands or die trying," he said. "And for that, I'm going to finally use the Brahmastra."

"But Brahmastra..." someone called out, "...where is it?"

"You'll see on the field."

Karna sighed, as he moved and he didn't hear any applause. Didn't see any smiles or signs of elation. It was all somber and quiet.

I wish they stay back.

89

Karna walked up to the centre of the field, where Jarasandha was sitting.

He was crouched. His men were yards away, with spears and bows ready. And so were Karna's men. They made sure they didn't interfere as the scorching heat beat down on them. Their eyes were locked and he could see the little, snide grin that Jara had on his face.

"I apologise for your brother," Karna said, as they circled around each other, not fighting, but just respecting each other.

"You know. Good. I didn't think he would be recognisable after the abomination he had become," Jara shrugged, but Karna could see a blanket of hurt and pain residing in him. "I was just thinking one thing, while walking here."

"What?"

"How it would have never begun, all of this, if you hadn't attacked my ship," he said. "You started this cycle of violence and retribution and unnecessary deaths and now I'm going to end it with your head under my arms."

Karna felt fear rattling inside him, but he didn't show it. He remained silent and his mother's voice echoed:

When blood is shed, it drenches everyone around it.

"But you started by killing my men…my people…"

"Because they rebelled and murdered my wife."

"Because you took their kingdom…"

"Because I had to grow my empire. I had asked your father for a share in timber production but he didn't want to cut it down," Jara sighed. "This can go on and on, as to who is to blame for today. The sun is high. And I hope you are ready. I respect you for taking a stand against Dhritarashtra, since he had come and must have offered you something. He's vile scum."

Karna nodded and chuckled, as they began to move around each other, sand slipping from their fingers, their chests bronze in colour and muscles protruding. "Well, that's one thing we can agree on."

"I never understand one simple fact though," Jara said.

"What?"

But Jara like a spider leapt at him from the ground up and grabbed him by the torso, lifting him up in air and throwing him, crashing on the harsh ground, where scars and wounds began to form on Karna's skin, as he shuddered in pain. It was quick and elegant like a dove, and Karna tried to come on his feet, when he saw Jara preparing for his next strike, but still away from him.

"Good one," Karna wiped the sand, as it split and swirled around him, as he came forward and they locked their arms against each other.

They both held their arms, as tight as possible, their veins popping out and they were both trying to push and shove each other, which Karna prevailed as he was tougher and younger tossing him on the side, Jara—like the spider he was—rolled over and grinned.

"Nice. Nice. You've learnt a thing or two. But wrestling is far more complex than that," he said.

"What didn't you understand?"

"Why aren't you using the famed Brahmastra?"

He knows.

"Because it's more complicated than that."

"Tell me," Jara said.

And Karna leapt forward, as Jara bent down and instantly grabbed his torso again, but instead of flipping him backwards, he had a tight lock, holding his head against his lower abdomen and circling him around in such a way that one would get confused, as he tossed him on the ground and Karna fell; the ground swirling with a lot of dust as Karna coughed and spat.

"Well..."

Karna began to think about the day when he had known the truth about the Brahmastra.

It was also the day he was expelled from the village of Parshuram.

One year ago...

"You can't do this, guruji," Karna was nearly tearing up. "I have done so much. I have learnt so much..."

"ALL LIES!" he rasped. And he was standing amidst hundreds of other priests, in a huddle, in a small common room, where a decision was made. "Your spirit is of a Kshtriya. The way you saved the villagers, no one would do that but a Kshtriya. A Brahmin would always see the bigger picture, but the Kshtriya is emotional. They go where their virtues lie. You do not embody the true essence of Brahmins and thus you are expelled."

"But I am, I am..."

"No, you are not. Calling you a Kshtriya is wrong, because we did some research, sent some emissaries and learnt the Karna we train is the Karna who goes by Vasu and he's a sutaputr. A son of a charioteer, a sarthi," Rambhadra shook his head, and though his voice betrayed him, his eyes didn't say he meant any of that. "You have constantly lied and for that you will be cursed. When you need the knowledge of your martial techniques most, that is the time you will forget them. I curse you and so do all of us! Banish thee!"

Karna clenched his jaw, and with a lowered gaze, he began to walk outside, hoping to not look back ever.

Present day...

A punch drove through the air and landed against his face, breaking his jaw as he fell down.

Karna grimaced, as a kick went against his chest and abdomen and he tasted the sand on the ground. And then Jara, grabbed him by the throat.

"This is your end, sutaputr. Hope you have enjoyed the run till now," he laughed.

Karna tried to free himself from this lock, but it was impossible, and thus he went with a quick save of his fist against Jara's face and he did it again, until the man began to bleed from his nose and fell back.

Karna leapt over him, sitting on him and began to punch him on his jaw, until Jara deflected it by putting both his hands together. And then he kicked him from behind by bringing his leg forward, as Karna rolled over.

His energy was depleting, draining fast.

"What is the secret of the Brahmastra?" Jara asked, coming on his feet and spitting blood on the ground. "I just want to know before I kill you. What are the blueprints? What is it? Tell me! How does one make it?" And he rushed like a bull, head on, and slammed Karna on the chest.

A crazy feeling of vomit came in his chest, but he let it rest as he fell on the ground and stayed there. Both men were tired under the heat.

But Jara didn't get around it. This time, he grabbed hold of Karna and began to choke him.

"Tell me, you piece of shit. You shall..."

Karna was choking, losing vision and blurriness was setting in...

One year earlier...

Karna was packing his bags and keeping in the anger and frustration. He would leave and never see it again. Someone knocked on his quarter's door. It was none other than Rambhadra, who was standing with a solemn face.

"I am sorry," he said.

"It was embarrassing."

"I know."

"I'll leave," Karna sighed, as he began to walk and bowed in front of his guruji out of respect and began to move.

"I am sorry. You shouldn't have lied."

"But you would have never taught me."

"Because perhaps, you are not ready."

"Why?"

"You give up quite fast. You are afraid of trying further, after you fail. Perhaps one day you might not, but today you are and thus I never told you the truth about the Brahmastra," he said. "But as a student who was tougher than a Kshtriya and a Brahmin, I have the right to tell you the truth about it. You should know, and perhaps use it one day."

Karna's eyes beamed. *Was he going to show it?* But Rambhadra didn't say anything. He just asked him to follow and Karna did so, quietly tracing his steps, as they came out where the red flowers were blooming and a brisk wind was blowing, with the flowers splayed out in the bright green grass, where it looked like blood majestically flowed. He took him to the branch, to a place, he had been to often but never noticed anything special about it, until now.

It was a pond. Where the fish swam.

"The Brahmastra is the greatest weapon ever created by Lord Brahma, since he's the creator of all," Rambhadra explained. "And when he had created the Brahmastra, he had known that this weapon, if achieved, could destroy anything, rule over anything, fight any enemy but it could be only achieved by the ones who were mentally ready for it."

"What is it?" Karna's breath was almost seizing as he was excited; elated.

"*Who* is it?" Rambhadra said. "The greatest of gurus like Bhishma Pitamah, Dronacharya learnt the true mastery of the Brahmastra because they knew the truth and the truth is in the pond, my dear child."

Karna looked down and there were some yellow fish, some wet leaves and his own reflection. "But I don't see a missile."

"Because there isn't any. For eons, the rumours about the Brahmastra being a missile were false because the truth is this," Rambhadra patted Karna on the shoulder. "The truth is your reflection is the Brahmastra."

"What?" Karna could almost laugh.

"When Lord Brahma created the Brahmastra, he had created it by making his own soldier one of the best; one of the brightest. The Brahmastra is the greatest weapon because it is the indomitable spirit of facing any enemy without fear in a human. The greatest weapon is the soldier itself," he smiled. "A sword is useless without the one who wields it, the bow is useless without the one who carries it," he paused, saying the final words that hit Karna like a brick.

"The weapon can be of the greatest dominance if it is wielded by a human who has no fear of failure."

Present day...

Karna could feel the lights going off and his breathing clamping up, not just because of the two tough wrestling arms wrapped around his throat but because he knew he was failing again…

I have to fight back. I have to…

Be a leader.

I cannot give up.

His eyes were barely open and his face was brutally bruised and he was going to die until…

He tightened his fist and smacked it across Jara's head. He fell on the ground, as Karna grabbed him by the leg, by pushing himself up and began to hurl him across the field with as much strength as he could muster. He limped, as Jara fell on the ground, holding his back as it hurt… when…

Karna yelled, gritting his teeth, as he smacked his head and threw him on the ground. With a quick push and a shove, he grabbed hold of Jara's neck and began to choke him.

"I'm going to kill you," Karna said. "I'm going to kill you for everything you have done, you bloody…"

And the man couldn't breathe. Karna could see his men didn't retort, and neither did Jara's soldiers, who looked worried but they were ordered not to interfere in Jara's fight.

Jara began to tap on the ground, as he tried to breathe, his face going red, his eyes red and he was gasping for breath.

"For whatever you have done, I will kill you. You have destroyed my home, my mother, my…"

And the man was gasping even further. Karna could feel how it felt to slowly make the spirit of a man ebb away.

"No...please...no..."

And then Karna imagined the faces—of Devi, of Satya, of all who have died. His anger grew and his chokehold became worse, as Jara was about to die...close to...

When the face of his mother came in front of him. In the cornfields. He was there. And he was crying. She had come and she had told him it was okay to be an outcast. Because those who were born to stand apart, often got humiliated as they grew up.

Karna could see her and she had said to him: "*So much of blood for these thrones. I do not care about whether Adhirath lost his crown. I care about the people losing their homes because of feudal powers. So promise me, Vasu, to free them when you grow older. Free them and don't let this promise wither even if I cry and beg you to come. The earth you sit on is far more important than your close ones.*"

"But you still cry at night, ma. The hurt. I shall hurt him the same way Jarasandha has hurt you."

"Won't you become like him then, my son?" She smiled. "Remember—when blood is shed, it drenches everyone around it. Never fight to overpower him. Fight to free Anga."

And he loosened his grip!

Jara began to take deep breaths and he spat and coughed and stood up as Karna rested next to him. He felt hurt and angry for not killing his opponent, but he also knew...

"You were right," Karna said. "I started this cycle of violence and it would have continued if I killed you. So I end it here. If you want to kill me, you can."

Jara looked up at Karna; his eyes grimacing with pain. "You are a fool! You should have done it when you had the chance. Do you think I would..."

And then there was a blast. A large one, at that.

"WE ARE ATTACKED!" Jara's men shouted.

And Karna smiled, as he saw Shanaya and hundreds of men moving towards the battlefield, and towards their camp.

"What just happened?" Jara's eyes widened.

"The deal with the Mlecchas," Karna smiled, "yeah, that has changed."

90

Jara was still on his arms and legs, just lying there as fire burnt, and his men were attacked and the people were scampering and running for safety, as the Mlecchas came in abundance, destroying the camps, disarming the catapults. The attack was swift, unexpected as everyone's attention was on the duel.

"You played me," he said, looking up at the boy. "You fucking played me!"

Karna smiled, a grin with blood trickling down his cheeks.

"How did the Mlecchas, those barbarians, turn back on my deal?"

"Well," Karna shrugged, "because I created a fake scroll in your name; and I took one of your men's bodies from the battlefield and the Mleccha leader's daughter went, to convince them further. They thought you would turn back on the deal once you were done with me..."

"But I never wrote anything."

"I know. It doesn't matter. You would have done it anyhow. Because war," Karna knelt down, pulling his hair up and it hurt, "is not won by honest, honourable people. It is won by shrewdness but also nobility. It is won by questionable ethics but also heroics of everyday life. War is balance."

"Do you think I will give up, stop myself from killing you?" Jara sighed. "After Mathura, I will come for you. You might have won this battle..." loud battle cries were heard and his voice went silent, "but you haven't won further. I'll come again and again, until I defeat you."

Karna looked positive. He didn't look scared. He didn't look as if it bothered him. In fact, Jara saw something in him; that he was ready to combat.

"I'll be waiting," and he left Jara's hair.

And they both stared at the face of the battle that was going on in the background, as Jara came on his feet and moved across Karna, in respite, as he shouted, knowing full well he had been damaged enough, destroyed and humiliated, but he knew he would come again.

But for now, and just for now, he shouted and everyone did listen: "RETREAT! RETREAT! RETREAT!"

91

Suyodhan had travelled a day further, when he was asked to camp with his father and he did so. At night, music played and dancers were brought in, and it was in the midst of the forest, where the roads were dead and not much was visible around. Unlike earlier, he didn't feel like going to the wenches or the maids, but remained in one corner. His father, with his ministers, sitting on his makeshift throne, was laughing.

Suyodhan saw Adhirath in a corner, and he was sitting next to the bonfire as hundreds of tents were established.

It had been a few days since they had left from Anga but since this was a large army, they would take time to reach Hastinapur. They would rest often and then move again.

Suyodhan had his reed jar in his hand as he drank wine from it and burped and drank more, until he heard his father calling out to him:

"Son, come! There is a message from Anga. I am sure you would want to hear what happened with your friend."

Suyodhan's eyes lit up, and he scampered to his father, who had gathered his ministers, even Adhirath. Suyodhan stood as the messenger who was panting and was on his knees in front of Dhritarashtra, said: "My lord, there is news."

"Of course. Tell me," his father promptly responded.

"Karna won."

Suyodhan raised his brows. And he gave a confused glance at Adhirath.

"What do you mean, he *won*?" his father spat, in frustration. "He can't win. He had no army..."

"He won the duel and the Mlecchas...they helped him again," the messenger said. "It was a surprise attack. But he won...Jarasandha already lost a lot of men, retreated finally, announcing that Anga was not worth losing so much over. Though he plans to return; when he will we don't know."

Suyodhan couldn't help but beam. And he was grinning, just like Karna's father. They both were smiling and they couldn't stop in front of the men, who were patting Dhritarashtra, who was bursting with anger, to calm him.

"That stupid, low caste dog," the king spat on the ground and threw the goblet, his wine spilling all over. "He won. He *won*. If that isn't a miracle, what is?"

Suyodhan didn't know about miracles. He never believed in them. They were all stupid for him. But he knew his father was right. Karna was a 'low caste dog'. Who showed that it doesn't matter where you come from, what your identity is.

If you have spirit and determination, you can achieve anything in this world.

Though he was sad that his friend had severed all ties with Hastinapur. Because one day, he wanted to sit on the throne, and he wanted Karna by his side.

92

Few days had gone by, and while Malinipur was a place of celebration, Karna was angsty.

He didn't know what to wear.

And he had lot of messages too. Lots of scrolls. A lot of interest. Lots of small kingdoms wanting to align with him after they had heard about him, with a small army, fighting a large foe. How he did it, was a matter of great intrigue and mystery.

But Karna didn't care.

"This kurta doesn't look good," Karna said, wearing the golden tunic and tossing it off.

Shanaya was getting dressed herself, and they both had decided they wouldn't take help from their manservants and handmaidens. They would dress together for the festival.

For the crown, by the priests and ministers, would be put on Karna's head finally, and he would be not just an interim king…but a king.

"Just wear your breastplate," she said. "It looks good."

"Well, you look good too," Karna said, as he saw her in a sari and her beautiful lines of linen and he came closer to her. "You are the most beautiful girl I've ever seen in my life."

"Well, that's a lie," Shanaya grinned. "Because you haven't seen many."

"Guilty."

They both laughed and Karna kissed her. "You were brave in convincing your father."

"It was your plan."

"But your execution," Karna smiled. "You are a good leader yourself. And I wish Devi was here," Karna felt sad, all of a sudden. "If only she was here, I would have given the crown to her. It is no use to me. And Satya, oh that man who had become a drunkard and then became sober for me—what a man but. Did what he was afraid of. Dying for his people, for the land."

Shanaya traced her fingers against Karna's cheek. "I know. To make you reach here, lives have been lost, but you know...they are looking at you from somewhere."

Karna nodded. Smiling. "I have to also see what Jarasandha is going to do now."

"Reparations. I have already sent soldiers out. They are saying he's resting and he's damaged. It will take years before he can even muster the strength to attack Anga. Our next step should be to form alliances with future kingdoms."

"I know," Karna smiled, as he walked to the window where the firecrackers burnt and the construction spots were organsied. He had sent a major army to Champa and told his people to shift there too. Soon, Champa would be populated and defences around it would be built.

"We also have to talk about our future trading..."

"Stop it."

"What?" she said.

"You have proved yourself to me."

"What?" she asked.

"I don't want to be the king, Shanaya."

For a moment, there was silence, until she sided next to him. "What do you mean?"

"I want Anga to be ruled by a queen. I am not fit to be a king." He held her hands, as he saw from the window, young kids playing and dancing on songs, and the capital from afar brimmed like Hastinapur itself. "I'll be around as your support, but I won't be here. All my life, my pursuit of chasing the promise I made, destroyed me. It made me cruel and angry. What Jara said—I started the war. He's right. I did. I brought death to this land, out of sheer determination to win. And in the process, I lost everything. I lost my uncle. I lost my people's hope. I lost Devi. But thank goodness I didn't lose you. I gained you and your stupid father who has drank himself to death," he chuckled, realising how Archimedes would always be a constant, unpredictable threat, but Karna was ready to forgive and forget, because he had realised there was no point shedding blood. "And I gained a..." he paused.

"So you won't be the king?"

Karna moved away from the window and looked through the scrolls. They were invitations, mails and messages, until his eyes fell on something spectacular. Something he never thought he would get.

It was a scroll.

From *her*.

Panchali.

Vasu,

I heard about your victory and I believe I will be able

to convince my father for my hand to you. And he will agree. Please respond to this and return to me and take me away from here. Please, Vasu. I really miss you.

I hope you have not forgotten me.

How could he? He loved her. He still did. But she was his past, she was someone who left him when he was a nobody, who didn't fight against her father but agreed to marry Arjun. But Shanaya, she was always there no matter what, no matter even if her father betrayed him, and he walked slowly to the hearth of his room, which burnt as he threw the letter in it.

"Who is it?" Shanaya asked.

"No one," Karna turned, smiling to himself. "About the king thing, I can suggest a likely candidate."

"And that is?"

"You."

"What? I'm a Mleccha…"

"You will be a good leader," Karna smiled. "I don't want to hold any status, but I will help you rule the city. I don't want to have the crown or anything of vanity. These things, they don't hold any significance for me anymore. But what does is…" he paused. "I have to meet someone before the coronation where I will announce your regality and subdue mine."

"But…" Shanaya was confused, as Karna kissed her on the lips and then on her forehead.

"I have to meet someone, my dear. Because I realised in the pursuit of achieving my goal, I gained something: I gained friendship."

And he went away.

Suyodhan had been exhausted from the journey.

But he was already here. And he had brought the wenches in his room and he bedded them for three days, until he got tired.

And while naked women lay on his bed, his window was awash with sounds at night.

He knew he had to get ready for the coronation, and he had come here for that even though most of his brothers didn't. They didn't like how Karna did what he did. Dhritarashtra didn't come either. But Adhirath did, taking a break from being a charioteer, to just be a father.

Suyodhan saw what the cracking of the windows was for, and he walked further, opening the drapes and noticed the breastplate first, and then Karna's beardless face.

"What are you doing here?" Suyodhan chuckled. "Don't you have a crown to wear?"

"I was feeling romantic," Karna grinned.

"You fucking fool," Suyodhan chuckled. "So that's how you get your girls? Throw pebbles at their windows. How original, my dear friend."

"Oh well," Karna shrugged. "I came here to tell you something."

"And what is that?"

"I swear fealty to your crown."

"But you said no to my father…"

"To your father, yes, but not to you. When you will rule," Karna said, "I will be there for you. Always. Forever. Till death."

Suyodhan narrowed his gaze. He could scarcely remember just a month back perhaps, this man had clearly said he would not help him. And now, he would. "What changed your mind?"

"I'm just a fool with a big heart."

"Ain't that true?" he laughed. "Why don't we ditch the coronation and drink ourselves to death?"

Karna nodded. "And people say romance is dead."

Suyodhan laughed. "But you do realise that by swearing fealty, you have to destroy the Pandavas with me. Along with me. Because they are..." his face contorted into a frown. "My enemies, no matter what."

"I know," Karna said, arching brows. "Do you have a plan?"

"Let me come downstairs," Suyodhan said, as he halted. "Well, there is one," he thoughtfully mused.

They both stood in silence, as Suyodhan with a smirk, said: "Well it does involve this architect fellow I met, Purochna, and something to do with a house of lac."

"That sounds stupid. I have a feeling it won't work out," Karna smiled. "But we can try. After all, it's all about giving your best."

To be continued...

Book 2

KARNA

THE SON OF SURYA